Melting Frosty
by Maggie Shayne

For Matt, Christmas has aroused painful memories ever since his father died, leaving his family all but destitute and Matt with far too much responsibility too soon. Holly lost her family in a tragedy—but found solace and strength in the holidays her family loved so much. So when Matt and Holly cross paths, it's more than fate—it's a chance for both of them to find the one perfect gift they have both searched for all their lives . . .

Charlotte's Web
by Erin McCarthy

For the longest time, Charlotte Murphy has burned for Will Thornton. But as far as Charlotte can tell, Will sees her only as a friend. Tired of waiting [illegible] Will [illegible] recognize her [illegible]s the sexy, wanton woman she truly is, Charlotte decides to fall back on her genes—and embrace the witch within h[illegible] Her newfound powers offer a temp[illegible] [illegible]t of who she wants. B[illegible]t does she reall[illegible] [illegible]o love her because of w[illegible]chcraft—or beca[illegible]

[illegible]ON[illegible]

Young Tamsyn has [illegible] [illegible]lace in her heart for her powerful fellow pac[illegible] [illegible] a dominant male leopard in the pack, the[illegible] [illegible]ate doesn't want to trap Tamsyn into the fie[illegible] [illegible] mating bond—a bond driven by the animal [illegible] sh[illegible] hardly had the chance [illegible] grow into a wom[illegible] [illegible]msyn knows what she wants for C[illegible]stmas, and s[illegible]ing to [illegible]t it . . .

continued . . .

Gifts of the Magi
by Jean Johnson

Steve Bethel and his fiancée, Rachel, could use a few miracles right about now—the family bed-and-breakfast is mortgaged to the hilt, the biggest blizzard in half a century is ruining the shortest day of the year, and their guests are canceling right and left. Then three strangers show up at what seems like the darkest hour, looking for a place to stay for the holidays . . .

An Enchanted Season

MAGGIE SHAYNE

ERIN McCARTHY

NALINI SINGH

JEAN JOHNSON

BERKLEY SENSATION, NEW YORK

THE BERKLEY PUBLISHING GROUP
Published by the Penguin Group
Penguin Group (USA) Inc.
375 Hudson Street, New York, New York 10014, USA
Penguin Group (Canada), 90 Eglinton Avenue East, Suite 700, Toronto, Ontario M4P 2Y3, Canada
(a division of Pearson Penguin Canada Inc.)
Penguin Books Ltd., 80 Strand, London WC2R 0RL, England
Penguin Group Ireland, 25 St. Stephen's Green, Dublin 2, Ireland (a division of Penguin Books Ltd.)
Penguin Group (Australia), 250 Camberwell Road, Camberwell, Victoria 3124, Australia
(a division of Pearson Australia Group Pty. Ltd.)
Penguin Books India Pvt. Ltd., 11 Community Centre, Panchsheel Park, New Delhi—110 017, India
Penguin Group (NZ), 67 Apollo Drive, Rosedale, North Shore 0632, New Zealand
(a division of Pearson New Zealand Ltd.)
Penguin Books (South Africa) (Pty.) Ltd., 24 Sturdee Avenue, Rosebank, Johannesburg 2196, South Africa

Penguin Books Ltd., Registered Offices: 80 Strand, London WC2R 0RL, England

This book is an original publication of The Berkley Publishing Group.

First edition: October 2007

Library of Congress Cataloging-in-Publication Data

An enchanted season / Maggie Shayne . . . [et al.].
p. cm.
ISBN 978-0-425-21785-6
1. Love stories, American. 2. Occult fiction, American. 3. Holidays—Fiction. I. Shayne, Maggie.

PS648.L6E48 2007
813'.08508—dc22 2007020572

PRINTED IN THE UNITED STATES OF AMERICA

10 9 8 7 6 5 4 3 2 1

CONTENTS

Melting Frosty

Maggie Shayne

The man in the overalls picked up the boxes, as instructed. He knew the situation. It was no surprise that the lady of the house wasn't at home. Looked like a nice family. It was too bad, it really was. He left the check, safe in its sealed envelope, stuck through the crack in the door, then carried the final armload to the truck. Just as he shoved it into the back, with the others, the hat fell out. It rolled past his feet in a most unusual way. He went after it, but it kept rolling, and then just as he bent to snap it up, a big gust of wind came out of nowhere, and scooped it up. It was carried away, over a house's roof and out of sight.

The man in the overalls rolled his eyes. Hell, an old worn-out hat like that wouldn't have brought much anyway. He returned to the truck, pulled the door closed, and secured the latch. Then he drove back to the second-hand shop with the dead man's clothes.

• *One* •

November 1992, Flint, Michigan

"YOU *SOLD* IT? *ALL* OF IT?"

Matthew stared up at his mother in blatant disbelief. Wasn't it bad enough that Dad had to die the day before Thanksgiving? That they had to bury him the day after? That their big meal on the day in between had consisted of deli meat, rolls, and about six casseroles brought over by neighbors and relatives?

She had to go and sell his stuff, too?

His mother blinked down at him. She seemed kind of in a daze, not all there, mostly numb. It seemed to him she could hear just fine, but what she heard wasn't making its way to her brain.

"I had to, Matt. The money situation isn't . . . it isn't good."

Yeah, he'd picked up on that much. He was twelve, not two. And he resented that his mother didn't seem to think he could understand things. He *did* understand. He heard and saw and understood. Dad had died broke. He'd racked up debts that Matt's mom hadn't even known about. There was no money. There were payments due. And the funeral had cost a bundle. He got all that.

"I know the money situation isn't good, Mom. And I could see selling the guns, the tools, the computer. But geeze, Mom, his *clothes?*"

"It was either sell them or give them away. And we need every penny right now. *Christmas* is coming."

And that was Mom. She wasn't worried about bills or taxes or losing the house or the car or even paying for the funeral. She was worried because Christmas was coming.

"We don't need Christmas this year," he told her. "We're not gonna feel like celebrating anyway."

"Oh, you're so wrong, Matt. We need Christmas this year more than ever."

He rolled his eyes, but thought about his kid sister, Cindy. She was only six, and yeah, she probably did need Christmas. But he didn't.

"There must be something you want for Christmas, Matt," his mother pressed on. "One gift. One special gift that could make this time a little bit easier for you. There is something, isn't there? Tell me."

He pursed his lips, cleared his throat because he didn't want her to hear his grief in his voice. He was fine. But . . .

"Yeah, there is something. Or was. Dad's hat."

"His hat?" She blinked, still blank, but a little less so. "That silly felt fedora he was always wearing?"

Matt nodded. "He used to joke about that hat being my inheritance. Anytime we were doing anything fun, he would be wearing it. Don't you remember? It was like—I don't know, it was like his trademark, that stupid hat. It meant a lot to him. Remember how he wrote his initials in it in permanent purple marker when we went on vacation, just it case it got lost?" He paused there, remembering the road trip, the theme park, the fun. And that hat, at the center of it all. "I want Dad's hat, Mom. It's a part of him."

His mother's dull, numb expression changed then. It changed right before his eyes. Her face crumpled, and a rush of tears flooded her eyes and splashed onto her cheeks, and then she lowered her head into her hands. "I'm sorry, baby. I . . . it went with all the other stuff. I didn't know. I'm sorry."

"Yeah, I figured." He sighed, wanted to be furious, but he couldn't stand to see her crying like that. Her shoulders were quaking.

"How am I going to do this?" she moaned. "I'm screwing everything up already and he's only been gone two weeks. How am I going to do this by myself?"

Matt licked his lips, reached out, and put a hand on her shoulder. "It's okay, Mom. It's just a hat."

"I'll try to get it back," she said. "It all went to a used clothing store, downtown. I can probably still find it."

"Just don't worry about it. It doesn't matter."

"Yes, it does," she cried. "Matt, I'm so sorry. I thought I could use the money to get you something nice for Christmas."

If he had to pick the moment when he'd decided to hate Christmas forever, that would probably be the closest Matthew could come. That moment, right then. Matt *hated* Christmas. He hated the entire holiday season. It had taken his father away from him, and then it had doubled the blow by taking the only thing of his dad's that he'd really wanted. And yeah, it was just a stupid old hat. But it was his dad's stupid old hat.

He hated Christmas. And he vowed that day, that he would *always* hate Christmas.

November 1992, Oswego, New York

Holly opened her eyes, and saw that she was in a place that was all white. Sunbeams spilled through the window like liquid gold, and angels stood all around her.

But they were not angels. There *had been* angels, only moments ago. That much, she knew. As she blinked her vision clear, the blurry shapes she'd mistaken as wings faded, and the men and women in white took on ordinary forms. The room really *had* been filled with angels. She only stopped being able to see them when she woke fully. But she thought they were still there.

A nurse was writing on a chart. Someone warm was holding her hand, and Holly looked up to see her Aunt Sheila sitting there in a chair beside her hospital bed. She looked like she'd been there awhile. Her hair was messy and her eyes red and puffy. She was staring down at Holly's hand as if she wasn't really seeing it.

Holly looked all around the room, and realized that what she'd been dreaming hadn't been a dream at all. "Aunt Sheila?" she said, surprised that her words came out in a dull croak.

The nurses in the room stopped what they were doing and turned to stare. Aunt Sheila's head came up, eyes met hers, and then filled.

"Baby," she said. "You're awake." She shot a look at the nearest nurse, who hurried out of the room muttering that she would get the doctor.

But Holly clutched her aunt's hand harder, and held her eyes firm this time. "Mom and Dad . . . and Noelle? They're dead, aren't they?"

Sheila didn't say anything. Instead she gathered Holly into her arms, and held her hard. She held her tight. Holly tried to be brave like her mom had asked her to, but she couldn't stop herself from bursting into tears. And in a second Aunt Sheila was sobbing, too.

They held each other and cried for a long time. They cried until they just about couldn't cry anymore. And then finally, Holly sat up in her bed, and wiped at her eyes. "You all thought I was going to die, too, right?" Holly said.

Aunt Sheila blinked her red eyes dry. "What makes you think that?"

"I think—I think I did, for a while. I was with Mom and Dad

and little Noelle. They're okay." She met her Aunt Sheila's eyes. "They really are, they're okay. You don't need to worry."

Sheila's tears spilled over anew, and she pressed her palms to Holly's cheeks, and kissed her forehead. And then she whispered, "Honey, do you remember what happened? There was a car accident. You were all in it. The doctors tried, honey, they tried their best."

"I know," Holly said. "But Mom wanted me to tell you that they're okay. I *saw* them. I was with them for a little while. But Mom, she told me I had to come back. She said there were really important things for me to do. She said everything happens for a reason. And she said you needed me, Aunt Sheila. She said death isn't real. And I know it's true, because I was there—only it's not really *there*, it's *here*. She's still here, she's still with us." She lifted her eyes, staring around the room, her lips pulling into a watery smile. "Can't you *feel* her?"

Sheila gathered Holly into her arms, and held her gently. The tears were used up, but the grief remained.

"They'll be okay as long as they know we are. I don't know if I could have been if I hadn't seen it all for myself. I crossed over with them. It was like walking them home. And it was beautiful, Aunt Sheila. If we fall apart, it's going to break their hearts, but we don't have to fall apart, because they're great. They're perfect, they really are."

Sheila nodded. "You're amazing, Holly, you know that?" She kissed her again. "So much like your mom."

"She wants us to remember her at Christmas," Holly said. "That was the one thing she made me promise to do for her. To always treat Christmas the way she did. She said she'd be there with me, every single year, as long as I keep that promise."

Sniffling, Sheila murmured, "She adored Christmas."

"And she never missed a Midnight Mass," Holly said. "Or a Christmas special on TV. *Rudolph*, *Frosty*, *The Little Drummer Boy*."

"And then there were the decorations." Sheila took a rumpled tissue from her pocket and blew her nose softly, shaking her head.

Holly nodded hard. "She shorted out the house last year when she added that full-sized sleigh and reindeer to the roof. Remember? Santa waved and the reins lit up and the bells jingled and the reindeer moved? But only for about a minute and a half. Then everything went black."

"I remember how mad your dad pretended to be when he had to hire an electrician to put the lights on their own separate breaker. He wasn't really mad, though. He loved having the house everyone wanted to drive past at night." They both laughed softly, sadly, but warmly.

There wasn't a nurse in the room whose eyes were dry.

"Sheila, look," Holly whispered. Sheila lifted her head and followed Holly's gaze to the window. Snow was falling outside. "The first snow of the season," Holly said. "Mom always said it has magic in it."

"We're going to be okay, Holly. You and me, I promise."

Holly nodded. "We will be. And so will they."

"They will. And we're gonna have a Christmas to beat them all," Sheila promised. "One to make your mom smile."

"She'll love that," Holly said. "I love Christmas, because she did. That's kind of what she left me, I think. I'll *always* love Christmas."

• *Two* •

Present Day, Binghamton, New York

HOLLY MADE HER WAY FROM THE KITCHEN TO TABLE SIX, with two breakfast platters, a carafe of coffee, ketchup, and maple syrup, all without batting an eye. She delivered the food piping hot and, as always, accompanied by a brilliant smile. "Anything else I can get you boys?"

Bub Tanner, as he was called, and that was the only name she knew, grinned at her, and rubbed his unshaven graying stubble with one hand. "I like how she calls us 'boys,' " he said.

"She's just flattering your ego, Bub," Tater said. And *that* was the only name she knew for him. "She knows we're both older than dirt."

"Speak for yourself, Tater." Bub reached for the carafe, but Holly beat him to it, filled his cup, and then Tater's, with the decaf they hadn't asked for.

"Enjoy your breakfast."

"Here, take this with you, hon, will you?"

Holly looked back to see Tater holding out his thoroughly

read newspaper. She smiled and took it from him. "Happy to get that outta your way," she said, and then she paused, because the paper was open to page three and folded in just such a way that one particular story was looking her right in the face.

"Oswego Welcomes Natives Home for Holidays," the headline announced. The story was a feel-good piece about all the people traveling in from out of town for the season, how good it was for business.

But that wasn't the way Holly saw it. Frowning, she carried the paper with her behind the counter, and into the kitchen. "Aunt Sheila?"

Sheila turned her wheelchair around—she'd been parked right next to the short-order cook, probably lecturing him on his technique—and smiled at her. "What, babe?"

"Look what Tater just handed me." She thrust the paper toward her, and Sheila looked at it, saw the story, lifted her brows.

"That's the fourth time this morning, Aunt Sheila."

Sheila nodded, tilted her head. "And how many signs did you have about your hometown yesterday?" she asked.

"Six."

"Right. Including the billboard for the school play, *To Oz We Go*."

"Oz We Go, Oswego. Come on, Aunt Sheila, it's almost blatant."

Sheila nodded. "You need to spend this Christmas at home."

"I don't know that I *need* to. And I don't want to leave you—but I feel like something . . . I don't know, *wants* me to."

"Which is why I called the Realtor."

"You did?"

Sheila nodded, and wheeled across the kitchen, toward the office door, with a quick glance back at Will, the new short-order cook. He met her eyes and there was . . . something.

Holly lifted her brows. "Was that—?"

"Office, Holly," Sheila said. She'd opened the door, and held it now, waiting. So Holly obediently went inside.

"The old place is empty," Sheila told her. "It's in rough shape, being that it's been empty for twelve years, but it's habitable, barely. If you want to go up there for a day or two over the holiday, I think you should. You haven't been back since the accident. Maybe . . . maybe it's time."

"But you'd be alone for Christmas. And we always do Christmas together. For Mom, you know. And—"

"We can do it up separately just as well. And I won't be alone." She said it with a meaningful glance at the doorway, which was still open. Will was whistling as he flipped flapjacks and smiled at her in a certain way.

Holly blinked and shot her aunt a look.

"Hell, I have MS. I'm not dead."

Holly smiled from ear to ear. Her aunt really did embrace life, in every possible way. She loved that about her. It reminded her of the way Mom had been. The way she was herself. It must run in the female line.

"I could take part of the decorations up with me," Holly said, mulling it over as she thought it through. "It would be kind of cool to decorate the old house like Mom used to. Even if it is in rough shape."

"I think she'd like that. The power will be turned on, a fresh tank of LP gas hooked up when you arrive. Key in the mailbox."

"You—you really did talk to the Realtor, didn't you?"

"I think you have to do this, Holly. You haven't been back there since you lost them. And your eyes are lighting up just thinking about it," Sheila said with a smile. "You've been taking care of me, taking care of everyone around here, ever since you came here, Holly. It's time to do something for yourself, even if it's only for a couple of days. Give yourself a present this Christmas. Okay?"

Holly heard the rumble of a motor and glanced up and

through the window, just in time to see a bus go past. Plastered to its side was an ad for the State University of New York at Oswego. She smiled, shaking her head. "I don't think the universe is going to take no for an answer. My hometown seems to be calling me. Guess I've got no choice."

Present Day, Detroit, Michigan

"Yes, I *do* have to go now," Matthew told his sister. "Yes, Cindy, I *know* it's Christmas week. But this is business."

She sounded heartbroken, but honest to God, if he had to sit through one more warm, cozy, family dinner at her house with her idyllic life and her doting husband and her chubby babies, he was going to swallow a stick of dynamite and a lighter and hope for the best.

"Honey, you know how I feel about the holidays. I know they're important to you, but 'to you' is the operative part of that sentence. This place is a bargain. I can't miss out, and if I buy it this week, when every other person in the market is taking the holidays off, I'll have the kind of edge you never get in real estate."

Spice that up with the phony-baloney goodwill of the season, and the Realtor likely wanting one more fat commission check before the end of the calendar year (to cover her holiday overspending, most likely), and he had it made.

People were idiots this time of year. He was smart enough to take advantage of that.

"Yes, Cindy, I'm flying. Right away? Well, yeah, seeing as how I'm calling you from the airport, I would say it's pretty much imminent. Yep, I'm renting a car when I arrive in Syracuse and driving up from there. And yes, we'll celebrate when I get back, I promise. There's no reason in the world I shouldn't be back in time for Christmas dinner. My flight leaves Christmas Eve, three p.m." He almost grimaced at the thought, but tried to make the words sound sincere all the same. "Have a great week, hon. I'll call you in a day or two."

He flipped the phone closed, cutting her off before she could dole out any more helpings of guilt, then slipped it back into his belt clip, and dragged his roller bag over toward the concourse, where the flight had just begun boarding.

As he got into his seat, he leaned back, closed his eyes, and told himself he really would do his best to get back to Cindy's in time for Christmas. Cindy *needed* Christmas.

And that thought brought to mind the other. The one from long ago, his first Christmas without his dad. And his mom's tearful explanation about how she'd gone to the secondhand clothing store and tried to find the hat, but that it was already gone. And the proprietor not only didn't remember who had bought it, he didn't even remember ever having seen it.

The hat was beyond recovering.

Just like his dad. Just like his childhood after that. Just like everything eventually was. Gone.

Just went to show what getting too attached would do for you. Things are fleeting. Here and gone again. There's no point getting too used to anything.

And holidays, he added mentally, are just plain stupid.

The wind blew the hat until it came to rest outside a truck stop just a few blocks from the dead man's house. And there it waited. Eventually, a long-distance driver came out of the establishment, burping in a very satisfied way and carrying a clipboard, a set of keys, and a travel mug full of Joe, piping hot and twice as strong.

He walked toward his rig, and almost tripped over the hat on his way. Then he paused and looked down at it, tipped his head to one side, and shrugging, bent to pick it up. It wasn't a bad hat. Nothing he'd wear, but the thing had character. He didn't really want it. He wasn't sure what possessed him to take the thing, but take it he did. He set it on top of the CB radio inside the truck, and let it ride there as he headed for his next stop in New York's southern tier. It was almost like having a friend along.

• *Three* •

All week long she'd been seeing signs, telling her to go home. And now that she'd arrived, she wondered why.

The house was not what she remembered. Of course, it hadn't been painted or maintained in twelve years. It showed the signs of neglect, too. There were a few shingles missing from the roof. One shutter had come loose and hung by its bottom bolts while the top of it veered out to the side as if threatening to jump. The white paint was peeling and chipped.

A car horn blasted, and Holly damn near jumped out of her seat, glancing reflexively into the rearview mirror. She saw a dark-colored sports car behind her, and even before she managed to put her own sunshine yellow VW Bug into gear to move out of the way, the hot little black car was pulling out and around her. It roared past, its windows too tinted to let her see the impatient jerk who was behind the wheel.

Licking her lips, she gently corrected her thoughts. For all she knew, the driver might have been late to pick up his little girl from some event, or maybe he was rushing a sick relative to the hospital. He could have a very good reason for his impatience, and she shouldn't judge.

She let the tense feeling run off her shoulders like water off a raincoat, and eased her Bug into the worn dirt driveway. It used to be pretty solid and bare. Now, grass and weeds had come up, and they brushed the underside of her car as she drove over them.

She brought the car to a stop and got out, then stood there for a moment as memories tried to sweep in. She could hear childish laughter—her own, and her baby sister's—drifting in from a long forgotten past. She could almost see them, bundled in snowsuits to the point where Holly could barely bend and little Noelle looked like the pink version of the Stay Puft Marshmallow Man. Her cheeks, cherry red, her nose and mouth covered by a scarf with snowmen all over it. She was walking, but only just, and holding Holly's hand, both of them in mittens as they tromped through the snow toward the place where they'd left the sled the day before.

She sighed and stared up at the two-story house. It was an ordinary frame house, nothing fancy, no real style or design to it. It was over a century old, drafty, poorly insulated, and probably needed a new roof and wiring and furnace and God only knew what else. It hadn't been in great shape when she'd lived in it as a child. She remembered her dad calling it a fixer-upper.

"Why do you want me here?" she asked the house, or maybe she was asking her mom. She wasn't sure. "What's the point?"

There was a roar, and then a horn. She didn't jump this time, just turned slowly to look toward the road where that same black sports car had returned, and sat there, growling like an agitated panther. Its tinted window slid slowly down, and she saw a man's face, hidden behind dark sunglasses.

Something wafted from him—a feeling—almost like a breeze filled with tiny electric sparks.

She lifted her brows. "You again?" she asked

He frowned, glanced at her car, and then back at her. "Yeah, sorry about that. I was in a hurry."

"Didn't do you much good, though, did it?"

"What do you mean?"

"Well, wherever you were in such a hurry to go, you're still not there."

He tipped his head slightly to one side, reached up to pull off his sunglasses, as if it would help him to interpret her foreign language if he could see her better.

"You should slow down. Learn to enjoy the journey. You never really get where you're going, anyway."

"Uh—well, where I'm going is the Best Western. And I sure as hell hope I'm going to get there."

She nodded, and thought he was only pretending not to get her deeper meaning. He looked intelligent enough. Dark hair, nice face. Deep chocolate eyes that made her tummy tighten up if she looked directly into them. And his mouth—well, she just wasn't going to look at that anymore at all. There was something way too sensual about those lips.

"I haven't been back here in twelve years," she said, "but unless they've moved it, you're pretty close." She pointed. "Back the way you came, five miles, then take a right at the light. You won't see it till you get around the big bend in the road."

He nodded. "Thanks." He slid his glasses back on, and she *thought* maybe he was giving her a more thorough look from behind them. It felt like it, anyway. Though she could be imagining it.

"Merry Christmas," she called.

"Yeah." He glanced at her, lips pulled tight, then pulled away.

She shrugged, and went up to the mailbox. The key was right where the Realtor had told her it would be. So she took it out, and let herself in, and didn't even take time to look around. She knew herself well enough to realize she'd get lost in memories if she did, and it would be dark in a few hours, so she settled for a quick glance at the note Ms. Sullivan had left on the door.

Welcome home, Holly. It was short notice, but I did what I could to give you a comfortable stay. The electric and water are on, but the furnace isn't. No time for that. So I had a face cord of firewood delivered for you—it's stacked around the side. You can use the fireplace to keep warm. I stocked the place with lots of bottled water in case the tap tastes rusty. Hot water heater isn't lit yet, but if you want to, go ahead. It's been checked out, and while not efficient, it is safe. If you need anything else, don't hesitate to call. Merry Christmas, Holly."

Ms. Sullivan had been a friend to Holly's mother. She wouldn't want any sort of payment or thanks for all she'd done, but Holly would find some way. Either that, or she would pay it forward by doing something extra-nice for someone else.

She folded the note and tucked it into her pocket to keep, taking only enough time to start a small fire in the hearth before she headed back outside. She still needed to unload her personal things, groceries and supplies from the car. She'd bought the fixings for a very traditional holiday meal. And all the decorations she'd brought along. She had a ton of lights to string before dark. The long night ahead would give her plenty of time to reminisce and explore her childhood home.

THE "FOR SALE" SIGN IN FRONT OF THE HOUSE WHERE HE'D stopped to ask for directions should have given him a clue, but Matthew had brushed it off as meaningless. The house he'd come to look over was unoccupied and had been owned by the bank for a dozen years. Its asking price had just been reduced by a bundle. That one had a Beetle-driving hippie type in residence. Tree hugger. He could spot them a mile away. Even leggy, blond tree huggers with eyes so blue you could spot them from twenty yards away.

Her looks had floored him. Her attitude had irritated him. He'd asked for directions, not a seminar on enjoying the journey. The nerve. And she'd capped it by tossing that useless, meaningless phrase "Merry Christmas" onto her farewell.

At any rate, he checked into the Best Western, which he'd been assured was the best hotel in the area—not that there were many. He was in a hurry, and starved to boot, so he didn't even look at the room. Just checked in, got the key, and asked the desk clerk the best place to get a decent meal that wouldn't take half the damn night.

She pointed to a chain restaurant across the parking lot. Matthew rolled his eyes, and headed there, walking because there was no point in driving that short distance, and the Carerra was probably safer where it was. He'd paid a premium to rent a Porsche for the two-hour drive up from the airport, and more for the insurance. He didn't want to have to use it.

He ordered a meal, then killed the time waiting for the food to arrive by phoning the Realtor to set up a showing.

Her reaction surprised him. "Uh—Mr. Reid—I, uh—it's the day before Christmas Eve."

"Yes, I'm pretty clear on the date, Ms. Sullivan. Do you refuse to show houses during the holiday season or—?"

"Well, no, of course not, I just—I had no idea you were coming into town."

"I didn't think it would be a problem. You said the place was unoccupied. Look, if you're too busy with your . . . holiday plans . . . I can swing by and pick up a key and some directions, and show myself around the place."

"No, it's not that."

"Well, what is it then?"

"I . . . I have a tenant there. Just for the holiday."

"A tenant?"

"Well, not exactly a tenant. More like a guest."

He blinked, completely puzzled.

"She lived there as a child, Mr. Reid. Her parents were friends of mine, and when she called asking if she could spend Christmas there, I thought there'd be no harm. It's her first time back here in twelve years and I thought—"

"Her first time back in twelve years?" he asked. And he immediately thought of the hippie chick in the bright yellow Bug, dispensing pearls of wisdom to hapless strangers. For some reason the fact that it was her made him a little more irritated than he already was. And he ignored the other feeling. The little trickle of liquid heat that simmered through him at the thought of seeing her again. That made no sense whatsoever. So as he did with all things that made no sense, he ignored it.

At least he knew where the house was now. "So are you saying you're going to give up a sale because you don't want to inconvenience a freeloader for an hour or two?"

"She's not a freeloader, Mr. Reid. And of course I don't want to jeopardize a sale over this. I just want to give her fair warning first, before traipsing in there with a stranger in tow. This is probably a difficult—"

"I have cash, you know. No financing needed. If I buy it, I can pay you just as fast as you can draw up the contracts."

"If the weather's not too bad tomorrow—"

"Weather?" He looked out the window. "It's as clear as a bell outside."

"We're supposed to get lake effect tonight. But once the roads are cleared tomorrow, I'll take a run over there and talk to her. I'm sure she won't have any problem letting you come in and see the place later in the day, again, weather permitting. All right?"

He rolled his eyes. His food arrived. At least the waitstaff in this town were fast. It didn't look as if anyone else was. "I'll call you tomorrow," he promised. Then he snapped the phone closed, and looked up at the waitress. "You keep things rolling this fast, and you're going to get a nice, fat tip."

She frowned at him, maybe a little insulted, but pasted a smile over it and filled his coffee mug. As she walked away, she paused to speak to another waitress, and he caught a few words.

"What are we supposed to get tonight? One to three?"

"I heard three to five."

He shrugged. It didn't sound so bad to him. He focused on his meal, which wasn't half bad, either.

• *Four* •

HOLLY STOOD ALL THE WAY AT THE END OF THE DRIVEWAY, staring back at the decrepit house that was currently lit up like a—well, like a Christmas tree—and smiling from ear to ear. It was dark outside, so the lights glowed even more brilliantly. It had taken her three solid hours. It hadn't been difficult at all, because her mom had everything down to a science where decorating was concerned. There were still little hooks all the way around the eaves of the house for hanging the lights. There were more around each window. She'd asked the Realtor ahead of time to leave a ladder in the storage shed, and she'd been delighted to see that Maureen Sullivan had taken the intiative to leave a few more things as well, including a bag full of extension cords, a hammer, and a box of nails.

Holly went back into the shed to return the hammer and nails to their spots, so Maureen would find them right where she'd left them. She flipped on the lights this time. She hadn't had to before—it had still been light outside.

The back corners of the shed were illuminated, and she spotted what she hadn't seen before: a giant box, taped shut. Her mother's handwriting was on the side of it. She'd written one word with a Sharpie marker. "Santa."

"It can't be," Holly whispered. Then she ran forward, falling onto her knees and tearing at the packing tape like a child tearing at her first present on Christmas morning. She got it loose, and pulled the box open. Then pawed her way past the bubble wrap and newspapers that lined the thing.

And then she sat back on her heels, smiling through her tears. Santa smiled up at her from his sleigh. She looked around and found the other box, the one that contained the reindeer. Everything was in pristine condition. After all, they'd used the set only that one year. The year before Holly's family had died.

"Aw, Mom. If I'd known this was still here . . ." She brushed her tears away. "No regrets, right? Okay. I'm putting him up on the roof, where he belongs!"

And with that, she carefully took Santa and his sleigh out of the box, carried them to the ladder, and laid them on the ground beside the ladder. Then she did the same with the reindeer. Finally, she searched the shed until she found a sack full of twine, and she strung it all together until she had a nice lengthy piece. She tied one end to Santa, climbed the ladder, and hauled him up.

The brackets that had held him and his crew in place were still there, right along the peak, though she crawled around feeling for them, because of the darkness. She made it work, though, and then hauled the reindeer up and was anchoring them to the roof, when the snow began falling, sticking to her hair, her shoulders, her eyelashes.

Headlights from the driveway drew her gaze downward.

* * *

"OH. MY. GOD."

Matthew could not believe that in a few short hours, the tumbledown farmhouse had turned into the tackiest display he'd ever seen. Lights lined the roof, up into the peak and down and along the edges. They lined every window, painting their borders in color. They outlined the door, twisted candy-cane-like over the railings that flanked the front steps, and marched all the way around the front porch. It looked like something out of a children's theme park.

He shut off the car, and opened the door to get out.

"Hello!" someone called.

Slowly, he lifted his gaze, following the sound of that voice, gazing through the tumbling jumbo-sized snowflakes until he saw her. That crazy, good-looking hippie was *on the roof*! His stomach knotted up. "What the *hell* are you *doing*?"

"Decorating." She shook her head. "As if that's not obvious. Do me a favor and turn your headlights back on?"

"Huh?"

"Car. Headlights. On." She thumped a fist on her chest. "Jane need light."

He almost smiled. Almost. He stopped himself barely in time. Instead he leaned back into the car and flipped on the headlights. They didn't help much, he imagined, but a little. She bent then and tugged, and he saw reindeer flying. Well, not actually flying. They were sort of rising, as she pulled them up by the rope.

And the snow, he thought, was coming down harder. "Look, it's gonna get very slick up there very fast. You need to come down before you break your neck."

"I promise I won't break my neck."

"You will if you fall."

"*Don't* make me think about falling. I wasn't even *thinking* about falling. Now you've gone and put falling into my head, which makes it possible."

"Huh?"

"What, you don't believe in quantum physics?" She turned, the rope slung over her shoulder now, and dragged the reindeer higher up onto the roof. Then she sat on the peak, one leg over each side. A position he thought was much more stable than her former one. So he relaxed a little. She stood the reindeer up, bending over their feet and fastening whatever device she'd rigged to hold them there. It worked great. She was more than a hippie, she was a female MacGyver, he thought. Then she made her way back to the edge and sat down beside the ladder, her oversized boots, which looked like furry moonboots to him, dangling over the side. She was holding something in one mittened hand.

"Would you do me a favor and toss me the business end of that extension cord?" She pointed as she said it, and he saw the heavy-duty cord twined at the bottom of the ladder, one end snaked toward the house, and he saw that it was already plugged into a heavy-duty, outdoor outlet.

He sighed. "I can't believe I'm going to be a party to this."

"What?"

"Nothing," he muttered. He went to the cord, unwound a length, and tossed the end up to her.

She caught it easily, a huge smile on her face. "Ready?" she asked.

"Not exactly."

She plugged it in. Santa's sleigh lit up like the runway lights at Detroit Metro. His reins glowed, his sleigh's entire shape was lined in lights, and they twinkled from key points on his suit. Every reindeer's harness glowed, illuminating its face. All nine of them. The traditional eight, plus one riding point with a glowing red nose.

"Happy birthday, Jesus," he muttered.

"How does it look?" she called. She was standing now, right

on the edge, turning her back to him to try to get a better look at the display. He lifted his hands in a "stop" kind of gesture, and grunted the opening syllable of a stern warning. But that was as far as he got before she fell.

He tried to catch her, but only resulted in breaking her fall a bit.

She landed on her back right at his feet.

Her eyes were closed. Not in an unconscious sort of a way, but in an "I'm scrunching up my entire face in agony" kind of a way.

"Ouch," she said. And then her face unscrunched and her eyes popped open. "Isn't this the place where you're supposed to be dropping to your knees, and lifting my broken body up and asking in a desperate, emotion-choked voice if I'm okay?"

He shrugged and remained standing. "You okay?"

"Yeah."

He extended a hand. "Help you up?"

"My hero." She clasped his hand with her mitten, and he braced while she pulled herself to her feet. "You're a romantic devil, aren't you?"

He chose to ignore her comment. "I t*old* you you were going to fall," he said instead.

"And that's why I did. Thanks a lot."

"You deserved it. This poor house would hide its face in humiliation if it could."

"I beg your pardon! This house *loves* to dress up and show off. It hasn't had the chance for a while. And I happen to think it looks great!" She stood staring at it, arms crossed over her chest, and then turned to look at him again. "Why are you here, anyway?"

"The place is for sale. I was thinking about buying it, and the Realtor refused to show it to me tonight. So I thought maybe you could give me the grand tour yourself."

She narrowed her eyes on him. "My ass hurts," she said. "I really don't feel like taking that giant ladder down and stashing it back in the shed."

He lifted his brows. "Uh-huh. And if I were willing to do that for you?"

"Then I'd ask you to bring in some firewood. Enough to last overnight."

"This is getting to be a pricey tour. And if I do both those things?"

"Then I'll give you the grand tour, and tell you everything I know about this house. And I know most everything about it. I grew up here."

He nodded. "Deal."

"Cool. I'm Holly, by the way."

"Of course you are."

She frowned at him, and he quickly said, "Matthew."

"Nice to meet you, Matthew." She looked up at the sky. "Man, I hope this isn't lake effect."

He looked up, too. "I heard that term in town, but then someone said it was only going to be a few inches."

"Phew. That's a relief. Tell you what, I'll put on some hot cocoa. You like hot cocoa?"

He didn't. It was too damn festive and Christmassy. But he didn't answer her, because his grumpy "no" might have made her change her happy little mind about letting him in at all.

The trucker opened the door of his rig when he arrived at his destination, in Binghamton. It was snowing there, and on a whim, he snapped up the old felt fedora and dropped it onto his head before climbing down from his rig.

But the wind had other ideas. It scooped the hat right off his head, and blew it crazily into the air, even as he gave chase, snapping his hands together overhead in an effort to catch it.

It was no use, though. The hat rose higher, and then sailed in a way he'd never seen anything that big sail before.

Shaking his head, he watched it go, and said, "Damn, that hat seems to have a mind of its own."

• *Five* •

HOLLY WENT INSIDE, RUBBING HER HANDS TOGETHER AND heading straight for the fireplace. Bending, she added the last two sticks of firewood in the house. She'd brought in only a couple of arms full—just enough to take the chill off and chase the dampness out of the house while she was outside stringing lights.

She tugged off her mittens and set them on the mantle with their ends hanging over the front to dry. Shrugging out of her coat, which wasn't damp at all, she hung it on a peg by the door, then she sat on the hearthstone to tug off her boots, and put them beside her, as close to the fire as was safe.

Sitting there, her back to the flames, she looked around what had once been the family living room. For a moment, she was swept into the past, to one Christmas morning long ago. The smell of pine, the twinkling lights, as she and her sister pounded down the stairs at about a quarter to dawn. The fireplace crackling, just like it was now. The presents, and paper and bows, and the candy canes on the tree.

Something tightened in her chest and she had a little trouble taking a breath. "Why did you call me back here?" she whispered.

Matthew came in, loaded down with more firewood than she could have carried in three trips, deposited it next to the fireplace, and then bent over and started stacking it more neatly.

Holly looked at him, then looked upward, her brows raised. "Really?"

"Really what?" he asked.

"I, uh—wasn't talking to you."

He frowned, looking around the place as if expecting to see someone else there. She shook her head, and crossed the room to where he stood. "Never mind. You just keep bringing the wood in. I'll take care of piling it neatly." And as she said it, she reached up to brush fresh white snow from his shoulders with her hand. "Looks like it's really coming down out there."

Her hand hopped from a pair of what she'd discovered to be nicely broad, strong shoulders, to his dark hair, where she continued brushing snowflakes away. But only for a moment, because he went very still and his eyes kind of slid around until they met hers.

Melted chocolate eyes. Yum, she thought.

Something crackled, and her hand went still in his hair. Whoa, that was something. And it was something potent, and delicious and exciting. And a little ridiculous. She didn't even know this man—and what she did know about him didn't exactly scream compatability. He drove an expensive car, too fast, was impatient, and thought her Christmas lights were gaudy. What was to like about any of that?

Her hand, she realized, was still buried in his hair. She drew it away, laughed a little to break the tension. "You ought to have a hat."

"Did, once," he said.

She frowned, tilted her head, and searched his face. There was something lost in his eyes when he said that.

He turned and headed back to the door.

Holly watched him go, then she felt the cold that rushed in as he went out, and rubbed her arms. She licked her lips. Was *he* the reason she'd been drawn back here? Was she supposed to meet him for some reason? Were they—*nah*. She added a few more chunks to the fire to distract herself from thinking along those lines, and got busy stacking the rest of the wood.

Twenty minutes later, they had enough wood to last for at least two nights, stacked neatly beside the fireplace. Matthew was shaking the bark and snow off his expensive black coat and taking off his boots by then. At least he hadn't *dressed* like a city slicker in a Porsche. He wore jeans, Timberland boots, heavy socks underneath them, a nice sweater over another shirt. The sweater was brown, the shirt, pale blue—at least that was the color of the collar.

He hung the coat by the front door, next to hers, then carried his boots over to set them beside hers near the fire. She'd already swept up the trail of bark and snow after he'd unloaded the last armful of wood, and wiped the damp spots from the floor with a handful of paper towels.

"Thank you," she said. "You really didn't have to do that, you know. I would have shown you around the house anyway."

"Oh, sure, *now* you tell me." He took a seat on the hearth, where she'd been sitting earlier.

She ran into the kitchen for the steaming mugs of cocoa she'd left out there, and brought them in. She handed him one and then sat down beside him.

"So," she said. "Grand tour begins in ten minutes. After you've had time to rest up, warm up, and drink your cocoa." She took a sip of her own. "Meanwhile, tell me what a guy like you wants with a tumbledown old fixer-upper in the middle of the booming metropolis of Oswego, aka 'Snowbelt Central.' "

He sipped his cocoa as she watched his face. A face that seemed get more attractive every time she looked at it. Hell. He lifted his eyebrows as he licked his luscious lips. "This is actually *good*."

"You sound surprised."

He shrugged and sipped some more. "I buy lots of old houses like this one. They usually sell for exceptionally low prices, 'cause they don't look like much. But if it's structurally sound, and the only work it needs is cosmetic, I usually double my money."

She blinked. "Double? Really?"

"Sometimes better."

She frowned, looking around at the house as she enjoyed her cocoa. "So what would you do to fix it up?"

"It's pretty much the same with every house. You slap on fresh Sheetrock, a couple of coats of paint, put some kind of flooring down, whatever looks good and costs least. Replace any windows and doors that need it. But only the ones that need it. You make sure the wiring and plumbing are up to par, maybe upgrade the heating system. Then you go to the outside, pop on some vinyl siding, hire a crew to spend a couple of days sprucing up the lawn, make sure the roof's intact, and voilà. It looks like a brand-new house."

"And how long does all that work take you?" She was thinking in terms of years.

He said, "Me? It doesn't take *me* any time at all. I hire contractors to do it. A job like this one—maybe three months, tops." He looked at her face and said, "Why are you frowning so hard?"

She tried to ease the muscles in her face, which had scrunched up into what must be a fairly unattractive scowl. "It just sounds so . . . cold. So impersonal. I mean, do you even pick the colors?"

"Of course I do. Siding's white. Interior, eggshell."

"Blaaah!" She made the sound long and expressive and stuck out her tongue as she emitted it.

"You, uh—have something caught in your throat?"

"You know I don't. God, the thought of this place—*this*

place—of all places being sided in white and painted . . . I can't even say it."

"Eggshell," he repeated. "Or maybe ivory."

"It's hideous."

"Well, I can see where the person who put up the lightshow from hell would see it that way, but really, plainly decorated places sell faster and bring more."

"Plain, maybe. Decorated? No. White siding and ivory paint do not count as *decorating*."

"Clearly not to you." He nodded toward the window, where multicolored flashes were turning the glass pane and the snowflakes beyond it red, then blue, then green, then yellow.

"Man, look at it snow." She slugged down the last of her cocoa, and got to her feet.

He did the same.

"Well," she said, turning, "where to begin. I guess you've figured out that this is the living room."

"Yes, that much is obvious. The picture window is going to be a selling point."

"Mmm. As would the plank floors. Dad was always going to sand them off and refinish them. Seven coats of poly, he used to say. He never got to it, but—"

"Vinyl flooring would be faster. Probably cheaper, too."

"They're maple," she said. "Maple floors are rare. Probably would be another . . . selling point."

"It's a thought." He examined the wide, worn-looking planks that made up the floor at the moment.

She ran her palms over the walls. "The Sheetrock does need replacing. But after sitting here unheated for so long—"

"It's to be expected."

"The sofa used to be here, by this wall. Most of the year there was a big old antique stand in front of that window, all covered in Mom's knicknacks. But once Thanksgiving passed, we'd move the table out, and that's where the Christmas tree went."

She turned. "There was a chair there, another one here, love seat over there. And the mantle was cluttered with pictures of my mom and dad and Aunt Sheila and Noelle and me. At least, it was most of the time. During the holidays, they got moved, too, and the mantle hosted Mom's Christmas village—until the collection got too big for it. That was the year Noelle was born."

"And then what?" he asked, sounding amused.

"Then we got a second dining room table. A *giant* one." She led him into the dining room as she spoke. It was just a big empty room now. Same plank floors, and worn-looking walls. "The one we used for actual *dining* was on this side of the room. And the one on the other side was Christmastown, USA. Mom would cover the table in that white, sparkly fabric that looks like fluffy fake snow. All her little buildings would be set up, just so. The church, the general store, the houses and shops, the ice-skating rink, the little miniature carolers that really sang. And there was a train that wound and twisted through the whole thing, with Santa in an engineer's hat, and a whistle that really blew."

"Wow."

It wasn't, she thought, an *impressed* wow. It was more of an "I-had-no-idea-people-were-so-sappy" sort of an exclamation.

She looked at him, awaiting a comment. He shifted as if slightly uncomfortable, then said, "I think the woodwork around the windows can be salvaged. That's a plus."

"Oh joy. Oh rapture." She said it in a deliberate monotone. "Kitchen next, I need more cocoa."

"Yeah, me, too," he said. "Make mine a double."

SHE SIPPED HER COCOA AS SHE LED HIM THROUGH THE REST of the house, filling every room with stories about her happy, idyllic childhood, and it began to seem as if every major event in her life was linked, somehow, to the holidays. Every Christmas memory ended with, "And that was the year Daddy got his raise." Or "And that was the year I learned to ride a bike." And so on.

She was a cheerful little thing, he had to give her that. Cheerful people, in his considered opinion, were only so because they didn't understand hardship. If you knew what life was really about, you couldn't go dancing through it with a butterfly net in one hand and an ice cream sundae in the other. Life sucked. It made you hard, once you saw that. This little thing, though pretty—okay, freaking gorgeous—and friendly, hadn't seen anything yet. Give it time. See how long her positive attitude bull lasted once she'd tasted the grit of real life.

She'd finished the tour. They were on the second floor, where she'd just given him a painstaking description of how she'd decorated her baby sister's room for the holiday with a miniature tree she'd picked out and decorated all by herself. It seems the young Noelle hated to go to sleep at night because she loved looking at the big tree downstairs and its twinkling lights so much. So little Holly had used her allowance money to purchase a small tree and a string of lights, which she had then erected in little Noelle's bedroom.

It was all so damn special, he thought with an inner grimace.

And then she added, "That was the Christmas they died."

They'd been standing there in that final room, which had been a toddler's bedroom, when she said it, and Matthew thought the bottom fell right out of his stomach.

He stared at her, and tried to speak, and thought he must have heard her wrong. "They . . . who?"

"Mom. Dad. Noelle. All of them." She gazed around the room again, her eyes damp in the glow of the single dim bulb. "Car accident. Icy roads, it was no one's fault. I almost went with them, but Mom sent me back."

"In the car?" he asked, thinking she'd narrowly escaped death because her mother hadn't let her go along on that fateful drive.

"No. I *was* in the car. I meant, I almost went with them to . . . well, you know. The other side."

"But your mom sent you back," he muttered.

"Yeah." She shrugged. "Aunt Sheila came and took me home from the hospital, to her place in Binghamton. This is my first time back here since." She sighed, and turned to look up at him.

He was shocked to see a fine sheen in her eyes, and yet, a wobbly little smile on her face. "You know, Ms. Sullivan said there was probably still some of our old furniture up in the attic. And I'm getting sick of having nothing to sit on besides that stone hearth." She turned and marched into the hallway as if she hadn't just revealed her deepest pain. "Come on, Matthew, you might as well see the attic."

The hat tumbled to the snowy ground when the wind let up, and moments later, a laughing child grabbed it and scooped it up.

"Look! I found the hat!"

"Aw, man, where did you get that?"

"It just came rolling up out of nowhere. Just like on Frosty!" The little girl's eyes grew very big then. "Hey, do you think it's a magic *hat?"*

"Yeah, Gracie. The snowman's gonna come to life and say 'happy birthday' the minute we put it on his head." Her older brother shook his head at her. "There's no such thing as a magic hat."

"I don't believe you!" she huffed. Then she marched over to the snowman they had built together, and tried to put the hat on his head. She couldn't quite reach, though. She was hopping, and swinging the hat uselessly. Then her brother lifted her up high, and she plopped the hat on the snowman.

And then she waited.

Her brother was waiting, too, she thought. Even though he said he didn't believe, he must wonder. They stood there, quiet for a long moment, but nothing happened.

"I guess you were right," the little girl said. "No such thing as magic."

"Hey, you never know," her brother said. "There could be. I mean, it's almost Christmas, right? Anything could happen."

He took her little hand in his, and led her home for dinner.

• *Six* •

Holly led Matthew along the hallway, carrying a flashlight she'd dug out of her backpack, which she'd left in one of the bedrooms, until she stood underneath the square in the ceiling that marked the entryway to the attic. It had always seemed a mysterious portal to her as a child. The attic was a whole other world; darker than the rest of the house, cooler in the summer months, hotter in the winter, when the heat gathered there and hung around. It was dusty, not as neat, filled with clutter and cobwebs and dust. It even *smelled* differently than the rest of the house.

And getting there was impossible without help. As a little thing, she'd been unable to reach the cord that hung down. Now, though . . . She stretched out her arm, stood up on tiptoe, and closed her hand around the plastic grip at the end of the cord.

"Wow," she said. "If that doesn't drive home how long it's been, nothing will." She glanced over her shoulder with a smile, but Matthew was only frowning at her. "I could never reach this before," she explained.

"Oh."

He seemed a little tense, was looking at her with a new intensity. Well, she guessed some people didn't deal well with it when you talked about death or loss. They were facts of life, just like the good stuff. There was no point in walling them off in some kind of soundproof room within your head. They were real.

Shrugging, she said, "Stand aside," and when she felt him move, she tugged the cord. The trapdoor came downward, and the attached ladder extended itself and slid to the floor all on its own. Holly flipped the latches on either side that would keep it that way, then stepped on up, aiming her flashlight beam ahead of her.

Cobwebs met her halfway, but she'd never been afraid of them, or of spiders for that matter, so she just brushed them aside and kept ascending, until she stood on the attic floor. She stepped to one side to make room for her guest, and shone her light this way and that, looking around the place with wide eyes.

He came up and stood beside her. "Man, there's a lot of stuff up here."

"Yeah." No need to elaborate. He'd stated the obvious. "Aunt Sheila and I sold everything that was worth much, just to help us get on our feet. She came back here while I was in the hospital and got most of my things out for me, so I wouldn't have to. And she told me she'd stored everything she couldn't sell in the attic and the shed outside. I just . . ."

For some reason her breath caught there, and her throat went real tight.

"You had no way of knowing what stuff was stored and what stuff was sold?" he asked.

She swallowed, nodded. "I never asked." Her voice was raspy, the muscles in her throat still clutching hard at her windpipe.

He cleared his throat. "I owe you an apology, Holly. I uh . . . misjudged you."

"People tend to think I'm either an airhead or that I've been living in a charmed little bubble. I promise, neither one is true."

"I got that. So how do you manage to love the holidays so much?"

"Not just the holidays. I love life." She shrugged. "Hell, I figure Mom didn't send me back here to be miserable. Mostly I think she sent me back to take care of Aunt Sheila."

"Your aunt's not well?"

"MS," Holly said. Then she met his eyes. "Don't look like that. You'd never know, aside from the wheelchair. Hell, I'm pretty sure she's having a fling with the new cook at our diner."

He tipped his head to one side.

"She loves life, too. Runs in the family, I guess."

He just looked at her, as if he didn't quite know what to make of her. She glanced at the TV—a big console model with a knob to turn the channel, and no remote control. "Noelle and I used to lie on the rug watching cartoons on Saturday mornings."

"I used to do the same thing with my kid sister, Cindy."

She nodded. "That TV was outdated, even then." Then she shook off the wave of sadness the memory brought. "What was your favorite?"

"My favorite what?" he asked.

"Cartoon. Mine was *Scooby Doo*."

"Oh. I don't know. I liked the Turtles a lot."

"*The Teenage Mutant Ninja Turtles*, you mean." She smiled. "I liked them, too."

He sighed, turned, and pointed. "There's a sofa. Should we take it downstairs?"

"You offering to help?"

He made a face at her in the glow of the flashlight. "No. I'm gonna leave and let a woman who just fell off her own roof try to manhandle a two-hundred-pound sofa down two flights, single-handedly."

"Don't even *think* I couldn't do it," she said.

He smiled, and it was the first relaxed, genuine smile she thought she had seen cross his face. "You know what? I don't doubt it for a minute."

"Shall we?" she asked.

He nodded. Holly stuck the flashlight into a back pocket, and they each got on one end of the sofa, picked it up, and began the awkward task of maneuvering it through the opening and down the ladder to the hall below, and then farther, down to the living room.

They lowered it to the floor, then positioned it just the way Holly wanted it, facing the fireplace, with a view to the windows.

"Perfect," she said with a satisfied nod.

"Anything else before I leave?"

"Yes, as a matter of fact, there is."

"Okay. Shoot."

She sat down, and patted the sofa until he sat beside her. Then she said, "Tell me why you hate Christmas."

Matthew lifted his brows and stared at her. "Now what makes you think I hate Christmas?"

"Are you saying you don't?"

"No. I'm asking how you knew."

She nodded, grateful for the honesty. She'd half expected him to deny it. "Your reaction to the decorations, your comments about the season in general, all that kind of stuff. It's pretty obvious."

"Well, obvious or not, it's not important."

She met his eyes, held them. "I think it is."

"Hell, Holly, don't be ridiculous. In less than a minute, I'm gonna walk out that door, get into my car, and drive back to my hotel, and you'll probably never see me again. So how in the world could my childhood traumas matter in the least to you?"

"They do." She drew a breath and then blew it out. "I think you're here for a reason. We both are. And I hate to let you leave before I figure out what it is. So it's something from your childhood, then. A trauma?"

Matthew got to his feet, looked down at her, and extended a hand. "It was nice to meet you, Holly. You're . . ." He shook his head. "One of a kind, I think. But I really need to get going."

She took his hand, but instead of shaking it, used it to pull herself to her feet. Then she went to the fireplace to get his boots and coat for him.

He sat on the sofa putting them on, and the silence was taut. She needed to break it. "So, are you going to put an offer in on the place?"

"Depends," he said. Both boots were on and he was bending over to tie them. Without looking her in the eye, he said, "Did you want to buy it back yourself?"

She looked around, felt herself getting misty. "I hadn't even thought about it. It's really not an option right now."

"I see."

"Why did you ask?"

"No reason."

"Liar."

He looked up from tying his boots, and met her eyes.

She went on. "You wouldn't buy it if I had said I wanted it, would you?"

"Sorry," he said. "You must have me mistaken for that Samaritan guy. Or maybe Santa Claus. I do what's best for me. Period."

"Oh, really? Then why did you ask?"

"Curiosity, that's all. Besides, I haven't decided yet if I want the place. It looks like a pretty good investment at first glance, but I never make a decision until I have my contractors inspect a place."

"Oh. So step two is to send them up here to take a look."

"That's right." He pulled on his coat, started for the door, paused halfway there, and turned back around. "Listen, are you sure you're going to be okay out here all by yourself overnight?"

She tipped her head to one side. "You *like* me."

"What are you talking about?"

"Why are you all concerned all of the sudden? You like me. Admit it."

"I have barely *met* you."

"Oh, so your concern for my safety here alone is based on you being what—that Samaritan guy, or Santa Claus?"

He pursed his lips, lowered his head. "Okay. I like you."

"I like you, too. Now don't worry. I've got plenty of food and water, the wood fire, lots of wood at hand, thanks to you." She gave him a nod as she said that. "And I have my cell phone. I'll be fine."

"Just thought I'd check."

"It's considerate of you."

He met her eyes, and they held for a long moment. For one, incredible second, she thought he was going to kiss her. But then he licked his lips and turned again toward the door. "Good night, Holly."

"Merry Christmas, Matthew."

He opened the door and headed through it, pulled it closed behind him. And then she was alone. She turned to face the empty house, and for just an instant, her heart whispered a longing. "Damn," it said, "I sure wish he had stayed a little while longer."

Knock, knock, knock.

Her head snapped up, and she spun to face the door, even as it opened. Matthew ducked inside fast, closed it hard, and stomped significant amounts of snow from his feet and his jeans.

He met her eyes, shook his head. "I hate to impose, kiddo, but I can't go anywhere. Not until it lets up a little."

Her smile was impossible to contain. She lowered her head to hide her face, and whispered, "Thanks," to the powers that be, for answering her wish. She tried to suppress the grin when she met his eyes again. "You can stay as long as you want," she told him. "Actually, I'll be glad of the company."

"Yeah. Every Christmas angel wants to spend her holiday with Ebenezer Scrooge."

"Exactly."

He looked at her with his brows lifted, but she ignored that and followed her instincts instead. She moved right up to him, wrapped her arms around his neck, and pressed her body to his. "I'm really glad you came back."

"Whoa." His arms closed around her waist, and he hugged her right back. When he straightened away, he seemed puzzled and, she thought, pleased.

And why wouldn't any man be pleased to be warmly, genuinely welcomed. She broke the embrace, and went to the window to peer outside. The snow was falling at a rate that brought back a lot of memories. "I think this is lake effect," she told him.

"And that's supposed to mean . . . what exactly?"

She kept looking out the window. "Depends on what kind of mood it's in, I guess. You up to another trip up to the attic?"

He peeled off his coat, hung it on the peg, and heeled off his boots. "What do you need?"

"There's a trunk up there, chock full of blankets and bedding, if memory serves. Maybe you could bring them down? And any oil lamps you see up there. I know there were a few. We might need them. After that, you might want to take a swing at opening that couch up. It's a sleeper sofa. Meanwhile, I'm going to dig through my gear for the portable radio I brought, and just in time so I can listen for a weather report while I cook us dinner."

"Don't tell me you're making a turkey with all the trimmings."

"Don't be silly. That's for Christmas Eve. Tonight, it's burgers and fries."

He sent her a look that registered surprise. "Huh."

"*What?*"

"I don't know. I guess I was expecting you to be a health food nut, if not a full-blown vegetarian."

"You should not judge people by their appearances," she said.

"You're right. I apologize." He started for the stairs.

She said, "Just a sec, Matthew."

He turned, and she lowered her eyes and shrugged. "I . . . um . . . the burgers?"

"Yes?"

"They're veggie burgers."

He was quiet for a second, but then he laughed. It was a deep, slow building chuckle, but it grew, and by the time she managed to lift her gaze to meet his, his head was tipped back and he was laughing loudly.

She laughed, too, and it grew, each of them feeding off the other's silliness, until their laughter died and they stood there, grinning foolishly.

And then his smile faded and he said, "So what about the turkey? Don't tell me it's tofu."

"Turkey, once a year, for Christmas dinner, is the only meat I eat. It's tradition."

"I guess that makes some kind of sense."

"Traditions meant a lot to my mom. Especially Christmas ones."

He nodded, holding her gaze, a smile still gleaming in his eyes. "You know, I honestly can't remember the last time I laughed like that."

"Then you definitely need to do it more often," she said.

"You might just be right about that."

Their gazes locked for a long moment, and then Holly dragged hers away and turned toward the kitchen. "I'm gonna start dinner and find that radio."

She hurried into the kitchen, where she had deposited boxes, bags, and two giant ice chests full of food. She fully intended to give herself, and her mom, dad, baby sis, and their former happy home, a full-blown, traditional, all-out Christmas Eve dinner. And she had brought *all* the trimmings. There was a new tank of LP gas outside, courtesy of Ms. Sullivan. Plenty enough for her to cook for a few days. The range was old, coppertone, and dated. But it was clean and it worked fine. She lit the oven to let it heat up, and then returned to her boxes and bags to dig for the little radio she'd brought along.

Once she had it working, broadcasting the station with the clearest signal, she took a package of frozen French fries from one of the ice chests. She lined a cookie sheet with aluminum foil, sprayed it with organic olive oil cooking spray, and spread the fries on it. Then she gave them another spray, sprinkled them in sea salt, and popped them into the oven. On a second tray she spread the veggie burgers, topped each of them with a slice of green pepper, a slice of onion, and a large thin slice of portabella mushroom. Then she added some tomato sauce and grated cheese blend to each, and slid them into the oven as well.

Finally the music stopped and the weather report came on. She went still, her full attention on the weatherman. Then she blinked, and looked skyward.

"I *said* I wished he would stay *a little while* longer."

The hat blew off the snowman's head, and tumbled to the ground. It rolled along until it hit the sidewalk, and then skittered on its brim, a few feet at at time, until it came to rest exactly in Bernie's path.

Bernie was cold. Way colder than he used to get in the wintertime. But then again, he was getting on in years. He was probably way too old to be sleeping in doorways and whatnot. He was on his way to his favorite diner—the one with the cute waitress who always managed to find something hot for him to eat, and gave it to him without making him feel like a charity case.

She was a rare gem, that waitress.

His stomach was growling in anticipation and he walked a little faster as he got closer to the diner. He tried not to show up there too often. Didn't want to wear out his welcome or take advantage of a kind heart. But there was just no help for it this morning. It had been a cold night, and he needed a warm meal in his belly more than he needed air.

His foot hit something in his path—and he looked down to see a black felt hat, just sitting there. Bernie looked up and down the sidewalk. He looked left and he looked right, wondering if the brisk, freezing wind had driven it off someone's head—someone who was, even now, running along the sidewalk to retrieve it.

But no. There was no one.

So Bernie hunkered down and he picked up that hat. He put it on his head, and it felt good. Warmed his ears a little. Moreover, he thought it looked pretty good, too.

He smiled, and stood a little straighter as he continued on his way to the diner.

• Seven •

MATTHEW WAS THINKING THAT IT WASN'T SUCH A HARDSHIP to be forced to spend another couple of hours with a pretty woman. She had that happy-go-lucky, little Mary Sunshine thing going on, yeah. And normally, people like that got on his nerves like nothing else in creation. But she was different. She wasn't one of those morons who were just too dumb to realize how shitty the world was. She wasn't one of those lucky idiots who'd never had any hardships and so thought the world was a bowl of freaking ice cream.

She'd had some hard times. Lost her whole goddamn family at the tender age of twelve. During the holidays.

Just like I lost my dad.

And yet, she loved the freaking holly-jolly-ho-ho-jingle-bell bullshit.

He had to admit, he was curious about her. Her reaction to such a similar tragedy was so totally opposite his own that he found himself wanting to know more. Wanting to know . . . *why*.

There was more than that, though, and he knew it. He was attracted to her. Big time. And it was tough to rein it in when she was so open about feeling it right back at him. Hell, that hug. And that crack about liking him. And the look in those big blue eyes every time they met his.

Damn.

She came into the living room, bearing big plates full of food, and his stomach reminded him how long it had been since his lunch.

"Well, it *smells* good," he said.

"You're gonna love it." She marched to the hearth, and sat down.

He got the message—she didn't want food and crumbs all over the sofa bed because she was going to have to sleep on the damn thing. Okay. He joined her on the hearthstone, and took the plate she offered him.

The burger *looked* good, too.

"Whole wheat bun," she said. "Best kind."

"I'll bet." He picked up a French fry, still piping hot and salty. She handed him the bottle of ketchup at her side.

"Come on, try the burger."

"Oh, all right." He finished the fry, then picked up the burger, which was pretty hefty with all the stuff she'd added to it. He wrinkled up his nose, preparing for the worst, and bit into the damn thing.

Grimacing, he chewed. Slowly, he felt his grimace vanish. And then he lifted his brows in surprise as he kept on chewing. And then he swallowed, and he smiled. "Well, I'll be damned."

"Told you."

"Oh, there'll be no living with you now, will there?"

"Uh, actually, Matthew, there kind of will."

"Kind of will . . . what?" He was lost.

"There kind of will be . . . some . . . living with me."

"Huh?"

"Where did you get the idea we were only going to get a few inches of snow?"

He frowned, glanced at the window. In the glow of her hideous holiday lights, he could see that the snow was still coming down, huge flakes, falling densely and rapidly. "I overheard the waitress saying it at the diner."

"Oh. And what did she say, exactly?"

"I don't know. 'Snow' and 'lake effect' and 'we're gonna get two to three.' Then the other waitress said, 'I heard three to five.' "

"Uh-huh." Holly shrugged, sighed. "Well, I hate to break it to you, Matthew. But, um, my best guess is they weren't taking about inches. They were talking about feet."

"Feet," he repeated blankly. Then his brain interpreted her meaning and he said it again. "*Feet?*"

She nodded. "According to the radio, it's going to go all night, three feet by morning, and possibly more. And I can't even imagine how long it'll take to get dug out, get the roads cleared, and so on, once it's over."

"You've got to be kidding me."

"No. It's pretty common up here. We're in the snowbelt, you know."

"I *knew*. I just didn't *know*, you know?"

"Oh, hell, yes," she said. "So, I guess you and I are going to be spending Christmas together."

Matthew looked up at the ceiling and muttered, "Dammit, when I said to get me out of spending another inane holiday with my sappy sister and her know-it-all husband and their whiny, sticky-faced kids, this is *not* what I meant."

"I was just having a similar conversation with the universe myself," she told him. Then she shrugged. "But you know, the gods love a good laugh. And this time I think the laugh's on us."

He sighed, but found it hard to be too upset about any of this. In fact, if he didn't know better, he might think he was almost . . . enjoying it.

Nah.

"I've got a three p.m. flight out of Syracuse tomorrow. Think I can make it?"

"If you do, you'll miss Christmas Eve dinner," she told him.

And then the hideous holiday lights outside flickered, and so did the inside lights. They flickered, and then they dimmed, and then they brightened up again.

She sucked air through her teeth and closed her hand on his forearm. And heat shot right up it.

"We'd better get those oil lamps lit, ahead of time. The power's not gonna last through the night."

Neither, he thought, was he.

Holly carried her empty plate into the kitchen, and her reluctant houseguest did the same. When she put a kettle of water on to heat, he crooked an eyebrow at her.

"No hot water?" he asked.

"It's gas, and it's not lit. I didn't bother. Probably just as well we don't—I mean, we've got a limited supply of gas. It's a new tank, but it's not a big one."

"You're using as much gas heating it on the stove as you would in the hot water heater."

"I am not. Why heat fifty gallons and keep them hot for the duration, when we can heat just what we need, when we need it?"

"Because I'm going to want a shower in the morning. How much propane is out there?"

"I don't know. A tankful."

"Yeah, but how big a tank?"

She shrugged.

"All right, I'll check while I'm out. If it's enough to last three days, we light the hot water heater. Deal?"

"What do you mean, while you're out? Why are you going out?"

"To see if it looks like I could make it back to the hotel."

"In that Matchbox Car you drove?"

"It's a Porsche."

"In this weather, you'd be lucky to make it in a Bronco."

"I'm just going to take a look."

She shook her head at that. "Fine, you win. If the notion of spending any more time in my presence is *that* intimidating to you, then—"

"Intimidating?"

She shrugged.

"Why would you think you intimidated me?"

"I haven't figured that out yet. I think you might be afraid of me. Or maybe of yourself. If you hang around me, you might just enjoy the holiday, and for some reason, you can't let yourself do that."

"Holly, there's absolutely no chance I'm ever going to manage to enjoy Christmas. But uh, just so you know, I was thinking if I could get back to the hotel, I'd try to talk you into going, too. If the power goes out—and three feet of snow. I just think it might be safer."

"Oh."

She watched through the doorway as he bent to pull on his boots, then his coat. Then he went to the door, and headed outside. She ducked aside to avoid the rush of wind and cold that came in when he left. Then she sighed and shook her head and tried not to wonder if he had been thinking one room, or two, at that hotel.

She took her teapot off the burner, and poured the steaming water into the waiting dishpan. Then she cooled it with some from the tap, and washed the handful of dishes from their shared dinner.

As she washed the dishes, she recalled standing here at the sink at the age of twelve, washing them after dinner and complaining loudly the entire time. "I don't know why *I* have to do them. *I'm* not the mom."

To which her mother had replied, "And just where did you get the idea that dishes were always the mom's job?"

Holly had frowned. Her father had just smiled to himself and averted his eyes. "Whaddya mean? Isn't it?"

"Well, let's see. Who dirtied these dishes?"

"We all did," Holly said.

"So then shouldn't we all clean them? Doesn't that make more sense?"

Tipping her head to one side, Holly thought on it. "I guess it does. But if that's how it is, then how come I don't just wash the ones I dirtied, and you and Dad and Noelle wash your own?"

"We could do it that way, if you want to. Noelle's too little yet, of course. But I think it's nicer to take turns. That way you get two nights off after taking your turn instead of having to spend time in the kitchen every single night."

Holly nodded slowly. "I guess you're right." Then she thought some more.

"Dad and I take turns doing dishes, but you make dinner every night, Mom. That's not really fair, either, is it?"

"No, it's really not," her mother said. "But your dad's a terrible cook."

At which point Holly had nodded hard, dried her hands on a towel, and marched into the living room, where her father had gone. "From now on, Dad, you and I should take turns with the dishes, and leave Mom out of it. She cooks every night. It would be more fair."

Her dad grinned at her and nodded hard. "You got it, kiddo. I think that's a great idea."

Holly smiled as the memory faded. She finished the cookie sheet and emptied the water, then grabbing a paper towel to wipe her hands dry, she went to the door and peeked out.

Even as she looked, he came tromping through what had to be six inches of snow already, toward the house. She opened the door for him just as he reached for it.

He stomped the snow off himself as best he could and came inside.

"So is it rude to say I told you so?"

"It's coming down so hard out there I doubt I could see to drive anyway. And there's so much snow in the road you can't tell where the shoulders are."

"And so you decided to try to leave anyway, because . . . ?"

"I didn't."

"I heard the motor—"

"Oh, that. No, I just thought if I could turn the car around, I'd have a better chance of getting out once the roads are cleared."

"Oh."

He peeled off his coat, shook it, and hung it on the peg by the door. He was pulling of his boots when she said, "Just so you know, breakfast will be on you. Both prep and cleanup."

He lifted his head slowly.

"We share chores in this house," she told him. "And I did dinner."

"I brought in the wood," he countered.

"I'll get the next load."

"If I make breakfast, we get to have meat."

"If you can find any meat in this house, besides the turkey, you're welcome to cook it."

"I might just go out and shoot something."

"If you can find a gun in this house—"

He held up a hand. "Yeah, yeah. I know. I was being sarcastic." His boots were off, and he carried them over to the fireplace, set them on the hearth, and then turned and went still. She'd taken all the blankets and pillows he had carried down the stairs and made up the sofa bed, and she had to admit it looked awfully inviting.

And he looked awfully nervous.

"There's no other bed," she told him. "Nothing that can be used for one, and if we divvy up what few blankets there are, we're both going to freeze."

"So we're gonna sleep together?" he asked.

She grinned broadly. "Yeah. You don't need to worry, though. Your virtue is safe with me."

"Gee, I'm very reassured."

"What, you don't trust me?"

"It's nothing personal. I don't trust hippies as a rule." He was teasing her.

She smiled even wider. "I don't think there are any such things as hippies anymore."

"I'm not sure we've come up with a slang word that describes you better."

"Fine. You call me Hippie. I'll call you Ebenezer."

"Whatever."

She shrugged and headed for her bag, which she'd slung on the floor near the stairs. "I'm going up to change."

"I'm going down to light the water heater," he said.

"It won't do any good. Power will be out by morning. You'll have a tank full of hot water and no electric to pump it."

"I'm willing to risk it."

"Have it your way."

She headed up the stairs with her bag, so she could change clothes in the bathroom. And while she was thinking about it, she ran the bathtub full of cold water, just so they could bail buckets full to flush the toilet if the need arose.

And it did. No sooner had she changed into her favorite flannel pajamas, than the lights flickered and died.

It was the bang, followed by a deep shout from the cellar that made her go running down the stairs blind, but knowing the house by heart.

• *Eight* •

HE'D FIGURED OUT THE INSTRUCTIONS, FOUND THE MAIN gas valve, cranked it on, and was holding a match to the pilot, his thumb on the required button, when the lights went out.

Just as they did, the hot water heater lit with a soft "whoosh" and he let off the button, watching the flame inside. It stayed lit. Good.

Or not so good, depending. If the lights stayed out this time, Miss Know-It-All upstairs would probably never let him hear the end of it. Then again, it had to come back on sooner or later. And when it did, he would have hot water for a shower. So there.

He put the cover back on the hot water heater's control panel, and rose, turning to make his way across the cellar to the stairway, but finding himself immersed in ink-thick darkness.

No problem, he could find his way out. It was straight ahead, about ten steps or so, and then—

He walked as he thought, and promptly banged his knee on

something solid as a rock with an edge to it, which caused him to yelp in pain.

Dammit!

Her footsteps pattered rapidly up above, and seconds after that, there was a light at the top of the stairs. "Don't move," Holly called. "Let me get down there with the light first."

"My hero," he muttered, returning her earlier comment to her, just as sarcastically as she had delivered it. But his knee was throbbing big time, and he thought he'd done some damage there. So, okay.

She was beside him a moment later, holding the flashlight and examining his face while burning out his corneas. "Are you okay?"

"Yep. Fine. Let's go upstairs."

"What did you hurt?"

"Knee," he said.

And he shouldn't have, because then she was hunkering down, holding her light as if she could see something, when his jeans covered it anyway.

"Hell, it's bleeding right through the denim. Come on, I can't do anything down here." She slid an arm around his waist, held him firmly against her side as she moved the both of them to the stairs, and then up them. He almost told her he didn't need any help. Right up until he stepped on the leg, that is. The second he did, he knew from the surge of pain that he *did* need help. And she was the only one around to give it.

Hell, just what he needed: to be dependent on a damn happy hippie—much less one so damn sexy he could barely keep his hands off her as it was. And to be stuck with her for God only knew how long to boot.

Just shoot me now, he thought. And then the thought faded, because she smelled so damn good. He hadn't been close enough before to realize it, he guessed. Or maybe she'd put some scent on when she'd been upstairs changing. Just for him?

* * *

HOLLY LED HIM TO THE FOLDED-OUT SLEEPER SOFA. HE SAT on its edge, tense as a bowstring. "Just relax. I'm not going to amputate, I promise." She met his eyes, tried to put a reassuring light in her own, but he didn't look reassured. He looked nervous.

"I'm going to get my first aid kit out of my bag."

"You brought a first aid kit?"

"Well, of course I brought a first aid kit. I never travel without one. Not that I travel much. Or at all. But I wouldn't, anyway, without a—" She shook her head. "Never mind. Take the jeans off. I'll be right back."

"I'm not taking my jeans off."

"Well, you're not sleeping with them on. You'll get the sheets all bloody, and they're the only ones we have." She ignored him, grabbing the second of the four oil lamps from the mantel, and lighting it. She'd already lit the first. Then she went to the kitchen, where she'd dropped the duffle bag she was pretty sure contained the first aid kit. She rummaged around until she found it, and came back to the living room.

He'd taken off the jeans and sat there looking obstinate, blood trickling from an inch-long gash in his knee.

"Hell. That must hurt like crazy." She hurried to him, kneeling in front of him and opening the first aid kit, which was a hard plastic minisuitcase chockfull of supplies.

"Damn," he said, looking down as she ripped open gauze pads with her teeth. "You could perform surgery with that thing."

"I filled it myself," she said. "It pays to be prepared. Hold still now." She pressed a few gauze pads to the cut. "Can you hold these here? Nice and hard. You need pressure on it so the bleeding stops. Okay?"

He replaced her hand with his on the pads. She got up and ran back to the kitchen, wet a fistful of paper towels in cold water because there wasn't time to heat any, and hurried back to him.

Then she washed the blood away from his leg. He had a hairy calf. Strong, too. Firm. It flexed when she ran her hands over it, washing away the blood. She liked it. She liked it very much.

"Your sock's all bloody, too," she said, trying to keep her voice from betraying her. She set the wet paper towels aside and took hold of his sock, peeling it off his foot, her fingers in contact with his skin all the way. There was something—a rush of warmth. Attraction. Pleasure. Something. She paused and lifted her head, met his eyes, wondering if he'd felt it, too.

He held her gaze, and the look in his made her aware of the suggestiveness of her current position. Kneeling in front of him.

Oh, yeah. He'd felt it, too.

He looked away before she did. Okay, so he felt it, but he didn't like it. Or maybe he liked it, but he didn't want to. Whatever. She washed the blood from his ankle, and then returned her attention to the knee, covering his hand with hers, lifting the gauze just enough to peek. It bled again when she did.

"I'm going to have to tape it up. Butterfly bandages should do the trick. It ought to have stitches, but I don't have a sewing kit on me."

"Not quite as prepared as you thought you were, are you?"

"You can bet I won't leave home without one again." He held the gauze while she unwrapped the butterfly bandages. "We should clean it first. I have peroxide. It won't hurt as much as alcohol would, but it won't be fun, either."

"Distract me then."

"How?" she asked, opening the bottle and trying not to hope he'd say something just slightly inappropriate. And yet hoping just that.

"You said you never travel. Tell me why."

She nodded at him to move the gauze. He did. She held a wad of fresh pads beneath the wound to catch the blood and excess, and then poured peroxide over it, saying as she did, "I don't like to leave Aunt Sheila. It's not like we can afford someone to take care of her, and she'd hate that anyway. I don't know, maybe now that she's apparently got a love life, he'll help out now and then."

Matthew's body went stiff as she poured, but then she quickly pressed the gauze to the cut again. "Okay, you hold it together and I'll tape."

He nodded, reached for an alcohol wipe and tore it open, then cleaned his hands with it. "Your Aunt Sheila—she's the one who raised you after . . . your family . . ."

"Yeah. I remember when I was in the coma, Mom telling me I had to go back." She applied the first bandage as he pinched the wound tight. It had to hurt. "She kept saying I had important things to do, and that there were people who needed me. She even specified that Aunt Sheila needed me. And it turned out, she really did. More than anyone."

"She was your mother's sister?"

"Yeah." She applied another butterfly.

"Your, uh . . . your family spoke to you. After they died, then."

A smile tugged at her lips. "I don't suppose you believe in that sort of thing. But they did. I mean, I was with them at first, when Mom said all that. But after I came back, she still . . . stayed in touch."

"How? You hear voices? See her in dreams?"

She put on the third bandage, sensing that this was important to him and answering carefully. "No. She sends me signs. All the time. Heck, that's why I'm here." She lifted her head. "You can let go now. It's all taped up." He took his hand away. She reached into the kit for more fresh gauze, tape, and a tube of triple antibiotic ointment.

"What did you mean, that's why you're here?"

"I kept seeing signs, telling me I should come home for Christmas. So I did. I didn't know why, or what the point was, but then you showed up." She applied a generous dollop of ointment, placed the gauze pad over it, and then taped it carefully in place.

"I showed up. You're saying you think I'm the reason she sent you here?"

"Well, you're the only reason I've seen so far."

"And what is it you think you're supposed to . . . uh . . . do with me?"

She lifted her head, met his eyes quickly, and smiled. "The only thing that comes to mind—besides the obvious . . ." He looked *really* interested when she said that, but she went right on, pretending not to notice, "Is that maybe I'm supposed to teach you how to love Christmas again."

She sat back on her heels. "All done."

He looked at the knee, nodded. "Nice job. Thanks."

"You can thank me by helping me decorate the tree."

He frowned, looking around the room. "You showed me every inch of this place, and I don't recall seeing any tree. Am I missing something?"

"My mother would *never* ask me to spend Christmas without a tree. We'll have one, somehow. Maybe one is growing close enough by so I can go out and get it when the snow stops. Or maybe Santa will bring one when he comes." She smiled and shrugged. "I don't know how we're going to get a tree, but I guarantee you, we'll have one."

"Ooookay."

She gathered up the wrappings, carried them to the fireplace, and tossed them into the flames Then she returned to the first aid kit, and packed it up, closed it, and set it in a corner for safekeeping.

"Does it hurt a lot?" she asked. " 'Cause I have pain reliever, if—"

"No, it's okay."

"So it's your turn, then," she said. She bent to the fire and tossed as many logs onto it as seemed wise, then replaced the screen and walked to the sofa bed. He was still sitting on the side, his feet on the floor, one sock on, one off. She crawled right past him and lay down, snuggled into her pillow, and tugged the covers up over her. She turned onto her side, to face him, waiting.

"My turn to do what?"

"Tell me something about you." She patted the mattress beside her. "And lie down, will you? I'm not all that bad, am I?"

He didn't answer, but he did peel off his sweater and shirt, leaving on a T-shirt. Then he lay down stiffly, on his back, pulled the covers to his chin, and carefully left a good four inches of space between the two of them.

"Not much to tell," he said. "I live in Detroit. I have one sister—married with two kids. I buy, renovate, and sell houses. I do okay."

He stopped there, as if that was everything. She rolled her eyes. "I mean something *real*."

"Like what?"

"Like why you hate Christmas."

He turned, just his head, nothing else, toward her. "I don't talk about that."

"Oh, come on. After the stuff I told you?"

He sighed. "Actually, it's pretty similar. Eerily similar. But purely coincidental," he added, with a lift of his brows and a nod of his head. "My dad died the day before Thanksgiving. The holidays have never been my favorite time since."

"How old were you?"

"Twelve," he said.

"How did he die?"

"Heart attack."

"So that left just you and your mom and your sister."

"Yeah."

"She younger or older, your sis?"

"Younger."

She nodded. "So how did you celebrate Christmas that year?" she asked.

He frowned at her. "You're a nosy little thing, you know that?"

She shrugged. "I already told you, I like you, Matthew," she said. "I'm starting to think I like you very much."

"Uh . . . yeah, well . . ."

"And I think maybe Mom knew I would. And I don't think there's any such thing as coincidence."

"Look, Holly, don't go getting any . . . ideas . . . you know about . . . you and me. This is just a couple of strangers stranded in a snowstorm."

"Yeah. I know." She moved closer; he didn't move away. She said, "Can I just try something? Just to make sure?"

"Try . . . what?" he asked.

"This," she said, and she closed her eyes and pressed her mouth to his.

Bernie wore the hat into the diner, and found himself a seat at the counter, not wanting to take up space in a booth. After all, he wasn't a paying customer. He was there in search of handouts, though his favorite lady never made him feel as if he was.

There she was now, coming right up to him, wiping her hands on a crisp white towel as she did. She was sick, he knew, but he wasn't sure exactly how. Only that she got more lame by degrees. She used a cane now, and he'd heard someone say she would be in a wheelchair before long. Her little niece sure had stepped up to the plate, though.

"Now, honey, you can't even imagine how glad I am to see you," she said. "I just had a fellow come in here—you wouldn't believe the manners. Ordered a full-blown breakfast fit to feed a lumberjack, then got all huffy 'cause I didn't get it to him fast enough and took his business elsewhere. I been back here wringing my hands thinking of all that food going to waste. I don't suppose you might have room for it, would you?"

He shrugged. "I'd be glad of it, Sheila."

Her pretty face broke into a full-blown smile. "Oh, thank you, hon.

Now, listen, it's gonna take a bit to warm it up for you. Why don't you head on back to that booth right there? It's next to the register. Gets too warm for most folks. And I'll bring it on back when it's ready. You want coffee or cocoa with that?"

"Cocoa would be good," he said. "If it's not too much trouble, I mean."

"No trouble at all." She had already hauled a heavy white mug from beneath the counter, and she turned to a big steaming pot that smelled like heaven, and poured frothy chocolate from it. She handed the mug to him and patted his hands. "My goodness, your hands are cold."

"Oh, they'll warm soon enough," he said, hugging them around the mug. "Thanks to you."

"Don't be silly, you're doing me the favor. Go on, go sit. I'll bring your food along presently."

Nodding, he got up off the stool and made his way back to the booth she'd indicated. He slid into it, grateful for the soft, cushioned seat, and the room to lean back and stretch out his legs underneath the table, and just soak up the heat wafting up from the register nearby. It felt good.

That Sheila, she was one in a million.

He took the felt hat off his head, and set it on the table beside him, remembering his manners late, but at least remembering them.

He wanted to give her something to thank her. But he didn't have much to give. Then again, he thought, glancing down at the hat, it would be no great loss to give her the hat. It was just the sort of thing she would appreciate, and he would be no more without it than he had been a few hours ago.

That was it, then. He'd give her the hat. He had a feeling it was the right thing to do. Odd, that. But there it was.

• *Nine* •

He did not expect Holly to kiss him. Hell, that was the *last* thing he expected. And his initial reaction was a sudden, desperate urge to jump out of that bed and run for the door.

He didn't act on it quickly enough, though, and so the second urge stepped up to the plate. And that one was to wrap his arms around her and pull her close and kiss her right back.

Which was totally idiotic.

And yet, he did it. He rolled toward her, twisted his arms around her tiny waist, pulled her close to him, so her chest was pressed to his, and opened his mouth to feed from hers. And she opened hers, too, and he let his tongue caress those lips and she opened farther to welcome it inside. Damn. Damn, he was on fire all of the sudden. And it was dumb and made no sense whatsoever.

Finally, he lifted his head back a little, though it was the last thing he wanted to do. "I, um . . . this isn't a good idea, Holly."

"I think it's a really good idea," she said. "Life's too short not to embrace gifts like this. And this is a gift, Matthew. Don't think for one minute it's anything less."

"I don't even know you."

She shrugged. "You're about to."

He was tempted. Sorely tempted. This was like some fantasy out of the Penthouse Forum. But it wasn't a fantasy. It was real, and she was real, and there were real reasons not to sleep with someone you didn't know. Particularly without protection.

And *that*, he thought, was the one argument that might save him. Both from her persistence and his own weakness.

"We don't have any—"

"Yes, we do."

He blinked at her. She smiled at him, her head resting on the pillow, her eyes sparkling with firelight. "You know how I was saying before that it always pays to be prepared?"

"Uh-huh." It was a croak.

"Well?"

"I, um . . . I'm not looking for—"

"Let's not question this, okay? Let's not analyze it or talk about it or, God forbid, waste it. Let's just enjoy it. Right now. In the moment. Can we do that?"

He had yet to meet a woman capable of any such thing. Then again, he thought, he had yet to meet a woman quite like this one.

"I can do that," he said softly. And now he got a little braver, reached out with his fingers to stroke a wisp of a blond curl from her cheek. And then he paused with that curl in his fingers, rubbing it. So soft. And her cheek, even softer. "Can you?"

"I've spent my entire life living in the moment. It's the only way I got through, sometimes."

He felt the surprise rinse through him at that admission—the admission that she had ever been less than perfectly happy. It was something he didn't imagine she let a lot of people see. And then he looked at her, *really* looked at her, and he saw beyond the happy, new age, positive-energy-spouting hippie. He saw a woman who'd been gutted, just like he had been. She was empty, and searching for something to fill that emptiness. She was vulnerable and needier than she knew. And right now, what she needed was him.

Unfortunately, he couldn't handle being quite that needed.

He stroked her cheek once more, then leaned closer, and pressed his lips to it. "I can't, Holly. I'm sorry."

Her eyes slammed closed. White teeth bit down on her lower lip. She rolled onto her back and flung a forearm over her face, probably to hide it from him. "It's okay. I understand."

"I'll probably regret it for the rest of my life, if that's any consolation."

"It's not, 'cause I will, too."

"I'm sorry," he said again.

"You should be."

"It's not that I'm not . . . attracted to you."

"Well, duh."

He frowned at her—well, *toward* her. She still had her arm over her face. "I don't follow."

"By 'well, duh,' I mean, 'obviously you're attracted to me' and 'who wouldn't be, anyway?' "

"Any man in his right mind would be," he said. "Maybe I just see more than they would."

"Suddenly the Grinch is Mister Insight?" she asked. "This oughtta be good."

"Would be, but I'm not going there. You going to be able to sleep?"

"Not much else to do," she replied. Then she rolled onto her side, away from him, punched her pillow as if it had done something to make her very angry, and lay still.

"I'm sorry, Holly."

"Stop saying that."

He sighed, tried to relax into the pillow, and closed his eyes. But he wasn't a bit sleepy. Mostly, his mind was busy conjuring what it would have been like. What he could have been doing, right then, instead of lying there, bored, wide-awake, and turned on in spite of himself.

Yep. He was an idiot.

EVENTUALLY, SHE SLEPT. SHE WASN'T SURE HOW. SHE'D been pretty much embarrassed to the roots of her hair to have offered herself to him so blatantly, only to have him turn her down cold.

Damn. She'd thought she had more sex appeal than that.

At any rate, she lay there stewing and frustrated until, finally, sleep had claimed her. And it seemed that sleep had its own ideas about what the two of them would and would not be doing in the comfort of the sofa bed.

Because when she opened her eyes, and she saw him opening his, they were lying, face to face. Close enough to kiss. They were tangled together. Her arms were around his neck. His were around her waist. Her leg was over his, his upper one was in between hers.

And before she could move, he was kissing her. Eyes falling closed, mouth moving to capture hers, arms curling tighter, pulling her closer.

"You don't have to . . ." she whispered when his lips slid from hers to her neck. And once he started kissing her neck, it was all over. That was her weak spot, right there. She thought wildly that she even liked his morning breath. It wasn't bad. Just real. Raw.

"I have to," he muttered against her skin. "Trust me, I have to."

She didn't have to be told twice. She arched her hips toward his, and he pushed back, then pressed her onto her back and slid his hand down the front of her pajama bottoms. She scrambled out of them to give him better access. Then she tugged at his clothes as they kissed some more, wrestling his T-shirt over his head. He pulled her pajama top free of its buttons, pushed it off her shoulders. And then his mouth was moving from hers, down her neck to her chest. She shivered when he found her breasts, mouthed them, suckled them.

Pleasure shot through her like fire through a dry forest. Heat so intense she thought she might go up in flames. He touched her, then his hand slid between her legs, not hesitantly, not timidly, but eagerly. And he groaned at the heat and wetness he felt there.

She arched against his hand, silently pleading for more, and he didn't make her wait. He rolled on top of her, slid inside her, and she quivered and sighed as he filled her. The sensation grabbed hold and wouldn't let go. She tipped her hips up to his and took all of him, until he drove the very breath from her lungs. And then again and again. He kept on kissing her the entire time they twisted and writhed and pressed into each other. Straining, reaching, taking, and giving. And all the while his mouth took hers. He kissed her as if he loved kissing her. As if he didn't want to stop. No man had ever done that before—kissed her all the way through sex. Open-mouthed, hungry, wet kisses. As if he wanted to devour her. As if he couldn't get enough.

It made her feel more wanted than she had ever felt in her life. And she wondered where he'd been hiding all this passion, all this fire. Thank God he wasn't hiding it now.

His hands slid underneath her backside, to hold her to him, tilt her up to take him, and he drove even deeper, and faster, and his kisses became more desperate. He was pushing her toward climax, and she reached for it, ached for it. And then, suddenly, he pulled back just slightly, tried to slow his pace.

"No," she whispered. "No, Matthew, don't stop."

"But I'm—"

"So am I."

She clutched his hips and rode him, moving against him as the wave crested, and crashed to the shore. Her entire body shuddered in sweet anguished ecstasy. She clung and she cried out, and then he was doing the same as he drove deep and held there, throbbing inside her.

They clung that way for a long time, and he kissed her again and again as her body sank into the most relaxed state of bliss she had ever felt. He withdrew after a time, rolling onto his side, pulling her close into his arms. She snuggled against him, content and sated.

Moments ticked past. Long moments as her body just hummed.

"We're very different people, you and I," he said eventually.

She stayed where she was, warm and cozy in his arms. "We have a lot in common, too, though. Not that I'm saying we have to, or—"

"I know." He sighed. She felt the rise and fall of his chest, his breath in her hair. Maybe she wasn't *entirely* sated just yet, she thought with a secret smile. "We had similar tragedies, centered around the holidays, when we were kids. But we reacted in entirely different ways."

"Will you tell me now? About that first Christmas without your dad?"

He was silent for a long moment. So long she began to think he wasn't going to answer her at all. And then he said, "Dad had this hat. This old felt hat he wore everywhere."

"Not a fedora," she whispered.

"Yeah. A black felt fedora. He always told me he'd give it to me one day. Like it was some kind of an heirloom or something. It was an inside joke between us."

"That's incredibly special."

"My mother sold it, along with all his things, to a secondhand shop so she could use the money to buy us kids Christmas presents."

"Oh, no."

"Yeah. It was just a stupid hat. But it meant something to me. I don't even remember what she bought me that year. Just that the hat was gone, and we couldn't get it back. And it got to me. I guess I resented Christmas over that, as much as anything else."

"I don't blame you. It must have been like losing that one last little piece of him."

She felt him nod. "That's exactly what it was like." He hugged her a little tighter. "Maybe it would have been easier if I believed . . . like you do. If he'd—I don't know—talked to me or showed up in a dream or sent me some kind of unmistakable sign, you know? But to me, it was like he was just gone. Just . . . gone."

"But he's not."

"See, that's where we're different. I don't really believe that."

"You're the kind of man who has to see things, touch them, to believe them," she said. "But I know your dad's not gone. I've been there, don't forget. And I'll bet he has sent you signs—you're just not seeing them. Because you're not looking for them. And you're not looking for them because you don't believe they exist. You think seeing is believing. But I know you have to believe first. *Then* you start to see."

He lifted his head and looked down at her. She met his eyes and smiled softly. He said, "I like you, Holly. In spite of myself, I think. But um . . . this—"

"Isn't going anywhere," she finished for him. "Because it's impossible. Because you have to go back to your life in Detroit, and I have to go back to my aunt in Binghamton. And because of a thousand other reasons. We don't have to go there tonight, though, do we? Let's just enjoy this for what it is, and not worry about what it isn't. That's what we both said we would do, isn't it?"

He nodded.

"So can I tell you something before we go to sleep?"

"Sure."

"That was the best sex I've ever had."

His smile was instant and full, and she thought, pretty damn self-satisfied. But he didn't return the compliment. He was probably afraid to, afraid she'd read too much into it if he did. But she wasn't going to put up with that. She jabbed him in the ribs a little. "You're supposed to say it was good for you, too, you know."

He snuggled down beside her. "It—"

His words were interrupted by the roar of a motor, and then a horrible crash and the sound of crunching metal. They both sat up in bed, stunned into immobility for just a second. Then they were scrambling for their clothes, lighting lamps. She ran to the window and looked out to see headlights, and the outline of a flatbed truck at a cockeyed angle off the side of the road, its nose crushed against a tree. The back of it was loaded with something, and covered in a white tarp.

"Oh, no."

Matthew was pulling on his boots, then his coat. "I'll see if the driver's okay."

"I'll grab the first aid kit and be right out," she told him, rushing for her own boots as he headed out the door. "God, who would try to drive in this?"

MATTHEW WAS WORRIED, AND TO BE HONEST, DAMN GLAD of the distraction, as he tromped through a good two feet of snow toward the wreck. Maybe the driver would be unharmed and would shack up with the two of them for the remainder of the storm. Maybe having a third party there would keep him from making any more asinine blunders like the one he'd made tonight.

Sure, Holly said it didn't have to mean anything. But he'd never met a woman yet who could have sex and not want it to mean something. And yeah, she was different from any woman he'd ever met before. But at the core, women were women.

And she had some kind of effect on him. Because damn, he had *never* had sex that good. And he never *ever* talked about that stupid hat. At least he never had, until tonight.

He hoped the driver was okay. And he hoped the guy would stay for a while.

As he neared the truck, the driver's door opened, and a man clambered out.

"Hey, are you okay?" Matthew called.

"Yeah, fine, fine." The man walked toward him, shaking his head. "I really thought I could make it through. Should have known better, but hell, tomorrow's Christmas Eve."

As he spoke, he zipped up his parka, pulled up the hood, turned to look in the direction he'd been driving. "Well, it's only another half mile. My place is just around the next bend in the road. Guess I'm hoofing it from here."

"You can't be serious."

"Damn straight I'm serious. I've got a wife and kids waiting on me."

"Look, at least wait until daylight. It can't be more than an hour away," Matthew said. "If another vehicle comes along, you could end up dead."

"Matthew's right," Holly called. Matt turned to see her hurrying closer, all bundled up from head to toe, her first aid kit in one hand. "Come into the house. We've got a warm fire. I'll make you some hot cocoa, and when it gets light, you can be on your way."

He rubbed his chin. "I don't know. I was due in hours ago. She's gonna be worried."

"Can you call? We have cell phones," Holly said.

"I have one, too. Home phones are out, I imagine. I couldn't get through." He shook his head. "Nope, I've got to go. Like I said, it's not far now. Too bad about the load, but it's pretty late to sell 'em now anyway. Still, one of 'em will go to good use."

He walked around to the back of the truck, untied the canvas, and flipped it back. Matthew smelled pine. And when the driver pulled a Christmas tree, all neatly bundled for travel, off the truck's bed, he just shook his head. "You've got to be kidding me."

"Well, I got a deal on 'em, you see. There's only a dozen. Lots of folks wait till Christmas Eve to get their trees, so I figured I could turn 'em around for a few dollars' profit." He eyed the nose of his truck. "Looks like they ended up costing me more than I thought." He loosened a string from the tree's bundled wrappings, used it to make a tow line with which to drag the tree home. A half mile through a blizzard.

"Hey, you folks have a tree yet?"

Holly smiled. "I think we do now," she said.

"Help yourself. Merry Christmas." The man turned and walked away, pulling the tree behind him.

Matthew watched him go. Then he heard Holly mutter, "Thanks, Mom."

He turned to look at her, and then at the truck full of trees, and then at her again. Her smile was as wide and bright as . . . hell, as a kid's on Christmas morning. "I told you. First, you have to believe." She ran through the snow, toward the truck, calling, "Come on, Matthew. Let's pick the best tree of the bunch!"

Sheila hadn't wanted to take the hat from Bernie, but sensed it was important to him, to his sense of pride. And besides, it was just exactly what

Holly needed. She'd only just reenrolled in school, and landed a role in the holiday play. She was playing a hobo, and this hat was the one missing piece her costume still needed.

So Sheila gave the hat to Holly. And Holly fell in love with it. Maybe, somehow, she felt its magic. At any rate, she never went away from home without it. She even took it with her on that fateful trip back to her childhood home, twelve years later.

• *Ten* •

By the time the sun came up, the tree was standing in the living room in a makeshift tree stand Matthew had constructed from an old pail he'd found in the basement, and was held in place by a few yards of twine.

"Now what?" he asked, surveying his work.

"Now, breakfast. I believe it's your turn to cook."

He studied her with his eyebrows raised, then, seeing that she wasn't kidding, he nodded. "Okay, breakfast it is."

"There's a pile of food in the big cooler in the kitchen. I never bothered with the fridge."

"Is there—dare I hope—coffee?"

"Of *course* there's coffee. And luckily, I brought the stovetop percolator."

"I'm not sure I know how to use it."

"Then I'll brew while you cook. Let's get cracking, we've got a ton to do today."

"We do?" He looked around the place as if in search of all the busywork she had lined up. "Like what?"

"Decorate the tree. Make Christmas dinner. And build a snowman."

"I was thinking more in terms of shoveling the driveway and cleaning off our cars."

She stuck out her lower lip. "You're in that much of a hurry to leave?"

He studied her face, sensing a lapse in her happy-go-lucky, Holly-Golightly mood. "We're going to have to eventually, Holly. It's stopped snowing. They'll probably clear the roads before the day is out."

She lowered her head, licked her lips, then nodded once. "Well, let's get on with breakfast then. If we're going to decorate the tree, make the dinner, build a snowman, clear the driveway, *and* clean off the cars, we'd better get a move on."

But the sadness remained in her eyes, despite her bright smile, as she hurried into the kitchen. Dammit, he thought. He knew it. He knew she was going to get all emotional on him, and want more than just a casual encounter. He hated hurting her. It was like kicking a puppy to hurt a bubbly little thing like Holly. But he couldn't help it.

God, he couldn't even imagine what else there could be between them. They were completely opposite in every way. Living with that cheerful, positive, upbeat, silver lining kind of attitude in his life would . . .

He was going to say it would be horrible. But he couldn't quite tell that big a lie, even to himself.

It just wasn't what he had planned. That's all.

By noon, the determined, stubborn, frightened man had shoveled the driveway to within an inch of its life. Yes, frightened, Holly thought. He was scared to death of her, she knew it. And not just of her, but of what she represented—belief. Faith. Reaching for the impossible with every expectation that it would be. He didn't want to believe in anything, because his past was full of pain. He was just avoiding more of that. Or he thought he was.

But he wasn't really living.

He wanted to get away from her so bad, she thought if they'd been stranded on a desert island, he would try to swim for it. If they were in a prison cell, he'd have gnawed through the bars. As it was, all he had to do was shovel some snow and wait for the plows.

He was cleaning off the cars now. Hers as well as his own. And he'd be done soon. Her time was running out.

She bundled up and headed outside. "Enough work for one day," she announced, snatching the snow brush from him. "It's time for some fun."

"You've got the tree all decked already?"

"What, you thought I was going to do it alone? No way. You, Ebenezer, are going to help me trim that tree. I've strung the popcorn and cranberries, though, and dinner's in the oven."

"Won't it be done awfully early?"

"Mmm. I figured that way you could eat with me before you take off. It hasn't snowed all day, and the plows have got to be out and making their way to us." She eyed the driveway, the cars. "And it looks like you've accomplished your chosen goals for the day. So all that's left . . ."

"Oh, not the snowman."

"Yes! The snowman." And with that she set the snowbrush beside the car, and ran into the snow. She started forming a snowball with the heavy, damp snow. "It's perfect for snowman building. And what a day. I mean, look at it, Matthew."

He did, she watched him. He looked up at the bluest sky imaginable, with the sun streaming down. It was, she suspected, about forty degrees. Pleasant and beautiful. While he was still staring up at the sky, she lifted her arm and pegged him square in the chest with the snowball.

"Hey!" He brushed the snow off, but even as he did, she bent to form another.

"Defend yourself, or suffer the consequences!" She fired again, but he ducked behind the car—her car, not his, she noticed. When he sprang up again, he was firing right back at her, and she took one to the side of the head before she found cover behind a drift. When she peeked up again, he was right on the other side, ready to nail her, so she pushed him hard, hands flat to his chest. He grabbed her wrists to keep from falling and wound up pulling her down in the snow on top of him.

They were both laughing, and then they both stopped. She held his eyes, licked her lips, prayed he would kiss her. And then he answered her prayer and did.

He kissed her, softly, then more deeply, and then his tongue swept into her mouth and she moaned around it. His hips arched against hers. She arched right back. They twined and tangled and fed from each other.

And then a roar made her lift her head. And she felt her heart break a little as the snowplow rumbled past, blasting snow out of the road like some kind of monster.

It felt like a monster to her just then.

There would be no snowman. No Christmas dinner with him. No trimming the tree. No more lovemaking. He was leaving; she could see it in his eyes when she lifted her face enough to stare down into them.

"I . . . can still make my flight," he said.

And why did it hurt so much when she'd only known him for such a short time?

She got up and turned toward the house, because her eyes were burning and she didn't want him to see that.

But he caught her shoulders, turned her around, and looked at her tears. "I'm really sorry, Holly. I never meant to hurt you."

"You're not supposed to leave. I know you don't believe in signs, Matthew, but we were meant to meet. We were meant to be together, here, like this. And I can't believe that the universe went to all the trouble to set this up, just to give us one night of great sex."

"Holly—"

"There has to be more to it than that. There *has to be*."

He sighed, and lowered his head. "It was coincidence. That's all. There's no deeper meaning, no universe plotting our lives. Things just happen, Holly. This . . . just happened. That's all."

She lowered her head, nodded. "Your keys are on the mantle. I'll get them for you." And with that, she walked back to the house, through the door. Angrily, she tugged off her mittens and brushed away her tears. Then she took the box she'd wrapped in old newspapers and decorated with a piece of pine all twisted around with a bit of her popcorn and cranberry garland. She picked up his key ring, and blinked her eyes as dry as possible, then she went back outside.

"What's this?" he asked when she handed him the box.

"It's a Christmas present." She shrugged. "It's stupid, really. Just something I thought . . ." She let the words die. "I, um—I put my phone number in there, too. I mean, at least that way, when you don't call, I'll know it's because you don't want to, and not because you don't know how to reach me."

"Holly—"

"Just go, okay? Just go, Matthew."

He sighed deeply. She couldn't keep the tears back any longer, so she turned and ran back into the house, fast, because she didn't want to lose it in front of him and make him feel worse than he already did. It wasn't exactly fair—she'd told him she wouldn't make anything out of this, and then she had.

And yet, she couldn't help it.

Leaning back against the door, she waited until she heard the Porsche start up and pull slowly away. And then she cried her eyes out.

• *Eleven* •

He managed to drive for about two hours before he had to stop for gas and food and to kick himself a little more thoroughly than he had been for the last hundred miles. What the hell was wrong with him? He was fighting the most irrational urge to turn the damn car around and go racing back there. And what good would that do? It wasn't like there was any future for the two of them. It wasn't like you could meet someone and fall in love in freaking twenty-four hours. It wasn't possible. It wasn't real.

Okay, maybe it *felt* possible. But that was nonsense. You couldn't form the basis of a relationship in one day. You *couldn't*. It just didn't happen. There was no such thing as love at first sight. Maybe infatuation. Maybe great sex even, but not love.

It didn't happen. And there were no signs, and he was not *meant* to be with her. It was all coincidence. That's all. Coincidence.

He sat in the car outside the diner, where he'd stopped for a quick lunch. He had an hour to spare before his flight, and only a few more minutes to the airport. But for some asinine reason, he couldn't convince himself to go inside. Not just yet. He was eyeing the box, the gift Holly had given him, and knowing that he wasn't going to get out of that car until he opened it. Because he was wallowing in feeling guilty for hurting her, and the gift, whatever it was, would certainly make him feel even worse, so he might as well take it.

Love at first sight. Bullshit. And this was just one more Christmas to add to the list of horrible ones. One more pile of the romantic crap people heaped on the holidays. If it hadn't been Christmas, she might not have been quite so vulnerable.

It was like she thought her mother had delivered him to her as a Christmas present. The way she did the tree.

And how about that tree, anyway? She said there would be one, and then there was. How the hell did that *work out?*

"Coincidence," he said. "Tell you what, Holly's mom. If you're so good at communicating from beyond the grave, why don't you send *me* a message or two? Or better yet, have my dad send me one. Prove to me this is real and I'll go back there so fast your freaking heads will spin."

He sat still a minute, caught himself waiting, watching, listening, looking all around, as if he *really expected* something to happen.

"Idiot."

Sighing, he took the bit of pine with its popcorn and cranberry strand off the package, and then he tore the newspapers off it. It was an old cardboard box she'd probably found in the attic. On the front was a folded sheet of paper. He unfolded it and read, "Thanks. Last night was the best Christmas present I ever got. This gift isn't the original, but I've had it for years, and I always loved it. I thought maybe you'd enjoy it, too." She'd signed it, "Love, Holly," and jotted her phone number underneath her name.

If he was smart, he'd crumple that paper up and toss it out the window.

But he wasn't smart, because he folded it and tucked it into his pocket instead.

Then he took the lid off the box.

Inside was a hat. An old, black felt fedora.

His throat closed off. He couldn't even breathe for a second. And he thought his hand was shaking as he picked the hat up out of the box and turned it slowly in his hands. My God, it was exactly—maybe a little more worn but—no. It wasn't the same hat. Of course it wasn't. But it was so like that old hat that lived in his memory—so very much like it that he couldn't help himself.

He turned it over, and looked at the tag that was sewn into the lining.

The initials were there. Faded, barely readable, but there. His father's initials.

He couldn't remember the last time he had cried, but right then, Matthew came close. His eyes were burning and so blurry that he could barely see. Because if this wasn't a sign, if this wasn't some kind of magic, he didn't know what was. He lifted his head, and whispered, "Dad?"

A truck pulled into the parking lot beside him. It was an orange truck and the men inside looked to be a road crew. There were signs in the back. One, the one facing him that caught his eye, read, "WRONG WAY. GO BACK."

A smile split his face. He nodded hard. "All right, Dad. I'm going."

He put the hat on his head, almost laughing out loud as he adjusted it to the same cocky tilt his dad always used. Then he turned the car around, and headed north on I-81.

Holly cried until she was spent, and then she picked herself up, told herself to stop being pathetic, and to do her best to enjoy Christmas. For her mom's sake, she could do that.

She decorated her tree, stringing the popcorn and cranberry

garland all over it, and topping it with a foil-and-cardboard star. At 4 p.m. the power came back on. She set her table—an upturned crate in front of the sofa, topped with a bath towel for a tablecloth. She'd brought some real china for the occasion, even had two tall taper candles, one red, one green, in crystal holders to add the finishing touch. And wineglasses, one of which she filled.

Her holiday dinner was keeping warm in the oven. Turkey breast, stuffing, cranberry sauce, mashed potatoes and gravy, mixed veggies, squash, and pumpkin pie. It was more than one person could hope to eat. More than four or five could probably manage, but she would try to do it justice.

But first, as long as the power was on, she decided to take a long, hot shower, and put on the dress she'd brought along. She always dressed for the holiday. And this one would be no different.

The shower was soothing, but she battled loneliness through the whole thing. If only Matthew would have stayed one more night. If only he would have celebrated Christmas with her.

Oh, but he was right. One more night would have only left her wanting another, and another, and more after that. It was probably better he left when he did.

She lingered in the bathroom, dried her hair, put on makeup and high heels. It was Christmas, after all. She donned the long red dress. It was pretty, slinky and clingy.

And then she opened the bathroom door and heard music. She blinked, wondering if she'd left the radio on, or if her mother was getting even more talented in cross-plane communications. "I'll Be Home for Christmas" was playing on the radio. It brought a teary smile to her face.

She walked slowly down the stairs, humming along, and stepped into the living room. All of her food was on the makeshift table. Her candles were lit, and the other lights were turned off.

Matthew was standing by the fire, staring at the flames, sipping a glass of wine. The hat was perched on his head. She froze, just stood there, staring at him, wondering if he was some kind of an illusion. When he looked up and saw her, he set the wineglass on the mantle.

"I'd have been back sooner, but I had a stop to make."

She wanted to rush into his arms. She wanted to burst into tears. She wanted to kiss his face off. But she forced herself to wait, to walk slowly to him, and not touch him. Not yet.

He took the hat off and said, "Where did you get this, Holly?"

"From my Aunt Sheila. She got it from a homeless man who used to frequent the diner. He found it rolling down the street, he said. I've always liked quirky things like that, so she gave it to me." She shrugged. "When you told me about your dad's hat, I thought this might be like it, so—"

"It's not just *like* my dad's hat. Holly, this *is* my dad's hat."

She blinked. "I don't—"

"He put his initials inside. They're there. This is the same hat."

She pressed her fingers to her lips.

"I think it's a sign. I mean, how could my dad's hat make its way from Flint, Michigan, to here? Why would it end up with you? Unless . . . somehow, we were . . . meant to . . ."

"Meant to . . . what?" she asked.

"I don't know. But I know I want to find out." He handed her a card, in a large envelope, and she opened it. A couple of kids, a boy and a girl, building a snowman was on the front. She opened it and read the inside. "You're why I love Christmas," it read.

Her tears spilled over, and she flung herself into his arms.

"I want to buy this house," he told her, holding her close. "But not to flip it. I want us to fix it up together, and spend time here together, and just . . . just see where things lead."

"You mean you don't know where they're going to lead?"

He stared into her eyes, searching them. "Do you?"

She smiled. "Yeah. We're going to live happily ever after."

He smiled slowly as he lowered his mouth to hers. "Okay."

Charlotte's Web

Erin McCarthy

• *One* •

"I JUST HAVE ONE QUESTION," WILL THORNTON SAID CASUally as he stood on a ladder and nailed fresh evergreen swags above Charlotte Murphy's front door.

"What?" Charlotte dragged her gaze off the seat of Will's jeans with a significant amount of effort, refusing to feel guilty. Lord, Will was slow sometimes. Her arms were straining under the weight of the boughs she was holding for him and her feet were getting cold in a hurry. Checking out the view he provided at eye level from his position on the ladder was fair compensation for the discomfort she was enduring.

"Who just grabbed my ass?"

Charlotte almost fell off the front step. "What? What are you talking about?" Okay, so maybe she had entertained the idea once—or nine hundred times—of cupping his backside and giving a nice, hard little squeeze, but she would never act on it. Probably. She was pretty sure. But definitely if she did, she would *know* it. Savor it. Make it count.

"Someone just copped a feel, and since I can see you out of the corner of my eye, and your hands are full, I was just wondering if you could tell whoever did it that it's not wise to grope a man on a ladder, unless she wants me to break my neck."

Glancing around to confirm what she knew, Charlotte frowned. "I don't know what you're talking about. There's nobody here but us." And her libido.

"Your sister did it, didn't she? That sounds like Bree." Will reached for another swag and Charlotte passed it up to him.

"Bree went shopping an hour ago." Which was classic Bree. Ditch out doing the Christmas decorating for their house with an excuse about getting pomegranates for a centerpiece. Like there were any pomegranates in the tiny grocery in Cuttersville, Ohio. Bree just wanted to peruse the bookstore, gossip at the hair salon, and stay out long enough to avoid having to drag all the boxes of ornaments out of the basement.

"Abby?" Will asked doubtfully.

"Abby! My baby sister, who is only seventeen, need I remind you, did not touch your butt, Will. No one did." For crying out loud, did he want someone to touch it? If she were a little bolder, she'd just reach out and smack it right now to really give him something to think about. But she wasn't bold. She was the opposite of bold—she was pastel pink on the color wheel.

"Someone did. I know what I felt." Now his voice sounded stubborn, his hammer pounding harder.

"Well, *I* didn't."

"Course not."

That was irritating. He didn't think she could, or would, or didn't think she *should*? How was it that he could suspect her little sister, a junior in high school, of grabbing him, but she was a no way, never happen? Was she so staid and boring and vanilla that it would never occur to him that she did actually have a sex drive, though it was well hidden and brought out only on special occasions like full moons and when the annual firefighters' hottie calendar hit the bookstore in town?

"Then I guess it was just wishful thinking, Will, because we're the only two people standing here."

"Huh," he said, leaning against the ladder for support and glancing left and right. "That's really weird."

What was weird was that never once in the last eight years had Will so much as suspected she liked him more than was appropriate for good friends. Yet she did. She loved him with a passion and urgency that was just downright embarrassing when she allowed herself to ponder it—or wallow, which was probably more frequently.

But he didn't seem to be on to her. To Will, she was just Charlotte, his best pal. Damn it.

Irritating as hell, but there it was. And she'd never had the guts to do anything but wait for him miraculously to come to his senses and figure out what was standing right in front of him. Which was a really sucky strategy, because so far Will hadn't been stricken with any epiphanies that they should really be Cuttersville's number one couple.

"Maybe it was the wind."

He scoffed and yanked another bough out of her arms. "Wind doesn't squeeze like that."

"Then it must have been a ghost," she said in exasperation.

She expected him to reject that ridiculous suggestion as well, but instead his brown eyes went wide. "That's a disturbing thought."

"There are no ghosts. I was kidding. Ghosts don't exist."

"Your grandmother said they did." Will took the last strand, much to her relief, and moved down the ladder so he could complete the arch around the door at the bottom left.

"My grandma—God rest her soul—was crocked. Sure she believed in ghosts, but she also said I'm a witch, and we know how crazy that is."

Will grinned at her, revealing his white teeth and dimples. How could he not realize how freaking cute he was? Charlotte thought it defied explanation that he didn't see the adoration that just had to be scrawled across her face. Apparently she'd missed her calling as an actress when she'd decided to open a coffee shop for a living, because Will didn't give so much as a hint that he saw her as anything but asexual.

"Yeah, you're not really the witch type."

"Who is the witch type?" And why did that suddenly make her feel lousy? It was that excitement thing again . . . she was neither a butt grabber nor a spell caster in Will's eyes. So what exactly was she to him? She probably didn't want the answer to that.

"Bree's the witch type."

"God, don't tell her that. She already thinks we should take up our 'heritage' and join a coven, and she's forever running on about her so-called empathic abilities." Charlotte stomped her feet a little to get the blood flowing. She wore only ballet flats, not boots, and the cold was seeping in. Ramming her hands deeper into the pockets of her black puffy coat, she waited impatiently as Will slowly pulled the ladder off the house and dropped it down.

"Actually, Abby acts devious enough to be one, too. She does that evil eye thing when she's mad at you."

"Again, don't encourage her, either. She's already gone completely Goth, right along with Bree. And Abby has been known to brag about the well-known fact that she was conceived in a cemetery." A source of mortification since Charlotte had been old enough to understand it, she had often wondered what kind of woman got it on in the graveyard. Finally, she had concluded that the answer was simply that the kind of woman who got turned on in a graveyard was her mother. As for her father, it was no secret to anyone that he happily gave his wife whatever she wanted, which explained both Abby's unusual conception and the fact that her parents were currently on a two-week tour of America's most haunted prisons. There was just no point in wondering sometimes.

Will lifted the ladder sideways and headed toward the garage with it. "Still amazes me that you have blond hair and your sisters are both brunettes. You don't look anything like them."

"I know. And you know how my mom feels about it. It drives her insane that I look like Malibu Barbie. Without the chest. Or the tiny waist. Or the bikini."

Will laughed. "Oh, I don't know. You might give Barbie a run for her money."

If that were a compliment, she'd take it.

"And I'm sure your mother doesn't care that you have blond hair."

"Yes, she does." Charlotte followed him, picking carefully over the snowy ground. "You know that Murphy girls are supposed to be weird. Interesting. Into crystals and piercings and flowing skirts. That's Bree and Abby. I'm odd blonde out who turned the tarot shop I inherited from my grandmother into a Caribou Coffee. That's blasphemy in the Murphy house, you know that."

Will figured there was some truth to that, but he also thought Charlotte worried too much. "They're proud of you, Charlotte. Even if they don't always get you." Will kept the ladder firmly in his hands so he wouldn't touch her. He was frequently tempted to touch Charlotte and almost always managed to control himself. Occasionally he couldn't resist and gave her a nudge or a shoulder rub or a quick peck on the top of her head, and she didn't seem to mind that.

The one time he had given in to hope and tried to kiss her full on the mouth, five years earlier, she had shot him such a look of horror, asking, "What are you *doing*?" that he had pulled back quick like and had never made that mistake again.

He was in love with Charlotte, and he suffered that knowledge in silence.

It was a hard lot in life and he saw no end in sight to the dilemma. Eventually he figured one of two things would happen. He'd either drop dead of sexual frustration, or Charlotte would fall in love with some schmuck and get married. If it was the latter, well, he'd have to pull up stakes and move out of state, because he could not watch her carrying on with another man. No frickin' way.

"What are you doing the rest of the day?" she asked him, with obviously no idea of the direction his thoughts had been running. "I've got to head to the shop in an hour for the Saturday night rush."

Since Charlotte had defied Cuttersville's fear of coffee with whipped toppings and her own family's franchise disdain, and opened a Caribou Coffee, the Midwest equivalent of a Starbucks, right smack downtown, her business had been booming. It had become a favorite Saturday night hangout for a lot of folks, young and old alike. Will thought her business savvy was amazing.

"I guess I'll just put up my own Christmas tree and call it an early night. I'm on morning shift tomorrow." Not that work would stop him from staying up all night if he had a good reason—he just didn't have a good reason. Unless Charlotte reacted the way he wanted her to his pronouncement, the way he knew she would.

She frowned at him. "You can't put your tree up by yourself! That's . . . that's . . ."

A cry for help? He was well aware what he was doing, and he should feel pathetic that he was playing off her sympathy, but he was too determined to spend as much time with her as possible to care. He shrugged and tried to look lonely, but stoic. "It's not a big deal."

"Yes, it is. Tree trimming is something you do with the people you lo— family and friends. I'll come over after work and we can do it together. It will be fun. I'll make you watch cheesy Christmas movies with me, because you know how much I love those."

She glanced down at his arms. "Are you going to set that ladder down? It must be heavy."

Yes. He was going to set the ladder down and he was going to close the three feet between them and he was going to put his mouth on hers, and slide his hand inside her jacket and cup her breast. His tongue was going in her mouth and taking possession, licking and sliding and mating, until she was weak with wanting him. Then when he stripped her clothes off and took her against the garage wall, she was going to understand, accept, embrace the fact that he wanted her as his friend, his lover, his life partner.

Or he could just shrug and lift the ladder onto its wall-mounted hooks.

But before he could do either, Charlotte's eyes went wide.

"Are you okay?" she asked. "You look sort of . . . angry."

It was lust, not anger. Pure sexual desire that threatened to make him lose control as she stood in the middle of the garage, her puffy coat covering all her curves, her fur-lined collar up around her ears, and her nose pink from the cold. He wanted her, he didn't know what the hell to do about it, and he was starting to get weird and desperate. But before he could formulate any sort of reply, he felt movement on his chest.

Thinking there was a spider or something crawling up his coat, Will swatted at it, glancing down.

"What are you doing?" she asked, taking a step forward.

"There's something on me." And crazy enough, even though he couldn't see a damn thing, his jacket zipper was actually descending. "What the hell?" It was just gliding right down, like someone was tugging it. It wasn't falling, it was being pulled. By nothing.

"Uh . . . Charlotte . . ."

"Your zipper's going down," she said, coming to a halt. "How is that possible?"

If he knew, he wouldn't be freaking out. He grabbed at it and tried to stop it, but the zipper was already undone at the bottom and the two sides of his jacket had fallen apart. "That was really weird. That's what it was like when I felt someone touch my ass. It felt totally real."

Charlotte was frowning. "There's no such thing as ghosts."

He was starting to doubt that himself, since he was the one being accosted. "I'm a cop, I don't believe in that stuff, either. But this is Ohio's most haunted town according to those paranormal investigators." Will shot an uneasy glance around the garage. It was an old structure, the garage originally a carriage house to the hundred-and-twenty-year-old Victorian Painted Lady that Charlotte lived in with her sister Bree. "And I know what I felt. And you saw what just happened."

"It was just a defect in your zipper." She was still frowning, her lips pursed together.

He would be willing to accept that if it made any sense at all, but it really defied the logic. "Okay, so let's just get out of here and we'll pretend nothing happened. I'm cool with that."

She nodded but didn't say anything.

Will took a step forward right as he felt the unmistakable sensation of his jeans unsnapping and the zipper starting to come down.

"Holy shit . . ." He stopped in his tracks and glanced down at his pants in disbelief. His black boxer briefs were showing.

Charlotte screamed. "Will!"

And just as fast as the zipper went down, it went back up, and though the snap seemed to struggle a little, it finally closed, too.

"Not only is this garage haunted, the ghost is a pervert," Will said, holding on to his pants with both hands. If Charlotte ever saw him naked, it was not going to be because some frisky spirit yanked his drawers and had him standing in front of her buck naked from the waist down.

"Maybe you should go," Charlotte said, wide-eyed. "I'll finish putting all these leftover lights and boxes away. I'll see you tonight at your place after I close the store."

Then her gaze dropped down to the front of his jeans and the tip of her tongue peaked out and slid across her bottom lip.

Yep. Time to go.

Will almost ran into Charlotte's sisters as he got the hell out of the garage and moved down the driveway, darting a glance back over his shoulder.

"Dude, watch it."

Abby was holding her hand out in front of her, preventing him from slamming into her. They had parked behind him on the street and he hadn't even noticed them getting out of their car.

"Sorry." Testing the zipper on his pants to make sure it was still up and locked in place, Will tried to focus in front of him and reestablish a hold on reality. "What are you two up to?"

"Panties shopping," Abby said, tossing her thick, dark hair over her shoulder, exposing a multitude of black and silver necklaces that looked like they were choking the life out of her. "And is your fly down or do you have to like go to the bathroom? You keep grabbing yourself."

"Excuse me?" Will blinked at her. What was with the Murphy sisters today? They seemed determined to make him uncomfortable, and he was equally determined to ignore the question about his crotch. "*Where* were you?"

"Shopping. I bought a bunch of thongs," Abby elaborated. She dug into the bag on her arm. "Black, and a pink pair, and one with cherries on it . . . You want to see?"

Only if he was a total sicko. She was a freakin' baby. "No, that's okay." He glanced over at Bree, wanting some help. Somebody needed to rein Abby in, and it wasn't going to be him.

Bree raised an eyebrow at him, a slight smile on her face. "Abby, Will doesn't want to see your underwear. He only wants to see Charlotte's naughty bits."

"*What?*" He didn't even know what the hell a naughty bit was, but he wasn't about to admit wanting to see it. Even if he did probably want to see it on Charlotte.

The middle sister, and by far the most straightforward, Bree shook her head, fingering the star hanging from her neck, on the outside of her black, capelike winter coat. "I've been pretending I didn't know this for about a million years, and I'm tired of keeping quiet. You're in love with Charlotte. It's totally obvious."

Shit. "To who?" Please tell him it wasn't obvious to Charlotte, because he was going to find himself seriously embarrassed if that was the case.

"To me. I'm empathic, remember? I can sense your feelings."

Right. Bree thought she was a witch who could somehow know accurately everyone's feelings. While Will wasn't going to accept that witches existed just as a matter of course, he wasn't inclined to flat out dismiss the possibility, either. But Bree had been saying that she was one ever since he'd met her and he'd yet to see her do anything magical. Even this revelation wasn't all that amazing. He imagined it wouldn't take much for someone to guess his true feelings for Charlotte if they spent as much time with him and Charlotte as Bree did.

"Can you sense that I don't want to talk about this?" He zipped his jacket back up and dug in his pocket for his keys.

"She loves you, too."

Will did not need to hear that. "No, she doesn't."

"She does?" Abby asked in amazement. "I thought they were just best friends."

"Hello. Yes, she loves him. As more than a friend. She wants him naked, and he wants the same for her. And neither one of them will make a move. Yet we all know they'd make the perfect couple."

It was really annoying and painful to stand there and listen to Bree feed all of his delusions. "Bree, just leave it alone."

"If she gave you a very obvious sign that she was interested, would you go for it?"

He wanted to scoff and tell her it would never happen, but he figured the best way to get her to lay off was to be honest. "Yeah. Sure. But short of her kissing me, with tongue, which is never going to happen, I'm not going to believe she's interested in me."

Bree smiled. That close-lipped knowing grin scared him.

"Trust me, Will-sie," she said. "Bree is going to make everything right."

God help him.

• *Two* •

CHARLOTTE SHOVED BOXES UP AGAINST THE GARAGE WALLS with manic fervor, her hands shaking slightly. She had mentally unzipped Will's pants. How the hell had she done that?

She had wanted it to happen. She'd visualized it happening. Then had watched the reality right before her eyes. His jacket, and then his pants, had come undone. The jacket had been wishful thinking. The pants had been some kind of a test to herself, to prove the jacket was a coincidence.

It wasn't. She had mentally demanded his pants unsnap, and they had.

She had the power to strip men with her mind.

Wow. That was truly mind-boggling.

But it had to be a fluke. A coincidence. Not real. Right?

Charlotte remembered how she had mentally chanted, "Down, down, down," while she had visualized Will's zipper descending. And then it had.

Yikes.

"What's the matter with you?" her sister Abby asked from behind her. "You're like throwing those boxes around."

Charlotte stopped shoving the huge empty Christmas tree box into the corner and grabbed the robotic reindeer and dragged him out, determined to be normal. She would put the deer in the yard, plug his ass in, and have a normal Christmas like normal people did, who weren't witches and didn't make men's pants unzip with their minds.

"I'm fine."

"No, you're not." That was Bree's voice now, sounding concerned, but Charlotte couldn't bring herself to look at her sister. Despite being totally different, she and Bree had always been close, and were only two years apart in age. Since they'd moved into their grandmother's house together the year before when Bree had inherited it, they'd gotten even tighter. Bree would know she was hiding something if she looked at her.

Apparently she knew anyway. "Charlotte, come on. You're really upset. Tell us what's wrong. Is it Will? We saw him in the driveway looking a little freaked. Did you guys finally give into the inevitable and make out or something?"

She wished. "No." Grappling with the deer, dragging him across the concrete floor, she glanced at Bree. "His pants just unzipped, that's all."

"Why would that make both of you freak out?" Abby asked, swinging a shopping bag in her hand. "You're like almost thirty and you've known each other for half your lives. I don't think seeing him unzipped would be that big of a deal."

It really wouldn't be if she wasn't totally in love with him and she hadn't made it happen by the sheer force of her sexually frustrated will. "I think *I* did it. With my mind. Which is impossible, of course, so clearly I've lost that same mind, and the fact that I have these feelings for Will is causing me to have a mental breakdown."

Bree held up her hand. "Stop right there. You're not having a mental breakdown. Now put down the damn deer and let's go in the house and talk about this."

"I have to finish with the Christmas decorations." Charlotte got the reindeer to the driveway and switched her hands to his ears, hoping it would be easier to pick him up that way. He wasn't heavy, just awkward.

Except that her sister yanked the reindeer away from her and slapped him down in a snow bank right next to the garage. "The deer can wait. There's almost a month until Christmas. We need to talk."

"No." But she already knew she'd lost. Bree was much more stubborn than she was and she would keep at her until she confessed the whole thing. Might as well get it over with because she did not like confrontation or having her sisters annoyed with her.

"Go in the kitchen and sit." Bree pointed at the back door.

"Fine." Charlotte figured she could use a little reassurance.

Five minutes later they were sitting around the big round table in the kitchen that Charlotte had painted a distressed white, settled in creaky ladderback chairs, teacups in front of them.

"So what happened?" Bree asked.

Charlotte clutched her teacup with a yellow rose pattern, letting the warmth seep into her flesh. "Okay, this is totally embarrassing."

"We know you dig Will. That's not a secret, so don't worry about it."

"I didn't know you dig Will," Abby said, making a face at her cup as she sipped the tea. "Bree knew, though."

Of course she did. Bree knew everything Charlotte was feeling. It was a creepy sort of ability her sister had, to get in tune with other people's emotions. She was a good judge of character as well. "Okay, I do sort of like him. A lot. For a while now. But he's not interested. So I was just looking at Will, thinking that it would be really, really nice to just unzip his jacket and run my hands across his chest. He has a nice chest, you know. Really, really nice. Muscular. He works out a lot. It's a cop thing." Charlotte set the tea down, no longer needing the extra heat. "And then his zipper just went down. Just like . . ." She gestured with her hand in front of her. "It was totally weird. So I thought, bizarre coincidence, right? So I focused on the zipper on his jeans, thinking while that's what I'd really like to see come undone, it was never going to happen. So I sort of mentally chanted the word 'down' and pictured it unzipping, and then it just was. The snap came undone, and the zipper went down. It was crazy."

Bree didn't back her up on that crazy thing. Instead she just nodded, looking satisfied. "So we finally know what your magical talent is. I've been waiting for years for some kind of indicator from you . . . Abby and I have known all along what our talents are. I can sense and alter other people's feelings, Abby can insert herself into other people's dreams, and now you can move objects. That's very cool."

Not cool. Charlotte rubbed her temples. "I can't move objects. It was just some kind of bizarre coincidental accident. Like the wind did it and I just thought I did it." Which was ridiculous and she knew it. The wind couldn't have managed what she'd seen. "And I've never moved anything with my mind before."

"This was different because you focused. You channeled your emotion—you are in love with Will, and love, grief, and anger are the most intense emotions we experience. All your want and desire was behind the urge to unzip his jacket, and then with the pants, not only did you want him physically and emotionally, you added a chant to your visualization. And it worked, obviously. You really need to hone and train your talent now that you're aware of it."

While she wasn't going to argue that all her want and desire had been behind the urge to strip him naked, she took issue with the outcome of Bree's conclusion. "I don't want to be a witch!

I'm not a witch." She wore sweater sets from J.Crew, for crying out loud.

"It's not like you have a choice. You are what you are." And her sister looked downright gleeful about it.

"Bree, I'm telling you, I'm not a witch. I have no talent to hone. I'm unhonable." Charlotte felt a little hysterical at the very thought of being Charlotte Murphy, the coffee-shop-owning witch.

"Now you have to go to the Jules festival on the winter solstice with us this year."

"Not." Bree had been trying to convince her to attend the witch ceremony for about five years and every year she flatly refused to go. Her sister gave her dire warnings about denying a piece of herself, but she usually dropped the subject after a week or two. But Charlotte had the feeling she was in trouble this year. Bree was going to hound her mercilessly now that she knew Charlotte had supposed magical powers.

Which she didn't. She was almost sure of that. Just to test it, she focused on her teacup sitting on the table and tried to move it. She even did an up, up, up chant while mentally focusing. Nothing. Whew. Major relief. No broom shopping in her future.

"Try something else," Bree suggested. "Try to move Abby's necklace."

You know, that was really annoying, how her sister could guess what she was thinking. "How did you know I was trying to move something?"

"I can sense your feelings, remember?"

"Or you just guessed because I got quiet."

"Is that how I know you chanted 'up' to the teacup?" Bree's look was smug, her black painted fingernails sliding through her equally dark hair.

A shiver rolled up Charlotte's spine. "I was just staring at it, that's how you knew."

"Try to move the necklace. Please."

"Fine, if it will prove I can't." Charlotte concentrated on the star dangling from Abby's neck on a black leather strap. She pictured it swinging outward toward her in a graceful arch, suspending in the air.

And almost peed her khaki pants when the necklace did just that.

"What . . ."

Her entire face went hot and her heart raced as she watched that star glint in the light from the overhead chandelier, a full ten inches out from Abby's neck. As Charlotte turned her head to the side to get a better look, terrified and fascinated simultaneously, the star turned onto its side, mimicking her motion.

"Dude," Abby whispered, her eyes crossing as she looked down, trying to see the necklace in front of her chest.

"Charlotte," Bree said, her voice low and awed.

Charlotte couldn't speak, her throat tight, her mind struggling to accept what she was seeing. "How can I be doing that?" It was utterly illogical. Yet she was clearly responsible for the movement. Even she couldn't deny that.

She didn't like it, but she couldn't deny it.

"I told you. It's your magical talent. And it's strong considering you've never used it before."

Charlotte pushed back her chair quickly and stood up. The necklace plopped against Abby's chest. "I don't want any magic," she said, knowing she sounded a little petulant, but feeling panicked. "I just want to be a normal family, a normal businesswoman who runs a Caribou Coffee. I want a freaking Bing Crosby Christmas just once, where everyone wears holiday sweaters and sings Christmas carols and eats sugar-and-butter-laden snowmen cookies. Is that too much to ask?"

Instead Murphy Christmas get-togethers involved tarot readings, offerings to the goddesses, and lectures from her mother on how the origins of Christian holiday traditions sprang from earlier Pagan and Druid worshipping. It was all very interesting, and she appreciated the open-mindedness of her parents, and how they wove spirituality and a respect for both nature and other humans into their daily lives. But having wassail wasn't nearly as exciting as pie and sugar cookies, and a Yule log was never going to replace a Christmas tree. That was why she tended to go overboard with the decorations now that she had her own house. Well, now that she was living in Bree's house, who allowed her to indulge in her love of snowmen, reindeer, nativities, and Disney character yard inflatables.

Christmas was about family, and she loved hers tremendously. But Christmas also showed very clearly how fundamentally different she was from them, and how isolated she felt sometimes as odd blonde out.

"That is a lot to ask actually. But I'm willing to have a traditional American Christmas with you—I'll even put on a reindeer sweatshirt," Bree said, though her face reflected her feelings on wearing emerald green cotton.

Charlotte thought Bree looked sincere, but she couldn't believe what she was actually hearing.

"I'm not wearing any reindeer sweatshirt," Abby said. "But I can sing Christmas songs and bake cookies."

"Are you guys serious?" Charlotte looked at her sisters and smiled, truly touched. "You'd do that for me?" That was so sweet.

"Of course we would. We love you. If this is that important to you, we're willing to put up with a little commercialism. I'm sure Dad will be cool with it, too, though I can't vouch for Mom."

"Christmas doesn't have to be about commercialism or giving tons of overpriced gifts. I just want to be together, and for once, I want you all to understand and appreciate what I like." Everything was always about everyone else's interests, never hers, and she was touched beyond belief that Bree and Abby were willing to suck it up and give her a traditional Christmas celebration. "You guys are awesome to do this. It means a lot to me."

"I just have one small request in return," Bree said, her green eyes lifting from her teacup.

Here it came. Charlotte braced herself. "What? You want me to go the Jules festival? Fine, I can do that."

"No. I want you to admit you're a witch. By casting a lust spell on Will."

• *Three* •

"*WHAT?* A LUST SPELL?" THAT WAS SO APPALLING, ON SO many levels, she didn't even know where to begin.

"Oh, now that's an awesome idea," Abby said, sitting up straighter and tossing her hair over her shoulder.

Who was this child? Charlotte glared at her baby sister. "No, it's not. I'm not a witch, and even if I was, why would I want to force Will into feeling lust for me? That's just . . . yucky." Humiliating. Desperate. Pathetic.

"Will wants you, Charlotte. Trust me. He just needs a push."

Did they have to keep making this harder for her? Every day she questioned, wondered, wished that Will could feel more for her than friendship, but he didn't, and at the end of every day she counseled herself to be content with what she had. She really didn't need them encouraging her futile dreams.

"He loves you. I can feel it."

"Stop it!" Charlotte was tempted to cover her ears. Bree's

words seared into her heart, inciting the dull ache there to a painful throb.

"How long have you felt this way about him?" Bree asked, her voice gentle, hand sliding across the table to touch hers.

Even though she didn't want to do this, even though she wanted to keep all her feelings neat and tidy locked away, even though she was embarrassed to realize how long she'd suffered in unrequited love, she also wanted the comfort her sister was offering. She wanted someone else to know how hard it had been, how unsure it had made her feel about herself, her future, wondering when she would ever give it up and move on.

"Remember when my dog died?"

"Trixie?" Abby's eyes went wide. "That was a long time ago."

"Yeah. Six years ago. And Will came over, and he said all the right things, and he took Trixie and buried her in the yard for me." Charlotte swallowed hard against the lump in her throat. "And I knew right then, that Will Thornton was a good guy, through and through, and that I loved him."

Crap, she was going to cry. She wanted him *so* bad she could just about taste him. It was *pitiful*.

"Then all the more reason to do the lust spell. Don't you want to know, once and for all, if there's a chance for you as a couple?"

"You guys really would be a good couple, now that I think about it," Abby said, dipping her finger into her tea and licking it. "You're both like really nice and into hard work and justice and all that."

Charlotte blinked. "Thanks, Abby. I think that was meant to be a compliment." Then she sighed. "But yeah, I guess I do want to know once and for all. I mean, I already know he doesn't feel that way about me, but I think I really need to see it in a totally obvious way. Maybe then I can figure out a way to move on, get over him. Because at this rate, I'm going to be ninety and still lusting after him."

"Gross," was Abby's assessment.

"Seriously gross," Charlotte agreed. For over five years she'd been holding her breath that someday Will would get married and start a family, and she needed to prepare herself for that inevitability.

Since she wasn't a witch, a lust spell wasn't going to work, and Will wasn't going to respond to any sexual overtures without a spell. But if, for some strange reason, the zipper thing wasn't a weird, crazy coincidence, and she did actually have some kind of magical talent, and a lust spell *did* work, she wasn't sure she could resist the opportunity to just once see what sex with Will would be like. Think of it as her gift to herself as she entered a lifetime of celibacy. A girl needed something to hold on to. Sex with Will would be a memory definitely worth clinging to for the next fifty years.

"So, how exactly do I create a lust spell?" She wasn't chanting naked in the woods in the snow. Her twin set stayed on, thank you very much. At least for the spell creation portion of the evening's activities. After the spell went into affect on Will, well, she could only hope.

"It's very simple, actually." Bree leaned back in her chair, eyes narrowed. "I need to collect a few things. What are you doing tonight?"

"I have to work, then I'm going over to Will's to help him put up his Christmas decorations. You know, his decorating is just pitiful. He doesn't even have a full-size tree. It's a tabletop tree." It was probably a bachelor thing, but it made Charlotte nuts. How could he survive without a wreath on his door? A person needed priorities.

"That's perfect. Okay, I'll meet you at the coffee shop at nine. We'll do the spell in the back room, then you can head over to his apartment."

Charlotte felt a niggling of doubt about this whole plan. She was either going to get lucky or make a total ass out of herself. She'd never been much of a risk taker. "And if I do this, you're going to let me do Christmas my way? And you'll cooperate?"

"Absolutely."

She was so not reassured.

BREE STEPPED INTO CARIBOU CARRYING THREE GIANT SHOPping bags, her nose running from the cold, as she searched the room for Charlotte. Abby was grumbling behind her, equally burdened.

"You know, it seems to me like we shouldn't even be doing this," Abby said, trying to shake her hair off her face without using her hands, since they were out of commission at the moment, busy holding all their purchases.

"Why not?"

"Because you're not supposed to do magic against someone's free will."

But that was the beauty of Bree's plan. "But Will consented, remember? He said he loved Charlotte, said he would respond if she gave him a clear sign. Magic should be used for the purpose of good, and this is definitely a good thing." She was quite proud of the way the whole thing was coming together. She was going to hook Will and Charlotte up if it killed her, because they truly were the perfect couple. If anyone should be married and popping out babies, it was those two. They were like Ward and June Cleaver for the twenty-first century.

"You're an evil genius," Abby told her.

"Thanks." Bree noticed several people she knew, including one of her coworkers at the library, and Abby's friend Brady Stritmeyer, who was sitting with the Tuckers—Danny; his wife, Amanda; and their daughter, Piper. There was another man with them, a stranger to Bree, and she didn't like the look of him as she waved to the group on passing by their table.

The new guy looked pretentious and boring, wearing a pink dress shirt—Lord, what man wore a pink shirt in Cuttersville—and wire-rimmed glasses. An expensive-looking watch was on his wrist, and he had cuff links in his shirt, of all things. At Caribou on a Saturday night. Everything about him looked expensive and insufferable, and there were papers spread out in front of him, like he'd been working. He was the only one at the table who didn't laugh or at least smile when Brady reached out and snatched Abby by the arm and pulled her down onto his lap.

Bree kept going, leaving Abby to chat for a minute. She found Charlotte behind the counter so she deposited her bags in the back room and came back to her sister. "Whenever you've got a minute, we're ready."

"Okay." Charlotte looked nervous as hell. "Give me five minutes."

"Sure." Bree didn't have any plans for the night. Since she'd broken up with her last boyfriend six months earlier, she'd been enjoying just doing a whole lot of nothing. The relationship had been emotionally and physically exhausting, constantly trying to keep up with Kevin's mood swings and PMS-like behavior, and she was still recovering. She leaned against the counter, inhaling the coffee bean aroma. The place smelled good, she had to admit. She glanced over at Abby, who was twirling her fingers in Brady's shaggy hair. "Hey, who's that guy with Danny and Amanda? The uptight-looking one?"

Charlotte looked over at their table, her hands busy wiping the back counter down. "Oh, that's their financial advisor . . . or is it he's their lawyer? I don't know, something like that, and he's in town from Chicago."

Figured. "Let me get the other bags from Abby and I'll meet you in the back room."

Her sister didn't really answer, just bit her lip. Bree was going to have to hurry before Charlotte wimped out on her. She was not going to tolerate Charlotte screwing up her own personal happiness out of plain old fear.

After a quick hello to everyone at the table, Bree told Abby, "Come on, bring that stuff in the back." She flashed a smile at Piper. "We bought Christmas decorations. Big, blinky ones."

"Cool," was Piper's assessment. She was a gawky kid, all legs and elbows, her hair an unflattering little bob, but she was a real peach. Bree saw her almost every weekend at the library, perusing for new reading material.

"Here, you take it," Abby said. "I'm going to the movies with Brady."

Annoyed, Bree took the bags Abby was shoving at her. "Is that you asking permission? Because it sounded more like you telling me, which isn't how it works." She and Charlotte were responsible for Abby while her parents were gone, and sometimes her little sister thought she was all grown up and then some.

Abby looked defiant, but she just said, "Can I go? Brady will drop me off."

"Can you?" Bree asked him, not really liking the way his hand was resting on her sister's thigh, but figuring she had no right to say anything.

"Yes, ma'am," Brady said, with more sarcasm than deference.

"Fine. Be home by midnight." She turned to go and accidentally looked straight into the eyes of the financial advisor/lawyer. A shiver raced through her when she realized she could sense his feelings. There was disapproval radiating from him. Toward her.

"Bree, have you met Ian Carrington?" Danny said. "He's our lawyer and a friend of Amanda's. Ian, this is Bree Murphy, the children's librarian over at the Cuttersville branch."

"And tarot card reader," Amanda added with a grin, her hand sliding down to her slightly raised stomach.

Bree had seen Amanda's pregnancy in the cards four months earlier. She gave a wan smile at Ian, who wasn't smiling at all. "Nice to meet you." Not really.

Apparently he felt the same way. He just nodded. "Likewise." But then he raised an eyebrow and glanced at her hands. "Children's librarian, huh?"

If it were any other guy under the age of thirty-five, she'd think he was checking her left hand for a wedding ring. But she suspected he was actually looking at her multitude of sterling silver rings and her black fingernails. That disapproval floated off him again, like a noxious cloud.

Pretentious jerk. She would have him know that Onyx was the hottest nail color of the season. Witches and nonwitches alike were wearing it.

"Yes. Children's librarian and tarot card reader." Deal with it. "Be home by midnight, Abby, I'm serious. I'll see you all later."

She had a spell to cast.

CHARLOTTE LOOKED AT ALL THE BAGS THAT BREE WAS DIGging through in bewilderment. "What is all this stuff?"

"It's camouflage mostly. You said Will doesn't really have any decorations. So I bought a butt-load of Christmas decorations. It's unreal how much tacky stuff they have on the market. So I bought a bunch of stuff and you can take it over to Will's and decorate his apartment. That way he won't think anything of you hanging up mistletoe."

"You've got to be kidding me." Charlotte had followed the plan until the mistletoe bit, than she had realized the plan was crap. "I'm going to look like a desperate *dork* if I hang mistletoe in Will's apartment."

Flinging herself down onto the microfiber faux suede sofa she had in her office in a soothing plum color, Charlotte bit her lip. "I can't do it, Bree. He's going to *know.*"

"Isn't that sort of the point?" Bree emerged with a sprig of mistletoe from a florist's box.

"That looks real."

"Well, duh. Fake isn't going to work. It's the live mistletoe that holds sexual energy."

"It's a plant. What is sexual about that?" Yet Charlotte found herself pulling back a little when Bree waved it in her face.

Bree laughed. "It's not going to make you spontaneously aroused or anything. You can touch it."

She was already aroused, and had been essentially every day since the very first minute she'd met Will on her twenty-first birthday, when he'd shown up at the Rampant Lion bar with his buddies, and caught her when she'd tripped getting off her stool, the embarrassing result of alcohol consumption and a poor choice of high heels.

"I don't need to touch it. Just tell me what to do. This whole thing is way too out there for me." *Way* too out there.

"Well, the mistletoe is associated with fertility, protection, friendship, good luck, and uninhibited sexual activity."

Hello. "Wow. Impressive little green twig. I just thought it was an excuse people used to make out."

"That, too." Bree pulled some ribbon out of another bag and started tying it around one of the branches. "But originally Druids used mistletoe to ward off evil spirits and to increase fertility because it stays green all winter long, even when the oak tree it grows on is dormant. Green is the color of growth and fertility."

Good grief. "I'm not looking to be fertile!" They needed to take things one step at a time.

"It's also the color of love and sex."

That she'd take. Both of them. In large quantities, please.

"Which is why I bought you a green sweater to wear." Bree finished tying off the red ribbon and pulled a cable-knit sweater out of another bag. "It's plain and boring, just the way you like your clothes."

How thoughtful. Charlotte rolled her eyes. Her clothes were not boring. They were classic, made from quality materials and designed to flatter her decidedly average figure. She was of average height, average weight, average backside, slightly above average bra size. She looked best in form-fitting sweaters with crisp cotton blouses underneath and a good old pair of cords or khakis and some boots with a kicky heel. Most of her sweaters were in pastels since she was blond, or occasionally when she was dressing up, she went with red. She never wore the emerald green Bree was shoving at her.

"This is furthering my conviction that I'm going to make an idiot out of myself."

"Why? It's not like I just gave you a push-up bra, a thong, and thigh-high stockings and told you to go for it. It's a cable-knit sweater, loser."

Charlotte yanked it from her sister's hand. "You're not being very nice to me."

Bree stopped pawing through yet another bag and looked at her. "Hey. I just want you to be happy," she said softly.

Shoot. Sister guilt. "I know. But you're freaking me out with all this stuff. And I really, really think Will is going to have a heart attack, run screaming, and never speak to me again if I try to drag him under mistletoe and chant his clothes off of him."

"No chanting in front of him—that would be a bad idea. We're just going to load this mistletoe with a nice little *hexensymbol* for lust. Then you can just pull it out and hang it up anywhere in his apartment and you'll be good to go. He will rip his clothes off all by himself, no chanting required."

Bree opened a pack of markers. "Now choose your symbols. Do you want sex, love, dominance, serenity, thrusting?"

Thrusting? The image of that both in actuality and how it might appear on paper rose up in Charlotte's mind. She reached up and redid her hair knot, mouth dry. "How many can I pick?"

"As many as you want."

"Then I'll take them all except for the dominance." Her friendship with Will was very balanced, and if they went beyond a platonic relationship, she wanted that aspect to remain the same. Then she added, before she totally lost her nerve, "And give me three of the thrusting ones."

"Dang, girl," was Bree's opinion of that. "You got it."

Charlotte could only sincerely hope that she would in fact be getting it before the night was over.

• *Four* •

Will dried himself off with a towel and debated calling Bree and asking her what the hell she had meant earlier when she'd sworn to take care of things between him and Charlotte. He'd been worrying about that promise just about every minute since, and had concluded there was really only one thing he could do.

He needed to tell Charlotte the truth about his feelings before Bree did. He was twenty-nine years old. It would be lame as hell if the woman he loved found that little fact out from her sister. Jesus, the only thing worse would be a note folded up and passed across the room.

Charlotte deserved better. She deserved him looking her straight in the eye and telling her he loved her.

Which was why he'd taken a shower in anticipation of her coming over to put up his Christmas tree. He figured a guy ought to smell good when professing love, and if Bree was at all right—which he had to admit, he was hoping she was—

then maybe, just maybe, they'd wind up naked before the night was out.

In fact, he was determined they were going to get naked. If she felt the same way about him, then he wasn't going to dance around the issue anymore. He was going to dust off his dormant seduction skills and show Charlotte where she really belonged, which was with him, in his life, in his bed. Forever.

Damn it.

He was a cop. He'd taken a bullet in the shoulder in a robbery a few years back. Why had he been such a freaking wimp when it came to Charlotte?

Because he hadn't wanted to lose her altogether. Having half of Charlotte, as a friend, was better than not at all, so he'd settled all those years. But no more. He wanted all of her.

His hair was bristle short, so it only required a quick rub for drying then he was done with it. Pulling on his boxer briefs, he opened the bathroom door to let out the steam and heard the phone ringing.

"Crap." If that was Charlotte canceling, he was not going to be a happy man. Or worse, the police station calling him in. He loved his job, but at the moment, he had a woman to seduce.

He grabbed the phone. "Hello?"

"Will, it's Amanda Delmar Tucker. How are you?"

The ex–Chicago socialite turned farmer's wife had also ventured into real estate in the past two years. Will had approached her about looking for a house for him. "I'm great, how are you? Feeling okay these days?" When he'd seen her a few weeks past, she'd been green around the gills from her pregnancy.

"Yes, the morning sickness is gone, thank God. I haven't puked that much since I was rushing my sorority in college and I just about had to drink my weight in cocktails to prove my so-called worth. How stupid is that? Why do we go along with lame things like that when we're eighteen? Anyway, the puking is past, and I have a house for you."

"Really? Where is it?" He had been going slow on the house search, wanting to be in town, but not really in one of the cookie-cutter subdivisions that had popped up in the last ten years. He didn't envision himself in a vinyl-sided box on Turkey Trail in the Pheasant Hills subdivision. He just wanted a solid house, with some character, and a place for him to toss his muddy boots by the back door. A garage for his weight bench and boxing bag. A house like the one Charlotte was living in with Bree, though maybe not so big.

"It's the gray house on Second Street. The Weeping Lady house. Jessie Stritmeyer wants to unload it now that she bought a condo in Florida and is going snow bird on us."

"Maybe she can say hi to my folks. They're living down in Florida now, too." Will immediately knew the house Amanda was talking about. It was on a street with a dozen other hundred-year-old Victorians. A five-minute walk from downtown, with big old oak trees lining the street in front of the sidewalks, the neighborhood was one of elegant wide porches and an eclectic mix of people. Families, singles, and older folks who were fifth-generation townies all lived there, along with the occasional yuppie newcomer who worked in management at the plastics plant, or the new-ager attracted to the reputation of Cuttersville as Ohio's most haunted town.

He'd like it there. As would Charlotte.

"When can I see it?"

"Whenever you want. Jessie left the keys in the mailbox and said you can go in whenever you feel like it. I guess she trusts you not to vandalize the place since you're a cop."

That was heartwarming, in truth, because Will had found out over the years Jessie was a shrewd businesswoman who trusted about no one. "Alright, thanks. I'll drop by tomorrow. I've never seen the inside."

"It's small. I lived there for two months when I first came to town. But it's in good condition, new roof, five-year-old furnace, and a damn good price. Plus it's charming, and all that."

There was a knock on his door. "Cool. Thanks. I have to go, Amanda. Charlotte's pounding on my door."

"Alright, tell her I said hi and that I love her for bringing Caribou Coffee to Cuttersville."

Will laughed. "I can do that."

He hung up and called out, "Come on in, Char, I'm getting dressed." Not waiting for her response, knowing she was comfortable letting herself in, he went back to his bedroom in search of pants. While he wanted to end the night naked, he didn't think it would go over well if he started things out in his underwear. Could be a bit awkward.

But he did hurry, just cramming himself into a pair of jeans and pulling on a random T-shirt. When he came out, Charlotte was staggering into his apartment, carrying two shopping bags in each hand. He rushed to help her.

"What's all this?" he asked, taking all four bags from her.

She brushed her hair off her forehead, looking a little flushed. "Christmas decorations."

"Oh." Will peeked in a bag. A giant glittery tabletop snowman stared back at him. "Wow, that was nice of you, sweetheart. You shouldn't have." Really. She shouldn't have.

"I wanted to. You need to get in the spirit of things." She smiled at him, and he knew he'd let her outfit his entire place in candy canes and angels, right down to his toilet paper, if she wanted. He was that whipped, and manly enough to admit it. "There are a few more bags in the car," she added.

More? Either that was a sign of how pathetic she viewed his life, or she cared enough to spend a ridiculous amount of time and money foisting Frosties on him. He was hoping it was the latter. Charlotte was heading back to the door but he sprang into action, not wanting her rushing around in the snow on his account. Beside, he didn't know what the hell to do with any of that stuff in the bags she'd already brought in. Decorating wasn't something he'd picked up on in the police academy.

"I'll get them. You stay here and start unpacking. Put everything wherever you want." Will shoved his feet into boots sitting by the door on a mat and held his hand out for her keys.

When she put them in his hand, she gave him a strange look, head down, eyes peeking up at him from under her pale eyelashes. "Okay," she said, and her voice was a little husky, her fingers brushing across his skin.

Holy crap.

Something had just changed between them. Bam. Just like that. It was different. Every day for ten years it had been the same—they were best friends, they cared about each other—but all of a sudden it was off. She was different. A little nervous, hesitant. Sly.

Alright then. This was good. He thought.

Will turned to the door. "I'll be right back." Because he was going to run.

CHARLOTTE LET OUT THE BREATH SHE'D BEEN HOLDING when Will went out his front door, his boots loud and aggressive as he obviously jogged down the stairs to the parking lot. She wasn't sure she could do this. He'd given her a funny look when she'd handed him her keys. Like he knew she was up to something.

Which she was. She had a mistletoe sprig in one of those bags loaded up with lust symbols, and if she were smart, she'd toss it in the trash pronto before Will even came back. And she would not visualize his zipper going down ever again.

If he ever dropped his trousers in front of her it was going to be of his own free will.

Which would be never.

Argh. She was back to the beginning again.

Charlotte yanked a snowman votive out of a box and plunked it down on Will's coffee table. She was noticing a snowman theme in Bree's shopping. That was the third happy chunky snowman she'd pulled out in one form or another. No mistletoe in this bag. She turned and searched a different bag. Not in there, either. A quick search revealed it wasn't in any of the four bags she had hauled into the apartment.

Would it be a bad thing if Will was carrying the bag with the lust-loaded mistletoe? Did he actually have to touch it, or if it was just in his vicinity, would it affect him? Could he be walking up the stairs, suddenly overcome with random lust, encounter the twenty-something waitress in 2B taking out her trash, and think it was her he wanted? Dang, Charlotte should have asked Bree for better instructions. All her sister had told her was to hang it up anywhere. That's it. Nothing else to go on.

So the only thing she could really do was act normal.

Which wasn't achieved by her yelling, "Give me those!" and yanking the final three bags out of Will's hands the second he crossed the threshold.

"Uh . . . okay." His eyebrows shot up. "Did I bring the wrong bags or something? I can take this back down if there's something personal in them."

Like what? Condoms or sex toys? Her face went hot. She was a wreck. An absolute appalling mess of a woman who was so in love with her best friend she was capable of mentally undoing his clothes. "Your Christmas present is in one of these."

It was a decent save, pulled straight out of her behind. His face relaxed.

"You shopped for me already? You must really like me." He swiped his finger over the tip of her nose and gave her a grin.

"I can live with you," she said, because it was an auto-type response and she was trying desperately to act nonchalant, friendly, and totally nonsexual. Then she realized how exactly that sounded—like she wanted to live with him or something—and mentally kicked herself. Whirling around, she burrowed into a bag, ripping out a couple of red pot holders. Pot holders? Why the hell had Bree thought Will would want festive Christmas pot holders? Will was a guy. He probably used a dishtowel and cussed in pain when he lifted a lid.

"You'd love living with me," he said, shaking up a snow globe and watching the flakes settle. "You could toss all my boring bachelor furniture and do an extreme home makeover."

If he only knew how many times she had mentally decorated a house for the two of them, right down to a locker in the garage for his sports equipment and a drawer to lock his gun in. "You would be in for the shock of a lifetime if you let me into this place with the authority to decorate." And was that her testing the waters? Because she actually felt like she was asking permission, like if he was willing to let her decorate for him, then in some way that indicated an emotional depth greater than friendship. It was a massive leap in logic.

"Why? You have good taste. Classy." His eyes dropped down to her chest. Briefly. If she hadn't been hyperaware, she might not have even noticed it. But there was no denying he had looked at her breasts. "Nice sweater, by the way. It fits you really well."

The lusty green sweater. Holy crap. It was working, because in eight years Will had never once commented on how her clothes sat on her body. "Thanks. It's new."

"I know. You've never worn it before." He glanced down at her chest again, she was certain of it. "Green looks good on you."

"No, it doesn't. Not really. I look better in red or pastels. But thank you." Where the hell was that mistletoe? The whole situation was making her nervous as hell. She couldn't go through with it. She couldn't sleep with Will to satisfy her own curiosity if he was doing it under the influence of magic. She would be way too aware the entire time that what she was experiencing was false.

"I think you look good in everything, actually. Except for black. You're too . . . feminine for black."

Okay. Charlotte glanced over at the man she'd known for

nearly a decade. The mistletoe must go. He was acting random and strange. And he was giving her a look that she knew. Couldn't misunderstand. She wasn't naïve nor was she clueless. That was a look of lust. It was in his rich, brown eyes. It was in the way he was standing, legs slightly apart in his jeans, the T-shirt straining over his muscular chest. He'd gone out for the bags without bothering to put on a coat, despite the foot of snow outside, which she found highly sexy. He'd always had very short hair, and it went well with the chiseled cheekbones, stubborn jaw, and the ever-present five o'clock shadow. Will was rugged, the epitome of masculinity, and for the first time in her memory, he was looking at her the way a man looks at a woman when he wants to get in her pants and do bad boy things.

Which aroused, frightened, and confused her. So when in doubt, avoid. "Where would you like to put your Christmas tree?" she asked him, standing straight up and assessing his apartment. "And why haven't you bought more furniture?" He only had one sofa, a paltry end table, a coffee table, and a flat-screen TV. Half the room was empty. And he had always eaten his meals on the couch or at the breakfast bar because he had no table and chairs. "You've been here almost five years, and you said you were going to decorate about two years ago."

"I didn't say decorate." He tossed the snow globe up in the air and caught it. "I said I was going to get new furniture. Men don't decorate. They buy stuff and put it in their apartments."

"Whatever you want to call it, you still haven't done it." Charlotte picked up the remote for his iPod and turned it on, searching the menu for Christmas music. He didn't appear to have any. Big surprise.

"Maybe I've been waiting for a woman to help me pick it out."

What the hell was that supposed to mean? He wanted a girlfriend? He had a girlfriend in mind?

"Know anyone who could help me out?"

"What, decorators? Probably." Will was walking toward her,

slow and steady, that look all over his face again. He was confusing her, and she didn't know what to think, so she backed up slightly.

"I can't afford to pay much. I was kind of hoping she'd do it out of the kindness of her heart, and so we can spend time together."

"Did you have someone in mind?" Charlotte wiped her sweaty palms on the front of her jeans, suddenly clued in as to where this was going. Possibly. Maybe. She hoped. Or feared.

"Yep." He was right in front of her, and the only piece of furniture of any size was somehow right behind her, trapping her against the back of it.

She leaned away from him from the waist up, but he just slid in closer, his legs trapping both of hers.

"I want you."

Hello. How many times had she wished he would say something like that? Now he had, and he merely meant he wanted her decorating services. Something was really wrong with that. Though honestly, he didn't look like he had window treatments on his mind.

"I never claimed to be an interior designer."

"I bet you have plenty of ideas. And you know what I would like. You know me better than anyone." His hand slipped around her waist.

He was touching her. He was holding her. He was really, really close to her, so close she could hear his breathing and smell his aftershave. Feel the hard press of his thigh against hers. Yep, he was holding her up close and personal. And her heart was going to crawl up her throat and choke her. Crap, she just wanted to relax and enjoy it. But it was wrong, wrong, wrong. It was all those sex symbols she'd drawn and tucked inside the mistletoe. It wasn't real.

Yet she just couldn't bring herself to shove him away. After all, this wasn't his fault and she didn't want to make him feel bad, or embarrass him. It's not like anything really inappropriate was happening. They were just cozy up against each other. So he was brushing his finger down her cheek. Big deal. They were friends. They touched. It was normal. Friends hugged, too. They kissed occasionally. Hello. Good-bye. Good luck. Missed you.

But not like that. Holy moly macaroni, Will had closed that little sliver of a space between them and had brushed his lips over hers. The first time was soft, quick, gone before she had barely registered it had happened. But then he was back again, and this time he wasn't playing around. His mouth came down firm, intense, taking her mouth in a hot, confident kiss that had her automatically responding, kissing back, desire igniting in every inch of her body. His grip on her waist tightened. She was too stunned to do anything but close her eyes and enjoy the moment. He tasted better than she could have ever expected, and the man knew what to do with his tongue.

There was no thrusting or pushing or awkwardness, just smooth, coaxing strokes of his tongue over hers, his warm, big body enveloping her everywhere. It was a hot and glorious contact that she let drag on and on, even when his hands dropped down and cupped her backside lightly. It was all good. It made sense to her when her eyes were closed and her lips were so happy, doing a delicious dance with Will. Everything seemed perfectly natural for a minute or two while her mind was mush under the influence of lust and longing.

But then his fingers brushed lower, down between her legs, from the back no less, in a blatantly sexual intimacy that ripped a gasp from her mouth, and sent a warm rush from her inner thighs. He'd made her wet. With just a kiss and a little butt groping.

And it had taken a lust spell to get him to so much as lip lock with her.

Charlotte broke the kiss, the embrace, and whatever else you wanted to call the sensual cloud she'd been floating in, and ducked under Will's arm to get the hell away. She was cheap and easy and she was in love with him. It would be wrong, wrong, wrong, with a capital *W* to sleep with him.

Will wiped his bottom lip as he turned, giving her a slow, sexy smile. "Where you going, Charlotte?"

At least she was pretty sure it would be wrong to have sex with him.

"That was feeling really good to me, and I wasn't finished."

Maybe it wasn't wrong. If he liked it.

A quick glance at the front of his jeans showed he liked it very much, thank you.

• *Five* •

WILL WAS FEELING OPTIMISTIC. ALONG WITH TURNED ON, hot and bothered, and good old-fashioned horny. Charlotte had let him kiss her. She hadn't balked or pinched her lips together or wrinkled her nose. Not only had she let him kiss her, she'd done some mighty nice kissing back, including touching the tip of his tongue with her own. And she hadn't seemed to mind his hands on her ass, if the way she had been pressing up against him was any indication.

She'd run eventually, but he had expected that. That was workable, fine, something he could overcome. As long as she was attracted to him, interested in taking their friendship to the next level, Will could deal with a case of nerves. But the minute he had pulled her shopping bags out of the trunk of her car and seen the mistletoe lying on top, tied with a ribbon and ready for hanging, he had known that Bree was right. Charlotte did feel something for him more than friendship and the mistletoe he'd scrunched up and shoved into his front pocket was proof. Why else would she buy mistletoe to hang in his place if she didn't want him to kiss her?

He was feeling so pleased that he didn't even mind that she didn't answer him at all when he told her wasn't finished kissing her, just dove back into her shopping bags with gusto, clearly flustered.

"I think your tree should go in front of the living room window. We'll move your coffee table over there and set it on top. That way everyone driving by on the road can see it, too."

"Good thinking," he said, leaning against the couch, just wanting to watch her for a minute. Charlotte was such a beautiful woman. Her beauty was fresh and natural, and while she cared about her appearance and took care of herself, she didn't primp and fuss and overprocess. She was also an intriguing blend of confidence and modesty, ambition and shyness, and he appreciated, enjoyed that about her.

"I brought my iPod, too," she said, yanking it out of her purse and holding it up in front of her like a shield. Her cheeks were flushed pink. "Christmas music. I figured you wouldn't have any."

"Wonderful." Will started toward her, but she moved again, practically jogging to the speaker he had sitting on his end table. "Charlotte."

"Hmm?" Her back was to him as she switched his player for hers. "Jingle Bells" blared out into his living room. "Oh, too loud. Sorry."

She bent over a little to adjust the volume, and Will almost groaned. Charlotte's ass in a pair of jeans was a beautiful thing. His mouth went dry just looking at the way the denim hugged her curves, especially at the apex of her thighs. "Are you just going to ignore the fact that we kissed each other?"

The song switched to "The Happy Little Elf." Now that was sexy. Not. He moved right up behind her, needing to kill the distracting music.

Charlotte whirled around and held the remote against her chest. "Yes, I was actually totally going to ignore the fact that we . . . you know."

"Kissed?" He almost laughed. She looked so embarrassed, you'd think they had done something downright kinky instead of just swapped spit for a minute.

She just nodded.

Will eased the remote from her hand and pointed it over her shoulder, shutting the music off. "I don't want to ignore it. I want to kiss you again."

"Why?" Her breath was coming in little urgent gasps, her hands still across her breasts even without anything to hold, and her chest rose and fell rapidly.

"Because it feels good."

"We're supposed to be decorating your Christmas tree."

"We can do that, too." He reached out and touched her cheek.

She jerked and tried to move away from him, clearly panicked.

He grabbed her hand and pulled her to a halt, then wrapped his arms around her. Giving her a soft kiss, he said, "Hey, what's the matter? It's me. Talk to me."

Her eyes closed briefly, then she opened them and met his gaze. Her blue eyes were troubled. "What are we doing here?" she asked.

"We're about to make love, Charlotte." There. He'd said it. No going back.

A strange little squeak came out of her mouth that he found incredibly cute. "We are?"

"Yep." Nothing he wanted more. Will lifted her hand and kissed her fingers, one by one. "Please say that I can."

Her skin was soft, her hand trembling a little. She smelled good, a soft fruity perfume scent, and he could feel the tension in her body. He wanted her to relax, so he stayed that way himself, nice and loose, and allowing a good foot of space between them. Lacing his fingers through hers, he leaned forward and brushed his lips over hers. She had a creamy, even complexion, her fair skin the only thing she shared in common with her sisters physically. Will loved the softness of it, the unblemished perfection of her jawline, adored her tiny pink lips, and the perky upturn at the bottom of her nose. She was a truly beautiful woman, inside and out, and he was a lucky bastard to have her as a best friend.

He was also an ungrateful bastard, because he wanted more. Burying his free hand in her hair, he kissed her jaw, the corners of her mouth, her neck.

"Will . . ."

Maybe it was meant to be a protest, but since she didn't follow it up with any rejection, or any body language that indicated she wanted him to stop, he choose to take it as a pleasure thing. Especially since her hand pulled from his, but she grabbed on to his waist, hooking her fingers through his belt loops.

He dipped his tongue into her ear and she gave a startled moan. Music to his ears. Better sounding than the corny Christmas songs she was trying to shovel down his throat. Hands free, Will went back to holding her ass the way he had been earlier, though tighter this time, pulling her forward, bumping her jeans against his in a rhythmic little grind that made his erection downright hurt. Wanting her was the freakin' understatement of the century. He wanted to eat her, to get inside her, to own her body with his, and to show Charlotte everything she meant to him.

It was strange to know her so well, to know her mannerisms, her laugh, her facial expressions, and hand gestures, yet to not know this part of her, the sexual side. To realize that there was something so elemental and huge that they had never seen in each other. Her responses were surprising him. He had expected tentativeness on her part, assumed he would have to coax her to respond, because Charlotte was a thinker. She was successful for the very reason that she was never impulsive. Yet she wasn't showing the least sign of hesitation, despite her earlier words. She was now moving her hips of her own volition, and she had arched her neck to give him better access. Her hands had made their way around the back of his jeans and were firmly gripping right and left. Not just holding, she was actually copping quite a feel off him, and it was driving his desire even higher.

Yanking her sweater down at the neck in total disregard for the fact that she'd told him it was new and he'd probably just stretched it to hell and back, Will sucked the swell of her breast above her white satin bra. Damn. He wanted more and so did she, given the way she was moving restlessly between his thighs and making little sounds of encouragement. It wasn't classy, but it wasn't hard to peel the front of her bra back and expose her nipple. Barely allowing himself a glance, Will flicked his tongue over it for a quick taste, then gave in to temptation, and completely enclosed her with his mouth.

Charlotte almost left her skin when Will sucked on her nipple. She had spent plenty a night visualizing just such a thing, imagining how it would feel, and planning her sexy and suave response. But she could never have known it would feel like fire and ice, like an orgasm and ice cream all at once, or that she would blurt out, "Holy shit!" instead of something witty and urbane.

It wasn't pretty, but it was exactly how she felt. Forcing her eyes open, she stared into Will's brown hair, brain trying to convince her that this was actually happening. She and Will were getting it on standing up in his apartment with one hundred or so snowmen piled around them and his Christmas tree not even assembled yet.

Crazy but true.

She needed to get a grip. Literally. If she didn't grab on to something besides his very fine butt, she was going to fall over. She needed to hold on to the table, but first she wanted just one teeny tiny little touch across the front of his jeans on her way past. If he was going to town on her chest—which she was really grateful he was—then surely she could just squeeze and take measure of what he had to offer. Well on her way to doing just that, she got caught on something by his front pocket.

Glancing down, she saw her finger had looped through red ribbon. "What's this?" She pulled back from Will to get a better look.

"What? Who cares?" He tried to pry back down the bra cup that had sprung back into place, but Charlotte stood straight up, recognizing what she was looking at.

It couldn't be. She yanked hard.

But it was.

He had the flipping mistletoe in his pocket.

"Where did you get this?" She dangled it in front of his face, horrified. He'd had the stinking mistletoe right next to his penis, of all things. That had to be seriously bad. And an obvious explanation for why he had kissed her, something he had never even hinted at before. For why he was even now reaching for her chest again.

"It was in one of the shopping bags," he said, pushing it out of the way and trying to kiss her again.

Charlotte dodged the lip lock. Her heart was pounding and she felt slightly ill. The poor man had no idea she was manipulating him into wanting her. She was evil and selfish.

"Why was it in your pocket?"

"I grabbed it thinking I could hold it up and steal a kiss." He grinned. "Turns out I didn't even need it."

Suddenly it seemed like Will had twelve hands and three mouths. He had a grip on her again and was nuzzling her ear, which was really distracting. The mistletoe was crushed between them, emitting a soft evergreen scent. "Will," she said, gathering every ounce of willpower she had. This had to stop.

"Hmm?" He made a sexy little sound, a cross between a growl and a purr as he nipped at her bottom lip.

It was so unexpected and arousing, that Charlotte shuddered, letting the ecstasy flood over her for just a tiny stolen second. Then she corralled her resistance and, in a move out of pure desperation, yanked her arm free from its position between their chests and pitched the mistletoe clear across the room, where it skittered to a stop in the kitchen.

He briefly glanced over in the direction she'd thrown. "What are you doing?" But he didn't really sound like he cared all that much. His eyes were on her breasts again.

Charlotte grabbed his cheeks and tipped his head up. "We need to talk."

She was squeezing his face kind of hard and his lips were bulging forward. "What?" he said, speech mumbled from her tight grip.

"This way you're feeling . . . you know, attracted to me. It's because of the mistletoe. Bree showed me how to put a lust spell on it." Charlotte winced and waited for his reaction.

"What?" he said again, looking at her blankly, his fingers resting on the neckline of her sweater, his intent clearly to pull it back down. "What the hell are you talking about?"

It sounded a little strange in retrospect. Letting go of his face, Charlotte pried her sweater out of his grip and pulled the neck back up, feeling more than a little bare, both literally and figuratively. "See, Bree thinks we're witches, right? You know that."

His eyebrow went up. "Yeah. So?"

There was just no reasonable way to explain this. "So she wants me to admit it, and in return she'll wear a reindeer sweater for Christmas." Not that Bree's clothes were the slightest bit relevant to the conversation at hand, but Charlotte was avoiding having to say out loud that she wanted Will in the worst way.

"Okay. Can't picture your sister in holiday gear, but whatever.

And you're actually willing to admit you're a witch? That doesn't seem like you."

"Well . . . I didn't have to say or do anything so much as I had to cast a spell. Which I thought wouldn't work, because I really didn't think I was witch. So I cast a lust spell on that mistletoe for you, knowing you wouldn't react to it, then I could show Bree I'm not a witch at all. But you did react to it. So I am a witch and you're just feeling desire for me because of the spell. It's all not real, this . . . physical attraction for me; it's the lust spell."

His face was still really, really close to hers. It was a good long five seconds before he responded. Then he said carefully, "Why would you try to cast a lust spell on me?"

Oh, shoot. She was going to have to admit it. There was nothing for it. Charlotte swallowed hard and whispered, "Because I wanted you to want me. The way that I want you."

There it was. He could do with it as he saw fit. Charlotte wanted to toss her dinner but she just sucked in a breath and waited for the blow.

Will touched her cheek. "Sweetheart."

Tears popped into her eyes. Damn it, she was going to embarrass herself by crying, but the way he said that, so sweet, so tender, it was like he was touched, and needed to let her down easy. It was awful, yet so like him. He'd never hurt her intentionally, and she'd put him in this awkward position.

"The mistletoe had nothing to do with me kissing you."

That wasn't what she expected him to say. "What do you mean? Of course it did."

"No, it didn't. I kissed you because I wanted to. Because I want you. Sexually. And I have for a long, long time."

She had fallen and bumped her head. She was dreaming. She had accidentally ingested hallucinogenic drugs without being aware of it. She had entered an alternative universe or fallen into a virtual reality world. Because it sounded like Will had just said he wanted her, too, and that was just impossible.

"No, you don't."

He laughed. "Yes, I do. And I'm damn glad to hear you feel the same way. Not to mention flattered that you would try to cast a lust spell on me. But honey, that wasn't at all necessary because I've been lusting after you for years."

"Years?" Was that her voice? She was downright squeaking. But Will was freaking her out. "But you've never once tried to do anything . . . you never tried to kiss me or anything. Are you sure it's not the spell?"

She'd hate it and drop to the ground and kick and scream if it *was* the spell from hell, but she had to be sure. There was no way she could allow herself to get all excited and worked up thinking there was a future for her and Will, then have it yanked away. She would, quite simply, die if that were the case. Overdramatic, maybe. But still the truth.

"I did try to kiss you once five years ago. Don't you remember? You gave me such a look of horror that I just flat out stopped. I thought you weren't interested at all, that being friends is all you ever wanted."

"You never tried to kiss me!" She would remember that. And she wouldn't have pulled back. God, what had she missed? It wasn't like a kiss attempt could really be mistaken for anything else, like reaching for a napkin, or pulling a stray hair off her face. It was impossible. She would have *known*.

"It was when I got shot."

One of the worst days of her life, second only to when her grandmother had died. Will had responded to a robbery alone, since Cuttersville's police force was small. They did all their patrolling solo, and that night he'd encountered a desperate twenty-year-old addict trying to break into the pharmaceutical supplies at the drugstore. He'd shot Will in the shoulder, but

Will had still managed to restrain and handcuff him before calling for backup. Charlotte had gotten the call from Will's mom, who was still living in town at the time, and she'd met them up at the hospital. "What about when you got shot?" Just the memory of the fear she'd felt before knowing he was okay made her mouth go hot.

"I tried to kiss you. In the hospital. I had one of those epiphanies, you know, from facing potential death, where I thought, 'Hey, I love Charlotte, what am I waiting for?' But you looked at me like I had lost my mind, so I let it drop." He had stepped back, putting space between them, and he shrugged, looking a little sheepish.

Now it wasn't just her mouth that was hot, it was her whole body, head to toe and every speck in between. She did remember, after all. "I thought you were hopped up on pain killers and didn't know what you were doing. I thought maybe you were dreaming. You were muttering incoherently. And did you just say that you love me?"

He nodded. Then he took her hand, his touch tender, his thumb smoothing over her skin. "Charlotte, I love you, totally and completely. As a friend, yes, but it's more than that . . . I love you the way a man loves a woman."

Charlotte was speechless, a big old grapefruit-size lump in her throat preventing her from swallowing or speaking. Not that she had formulated a coherent response anyway. She couldn't really see, either, because tears had completely blurred her vision. So she stood there watery and wordless and shook her head, overwhelmed. This was real. He was real. The love she felt was real, and now he was telling her she had his, too.

Squeezing his hand back and breathing really hard, she managed to force out, "I love you, too," before dissolving into full-blown sobbing. She didn't mean to. Didn't want to. But the emotion she felt, the relief, the joy, the hope, was overwhelming, and she just lost it.

Will pulled her close against his chest. "Shh, sweetheart, it's alright. It's all good. These are happy tears, right?"

She nodded, face squashed against his T-shirt. "Uh-huh." Wiping her tears on the cotton of his shirt, she sucked in air and tried to get control of herself.

"Alright, then." He tipped her head up, forcing her to look at him. "Then can I make love to you?"

Hell, yes. "Absolutely." Only she couldn't stop herself from darting a quick glance over to his kitchen, where the mistletoe was lying.

He grinned. "Should I go get it? And how exactly did you cast a spell on that thing anyway?"

"It doesn't matter. Just leave it." Bree would be disappointed that it hadn't worked, but Charlotte couldn't say she was. Will wanting her all on his own was far better. There was really no comparison.

"Sure it does. I'm curious." He went over to the kitchen and picked it up. Groaning when he made contact, his eyes rolled back in his head like he was suddenly experiencing intense pleasure.

Charlotte was horrified for a split second, then Will laughed.

"Just kidding." He winked at her.

"Not funny." Though he was so damn cute, it wasn't like she could even work up any real irritation. He loved her. He. Loved. Her. She was going to be flying on that for about a month.

"Yes, it is." Will was inspecting the mistletoe. "What's this white ribbon for? It's all twisted inside the branches and you drew little pictures on it."

"Those are symbols." Charlotte crossed her arms and tried to be nonchalant about the whole thing.

"Symbols for what?" He twirled it around, running his finger down the ribbon. "This is a blue wavy line. What's that mean?"

"Serenity. In our relationship."

He glanced over at her, looking touched. "That's very sweet."

"Your friendship brings me happiness." They were only a few feet apart, but Charlotte felt the energy between them, the new awareness of each other, a sort of strumming electric attraction and excitement, a giddy sense of anticipation and security. They were no longer just friends. They were about to become lovers and they were in love. It was a powerful moment, just locking eyes with Will and letting him see the truth.

"Yours does, too, Charlotte, more than I can say." He cleared his throat and tapped the next symbol. "This is a crazy-looking *H*, or I don't know, like a arch of some kind. What's that mean?"

"That's the bluebird of happiness. It's for love."

Will tilted his head slightly. "This sounds more like a love spell than a lust spell."

She had to be honest, with him and herself. "Maybe it was both."

"I think they really go hand in hand, don't they? One works best with the other."

"That's true." And she loved him even more for understanding.

"So what's lusty on here?"

"The hexagram is the symbol for sex." Which she wanted to actually be doing instead of standing there talking about it.

"Okay, you have two of those. And three male symbols."

Yes, she did. Charlotte felt her inner thighs moisten, the tight ache she'd been feeling all night building and growing in anticipation. "Those are the phallus of thrusting symbols."

Will sucked in his breath, his look so hot, so aroused, that it felt like he was stroking her from across the room, like his fingers were already inside her body, invading and pleasuring her.

"Are they now? And you felt the need to put three of these on here? More than anything else, I see." Will started toward her, stalking her, an impressive erection already pressing against the front of his jeans. "Why is that, sweetheart? Are you saying you want me to thrust my cock up inside you?"

Hello. Charlotte's nipples tightened and she shifted restlessly. "Yes, that's what I'm saying. That's what I was hoping for, even when I thought it could never happen."

His hand brushed against her waist, thigh rustling against hers. "It's going to happen. Right now."

• Six •

WILL HAD INTENDED TO TAKE IT SLOW, SENSUAL, SWEET FOR their first time. But then Charlotte had blushed, her cheeks pink, her lips wet and parted, and she had just tossed off that admission of having put phallus-thrusting symbols on her mistletoe ribbon.

He'd heard "phallus" and "thrusting," along with her wanting him, and his brain had ceased to function. All commands were coming from below the belt now, which was why he just about attacked Charlotte, hands sliding all over her thighs, her ass, her waist, while he kissed her hard, sucking and tugging and thrusting. Her hands went into his hair, gripping hard, as they rocked and slapped together, tongues entwining, skin hot, breath rushed and urgent. Pulling back slightly, Will ripped his shirt off over his head and dropped it to the floor.

Her eyes widened and she dropped her touch to his chest, stroking over him with such appreciation and curiosity that Will groaned. Her lips were wet and shiny from his kisses, skin flushed with pleasure, legs spreading apart as she tried to get closer to him.

Charlotte had a raw sensuality that he had never seen, never even guessed existed, and he wanted to see more, wanted to see how hot she could get, how far she'd go. They were going to have a hell of a lot of fun exploring that in the next few months.

Shoving up her sweater, Will pulled and tugged until it popped off over her head, her head sticking up, her arms flailing as she tried to get free. Then to his total amazement, she reached back and unhooked her bra and tossed it to the side, exposing her very lovely breasts, bare shoulders, and flat belly to him. Will forgot to breathe.

Then he couldn't prevent a guttural growl from coming out of his mouth as he bent over and took her nipple into his mouth, cupping the soft weight of her breasts with his hands. She gasped, pinching his shoulders. That sound, the way she expressed her pleasure, her voice the same one he knew so well, yet so different, was as big of a turn-on as the taste of her tight flesh under his tongue.

Sliding his hand down, he caressed the front of her jeans, back and forth, feeling the soft give of her body beneath his touch, regretting the thickness of denim. It was just a hint, a tease, so he unpopped the snap and tore her jeans and panties down all in one desperate motion. Lacking in any sort of romance or finesse, definitely, but he was about to suffer bodily harm from excessive arousal. He'd make it up to her later.

Charlotte was obviously of a same mind, because she gave him a hand by stepping out of her jeans. Kicking them to the side, she dropped down to her knees, before he even got a glance at her nakedness. Her knees. Hands reaching for his fly.

Holy shit. He hoped he knew where this was going.

It was. In two seconds she had his cock out and in her mouth. No hesitation, no playing around, no lick, no flick, just deep down into her throat, enclosing him in her slick, moist heat. He grabbed her head for balance and closed his eyes. "Damn, sweetheart. You're killing me."

She pulled back completely, mouth shiny, eyes hooded and still trained on his erection. "I've been wanting this for a long time."

Then she enclosed him again, forcing a quick, hot rhythm on him that had his balls tightening and his teeth grinding. It was so fucking good, but too much, too soon. He jerked away, and shoved his own jeans down and dropped onto his knees. Charlotte rested in front of him, lips puffy, chin glistening with moisture, her chest pink with excitement and exertion. Giving her a searing kiss, Will put his arm around her shoulder and urged her back onto the carpet.

Pausing to take a look, to savor the moment, to run his gaze over her beautiful, sexy body, Will whispered, "You are amazing."

She gave him a brief smile and mouthed, "I love you," soundlessly.

It about tore his heart out, and he felt the most overwhelming sense of tenderness and gratitude toward her. He couldn't imagine his life without Charlotte. He wanted her forever, as his, body and soul. Time to slow this down, get control, make love to her slowly and completely.

Then she spread her legs in a seductive offer.

All plans went out the proverbial window. He accepted that he was a selfish brute as he trailed his fingers through her damp curls, swirling around her clit, and opening her for him. She gave little gasps of pleasure and wiggled her hips, drawing her legs farther apart and exposing her pink, moist sex to him. Will put his palms flat on the carpet, moved between her legs, and thrust inside Charlotte, filling her completely.

He paused to regroup, mouth dry, erection throbbing at the first feel of her body wrapping around his, at the sight of her beneath him, chest heaving, eyes rolling back in pleasure, hair damp with sweat, nipples peaked and deep red. He wanted to savor, but he was too on the edge, too out of control.

And when she said, "Will, please, God, you feel so good," he gave up trying to stop himself. He just pounded into her, over and over, gritting his teeth and closing his eyes. She made frantic little sounds of pleasure, her cries getting louder each time he sank inside her, and Will knew she was almost ready, felt her legs squeeze around his thighs and her inner walls tense, constricting on his cock. Then she came, back arching up, eyes wide in shock, cry petering off into a strangled gasp, her hips stilling, even as he felt the tremors deep inside her. It was beautiful, surreal, arousing as hell, and he stroked through her orgasm and straight into his.

Charlotte watched Will above her, and couldn't imagine that she could ever love him more than she did. She had wanted this, hoped for this, hell, pined for him and a moment like this, but never could she have imagined that when it actually happened, she would feel this whole, this loved, this completely and deeply happy.

Almost as good as the sex itself was the way he collapsed on the carpet and pulled her tight in next to him, her legs entangled with his. Almost. The sex had been really hot. But it was sweet and comfortable, serene, lying naked with him, the hard planes of his chest warm beneath her hand, his body still partially inside hers.

"I completely forgot about a condom," he murmured, his hand stroking her back slowly. "I'm sorry, that was totally irresponsible."

"It's okay, I forgot, too." And truthfully, Charlotte wasn't worried about it. She knew Will and where he'd been and it wasn't anything to be concerned about. As for getting pregnant, she was twenty-nine years old, a successful business owner, and involved with her best friend, the man she loved. A child wouldn't be a crisis. In fact, she got a little warm and fuzzy inside at the thought of starting a family with him someday. "Would it be awful to say I'm glad we didn't have latex between us for our first time?"

"It's not awful, considering I was thinking the same thing, but it sure as hell isn't politically correct." He sighed, and kissed the top of her head. "Damn, sweetheart, that was a good time."

She laughed, feeling too satisfied to move. Ever. Despite a shiver that went through her from being naked in December on the floor.

But Will noticed and said, "You cold? Let me grab a blanket." He slid out from under her and walked toward his bedroom.

Charlotte rolled onto her side, resting her head on her arm so she could have a clear view of his tight butt and muscular thighs, his strong back, and chiseled forearms. Will was a fine man in more ways than one, starting with his intelligence and compassion, and ending with that naked ass in front of her. It made her want to lick her lips and start all over again.

But he disappeared into his room, and when he returned a minute later, he was wearing jeans and holding a blanket in his hand. Her disappointment at having him covered was profound. He looked amazing in jeans, she'd give him that, but she'd been gawking at him clothed for eight years. She'd wanted to linger a bit on his nudity, really get a good eyeful before he covered it all back up. She would have to content herself with the knowledge that she'd be seeing a whole lot of his bare body from there on out.

"I know it's freezing outside," he said as he dropped onto the floor and spread the blanket over her and brushed her hair back off her shoulder. "But would you want to go for a ride? There's something I'd like to show you."

She had absolutely no interest whatsoever in getting dressed and going outside in the snow and freezing wind, but if he had something to show her, she wanted to see it. "Sure." Trailing her fingers over his bare chest, she smiled at him. "Then when we get back, we can finish putting your tree up. And other things."

"What other things?" He grinned.

"I'll leave it to your imagination."

"I have a very good imagination. I've spent a good long time picturing all the things I can do to you." His eyes had darkened.

Sounded perfect to her. "Then let's go. Sooner we go, sooner we get back."

Will liked the gray house. It was small, Amanda hadn't exaggerated about that, but it was double the size of his apartment, and it was structurally sound. It had two bedrooms, and a funny little extra room that must have been an outside sleeper porch originally, one and a half baths, and a kitchen, dining room, and living room. Lots of thick woodwork, a brick fireplace, and an old milk chute cut out in the kitchen wall.

"What do you think, sweetheart?" Will stopped in the living room and looked at Charlotte. Her opinion meant everything in the world to him, because he had every intention of seeing her living in the house with him.

She had walked through the whole house with him, quiet, but eyes sharply inspecting everything. She'd seemed surprised he was considering buying a house, and maybe a little offended he hadn't told her. It hadn't been a secret, he just hadn't been sure. He'd been waiting for something before he made that big investment. Now he knew just what that was. He'd been waiting for Charlotte. To make the decision to buy a house together.

He'd almost given up on that dream. But now here it was, right in front of him, everything he had ever wanted.

"It's cute, charming. I like it, Will." She ran her hand over the fireplace mantel, still the original oak. "It has character. Good bones."

"Good. I'm glad you think so, because I like it, too." Will searched for the right words to convey to Charlotte what she meant to him, how she was his family, his life, his heart. "And I only want to buy this house if you can picture yourself living in it with me."

Her head whipped around and her eyes met his, wide with shock. "Excuse me?"

Will didn't even hesitate. They'd wasted enough time, he didn't intend to waste any more. "Charlotte, I know this is moving fast, but we know each other better than a lot of people who've been dating for years. I am completely and totally in love with you . . . You are my very best friend, you are amazing, and I want you to live with me. In this house, or a different one, if you don't like it. But I want you with me, now, forever."

He closed the two feet between them and took her hand. "Will you marry me?"

Even he hadn't known he was going to say that last bit. But it just came out, right and strong.

Charlotte thought Will's proposal was the most beautiful thing she'd ever heard in her entire life. It should have felt surreal, strange, that after all those years of just being friends, they would leap straight to a commitment, but it didn't. She knew, without a shadow of a doubt, that Will Thornton was the man for her. And now he was going to be her husband.

Tears popped into her eyes and she touched his cheeks, studying his strong, handsome face. "Yes," she said, nodding her head rapidly. "God, yes, I will marry you."

Then she was kissing him, or maybe he was kissing her, she wasn't sure which, and it didn't really matter because they were together, as one, and it was a kiss of pent-up love, past frustrations, present passion, and future happiness.

"I love you," he whispered, pulling back a hairbreadth.

"I love you, too." And all the amazing things his tongue was suddenly doing to her neck.

"This house still has some furniture in it since it was a rental," he said as his tongue splayed across the swell of her breast, her neckline stretched down again. "Couch or bed?"

"Will! This is Mrs. Stritmeyer's house . . . we shouldn't."

"So? We're buying it, aren't we? It's going to be our house soon."

Their house. Holy crap. She almost had an orgasm just at the thought of that. Waking up with Will. Eating dinner every night with him. Sharing a bed, a shower . . . That image went straight to her inner thighs. "Shouldn't we look at other houses?" It was a struggle to feel practical when his hand was sliding over her clitoris through her jeans, but she forced the words out.

"I did. Didn't like anything else." Then he buried his head back in her breasts. "Besides, don't you know the story? This is the honeymoon house. The original owner built it for his bride."

How romantic was that? She almost melted right then and there, but Charlotte had heard a different version. "I heard it's haunted . . . that the lady cries in the mirror upstairs because her husband left. That's downright sad."

"She cries from missing him because they were so in love. That's romantic. We can bring love back to this house, sweetheart." He peeled her bra down and licked her nipple. "Starting right now."

"Okay." She did like the house. And it was the spot where Will had proposed. And he was doing really amazing things to her nipple, which made really just about everything make sense. "Let's buy it."

"It might be cool living in a haunted house, as long as this ghost isn't yanking down my zipper like the one in your garage."

Whoops. Guess she had never really discussed that with him. She really wasn't at all sure how he was going to like the idea of having a witch for a wife. Not that she was exactly witchy, but still, he might not be comfortable with her strange new ability to levitate objects. She wasn't comfortable with it, come to think of it.

"That wasn't a ghost, baby."

"Well, something did it. I didn't imagine it. Or the fact that someone grabbed my butt."

Had she done that, too? Charlotte didn't see how that was possible, but at the same time, she'd been waxing quite poetic about his ass right at that particular moment. "You see, the thing is, you know how Bree thinks I'm a witch?"

"Uh-huh." His mouth switched to her other breast.

Like it wasn't hard enough to force out the words. He was seriously distracting her.

"Bree says I can move objects. She says I unzipped your pants with my mind."

Will went completely still, tongue on her nipple. His breath blew hot on her slick skin, making her nipples firm even more. "Say that again."

She really wanted to just forget the whole thing and go back to foreplay, but he had obviously gotten distracted by the whole "I'm a paranormal freak" thing she'd just thrown at him. "I unzipped your pants. I was, well, interested in you, sexually, you know, and I envisioned your jacket opening, and it did. Then I pictured your pants unzipping and they did. I'm sorry." She really did feel contrite about that. It wasn't fair to unzip his pants without warning and she was going to have to learn how to control her so-called talent.

Will stood up, leaving her chest half uncovered. "So, you're saying *you* did it? Did you know you could do stuff like that?"

"No. I'm still not convinced I can."

"Unzip my pants now."

"Will!" Charlotte felt her cheeks burn, and she wasn't sure why. "I don't think so."

"Come on. I want you to." He stood with his legs apart and hands loosely at his sides. "Unzip me. Take what you want."

Oh, my. That was a little hard to resist. Charlotte stared at his snap and zipper, pictured them opening for her. Pictured what was behind them. Pictured wanting him, undressing him. She chanted down in her head over and over, concentrating on the metal button, vision blurring.

And the button popped open. The zipper went down.

"Whoa," Will said.

Charlotte felt a strange sort of pride in her accomplishment. "I can't believe I can do this."

Will grinned, peeling off his winter jacket and tossing it to the floor. "Think of how many ways you can take advantage of me."

"You don't mind that I have a freakish ability?"

"Hell, no. That is seriously hot, sweetheart. Just don't ever get mad at me and wing dishes at my head."

"I'm not a dish-throwing kind of girl."

"I know." Will sat down on a fussy Victorian sofa in front of the fireplace. "But you're not really the nice girl you claim to be, either. You have a naughty side, too."

"Maybe I do. More than I realized." Because she was already stripping her jeans off, just like that, and climbing onto his lap. "We'd better make it quick," she told him, even as she ground her panties against his erection. "The heat's not on in here. And you never know who might show up."

"I can be quick."

He wasn't lying. He had somehow managed to spring himself free, and while he kissed the stuffing out of her, he got her shirt up, bra unhooked, and panties pulled to the side. Before she could barely blink, his finger was inside her, stroking her incoherent. Charlotte plunged her tongue into his mouth, needing to taste him, her hands in his hair, holding on. God, she loved him. She never wanted to let him go.

Desire spiraled into desperation. Normally, she'd always thought of herself as a little bit sexually inhibited, but none of that was in evidence with Will. She just felt, reacted, took. Ripping his shirt up, she pressed her bare chest against his, dragging a moan from both of them at that wonderful collision of hot flesh on flesh.

Will lifted up her hips and brought her down onto him with one smooth motion. Charlotte couldn't have even explained what exactly happened to her panties. Somehow they were sideways, enough out of the way to accomplish the primary goal, which was him deep inside her. She let her head drift back as he lifted up into her, the angle pressing his pelvis into her clitoris in a frantic tease. Charlotte lifted her hips and slammed down onto him, meeting him thrust for thrust, frenzied and determined. She needed it hard, needed to feel all of him, needed to take them there together.

So much for slow again. Will figured maybe eventually they'd get there, in about a year. He just wanted Charlotte too damn much to have any sort of patience whatsoever. She seemed to feel the same way, given the way she was bucking up and down on him, her breasts brushing against his chest, her ass soft and sexy on his thighs. When she came, Will thought it was the most beautiful thing he'd ever seen. She was so honest in her appreciation, her cries loud and unrestrained, her eyes rolled back, her fingers gripping his skull.

Her convulsion jerked his head back, and that was all it took to make him join her. Will pulsed into her, straining, holding her at the waist, wanting her still so he could fill her as completely as possible. It had some solid staying power, and Will finally collapsed back against the sofa and let out a little laugh.

"Was that quick enough?" he asked, blinking hard to focus on her.

Her skin was shiny and pink from exertion and pleasure. "That was perfect." She grinned and leaned forward to kiss him softly.

Will stroked her back lazily. Then heard a car door slam. "Uh, sweetheart, I think someone's in the drive."

She leapt off him with a dexterity that was impressive, tucking and adjusting and pulling her jeans back on. Will did the same and he was just slipping back into his jacket when they heard the front door open and giggling.

"You can see my new thong," a female voice said.

Uh-oh. Will knew that voice. He darted a glance at Charlotte, whose face had lost all the flush from their lovemaking and every other ounce of color.

Abby and Brady Stritmeyer came into the room, laughing and kissing and pawing at each other's clothes.

"Abigail Murphy!" Charlotte said, her voice filled with horror.

Abby's head snapped up and her eyes went wide. "Charlotte?" she said in a tiny voice.

"Shit," Brady said, quickly pulling Abby's shirt back down.

"What the hell are you two doing?" Charlotte asked.

Will figured that was obvious, but he kept his mouth shut.

"The, uh, movie sucked, so we left halfway through. Brady's grandma owns this house, so we came to talk." Abby was blushing, but she was also holding her arms crossed over her chest defiantly. "I don't have to be home until midnight. What are *you* two doing here?"

"I'm buying this house," Will said. "I wanted Charlotte's opinion." And her body, but that was irrelevant. "And I wanted to ask her to marry me, so I did."

Abby dropped her arms, defiance disappearing. "Are you serious? Ohmigod! That rocks, Will!" She ran to her sister and bounced on the balls of her feet. "Did you say yes? Tell me you said yes?"

Charlotte smiled and accepted her sister's hug. "I said yes."

Then Abby was squealing in delight, so Will took the opportunity to sidle up to Brady, who shot him a wary look.

"Congrats, man," Brady said.

"Thanks. And keep in mind I'll be Abby's brother-in-law. And I'm a cop. I carry a gun." Then he smiled at Brady. "Just a friendly reminder."

"Got it."

"What is going on here?"

Bree joined the party, looking annoyed and cold, snow all over her feet, shod in impractical open shoes, her skirt hovering somewhere around her knees. It wasn't the best choice of outfit for December, but Will didn't think Bree went in much for practical. Stubborn was more her style.

"What are you doing here?" Abby asked.

Will was wondering the same thing. When he'd brought Charlotte to see the house, he hadn't expected they'd be throwing a housewarming party in it that night.

"I saw you and Brady drive past the house, and since you were supposed to be at the movies, I wanted to know what you were doing here."

"You followed me?" Abby frowned. "You so need a life."

Bree glared at her little sister, and Will saw the whole conversation going bad places. He slipped his hand into Charlotte's and pulled her by his side. "I brought Charlotte here to show her this house because I was thinking about buying it."

Bree blinked, studying him. "You're going to, aren't you? I feel all these weird happy waves from you, and . . ." Her mouth dropped. "You and Charlotte had sex, didn't you? I can sense it."

That was kind of disturbing. He didn't think he wanted Bree sensing it every time he and Charlotte got busy. But since Charlotte was now blushing a violent red, he figured it was obvious anyway. He said, "Charlotte and I are buying this house together. We're getting married."

Damn, that felt and sounded so good when he said it. He was having happy waves. Big ones. He pulled Charlotte even closer and wrapped both his arms around her. He never wanted to let her go again.

"Charlotte, is he serious?" Bree asked.

Charlotte looked at him and Will felt his breath catch. There was no mistaking the look she was giving him—it was tender, filled with love, and edged with lust.

"Oh, yeah, he's one-hundred-percent serious."

And she kissed him right there, in front of her sisters. Which, for Charlotte, was a serious sign of affection.

He whispered in her ear, "How powerful a witch do you think

you are? Can you make them move right out of this house? I want to work on your lust spell some more."

Charlotte pulled back and gave him a saucy smile. "I can handle this." She glanced over her shoulder. "You all need to leave because Will and I want to be alone."

That worked.

• *Seven* •

A WEEK LATER CHARLOTTE FIGURED LIFE DIDN'T GET ANY better. She and Will were hosting a Christmas party in the gray house and they were surrounded by family, food, and holiday music. They'd made an offer on the house and were set to close in a few weeks. Jessie Stritmeyer had happily agreed to let them have their first Christmas party in the house, despite not having moved in yet, and she'd even given them their first housewarming gift—a rather obscene-looking cactus.

Charlotte's mother was chatting happily away to Will's mother, who had come back from Florida for a week to celebrate Christmas. Mrs. Thornton, bless her heart, actually seemed interested in the running commentary Charlotte's mother was delivering on her haunted prison tour adventure, complete with cold spots and rattling manacles.

Abby reached around Charlotte for the cookie tray resting on the coffee table. "These rock." She bit the head off a blue frosted angel and chewed.

"Thanks." Charlotte had baked six dozen cookies in a sort of love, sugar, and sex high after she and Will had spent a rather industrious morning getting to know each other just a bit better. Yet again. "Nice T-shirt."

Her sister grinned. "It's Christmas themed."

It was, but somehow Charlotte didn't think a shirt that featured Santa being enthusiastically whipped by his reindeer was really traditional in the truest sense. Charlotte sank back into the sofa and watched Will, her father, Mr. Thornton, and Brady Stritmeyer inspecting the door in the dining room that led to the backyard. She heard them tossing around thoughts like installing better insulation, a new track, and a dead bolt. They were in collective man heaven inspecting the house and laundry-listing all the repairs it needed.

Bree was sitting on the other side of her, wearing the tackiest, most appalling sweatshirt Charlotte had ever seen. Suffering from multiple personality disorder, the shirt was green, red, gold, plaid, striped, decked out with bows, lace, raffia, and featuring at least three Christmas scenes on it. It looked like a craft fair had vomited on her sister's chest, and she had to admit, Bree looked better in black.

"Are we going to burn this shirt together after today?" Charlotte asked her, knowing her sister had picked the hideous thing to wear to prove a point. Charlotte couldn't expect her sisters to change any more than she herself wanted to change. Just because they didn't share the same taste in clothes didn't make them any less sisters.

"I was hoping." Bree grinned. "I think I might actually need therapy after wearing this."

"Thanks for doing it." Charlotte crossed her legs and took her sisters' hands in hers. She squeezed, feeling deliciously, ridiculously happy.

"Hey, by the way, what did you do with that mistletoe and the ribbon?" Bree asked.

"It's shoved in a drawer."

"If you don't want it you have to destroy it piece by piece since you put a spell on it."

"That's sounds dangerous. How about I give it to you and you can do it." "Destroy" was not a verb Charlotte acted out intentionally.

"Okay. I'll take care of it."

Charlotte was still gripping their hands, unwilling to let go just yet. Will glanced over at her and smiled. Dang, he was so cute. She imagined running her fingers over his tight butt, sliding around to the front and stroking him into thick, throbbing hardness.

Suddenly Will's eyes went wide and he took a step backward, like he was evading something. A glance showed he had an erection before his hands moved in front of it to block the view. Holy crap.

"Careful, Charlotte," Bree whispered, her voice gleeful. "Together the three of us are more powerful than one."

Huh. It was a little scary to imagine what the three of them could do together, but it didn't stop her from looking at Will and still thinking naughty thoughts.

He grinned at her. *Later,* he mouthed.

Definitely later. And forever.

Beat of Temptation

Nalini Singh

For the Sexy Regency Cave Club:
Sharyn, Peta, and Nicky,
and honorary members, Doug and Rob.
Thanks for the Christmas memories.
(I'll never look at a cave the same way again!)

• *Happiness* •

THE PSY COUNCIL TRIED TO OUTLAW CHRISTMAS ONCE.

It was in the year 2019, four long decades after the implementation of the Silence Protocol. The Protocol itself arose out of the overwhelming incidence of insanity and serial killing in the Psy populace. Driven to the edge, the Psy made a choice. They conditioned their young to feel nothing—not jealousy, not rage, and definitely not joy at the thought of Christmas morning.

So it was that by 2019, only ice ran in the veins of the Psy politicians who wanted to make Christmas illegal. Since the Psy race controlled government then as it does now, *Law 5198: Deletion of Christmas and Associated Holidays* was near certain to pass.

There were a few minor hiccups. Some elderly Psy—those who had been too old at the inception of Silence to allow for true conditioning—weren't certain they wanted the holiday outlawed. But the old ones were few; the last, unwanted vestiges of an emotion-filled past the Psy preferred to forget. They were ignored, their fading voices drowned out by the Silent majority.

Law 5198 was read into the statute books and life moved on.

Except that the humans and changelings, the other two parts of the triumvirate that is the world, took no notice. Christmas trees went up as usual, gifts were bought, and carols were sung. Human business owners did a roaring trade in mulled wine, fruit cake, and roasts with all the trimmings.

In comparison, Psy who owned interests in companies that usually profited from Christmas suffered a sharp drop in income—*Law 5198* meant they could no longer advertise their products in conjunction with the outlawed holiday.

The Psy Council found itself faced with both a mass revolt by the other races, and considerable opposition from the very businesses that backed up its regime. Psy might not feel, but they also did not appreciate their profit margins being compromised. The businesses weren't the only ones who felt the negative impact of *Law 5198*—Enforcement could find no way to prosecute everyone who violated the law against Christmas.

The churches simply acted as if the law didn't exist. But they, in their solemn dignity, weren't the worst offenders. The changelings, in particular the nonpredatory deer species, took great amusement in walking the streets in their animal forms, dressed up as Santa's reindeer.

Then the horse-changelings decided it wouldn't hurt their pride to be harnessed two by two to large sleds in order to transport shoppers around the cities. Finally, the humans, the weakest of the three races—with neither the psychic powers of the Psy, nor the animal strength of the changelings—came up with the killing strike.

They changed the name of Christmas to the Day of Happiness.

It was unacceptable for Psy to feel happiness. Those who did had their minds wiped clean and their personalities destroyed in a horrifying process known as "rehabilitation." But it wasn't illegal for anyone else to celebrate happiness. And if they wanted to do it by singing songs, gathering with loved ones, and attending certain ceremonies dressed in their Sunday best, well, that wasn't illegal either.

The powerful, deadly Psy Council was used to instant obedience in all things. However, in the year 2021, the Councilors admitted that wasting Psy resources to ensure compliance with *Law 5198* made no financial or strategic sense. The law was quietly repealed.

Now, some forty years later, Christmas is a celebration unlike any other. Though the Day of Happiness was retired soon after the repeal of *Law 5198*, changelings and humans have always known that they are one and the same thing. Of course, happiness isn't guaranteed by the magic of Christmas. Sometimes, a woman has to fight with everything in her, with her pride and her fury, her love and her anger, with her very soul, in order to claim the joy . . . or the man, meant to be hers.

• One •

Tamsyn looked across the Pack Circle to the men and women who stood on the other side. Lachlan, their alpha, his hair going the white of wisdom and age, was saying something to Lucas, who was barely fifteen but carried the scent of a future alpha. The past and the future side by side. One day soon, Lucas would lead them. Everyone knew that. The boy had been drenched in blood, his parents murdered in front of his eyes. But he would lead. It didn't matter that even if they waited a decade, he'd still be far too young.

Just like Tamsyn was too young at nineteen to be the senior healer for the DarkRiver leopard pack. Her mentor had been Lucas's mother, Shayla. The attack on Lucas's family had not only stolen their healer, it had left DarkRiver in a state of constant alert. That didn't mean they had given up. No, they were quietly building their strength until the day they could destroy the ShadowWalkers—the pack that had murdered their own.

She knew Nate would be one of those who went after the

rogue pack when the time came. He stood tall and strong beside Lachlan, his concentration on whatever it was they were discussing. At twenty-nine years of age, he was one of the pack's top soldiers and would soon be a sentinel, assuming Cian's position when the older man retired from active duty. The sentinels were the pack's first line of defense. They were the strongest, most intelligent, and most dangerous predators of them all.

"Tammy, you're back!"

Startled, she looked away from Nate and into Lysa's bright green eyes. "I only got in an hour ago." Even now, she didn't quite believe she was home—the six months she'd spent at the teaching hospital in New York had been the hardest of her life.

"So the course is over?"

"Yes. That part of it anyway." She could finish the rest of her medical training in nearby San Francisco. Most changeling healers relied on their inborn gifts, but Tamsyn had made the decision to study conventional medicine as well. It was one more way to compensate for her inexperience, for the healing gifts that hadn't yet matured to full strength. She refused to allow her youth to disadvantage her pack.

"Nothing went wrong while I was away?" She'd hated leaving DarkRiver in someone else's care, though she fully trusted the healer who'd stepped in to hold the fort during her absence. "Maria?"

"She left this morning. Itching to get back home exactly like you." Lysa smiled. "It was nice of Maria's pack to lend her to us and she was great, but damn, I'm glad to have you back."

Tamsyn returned her friend's fierce hug. "I'm glad to be back."

Lysa set her free. "Go on. I know you're wanting to catch up with Nate."

"No." She glanced over her shoulder. "He's busy with Lachlan."

"The man's your mate, girl. You can drag him away."

Mate. The word made her heart skip as it had since the day she'd turned fifteen. That was when the mating instinct had awakened, when she'd realized she was one of the lucky ones—she'd been born into the same pack as her mate, had known him since childhood. "It's not official yet."

Lysa rolled her eyes. "As if that matters. Everyone knows you two are meant for each other."

Maybe, but they were nowhere near to consummating the relationship. Nate was determined she get the chance to explore her freedom before settling down. What she had never been able to make him see was that he *was* her freedom. She didn't want to be apart from him. But Nate was stronger than her. And at ten years her senior, he was used to giving orders and having them followed.

"I should freshen up," she said, dragging her eyes away from him a second time. "I just dropped off my bags before coming here." Searching for him.

"All right. I'll see you after you've settled in." Lysa smiled. "I have to go talk to Lachlan about something."

Nodding good-bye, Tamsyn began to move away from the large clearing ringed by trees that was the pack's outdoor meeting place.

Nate had seen Tammy arrive, waited for her to come to him. And now she was walking away. "Excuse me," he said to Lachlan, no longer caring about the discussion at hand. Some Psy named Solias King was apparently making what he thought were discreet inquiries about DarkRiver's territorial reach and ability to defend itself. Lachlan was fairly certain the man wanted to steal their land.

"This is important—oh." The DarkRiver alpha looked up and followed the path of Nate's gaze. His frown turned into a grin. "No wonder you're distracted. Guess we won't be seeing you for a while. We'll have to track this idiot down ourselves."

Good-natured laughter followed Nate out of the Pack Circle as he tracked his mate's scent through the trees. He caught her in under a minute. The second his palm clasped the back of her neck, she froze. "Nathan."

Her skin was delicate under his hand and he was very aware of how easily he could damage her. With her hair swept up into a long tail, her neck appeared even more vulnerable. He rubbed his thumb over the softness of her. "When did you get back?"

"Around four."

It was now five-thirty and winter-dark. "Where have you been?" The leopard who was his other half didn't like that she hadn't come to him first.

She turned her head, eyes narrowed. "It's not like you left a note as to your whereabouts."

His beast calmed. She'd gone looking for him. Gentling his hold, he slid his hand to the side of her neck and pulled her to him. She came but her body was stiff against his. "What's the matter?"

"Juanita was very happy to tell me where you were."

He heard the jealousy. "She's a friend and a fellow soldier."

"She was also your lover."

The beast wanted to growl. "Who told you that?"

"I'm a decade younger than you," she retorted. "Of course you've had women. I don't need anyone to paint me a sign."

The jagged edge of anger turned his next words razor-sharp. "I haven't taken a lover since your fifteenth birthday." He was a healthy leopard male in his prime. Sexual hunger did not sit well with him. But neither did cheating on his mate. "And if someone's telling you different, I'll tear out their throat."

She blinked. "No one's telling me different." Her voice was husky. "But I don't like knowing you've had other women in your bed, that they've touched you, pleasured you."

Her bluntness shocked him. Tamsyn did not talk to him like that. "What exactly did you do in New York?" The possessive fury that hit him was close to feral, a harsh thing with claws and teeth.

Her mouth dropped open. "I don't believe this!" Breaking his hold with a quick move of her head—a move he'd taught her—she faced him, hands on her hips. "You think I would—" She gave a little scream. "You know what, if I had, whose fault would that be?"

He folded his arms to keep them from hauling her back against his chest and proving to his beast that she still belonged to him. "Tamsyn."

"No. I've had it up to here!" She jerked the edge of her hand to below her chin. "All the other females my age are taking lovers left, right, and center, and the only thing I get is frustration!"

Her raw need was simple truth. Newly mature females were very sexual, their scent intoxicating to the young males. Then there was the fact that the mating heat had shifted Tammy's natural hunger into higher gear. He could taste the woman musk of her, the lush ripeness just waiting to be bitten into—it was an exhilarating blend, and one he alone had the right to crave. Even the idea of any other male lusting after her pushed his temperature into explosive range. "If I take you," he said quietly, "it'll be for life."

"I know that! And I accept it. I need to belong to you—in every way."

His cock wanted to take her up on it. But she was *nineteen*. She didn't understand what it was she was committing to. He wasn't some kitten who'd follow her around with his tongue hanging out like the young males did with the females. He'd take her and he'd keep her. Sexually, he was far more mature than she was, and a leopard-changeling's sexual needs only grew more intense with time. "You don't know what you're asking."

"Dammit Nate, I'm sick of needing you so much I can't sleep." Her hands fisted by her sides, caramel-colored eyes rich with heat. "I'm sick of stroking myself to sleep."

Jesus. The images that hit him were hot and erotic and so detailed they threatened his beast to madness. "We've had this discussion before," he reminded her. "You're carrying too much responsibility as it is." Shayla's murder had forced Tammy to step into the older woman's position—as DarkRiver's healer—at seventeen years of age. She'd never had a chance to be a juvenile, to mess about, to play and roam. "I've seen exactly how wrong things can go if leopards bond before they're ready."

"We are not your parents," she spit back.

He went silent. "I told you to never bring up my parents again."

"Why not?" She was trembling. "They're the reason you're being so stupid. Just because your mother was miserable after deciding to take a permanent partner at age eighteen doesn't mean I will be."

His mother had been more than miserable. "She committed suicide." If not in truth, then in effect. Her drinking had escalated to such an extent that even her tough changeling physiology hadn't been able to repair the damage.

"We are not your parents!" Tamsyn repeated, her voice breaking on the last word. "You're my *mate*. And I'm yours. Your mother and father didn't have that connection."

No, his parents had fallen in love the old-fashioned way, without being driven by the mating instincts of the leopard. It happened like that sometimes. Though mating wasn't uncommon, not every changeling found his or her true mate, the one with whom they could bond on a level that was almost psychic. "Mating will demand more from you than a nonbond relationship ever would," he told her, cognizant of the terrifying animal fury of his hunger for her. "I don't want you walking into that before you're ready."

"And you're the one who decides if and when I'm ready?"

"I'm older and more experienced." She had years to go before she caught up.

She seemed to be gritting her teeth. "Fine! Enjoy yourself in your perfect little world where everything goes according to your plans. Don't blame me if I get sick of waiting for you!" She turned and began to stalk through the trees.

"Tamsyn." He used the tone of voice that made even the rowdiest juvenile stop and pay attention.

She kept walking.

"What the hell?" Striding after her, he caught up just in time to see her clothes disintegrate off her body as she shifted into leopard form.

He froze, stunned as always by the beauty of her. Her pelt was glossy, the dark rosettes defined luxuriantly against the gold. Suddenly, she looked over her shoulder and gave him a look that could only be described as haughty. Her eyes were green-gold, not caramel, in this form, but they were very definitely all female.

He growled at the implied challenge. She snapped her teeth in response and took off. He almost went after her—his claws were already out by the time he brought himself back under control. If he ran her down in his current state . . . well, she wouldn't be complaining about stroking herself to sleep again.

Oh, hell.

Now his mind was so full of images of soft feminine flesh and long stroking fingers that he was in danger of bursting out of his pants. "Shit." Turning in the opposite direction from her, he ran toward a nearby waterfall. An ice cold bath was exactly what he needed to knock some sense into his head.

He wondered if she moaned when she brought herself to orgasm.

• *Two* •

Tamsyn shifted back into human form near her parents' home. They lived fairly close to the Pack Circle and it was where she was staying for the time being, her life in limbo—she should have been living with Nate by now. Eyes stinging at the reminder of his rejection, she went to retrieve some clothes she'd hidden for just such contingencies. Nudity was no big deal in the pack, but she was already going to be a crybaby. At least she could be a clothed crybaby.

Dressed, she walked to the front door. Her mother opened it before she could knock. With her dark hair and pale brown eyes, Sadie Mahaire was an older, smaller version of Tamsyn. It was Tamsyn's father who had given his daughter her height. Her mother took one look at her face and opened her arms. "Come here, my darling."

Sobbing, Tamsyn went into her mother's embrace. "I don't know what to do, Mom," she said, what felt like hours later. She was lying on the sofa, her head in her mother's lap and her legs curled up on the cushions. "This need I have for him, it's clawing me to pieces. But . . . but he doesn't seem to feel the same." That knowledge crushed her, made her feel as if she were bleeding inside.

"Oh, yes he does." Sadie stroked Tamsyn's hair off her face with gentle hands. "He's simply had longer to get used to it."

"Longer? How? The bond awakened at the same instant in both of us." He'd come to the door on her fifteenth birthday and she'd felt something in her snap taut, a connection so strong, it vibrated with how utterly *right* it was.

"Yes, but you were fifteen. Your sexuality was young, immature."

She remembered the wave of heavy warmth that had uncurled in her stomach whenever she'd been around Nathan, the soft ache in low places. "I wanted him even then."

"But as a girl wants, not as a woman." Sadie pressed a kiss to her brow. "He, on the other hand, had to have had a brutal time of it. You were a baby and he'd never have allowed himself to touch you, but he was a man and his beast knew you were his mate."

Tamsyn began to see what her mother was saying. "He had to learn to chain the mating urges of the leopard, wait until I was ready." For the first time, she understood the pain it must've caused him. "And he couldn't be with any other woman."

"Mates don't cheat." Sadie sighed. "That's a very good thing, but it's also a hard thing to bear when things don't work out perfectly. But you understand about Nate now, don't you? He's as hungry for you as you are for him—it's just that he's had years to build up his will against the need."

"He's going to be a sentinel, Mom," she said, proud but afraid. "You know the kind of men who become sentinels. His will was already as strong as steel before he found out about the bond. Now I'm pretty certain it's unbreakable." She rubbed a hand over her heart, where the bond was a savagely twisted knot. Though it was meant to be an instinctive link, Nate had somehow learned to block it. Her animal heart kept reaching out to him . . . only to slam up against a solid wall of resistance.

"Oh, my baby." Sadie squeezed her shoulder and Tamsyn sat up, wiping away the final evidence of her tears. "Now listen," her mother said, pure love in her expression. "The man's will might be unbreakable for some, but not for you. You're his mate. You have a direct line to his soul."

"But he won't listen. He's made up his mind that we're going to wait and wait and wait and—" She shook her head, shoulders hunching in defeat. "I know he's thinking in terms of years, not months." A wait that long would drive her insane. She wasn't being overly dramatic—the lack of tactile contact between her and Nate, the denial of what their beasts craved, it physically *hurt*. "And it's not like I'm some sexy little thing that can seduce him." It was out before she could feel embarrassed.

"You're beautiful." Sadie's voice was full of maternal pride. "You have courage and strength and such spirit."

Tamsyn didn't have the heart to tell her mom that while those qualities might be nice, they didn't exactly make her a knockout. Her hands were practical healer's hands, her hair a plain brown, and her eyes . . . well, her eyes were okay. Sometimes she thought they looked like dark amber. But what man would care about her eyes when women like Juanita with their seductive, curvy bodies were sashaying around? Tamsyn was all legs and strong bones. More horse than leopard, she thought morosely.

"If you give up," Sadie said, cupping Tamsyn's cheeks with soft hands, "you'll regret it for all the long, lonely years that follow. So will he. Nathan thinks he knows what he's doing, but starving the bond will destroy both of you."

"How do I reach him?"

"That's for you to figure out." Her mother smiled. "But I'll give you a hint—he's a man. Treat him like one."

* * *

Two hours later, Tamsyn still hadn't a clue about what she was going to do. Frustrated in more ways than one, she stomped downstairs with the intention of finding something with which to take her mind off Nate. Maybe her mom was quilting and needed an assistant. But the house proved to be empty. Sadie had left a note tacked to the back of the front door.

Your father and I decided to go for a bit of a roam.

Translation: They were off feeding their animals' need for the wild and who knew when they would be back. It could be days.

"Great," she muttered, feeling sorry for herself. Trudging back into the living room, she had the beginnings of a good sulk going when she spied a box on the coffee table with her name on it.

Another note:

Tammy, darling, I thought you might like to do these while things are quiet (and you're sulking). We could do with some new ones. Love, Mom

Opening the box, she found it filled with homemade Christmas decorations. She smiled, unable to resist their magic. Every year until the horrible day when a bloody nightmare had forced her to step into the position of DarkRiver's healer, she had made these with her family. There were silver cardboard angels and beads strung on fishing wire and beautifully detailed paper dolls. But what held her attention were the round glass ornaments.

Each was meticulously painted with scenes from fairy tale and legend. Most had been done by Tamsyn and her mother as they sat side by side for hours, her father content to "supervise." She smiled. Every ornament held a memory of happiness, of love. Her hand found one decorated with the image of a running panther. She stilled.

Healing's not just about bones and cuts, Tammy, sweetheart.

Tears pricked her eyes at the memory of Shayla's patient voice. Lucas's mother had been a black panther like her son. She had also been Tamsyn's teacher, her friend—a friend whose advice and guidance Tamsyn missed desperately. But today, in this moment, it felt as if Shayla stood right beside her, telling her the truths she needed to hear.

This would be the second Christmas since the attack. No one had been in the mood to celebrate the first, but perhaps it was time to heal her family, her pack.

Even if she couldn't heal herself.

Her eyes narrowed at the self-pitying thought. "Snap out of it," she ordered herself. Sulking be damned—she would not let Nate's idiocy ruin this Christmas for her. And she was going to make sure he knew it.

• Three •

Solias King was a Tp-Psy, a telepath with a Gradient 8 ability. That meant he was strong enough to use mind control should he ever decide to. Solias had done so before—politics didn't allow for such niceties as high moral principles.

His current plans, too, would have been far easier to implement had he been able to utilize his telepathic abilities to coerce and persuade. Unfortunately, changelings had rock-solid natural shields. He *might* be able to turn one of them—and that with considerable effort—but he couldn't control the entire DarkRiver pack. "But it shouldn't be necessary."

"What, sir?" his aide and son, Kinshasa Lhosa, asked.

"Nothing of note." Solias turned. "Do you have the details?"

"Yes." Kinshasa passed them over. Despite his youth, the eighteen-year-old was extremely efficient. Solias had made a good investment when he'd entered into a reproduction contract with the Gradient 7 Tp-Psy who was Kinshasa's mother. Both

Kinshasa and the second child from the contract were high Gradient minds, powerful in their respective abilities.

"Give me a précis."

Kinshasa spoke from memory, his dark skin unlined. "The land in question is perfect for your needs. You can locate a small comm station and office there, then use it as a base for further expansion."

"The leopard pack?" Solias didn't trust Kinshasa—he trusted no one, blood relative or not. But the boy was undoubtedly good at research. "Will they pose a problem?"

"No," Kinshasa said, his tone holding the cool emptiness of Silence. "DarkRiver is a small group with no real presence. If we were going up against the SnowDancer wolves, it would be a different story. They're somewhat more aggressive."

That was why Solias hadn't looked into "acquiring" wolf land. "Begin preparations for development." The leopards—animals shackled by the choke of emotion—were clearly no threat.

"Yes, sir." Kinshasa paused. "There was another matter, sir."

"Yes?"

"The Psy Council has requested a meeting with you."

Solias nodded. "Forward me the details." The Council was likely interested in the details of his political aspirations—power never changed hands without the Council's approval. If Solias played his cards right, he might not only take over the leadership of San Francisco, he could rise to the Council itself.

The Councilors would appreciate his firm hand with the animals. And if it all ended with a few dead leopards thrown into the mix, so much the better.

• Four •

Having half-frozen himself in the icy chill of the waterfall, Nate finally hunted Tamsyn down well after sunset. It wasn't that he didn't know where she was. It was that he wasn't sure he could face her without doing something stupid. Like yelling, "What the hell are you doing up there?"

Her eyes were night glow as she stood on a tree limb several dangerous feet off the ground, in human form. It would have been another matter if he'd found her there in leopard form. That was normal. The same couldn't be said for a woman with a rope of Christmas lights slung over one shoulder. Now, that woman snorted and began to string the lights around and along the boughs above her head.

"Tamsyn, I swear to God," he grit out, tracking her so he could catch her if she lost her footing, "if you make me come up there, you won't be sitting without wincing for weeks."

"You won't lay a hand on me, Nathan Ryder," she said. "That's the problem, as I recall."

She was right, of course. He'd rather cut off his hand than hurt her. "Fine." Slicing out his claws, he prepared to scale the tree and drag her down to safety.

"Don't you dare mess up my Christmas tree."

He stopped. "Your *what?*" The fir was so tall it seemed to touch the night clouds. Only a crazy woman would attempt to decorate this. But instead of asking if she'd lost her mind and chance getting his head bitten off, he decided to point out another fact. "It's not Christmas for weeks."

"It's a big tree." She continued walking along the branch as she strung the lights. "If you're not going to leave, make yourself useful and string the other side. There are more lights at the bottom of the trunk. Don't insult my cat by playing catcher."

Knowing she was right about her leopard being agile enough to ensure she'd always land on her feet, he looked down, then wished he hadn't. "Where did you get this many lights?" He picked up the heaviest rope, shoved it over one arm, and started climbing.

"People liked the idea of a giant Christmas tree."

"It'll draw Psy to the area like magnets." The other race knew nothing of the pack's network of lairs and aeries. It was a form of protection against the Psy hunger for power. "You want to announce our Pack Circle?"

"I'm not an idiot." The words were blades. "The lights are special low-impact ones. They won't even show to the top of the tree, much less put out a detectable heat signature."

He wondered if insanity was catching. "I can't believe I'm having this conversation with you. It's ten o'clock at night."

"Feel free to leave if it's past your bedtime."

The bite of sarcasm made him grin. His cat liked being near Tamsyn, no matter her mood. And he was animal enough to appreciate her claws—no leopard wanted a weak mate. "So, what are you planning to do for an encore? A parade of giant jack o'lanterns? Maybe we can use them to scare off the wolves?"

"Good idea." He could hear her smirk. "Shouldn't you be out doing important sentinel stuff?"

"I'm not officially a sentinel yet." Though he was already being allocated most of Cian's work as the other man concentrated on his role as advisor to Lachlan and trainer to Lucas. "I have the night off."

"And you're here? What, Juanita was busy?"

He let her hear the angry rumble of his growl. "Are you really accusing me of cheating?"

"Not possible to cheat on something that doesn't exist."

"Tamsyn," he began, intending to tear into her. Then his beast suddenly realized something. "You're still jealous of a relationship that was over years ago." He couldn't understand why, not when he'd made it plain that he'd been celibate since the mating bond snapped into being.

Silence for several minutes. "It hurts me to know a woman who's been allowed full skin privileges with you—while I'm not even worth a simple kiss."

He froze at the amount of pain in that single statement. "Don't you *ever* compare yourself to any other woman," he said, his beast raging at the mere idea. The instant he'd realized she'd been born for him, it had blinded him to anyone else.

She didn't answer.

"Tammy."

"I don't want to talk anymore."

He was certain he heard tears in her voice. It shook him. His strong, beautiful mate never cried. "Tammy, don't."

"Don't what? Decorate my tree in peace?" The acerbic edge was back.

"I thought . . ." He shook his head, relieved. "What's next, after the lights?"

"Ornaments. They'll take a while. I'm going to get the kids to make one each."

He jumped easily to the ground and picked up the last rope.

Stringing that took far too little time though he tried to stretch it out. Tamsyn was waiting for him when he jumped down the second time. "Thanks."

He fisted his hands to keep from stroking the delicate line of her profile. "You going to turn it on?"

"Not until it's ready." She shoved her own hands into the pockets of her jeans. "I better get inside. It's chilly."

He was one step from pulling her into a hug, would have done so for any other packmate who needed it—touch was the cornerstone of who they were. But if he touched Tamsyn, it wouldn't stop at a simple hug. He'd take all of her, claim proprietary skin privileges from head to toe, spending extra time on every seductive feminine curve in between. His voice was leopard-rough when he asked, "What are you doing tomorrow?"

"Working with the kids on the ornaments. Going over some study papers." She turned on her heel. "Good night, Nate."

He frowned. "You're still angry."

"No." She gave him a tight smile. "But I'm also not a sucker for punishment. You might have had years to get used to resisting the full brunt of the mating heat, but I haven't. So help me out and keep your distance."

"KEEP MY DISTANCE." NATE PACED ACROSS THE LENGTH OF his living room and back. "Keep my distance." He was her mate—she *belonged* to him—and she'd told him to keep his distance.

Something growled deep in the forests that surrounded his home and he wondered which one of his pack was running under the moon. If he'd had to bet, he'd have said either Lucas or Vaughn, or maybe both. The two were still juveniles, but both had already seen death firsthand, been scarred by their losses. Now they waited to grow up so they could claim vengeance.

He would go with them when it was time to destroy the

ShadowWalkers. The younger males would be fighting their demons, but he would be fighting for his mate's right to be safe. Something dark and almost violent in him tightened at the thought of her, a sense of complete rightness filling his soul. She was his, wouldn't ever be anyone else's. The reminder calmed the visceral hunger of his beast.

He would never forget the moment when he'd realized what she was to him. Because of the disparity in their ages, they had had different friends, moved in different levels of the pack. But he had always known who she was, adored her in a way that was everything good—her laugh soothed the rough edges of his beast, her smile made him want to smile in turn.

On the night of her fifteenth birthday, she had hosted a small sleepover party at her parents' home. He'd dropped in to wish her a happy birthday. It had been no fleeting impulse—he'd become used to swinging by to check if she was okay, especially during the times when her parents were out. As soon as she had opened the door, he'd felt the bond snap taut. The knowledge had been in her eyes, too, shocked and bright.

He'd touched her then, cupped her cheek with his hand. She had leaned into him, soft and welcoming and everything he had ever wanted. He'd known that, at that moment, he could ask anything of her and she'd give it to him. That was what had made him draw back. "Not until you're ready," he'd said, ending the contact.

It was a promise he refused to break.

Tamsyn thought he was being cruel. She hadn't seen what he had with his parents. His mother had been too young, his father too demanding. Within a decade, they had destroyed each other and themselves. The idea of doing that to Tamsyn was his worst nightmare. Because he knew he was too much like his father—he would not be an easy man to mate with. He'd expect total devotion, demand complete sexual surrender, take absolute possession.

Tonight, his body hungered for her with a fury that was more animal than man. The cat had wanted her from the first. To the leopard, she'd smelled mature at fifteen, but the man had known she was nowhere near ready. Now . . . now he could have her—if he was willing to look into her eyes for the rest of his life and know he'd stolen what little freedom she could have had.

"No." He would not do that to her. She might be frustrated and annoyed with him, but she'd forgive him. It was what mates did.

TAMSYN WAS NEVER GOING TO FORGIVE NATHAN FOR PUTting her through this! "I can't stand it!" Her skin was so sensitive even the sheets felt abrasive. The flesh between her legs was swollen with need and there was only one man she wanted to rub against, only one thing she wanted to do. Unfortunately, Nate didn't want to play.

Why had he turned up tonight? To torture her? Her beast had become drunk on his scent, addicted to the proud masculine taste of him. It wanted more. So much more. Maybe that was why he'd come over—because his beast was starving, too? She snorted. More likely he'd come to tell her off for daring to turn her back on him this afternoon.

Nate was used to obedience. Particularly from her. As a fifteen-year-old, she'd taken everything he said as gospel. At sixteen, she'd given him the occasional moment of lip but had always accepted his decisions in the end. And he'd never let her down. He'd been her rock . . . especially after that dark day two years ago when she had failed to save Lucas's father.

"Carlos wanted to die," Nate had whispered in her ear, holding her tight as she sobbed over the loss. He'd still held her then. "He didn't want to live without Shayla."

It hadn't taken away her sense of failure, but she'd understood. The bond between mates was beautiful, powerful. Separated mates could live without each other, but it hurt. As she knew too well. And she shouldn't! Unlike those whose mates had been lost to death, Nate was alive but wouldn't touch her.

That was so incredibly wrong. Changelings weren't Psy. Touch was as necessary to them as food and air. Tamsyn thought nothing of hugging and kissing a fellow packmate who needed reassurance. That her mate wouldn't even give her that . . .

"I don't care," she lied into the dark. "Hell, yes I do." Shoving off the sheets and blankets, she slid off the bed and went to get a glass of water. Ice cold water. God, even her skin ached.

Filling up the glass, she took it and herself to the front window. Her plan—to distract herself by admiring her tree—disappeared the second she saw the leopard asleep on one of the branches. She couldn't make out his markings but she already knew who it was. Nathan. The man wouldn't take her as his mate in truth, but he thought he had the right to protect her? Damn him. Slamming down the glass, she was halfway to the door when she looked down at herself.

All she wore was an old football jersey. It was Nate's. She'd stolen it from him in a blatant bit of thievery, needing his scent around her. But big as it was, it gaped over her full breasts and only hit her midthigh. Maybe she should change. And it was freezing outside.

Nate probably wouldn't appreciate her walking around half-naked any— She slapped her forehead. "Tamsyn, sometimes you're an idiot." Of course he wouldn't appreciate her walking around half-naked. The sight of so much skin might incite his beast, tempt it enough to overpower the man's will.

Her lips curved.

• *Five* •

SHOVING HER FEET INTO A PAIR OF FLUFFY SLIPPERS, SHE stamped outside and to the tree, knowing he'd have woken the second she opened the door. "Nathan, you get out of here right now!" She hugged her arms around herself, well aware the move plumped up her breasts, creating a deep cleavage.

The leopard growled at her, its green eyes dangerously bright.

"Don't you growl at me," she said and her breath turned the air to mist. "You don't get to pick and choose which parts of the mating deal you want. It's all or nothing. *Go away!*"

He padded along the tree limb and leaped to the ground by her feet, a stunning creature she could stroke for hours. Then he butted at her legs, urging her inside the house.

The touch of his fur against her skin made her shiver. "I'm not leaving until you're gone." She'd meant to tease him, but already, her own leopard was scraping at the insides of her skin, so darkly needy it scared her.

He bared his teeth and gave a short, husky roar meant to snap her to attention. His eyes told her to get her little butt back inside or he'd do it for her. She hoped he would. Because if he shifted now, he'd be naked. Skin to skin contact at last. Her thighs trembled, but she somehow found the strength to stamp her foot and point away from her home. "Out! Leave!"

He began walking toward the house. She frowned, wondering what he was up to. He got to the door and looked over his shoulder. She wasn't going to fall for that. Then he walked inside. Her eyes wide, she hotfooted it inside, closing the door behind her.

The leopard was sitting in front of the currently unlit laz-fire, the artificial heating system designed to resemble a live blaze—but one that had zero chance of getting out of control. He glanced at her, his eyes night-glow in the darkness.

"Good idea," she said, half-frozen. Kicking off the furry slippers, she turned on the laz-fire. The flames shot to instantaneous life. "Brr." Rubbing her hands together, she sat down beside Nathan. She couldn't quite think straight but that was okay. Nate was in her house. He was here. And they were alone.

He butted at her hand with his head and she began to stroke him, her body warming up from the inside out. "What were you doing out there, Nate?"

He lay his head on her thigh and growled softly in response.

"It's because my parents are gone, isn't it?" She sighed and tried not to tremble at the proximity of him. He was so lethally beautiful, his body pure muscle under her strokes. "When are you going to accept that I'm a grown-up? Huh?"

No response. The steady rhythm of his breathing told her he'd fallen asleep. She couldn't bear to wake him. Tears pricked her eyes. If she shifted, they would both be cat and . . . No, she thought. She wouldn't use the animals' driving need against Nate.

It was the man who wanted to give her "freedom" and it was the man she had to convince. The animal already knew what was right. If only Nate's human half hadn't gotten in the way. Except, of course, she loved that part of him, too. Sighing, she stroked her fingers through his fur over and over.

It was a long while later when she curled up beside him and went to sleep.

NATE WAITED TO LIFT HIS HEAD UNTIL HE WAS ABSOLUTELY sure Tamsyn was fast asleep. The last hour had been both pain and pleasure, torture and redemption. The animal couldn't understand why he didn't claim her. One thought, a split-second shift into human form, and he could take her right there on the softness of the rug.

The temptation was shockingly strong.

She was the most exquisite creature he had ever seen. A long, tall drink of woman. He could spend all night stroking his hand up and down the sleekness of her thighs—exposed by that jersey she'd stolen years ago.

He'd known, of course. It had given him pleasure to think of her covered in his scent. Since he hadn't seen her wearing it around, he had guessed, *had wanted*, it to be her nightwear of choice. His claws dug into the rug as he shifted his attention to the proud thrust of her breasts. There was no question about it—Tamsyn was every inch a woman. And so heartbreakingly young.

No one would think to look at her that she'd been their healer for two years already. Oh, the few packs they had trusted after Shayla's murder—packs with men and women seeded from DarkRiver—had sent senior healers to complete her education, but it was Tamsyn the pack looked to. She was their own and she was deeply trusted.

Because she had never let them down.

He remembered her at seventeen. Her mentor was dead and Shayla's mate, Carlos, lay critically injured. Their son, Lucas, remained missing. Tammy had been so slender back then, a fragile reed he'd thought would snap under the weight of the dying sentinel's wounds. But she hadn't broken. Instead, she'd put every inch of her abilities into healing Carlos.

She hadn't been able to save his life, but she had given him the strength to whisper his final words—ones that told them Lucas was still alive. Tammy had been completely drained by the effort to save Carlos, but when they had rescued a badly injured Lucas, she had somehow found impossibly more to give. And she'd kept doing it for weeks.

She had slept only when Nate forced her to, worried she'd collapse under the strain. Even then, she would crawl out of bed after a few hours at most. Finally, Nate had had to half-kidnap her. He'd held her in his lap and told her to sleep. And she had, curled up trustingly in his arms.

The girl who had been that slender reed was gone. She'd grown into a woman of courage and beauty, but one who had never been given the chance to be a juvenile. Leopards valued their freedom to roam—many left the pack and came back after spending time in the wild. He, too, had left DarkRiver for several years in his late teens. Tammy had never had that choice, her wings clipped at fifteen.

Backing away from the lush temptation of her, he dragged an afghan off the couch using his teeth and pulled it over her. It would've been easier in his human form, but he didn't trust his willpower that much. One touch was all it would take. He'd crumble like so much dust.

He decided to keep watch over her from the outside.

Tamsyn woke up warm . . . and alone. It hurt. "I could hate you, Nathan." Getting up, she hugged the afghan around herself and stared into the laz-fire. Her internal clock told her it was morning, sometime around six. Despite the fact that she'd done all she could to entice Nate, he hadn't so much as kissed her.

Was she that disgusting to him?

A sob caught in her throat. It was the first time she'd considered that Nate's recalcitrance might spring, not from his overwhelming protectiveness, but because he didn't *want* to be tied to her. Her lower lip trembled. She hugged the afghan even tighter around her body in a vain effort to ward off hysteria.

Being unwanted by a mate was a nightmare beyond comprehension. Mating wasn't marriage, wasn't infatuation, wasn't a connection you ever broke. She was tied to Nate on the level of her soul. More than that, she loved him. Some people said that there was no difference between the bond and love, but she knew there was. It was one thing to be compelled toward Nate, another to adore him like she did. She loved everything about him, from his strength to his laugh to his unashamed masculinity.

But what if, for Nate, the bond was simply a compulsion? One he couldn't dissolve, but that he wouldn't have chosen if he'd been given the choice? She was hardly a prize, she knew that, had always known it. Added to that, Nate was older, more experienced. Maybe he'd expected and wanted to find a mate who could match him, a woman who'd seen far more of the world than just their small corner of it.

In contrast, Tamsyn had always been tied to DarkRiver. That didn't matter to her. She was a woman of home and hearth. It was the way of most healers. They liked to be near their people, their lands. Healers built permanent homes before most others, took in any who needed their help, and cherished those who were their own. The months in New York had almost torn out her heart, she'd been so homesick.

But Nate had roamed. He'd left the pack for years as a juvenile and come back a man, strong, loyal, and with wild horizons in his eyes. What did he see in hers? Home—calm, steady, enduring. But not very exciting. No wonder he didn't want her!

Tamsyn had worked herself into quite a state, something that would've flabbergasted those who knew her, when the comm console chimed. It was the emergency code. She blinked and snapped to attention, the healer in her taking over. "Talk to me."

Juanita's face appeared onscreen. "Dorian broke his arm while we were sparring near the Circle. It's pretty bad."

"Don't move him." Turning off the screen, she got up, changed at the speed of light, grabbed her emergency supplies, and headed out.

The cold air cut across her cheeks as she ran. If Dorian hadn't been so close by, she'd have taken a vehicle. But at this distance, her changeling speed was faster than the vehicle would have been on the rutted forest roads. The roads had been damaged on purpose. It was another line of defense, meant to bog down the unwary. DarkRiver was never going to be caught off-guard again.

She found Juanita crouched beside Dorian, who was sitting propped up against a tree. Though the woman looked concerned, Dorian's face betrayed nothing. Barely into double digits, the boy was better at hiding his feelings than most adults. "What were you two doing to break that arm?" she asked, going down beside him.

"Karate. Brown belt. San-kyu," Juanita answered.

Tamsyn didn't berate the other woman for using such advanced techniques against a boy. They all knew Dorian was no child. He'd been born latent and had no ability to shift into leopard form. Perhaps it was something that might have been held against him had he not made it his mission to become so dangerous, no one would dare treat him as anything but another cat.

"A single break. Clean," she told him. "You were lucky."

Pure blue eyes looked into hers. "How long till I can use it?"

"As long as I say." She put a pressure injector against his arm before he could object that he didn't need the anesthetic. Then, using the portable deep-tissue viewer to double-check the conclusions of her healing gift, she set the break and encased it in a lightweight but durable cast. Dorian had normal changeling strength and healing capacity—he'd regain the use of his arm far sooner than a human or Psy would have in the same situation.

"Nita, can you give me a minute with Dorian?" She glanced at the beautiful woman.

Juanita nodded. "I have a perimeter watch to take over."

"I'll make sure he gets home."

Dorian scowled as they talked about him but didn't say anything until Juanita had disappeared into the trees. "What?"

Shaking her head at that stubborn male expression, Tamsyn moved to sit slightly behind him. Then she threw her arms around his neck and leaned down to press her cheek against his. "San-kyu, that's the third level, isn't it?" With the dominant males—or with the young ones who would one day be dominant—you had to tread carefully. Demanding would get her nothing from Dorian.

He softened a little. "Yep. I'm going for black next month."

"Impressive. When I left for New York, you were still on the first level of brown."

He let her tug him further into her embrace. Touch was at the heart of a healthy pack. It was what bound them together, what gave them their strength. Smiling, she raised her hand and began to brush her fingers through his incongruously silky blond hair as he lay against her.

"I'm going to be past Juanita's level soon." It was a small boast and it was perfectly normal. Whatever had happened to break his arm, it hadn't bruised his pride too much.

She grinned. "Then who are you going to beat up?"

He actually smiled. "You want I should do Nate for you?"

It seemed the whole pack knew how things were between her and Nathan. "Brat."

"Yeah, but you like me."

Laughing, she pressed a kiss to his cheek before rising. He followed, his bones showing the promise of a height that would top hers by several inches at least. "Look after yourself, Dorian. If I see you one more time this year, I'm going to do something nasty like pull healer rank and ground you."

"Like you wish you could ground Nate—maybe in your bedroom?"

"Dorian!"

Mischief in his grin, he backed away from her before turning to run off through the trees. She kept her smile hidden until he was gone. Then she bent down and began to gather up her supplies and equipment. She was pleased. Her medical training had come in very handy today. Otherwise she'd have used up healing energy to no useful purpose. What she did came from inside her—she had to conserve her strength for the worst injuries . . . as had happened with Carlos.

Leaves rustled to her left and she looked up to see Juanita step out. "Did you see my—ah, there it is." Nita picked a slender black timepiece off the ground. "Took it off while we were sparring. That boy is dangerous when he gets going."

Nodding, Tamsyn continued to put away her things. Nita was the last person she wanted to chat to, especially after the horrible realization she'd had that morning. Then the other woman went down on her haunches beside Tamsyn.

"Hey, Tammy. I need some advice."

Her healer core came to the surface, consigning the sick ugliness of jealousy to one tiny corner. "Is something the matter?" She looked into that sensual, exotic face and no longer saw a rival, but a packmate who might need help.

"You could say that." Dark eyes twinkled. "I'm wondering how to bring up Nate without putting my foot in it."

• *Six* •

Tamsyn froze. "What about Nate?" she forced herself to say.

"Look"—Juanita tapped a finger against her knee—"he's a wonderful guy and we had some fun together—"

Tamsyn shut her bag and prepared to get up.

Juanita stopped her by holding onto her upper arm. "But that's all it was. Fun. We were friends then and we're friends now. Nothing more."

"Okay. I have to go." She was so hungry for Nate's touch that even the idea of him with another woman bruised her raw.

Juanita didn't release her. "You're not listening, Tammy. I'm telling you that that man never looked at me with the kind of wild heat with which he looks at you. He never craved me, not like he craves you."

Tamsyn stared at the other woman. "He left me," she found herself saying. "I was all but offering myself to him on a silver platter and he left me. He doesn't crave me."

Juanita laughed. "The man wants you so much, he's driving all the juveniles crazy. You know how sensitive they are to sexual hunger, and right now, Nate is a six-feet-plus shot of pure animal need. And he's not interested in anyone but you."

"But—"

"But nothing." Juanita stood and waited until Tamsyn, too, was up before continuing. "Don't take this the wrong way but you're young."

How else could she take it? "I'm more mature than people years older."

"Yes, you are. I wouldn't hesitate to come to you for advice on a thousand things." Juanita's matter-of-fact words took the wind out of Tamsyn's sails. "But there's one area in which you are a babe in the woods."

"Men," Tamsyn whispered, embarrassment a blaze across her cheeks.

"Yep. You were one of the lucky ones—you found your mate early, but that came with a price." Juanita didn't need to spell it out. "So trust me when I tell you the man is dying for a taste of you."

Tamsyn ached to believe. "He's very good at hiding it."

"Of course he is. He's stubborn and he's dominant. He wants to do this *his* way. It's up to you to change his mind. Please do it before he drives everyone insane."

Taking a deep breath, Tamsyn swallowed her pride and put her faith in the bonds of Pack. "You have experience. Teach me what I need to know."

Juanita grinned. "I thought you'd never ask."

A DAY AFTER HE'D LEFT TAMMY SLEEPING BY THE FIRE, NATE returned from a meeting with Lachlan to find the area around her home crawling with children. Not all of them were exactly underage. "What are you doing?" he asked Cian, who was sitting on what looked like a bench and table set stolen from their alpha's backyard.

The older man grinned. "Making Christmas decorations, what does it look like?" He returned to painting the small glass ball in his hand.

"Why?" Nate insisted.

Cian scowled at him. "Because Tamsyn said I had to."

"She's less than half your age."

"Have you tried to argue with her when she wants to get her own way?" Shaking his head, Cian returned to his task. "Besides, it's kind of fun. And she's got the juveniles interested in something other than raising hell, which makes our job easier."

Now that Cian had mentioned it, Nate realized just how many of the older kids were present. Even arm-cast-laden Dorian appeared to be having fun. Nate watched as the boy bent down to help a five-year-old paint something on her globe. When she smiled, so did Dorian.

Turning his head, Nate found Lucas sitting with another group of young ones. Several cubs were trying to use his body as a climbing frame, but from the sharp grin on his face, he didn't seem to be worried. He called out to someone else and Nate's eyes followed his gaze to locate another unexpected addition to Tamsyn's gathering. Vaughn. He was even worse a loner than Dorian. But there he was, patiently helping several of the three-year-olds.

"They're happy," a feminine voice said from beside him.

He looked down. "You did good."

Astonishment was open on her face. "Oh." A pause. "Thank you."

He scowled. "What's wrong with me complimenting you?"

"Nothing." She shrugged, her breasts pushing out against the softness of her black cowl-neck sweater. "You just don't do it much."

He reached out to pinch a bit of her sweater with his fingertips. "What is this stuff?" It was so damn strokable he was having a hard time keeping himself from doing exactly that. Shaping his mate's body with his palms seemed like the best idea he'd had all day.

"Angora blend." She pulled away from his touch and took a step backward. "Do you want to paint an ornament? Or you can help the children."

He didn't like the distance she'd put between them. "What's the matter with you?"

Something flickered in her eyes before her lashes lowered to screen her expression. "I'm living my own life. It's what you want, right?" A small smile. "I'm finally beginning to appreciate what you've been trying to tell me." With that, she went off to check up on a group of giggling teenage girls.

Nate wondered if he looked as sucker-punched as he felt. She'd pulled that stunt out of nowhere. All these months of fighting him, of demanding he accept their bond, and she was suddenly going to fall in line? Right. He'd believe that when he saw it. Tamsyn had called him every day from New York—she couldn't shut him out if she tried.

Twelve hours of near-silence later, long after everyone else had left, he grit his teeth and handed her an ornament. "This is the last finished one." Many had taken theirs home to complete.

"Thanks." She hung it on her damn tree before jumping down from the branch on which she'd crouched. "I think it'll look fabulous when it's done, don't you?" Without waiting for an answer, she turned to walk up the path to her door.

"Where are you going?" He barely kept the growl out of his voice.

She threw him a confused look. "It's dark. I'm going to have a bath and dinner."

He waited for the invitation to join her. It didn't come. "Your parents aren't back."

"Oh, don't worry." A tight smile accompanied her words. "A few of my girlfriends are dropping by tonight."

"Who?"

"Friends. Actually, do you mind not coming by at all?" she asked. "We can hardly talk girl-talk if we know you're out here skulking."

His temper wasn't easily stoked. But it was smoking now. "Skulking?"

She gave him an airy wave. "You know what I mean. We'll be fine. I even asked some of the other soldiers to swing past during their night watches. You should go do your own thing." A few seconds later, her door shut behind her.

He didn't move, rooted to the spot by pure disbelief. She'd told him to get lost. Nobody told him to get lost. Especially not his mate. He'd taken the first step up the path to her home when he felt someone walk out of the woods behind him. He turned to find Juanita. "What?" It was the leopard speaking.

"This is part of my night route." She gave him a curious look. "What are you doing here?"

What kind of idiotic question was that? "Looking after my mate."

Juanita scowled. "You're on the eastern perimeter, Nate. If you wanted a change, you should've told Cian. We'll have a gap there otherwise and you know we can't afford to. Especially not with Solias King's men sniffing around."

He knew she was right. "Cian factors mates into the watch assignments."

"Yeah, but you haven't claimed Tammy. He probably thought you wanted some space from her—you're getting more and more irritable." Her tone was blunt. "Look, I'd take the eastern for you, but I'm pulling a double anyway and I'd prefer to stay close to home."

There was nothing he could say to that. He was one of the most experienced soldiers in the pack, and as such, he had a job to do. "Don't let anything happen to her." It was half warning, half threat.

Juanita's response was a raised eyebrow. "Tammy's no cub. She can handle herself."

Tamsyn put out the snacks with trembling hands. She couldn't believe she'd "ignored" Nate all day. The act had stretched her nerves to screaming point, the compulsion to speak to him as powerful and as intrinsic as her heartbeat. She was obsessing over their parting words when the soft buzz of the doorbell sliced her thoughts in half.

Taking a deep breath, she opened the door. "Oh, it's you."

Juanita grinned. "I told you it would work."

"He's furious." She looked over the other woman's shoulder, hoping to see Nate. "I thought he was going to march up here and demand I—"

"Precisely." Juanita put her hands on her hips and shook her head. "He's used to demanding something from you and getting it."

"Isn't that what mates do?"

"Sure. But he's being an ass about it. He's not exactly meeting your demands, is he?"

Tamsyn scowled on Nate's behalf. "You don't—"

"Don't you dare defend him," Juanita ordered. "And don't you back down, either. You're just giving him a taste of his own medicine. This is what he's been doing to you for over a year. Let him see how he likes it."

It made sense, but Tamsyn wasn't a soldier, to think of love like strategy. Her heart was that of a healer—gentle and easy to forgive. "He hates it."

"Good." The other woman grinned. "If you don't allow him access to you anytime he wants to feed the animal's need to be close to you, he's going to get desperate sooner rather than later. Then he'll jump you and, bang, we'll all live happily ever after."

Tamsyn nodded. She liked the idea of being jumped by a sexually hungry Nate. "If he doesn't do it soon, I might attack him myself." Her sensitivity to his proximity was getting worse, the mere sound of his voice enough to melt her to damp readiness.

Juanita grinned. "I give him a week."

TWO NIGHTS LATER, TAMSYN DECIDED JUANITA WAS A GE-nius. Nate was scowling at her from across the Pack Circle, such violent need in those midnight blue eyes that she could feel her stomach twist itself into a thousand knots.

"Stop staring at him," she muttered noiselessly to herself. She hadn't said much more than hello to him for the past forty-eight hours, but if she didn't keep her eyes to herself, he'd figure out just how hard it was for her to maintain her distant air. She ached for him and the ache was a pulsing beat in every inch of her skin . . . and worse in lower, hotter places.

Breaking the connection through sheer effort of will, she focused on the dancers in the middle of the Circle. They were part of an impromptu gathering sparked by the full yellow moon, a happy diversion from the general air of wary alertness that had gripped DarkRiver since the attack by the ShadowWalkers. That wasn't to say that their defenses were compromised. Those on watch were being spelled by off-duty packmates so everyone could join in the fun.

And it *was* fun—warm, friendly, brilliantly alive. Several people had pulled out instruments and the music was energetic and strong. She clapped along with the players, and when Lucas came to offer her his hand, she took it with a smile. "Watch out, I've got two left feet."

He grinned, the savage markings on one side of his face—markings he'd been born with—making him look more panther than boy. "Good thing I don't scare easy."

Laughing, she let him swirl her around in an energetic dance that required enough of her concentration that she almost stopped thinking about Nate. When the tall juvenile snapped her back into his arms, she was breathless. "You're in a good mood," she said, glad to see him happy for once.

There was darkness in Lucas, such darkness. She knew it would be there until the day he took vengeance on those who had stolen his family from him. He was four years younger than her, but looking into those eyes, she saw not a child but a man. Lucas would one day be an alpha of incredible strength, of that she had no doubt.

He held her closer, touching her with the easy friendliness of Pack. She rested her cheek against his shoulder and swayed to the gentler beat that had replaced the pounding dance music. "So?"

"So I thought you needed to be held." The words were blunt, the tone affectionate.

"Thank you. I did." There was no need to lie. Not with Pack.

"Dorian said you don't want us to beat some sense into Nate." He sighed as if in disappointment. "Are you sure?"

She laughed at his teasing. "I like him in once piece, but thanks for the offer."

"Do you want to dance with him? 'Cause he's heading this way."

• *Seven* •

SHE SMELLED THE RICH EARTHINESS OF NATHAN'S DISTINCTIVE scent before she could answer. It hit her system like a drug. An instant later, the heavy weight of his hand dropped on to her hip. "Luc. Go find a girl your own age."

Lucas released her. "I think I like sexy older women—why don't I keep Tammy and you find someone else?"

Nate's growl was met with unrepentant laughter as Lucas threw Tammy a wink and walked away. She paid little attention to the exchange, her entire body focused on Nate as he placed both his hands low on her hips and pulled her back against his chest. "What the hell are you wearing?" He spoke against her ear, breath hot.

It was an effort to think. "Jeans and a sweater. Is that a crime?"

"The sweater is orange and anyone can see down your cleavage."

She forced herself to laugh. "Nate, the vee isn't that deep and the color is soft peach, not orange." It went beautifully with her hair and eyes, throwing up golden highlights she'd never have believed possible.

"It's fucking painted on your body, just like your jeans."

"Watch your mouth, Nathan Ryder." Firming up her tone, she put her hands over his and began to sway against him. It wasn't a calculated act—her body simply craved the contact. "I'm nineteen years old. This is what women my age wear."

His breath seemed to catch for an instant. "You don't."

No, she didn't. It had always seemed to her that she shouldn't aggravate the situation between them by being deliberately sexual. But tonight, she'd followed Juanita's advice again and gone wild. The jeans—brought on a whim in New York—shaped her butt, and from the good-natured whistles she'd inspired in male packmates, it wasn't a bad butt.

As for the long-forgotten sweater, baggy when she'd been a gangly thirteen, it was made of a soft, strokable material that did feel painted on over her now-womanly figure. That was the point. It was meant to make it hotly clear to Nate that she was a sexual young female, not a nun happy to wait for him to make up his mind.

"I decided it was time to change my personal style." She moved against him again, exquisitely aware of the unforgiving ridge of his erection. "Have some fun before we settle down, exactly like you wanted."

"Stop that." But he didn't do anything to halt her subtle erotic movements. "This kind of fun isn't good for the blood pressure of the other men." He pulled her even closer.

"They know I'm yours," she murmured, feeling her skin flush. "Only yours."

"Then why are you dressed like an invitation?"

For you, you idiot, she wanted to say. "I wanted to feel sexy." She shrugged. "I haven't had much of a chance to explore that side of me." That, at least, was true. Between Nate's pigheadedness and her responsibilities, she hadn't had much play in her life. She did so want to play with Nate—silly, intimate, affectionate games.

His hands tightened. "And what are you going to do after getting yourself all heated up like this?" It was a half-growled question, but she knew him well enough to know that that roughness was an indication of need, not anger.

She tilted her head, looking up at him as he looked down. "I bought a friend."

He seemed to choke for a second. "A friend?"

"Uh-huh. He vibrates." It was a whisper meant to carry to his ears alone. "I think I'll try him out tonight."

His fingers were pressing down so hard, he was probably going to leave bruises. She didn't care. Not when he was burning her up with the heat in his eyes. "Don't."

Raising her arms, she linked them behind his neck. "Why not?"

"Your first time shouldn't be with *that*."

She shrugged. "I'm getting older, Nathan. I have needs." Dark, clawing needs. Needs only he could fulfill.

"Promise me you won't use that stupid toy."

"It's not stupid." She rubbed against the hardness of him and heard him suck in a breath. "It's smaller than you, though."

"Christ." Pulling her arms off his neck, he spun her around so she faced him. "Don't. Use. That. *Thing*." It was an order.

"Why not?" She pressed into him, the leopard in her inciting a desire to taunt, to torment. "Lots of women do it."

Eyes going cat, he leaned down to speak against her ear, his lips teasing a suddenly sensitive portion of her anatomy. "If you promise not to use it on yourself tonight," he whispered, "I'll use it on you."

Her legs threatened to collapse. "When?"

"Promise first."

She was weak, so weak where he was concerned. "I promise I won't use it tonight."

He nipped at the shell of her ear and it was then she realized he'd danced them to the farthest edge of the Pack Circle, well away from the reach of the temporary lights. She whimpered and held on. "Nate."

"Shh. It won't be that long, baby." His hand stroked over her back, a rigid inflexibility to his body that hadn't been there before. "You need a little more time."

A nauseous feeling twisted through her. "Nate, you said you'd—"

"When the time is right." There it was again, that tense restraint . . . as if with her surrender, he had found control.

Anger and pain mixed a caustic brew inside her. "Well," she said, wrenching away from him, "I only promised not to use it tonight."

"Tamsyn."

"And," she continued, "I'm not going to fall for that dirty trick again." She began backing into the Circle. "I'm sick of being teased and left wanting. Tomorrow night, I'm taking care of business."

TAKING CARE OF BUSINESS.

Nate glared into his morning coffee and then at the duty roster he'd just received from Cian. Punching in the sentinel's code on the comm console, he waited for Cian's face to appear. "What the hell are you on? This roster is a joke!" He was so pissed, he consigned seniority and rank to Hades.

Cian blinked. "I heard you wanted to be on the perimeter, away from Tammy."

"I don't recall asking for that particular *favor*."

The other man winced at his tone. "You do make a point of avoiding her whenever she comes after you." He frowned. "Though she seems to have stopped doing that lately."

That observation made Nate's incisors threaten to erupt. The leopard was not happy with Tamsyn right now. Neither was the man. They both wanted to bite. To dominate. To mark. "Switch me with Juanita."

"You sure?" Cian scowled. "You're not exactly in a good mood. Do you want to be around Tammy?"

It was an insult—as if he'd ever hurt her. "If I had wanted advice, I'd have asked for it. Switch."

"Fine." Cian threw up his hands. "I'll tell Nita."

"And mind your own damn business from now on." Turning off the comm, he finished his coffee and headed out. He was hungry, but he figured Tammy would have something—she was the best cook in DarkRiver.

His new watch area was in the immediate vicinity of the Pack Circle and included Tammy's home among a few others. On his first pass, it appeared she was still asleep, but he caught the sharp freshness of tea leaves on the second pass. Since he'd remained in human form, it was easy to walk up to her back door and knock.

He knew she had to have scented him, but she peered out suspiciously from the kitchen window before opening the door with a scowl. "What are you doing here?"

Okay, so she was still mad. His cock throbbed at the memory of the events that had led to their fight. He wanted to put his hands on the sweet curves of her bottom, crush her to him, and kiss the hell out of her bad mood.

"Good morning to you, too, sunshine," he managed to say through the chokehold of desire. It was torture being near her, but that was infinitely better than the distance she'd maintained over the past few days.

"You're just hungry." She snorted and turned away, leaving the door open.

He walked in to find her at the counter, cutting slices of bread from what looked like a home-baked loaf. He forced himself to stand to the side instead of going behind her and bending down to draw in the lusciously feminine scent along the line of her throat. "Only bread today?"

She lifted the knife and pointed it in his direction. "Do you want to get fed or not?"

"I love bread." He knew how to stroke his mate when she needed stroking. His mind immediately took the image and ran with it, ratcheting his hunger past explosive. "Why are you half-dressed?" She was wearing his old football shirt and those ridiculous pink fluffy slippers. Sexy and adorable. A killer combination.

"I was minding my own business in my own house. You're the one who decided to intrude." She slapped some butter onto a slice of bread and shoved it in his direction.

He decided not to ask for jam. "Bad night?"

"Nate," she said very quietly, gripping the edge of the counter with her hands. "Did you come here to gloat?"

He put down the half-eaten piece of bread. "What the hell are you talking about?"

"You know exactly what I'm talking about!" She turned and poked at his chest with a sharp finger. "Look, I can make stupid, virginal Tammy Mahaire so hot she doesn't know which way is up. I can leave her gasping for me and walk away as if it doesn't matter!"

"Hey." He grabbed at her hand, but she pulled away. "I didn't mean anything like that. I didn't have a good night's sleep, either."

"Oh, that makes it all right!" She threw up her arms. "We were both miserable. Whoop-de-frickin'-do!"

There was no missing the sarcasm. It dripped from every word. "What the hell is it with you lately?" He succeeded in trapping her against the counter.

"Nothing!" She shoved at him but he was far stronger. "Go away. Go away and leave me alone. Don't you get that? How many times do I have to tell you?"

"You don't get to do that—I'm your mate."

She stopped fighting, her chest heaving. "No, Nate, like I told you before, you don't get to pick and choose which parts of the mating bond you want to accept. As far as your treatment of me goes, I'm not your mate. I'm simply another young, uninteresting female."

"Don't be an idiot."

"I'm not. I'm sexually frustrated." She narrowed her eyes. "But as we discussed last night, that can be easily fixed."

He snapped. How could she possibly think to replace him with some mechanical object? Masculine pride, pure need, and raw heat made for a volatile combination. "Sex? That's really what this is about?" He pushed harder into her, crushing the softness of her thighs under his.

Instead of backing off, she pushed *into* him. "Yes! Yes! Yes! Clear enough for you?"

"Fine." Grabbing her waist, he lifted her onto the counter, spreading her knees wide in the same move. Something fell to the floor and shattered, but he didn't give a shit. "You want to fuck, we'll fuck."

A hint of uncertainty moved over her face. "Nate—"

He closed his hand over the bare skin of her upper thigh. "You're backing off? Don't want me now that you're faced with the reality?"

Her lower lip quivered. "Not like this," she whispered. "Why are you being so mean?"

The protective male core of him couldn't bear to see her looking so emotionally bruised, but they had to have this out. He couldn't handle being pushed the way she'd been pushing him since her return from New York. "I'm trying to give you something—I'm trying to love you the only way I know how, and you're rejecting it because you're hot for sex?" That hurt him. Her freedom was the biggest gift he could give her. Some days, the cost it demanded threatened to drive him to murder.

"No, Nathan, no." She cupped her face in his hands. "I just need you—all of you—so much that I'm going crazy. I need your laugh. I need your company. I need you to sleep beside me and I need you to wake when I wake. I need you with everything in me."

"Then stop with the sex talk. It's not you."

Her hands dropped to his shoulders. "It's not me?" A soft question.

"No. You're warm and practical and loyal. You don't go around flaunting yourself like a—" He caught himself before he said something unforgivable.

"Why don't I finish it for you—like a bitch in heat—that's what you were going to say, wasn't it?"

• *Eight* •

"Damn it, Tammy, don't look like that." He was the one who cupped her face this time—her spine was straight, but she couldn't hide the hurt in her eyes. "All this, the way you've been talking and dressing, it's not anything normal for you and you know it."

She looked at him through her lashes. "Yeah. Don't know what I was thinking."

His beast didn't like the flatness in her tone. Reacting instinctively, he bent until their foreheads touched. "Come on, where's my sweet Tammy?" He missed the woman who had become his closest friend over the years, the one with whom he could totally lower his guard. It was something he hadn't been able to do since the day she'd started pushing at him. "Tamsyn?"

"I'm fine and I'm also late." She gave him a shaky smile, then pressed her hands gently against his chest. "Some of the kids will be here soon to finish up their ornaments. I'd better get dressed. I'll talk to you later, okay?"

"You sure you're all right, baby?" His leopard was pacing inside his skull, growling that something was wrong.

"Just a headache. Lack of sleep, you know." She shrugged, making the former point of contention a joke. When her lips curved upward in a deeper smile, the leopard relaxed.

"Yeah, I do." Laughing, he helped her down from the counter, then lifted her over the mess of the broken jam jar on the floor. "Go get changed. I'll clean this up and head out to continue my watch."

"Here." She reached out, picked up a muffin from a tin, and gave it to him. "I made them for the kids."

He bit into it. "Good thing I got here first."

TAMSYN LEFT THE ROOM TO THE SOUND OF NATE'S chuckle. The knives of pain inside her stabbed with brutal force, but she kept her composure until she heard him leave the house. Then she sat down on her bed and cried. The tears weren't of frustration or simple hurt. They were the shattered cries of a broken heart.

Juanita had been wrong. The mating heat might have forced Nate into wanting her, but he didn't actually see her as a sexual, desirable woman. He saw her as comfortable . . . practical. Warm, loyal Tamsyn. If the bond hadn't thrown them together, he'd probably never have looked at her twice, not as a man looks at a woman.

She might have lain there for hours, but she couldn't bear to disappoint the kids. So she got up and dressed. What she saw in the mirror simply reinforced her earlier conclusions. Dressed in a pair of old jeans and a thick white sweater, with her hair pulled back into a ponytail, she looked young and . . . ordinary.

She was no temptress. She was safe and sensible, the one that juveniles came to for help without judgment, and mature women for ideas about how to handle rambunctious infants. Even senior packmates didn't blink at asking her advice on Pack issues. Because she was trusted, both for her steady temperament and for her loyal heart. None of which was bad. Only she didn't want Nathan to see her as that—she wanted him to see her as she saw him. As a lover, a playmate in the most intimate of arenas.

But he didn't. And that blow cut so deep, she could barely think.

Something registered in her consciousness. A second later, she picked up the high-pitched sounds of children's voices. The healer in her took over—there was no time for self-pity. Wiping her eyes with the backs of her hands, she went to the bathroom and splashed cold water over her face. Then she used her healing abilities to get rid of the redness around her eyes.

The doorbell rang.

Pasting on a smile, she walked down and opened the door. The kids' bright and excited faces turned her faux smile real, but nothing could heal the open wound that was the jagged beat of her animal heart.

NATE SAW TAMSYN AGAIN THAT DAY, BUT IT WAS HOURS later and with several others as they sat around her kitchen table eating dinner. She'd chosen not to sit next to him, but he could understand why. The awareness between them had only gotten stronger since this morning, until he could scent nothing but the sensual promise of her. She was everything he had ever wanted—that smile, that acerbic wit she seemed to show him alone, and lord help him, that body—and she was his. No other man had the right to her.

His beast wanted to roar its claim, but he fought the impulse. He'd wait. He'd wait . . . but maybe not as long as he'd initially planned. He'd give her another six months of freedom at least, let her live some of her dreams. She could go roaming if she liked, explore a bit of the wild. It might be dangerous, but Tamsyn was smarter and more mature than most of the other young leopards. She'd be fine.

The cat in him didn't like the idea, knew how badly it would hurt to be parted from her, but it had to be done. He never wanted her to turn to him—as his mother had turned to his father—and accuse him of stealing her life. That would destroy him. Because she *was* his life. The thought of crushing her spirit was his personal nightmare.

"Are you going to eat or do you plan on staring at Tammy the whole night?" Juanita passed him the potatoes.

"I can stare if I like." It was his right.

Rolling her eyes, she called out to Tammy. "Hey, where's that dress you were going to wear tonight?"

Tammy colored. "I changed my mind."

"You look fine to me." Dressed in black slacks and a pale blue cardigan, she appeared soft and touchable. Strokable. Shit. His mind was going off track again. Before long, he'd start thinking about unbuttoning that cardigan and kissing his way—

"Great," Juanita hissed, breaking into the taut eroticism of his newest daydream. "Tell your mate she looks fine."

"What the hell's wrong with that?" He took the peas she almost shoved into his chest. "She looks—" He cut himself off before he said what he wanted to say, which was "pretty enough to bite into."

Juanita shot him a disgusted glance before turning her attention to the packmate on her other side. Ignoring her, Nate went back to the pleasurable task of watching Tamsyn. The beast bucked to taste her. *Six months*, he told it. *Six more months and then you can have her. In every way. And over again.*

BUT A BARE WEEK LATER, HIS HUNGER FOR HER HAD GOTTEN so bad that he had Cian reassign him to the perimeter. Tammy was no longer trying to flaunt herself at him—if anything, she seemed to be going to great lengths to give him space. Paradoxically, that only amplified the building pressure to mate, to touch and taste and claim. Without the control provided by the vivid scars of memory, he'd have given in a hundred times already.

Still, he couldn't keep from going to her each morning, just to see her smile. "Hey, sweetheart, any muffins today?"

She gave him one, but there was no smile on her lips. "How's the Solias King situation? Any decisions?"

"We're planning to make a move in a few days." He'd already told her what they intended to do—she was his mate, and more than that, she was damn sharp, an integral part of the steel backbone of the pack. "You want to come along? Be a nice run." He wanted to feel her beside him, strong and hotly female.

She shook her head. "This isn't working, Nate."

The quick change in subject rattled him. He put down the food, belatedly aware of the bags under her eyes, the lack of light in her face. "We'll get past it."

"Not living so close." She shook her head. "One of us has to leave."

He'd thought about setting her free to roam, but now that it had come down to it, he found he couldn't let her go. "Don't make any impulsive decisions. It'll die down."

"No, it won't. Don't lie to me," she snapped, folding her arms. "We're experiencing the final stages of the mating dance and it's going to keep getting worse, especially if our beasts continuously sense each other's presence. I was thinking I should go to—"

"Just wait." He fisted his hands to keep from touching her. "I'll talk to some of the other mated pairs. Maybe there's something we can do to lessen the impact."

"I thought you wanted me to go out into the world?" Her voice was soft, her skin flushed with need. "Isn't that why you keep pushing me away?"

"Stay." That single word held his heart.

• *Nine* •

Stay, he'd said, but Tamsyn knew he didn't mean it the way she needed him to mean it. The mating instinct urged him to protect her and so he wanted her in sight. It didn't make him happy just to see her. Not like it made her heart bloom simply being in the same room as him.

If the mating urge died tomorrow, there would still be no other man for her. He was her one and only. But she wasn't his. Her throat feeling as if she'd gotten a rock stuck in it, she left the parking garage in the city and crossed the street.

She'd promised the kids she'd get more lights for the tree, but now that she was here, she decided to pop into the bookstore, too. Nate liked reading. She knew exactly what to get him for Christmas. That thought made her want to cry again. Her nose grew stuffy with withheld tears as she strolled through the small and expensive hard-copy section. Most people bought the downloads, but she wanted to give Nate something he could hold, something that made him think of her.

Her choice was sold out, so she went to one of the consoles and ordered in another copy. That done, she picked up her other purchases and began to make her way to the exit.

That was when she saw her.

The Psy woman—a stranger with eyes of darkest brown and skin the same rich shade—was occupying a booth near the door. Dressed in a black pantsuit teamed with a white shirt, she appeared a serious business professional. But then again, all Psy seemed to wear variations on the same theme. Tamsyn had never seen one of the psychic race in any color, excepting white, that didn't fall in the range from deep gray to brown/black.

On any other day, she would have kept walking. But today, she didn't, her motive a mystery even to herself. "Excuse me," she said, coming to a standstill near the woman.

The Psy looked up. "Did you want the terminal? I'll be finished in approximately one minute." She glanced over Tamsyn's shoulder. "There are several others that appear free."

"No, I don't want the terminal." Tamsyn looked at her, at her human-seeming eyes, her clear skin and shining fall of jet-black hair. There was nothing that marked this woman as different, as Psy, part of a race that had eliminated its emotions. "I wanted to ask you a question."

The stranger considered her request for a second. "Why are you asking me?"

"I need to ask a Psy and you're the only one here."

"I can't fault your logic." She tapped her finger on the screen to complete her purchase, then turned to give Tamsyn her full attention. "Your question?"

"Do you ever cry?" It seemed imperative that she know the answer.

The Psy didn't react to the oddness of the question—if she had, she wouldn't be Psy. "Even those of my race have little to no control over certain physiological reactions. If, for example, a foreign object were to accidentally enter or touch my eye, that eye would certainly produce fluid in an attempt to excrete the intruding matter."

Tamsyn frowned at the clinical description of such a wrenching, heartbreaking act. "No. I don't mean that. I mean, do you *cry*?"

The stranger looked at her for several long moments. "As you chose to approach a Psy, you must know the answer to that question. However, I'll respond as I see no possible negative repercussions from doing so." She picked up a slim electronic pad from the desk near the terminal. "No. We do not cry out of fear or sadness, anger, or rage. We do not feel, therefore, we do not shed tears."

"Don't you miss it?" Tamsyn asked.

The Psy ran her gaze over Tamsyn's face. "Judging from the redness of the blood vessels in your eyes and your stuffy nose, I believe I can say with certainty that crying is in no way a positive experience. Why would I miss it?"

"No. I meant . . . don't you miss feeling?" Love and hope, joy and need.

"I can't miss what I've never experienced," the other woman said, as if that should have been self-evident. "My race chose to eradicate emotion for a reason. Those with emotions are weak. We're not. It's why the Psy rule this planet." With that, she gave a curt nod and left.

Tamsyn stared after her, the words circling around and around in her head. *Those with emotions are weak.* She saw the reflection of her drawn, listless face in the terminal and found herself agreeing. For a frozen heartbeat, she wished she were like that Psy woman. Cool, controlled, focused. No attachments, no hopes, no dreams.

And no Nathan.

Her eyes, which had started to close, snapped open. "No," she whispered fiercely. She would not, could not, live in a world where Nathan didn't exist. He might make her cry as much as he made her laugh, but she couldn't imagine waking up one day and having emptiness where he was.

She didn't know much about how and why the Psy race had stopped feeling, but it had to have been a terrible thing that had driven them down this path. Her healer's soul ached for them—for the love they would never touch, but she knew she couldn't help them. Not when they barricaded themselves in their high-rises, their minds shut to the possibility of hope.

It's why the Psy rule this planet.

Tamsyn shook her head. The stranger was wrong. The Psy might rule, but their world was limited to towers of steel and glass. They knew nothing of the joy of running under a full moon and listening to the music played by the wind, of feeling the sensation of a packmate's fur against human skin, of the sheer life that existed in the forests that were *her* world.

But the woman had been right about one thing—how could you miss something you had never experienced? Nathan had never been hers. Their beasts might cry out for each other, but if the human half of Nathan chose to repudiate that bond, who was she to stop him?

SHE LEFT THE NEXT DAY. THERE WAS NO OTHER WAY. IF SHE remained within reach, Nathan's beast would eventually push him over the edge. And she couldn't bear to lie with him knowing their intimacy was nothing more than the result of a physical compulsion. It would be a glimpse into her own personal vision of hell.

Her friend, Finn, was more than happy to fly in on short notice.

"The healer in our pack's not even forty, so I'm not going to get to do anything serious for a while," he told her when she met him at the airport and escorted him into their territory. Dark-River wasn't known for its friendliness toward unknown males.

They couldn't afford to be, not after the attack by the ShadowWalkers.

"I know," she said. "That's why I asked you rather than Maria."

He gave her a smile but his eyes were watchful. "I appreciate it."

She ignored the unasked question. "I'm going to introduce you to the alpha. He knows you're coming, of course, but the hierarchy has to be maintained." The laws of rank and hierarchy were there for a reason—they balanced the predatory nature of their animal halves with order.

Finn nodded. "I'll feel better once he adopts me into DarkRiver. It wouldn't do for one of your pack to slice me up because they figured me for an intruder."

Since she thought the same, she made sure to take him to Lachlan first thing. Even with that delay, she was ready to be on her way out of DarkRiver territory by late afternoon. "Take care of my people, Finn."

The twenty-one-year-old healer didn't bother to conceal his worry this time. "What about you, Tam? Who's looking after you?"

"I'll be fine." She tightened her hands around the straps of her bag. "It might be permanent, you know that, right?"

"Yes." He stroked his hand over her hair, offering comfort in the changeling way. "But it shouldn't be. You were born to be DarkRiver's healer."

"I can work with another leopard pack." But Nathan couldn't be replaced. Not when it was clear that Lachlan was preparing Lucas to step into his role as alpha sooner rather than later. When the time came, Lucas would need to rely on Nate's experience and rock-solid advice. "Try it here," she made herself say. "If everything works out . . ."

"No rush." Finn's tone was gentle. "I'll hold your place until you come to your senses. Then I'll happily return to the civilized world of our territory instead of this jungle."

She smiled at his joking, but as she walked away, she had the sick feeling she might never return. When she neared the fir she'd strung with Christmas decorations and lights, her eyes stung. "I'm sorry, Shayla," she whispered to the ghost that reproached her for leaving her pack when it still needed her.

They would be okay, she told herself. She'd started them on the road to healing. All they had to do was follow it. Tempting as it was to pass by quickly, she made herself look up. There was the ornament Vaughn had painted, right next to the one by Cian. Around them wove the string of lights Nate had hung after he'd growled at her for putting her fool neck in danger. And there was the star she'd almost thrown at him, she'd been so mad.

"Oh God." Blinking, she looked away . . . and kept walking.

• Ten •

NATE RETURNED HOME CLOSE TO DAWN, COMING FROM A night raid to "suggest" Solias King look elsewhere for his development. The damn, encroaching Psy would follow their advice, of that Nate was certain. Even in leopard form, he wanted to grin.

He'd stood watch for hours as Cian and a couple of others with tech training had methodically taken apart every piece of Psy equipment already onsite. While that might have been enough, Nate had gone a step further and buried several of the most expensive pieces in a section of DarkRiver land that bordered SnowDancer territory. No Psy would dare venture that close to wolf land. The feral pack had a reputation for ripping out intruders' throats and using the bleached-out bones as fence posts.

Just in case Solias King missed their point even after all that, they had also removed the semipermanent survey markers and disabled the rudimentary comm tower erected a few days ago. It was why DarkRiver had allowed the thing to go up in the first place—so they could destroy it, and in a fashion that made it clear they would brook no further trespass on their lands.

Nate was particularly proud of the crowning touch. Inspired by Tammy, he'd taken along a large Christmas ornament—an old-fashioned picture of the man in red and white—and hung it from the now useless comm tower. Then he'd wrapped a string of blinking multicolored lights around the metal skeleton.

He couldn't wait to tell Tammy—she'd bust a gut over it. Taking on the Psy wasn't usually a laughing matter, as the cold psychic race didn't hesitate to kill. But from everything they had been able to unearth, it appeared that Solias King's darker impulses were currently being curbed by his political aspirations. He couldn't afford to come down hard on the changelings. Any violence and his own Council would turn against him.

Nate had no illusions that the Psy Council cared about changelings, but they damn well did care about their bottom line. And that would suffer massive depreciation if people thought the Psy were declaring a racial war. The Council would never allow such a panic to start over a small piece of land in the territory of what they considered a minor pack. Nate had a feeling DarkRiver wasn't going to stay minor long, but until then, they could and would use the Council's sense of arrogance to their advantage.

Shifting the second he cleared the doorway to his home, he pulled on a pair of jeans and an old cable-knit sweater. He had to see Tamsyn, no matter the ridiculously early hour. The royal blue sweater had been a gift from her. Maybe it would thaw her mood—she'd been more than a little distant when he'd dropped by this morning.

But his hopeful frame of mind disappeared the instant he got near her house—the area was blanketed in the scent of an unfamiliar male.

Unbidden, scenes of the carnage that had taken their last healer from them filled his mind. "Tammy!" He pounded on the door. "Tammy!"

The door swung open to reveal a young male. "Hel—" His voice cut off as Nate gripped him around the neck and lifted him off the floor.

"What have you done to her?" He tried to ignore the fact that the male was dressed only in a pair of pajama bottoms, his hair mussed.

I'm sick of stroking myself to sleep.

No, she wouldn't do that to him. The agony he felt at the thought of Tammy, *his* Tammy, with anyone, much less this runt, was enough to call the beast to the surface. His eyes shifted to cat. He couldn't hear anything through the pounding roar of blood in his head, was dangerously close to killing.

The single reason he didn't do so was that his leopard suddenly started scrambling to find Tammy. He threw aside the other man and strode into the house, preparing himself for what he would find. If she was in bed— Something tore inside him.

He wouldn't hurt her. He could never hurt her.

But that boy was going to die a slow, cruel death.

He shoved open the bedroom door . . . and found the bed made, with no signs of recent occupation.

"I slept on the couch," a raspy voice said from the doorway.

He turned to find the stranger supporting himself against a wall, one hand rubbing at his throat. "Didn't seem right to sleep in Tam's bed."

Tam? The leopard growled, harsh and vocal. "Who are you and what are you doing in my mate's house?"

The other man's eyes widened. "Mate? She never—" He slapped up his hands, palms out, when Nate started advancing. "I'm a healer. Name's Finn."

That stopped Nate midstep. Healers, even enemy healers, had automatic protection. Only blood-hungry packs like the

ShadowWalkers broke that rule. "We already have a healer." Claws raked his gut, twisted through his body like hard fire.

"She asked me to fly in and take over for a while." Finn coughed a few times. "Said it might be permanent. Our pack's got a senior healer and another apprentice, so they were happy to let me go."

"I *said* we already have a healer." Nate glared.

Finn didn't back down. "Not anymore you don't. She left."

The beast wanted to lash out, to tear and scar. "Where did she go?"

The healer held up his hands a second time and Nate wondered what the other man had seen in his eyes. "I swear I don't know. I figured she'd talked it over with your alpha—maybe a sabbatical or some extra training. She introduced me to him."

Nate left on a mission to find Lachlan, but it was Lucas he ran into first. He would have pushed past except that Lucas stepped into his path and said, "Looking for Tammy?"

Nate stilled. "You knew she left?" At that moment, the first rays of the rising sun hit the tree line, throwing light across Lucas's savage facial markings.

"Didn't you?"

"Damn it, Luc. Answer the damn question."

"Sure." The juvenile folded his arms. "I heard her ask Nita to drive her out of the territory."

The urge to grab Lucas and shake Tammy's location out of him was so strong, Nate looked away and took a deep breath before saying, "And neither of you tried to stop her from leaving?"

"Why would we?" Lucas's tone was hard. "You made her cry, Nathan. You made your mate cry and then you didn't hold her."

The blow hit him with bruising force. "Where is she, Lucas?"

"I don't know—you could ask Nita, but I don't think she's around." He glanced at the sun-touched trees. "I have to get to the Circle for training."

Nate didn't try to stop him from leaving, and was still standing there when Cian appeared out of the shadows. "Nate? You after Lachlan? I just left him—he's free for the next half hour or so."

"I'm trying to find Tammy."

Cian's face showed instant comprehension and not a little anger. "What the hell are you doing to that girl, Nate?"

"What's right for her." Cian didn't understand what it was to watch a woman fall out of love with her man, turn bitter and self-destructive . . . and finally, suicidal. He'd held his mother's dead body. He refused to hold Tamsyn's. "She's too young."

"She was too young when Shayla died. But did you hear her complain?" The sentinel's voice was a whip. "Seventeen years old and she took on a position most people don't touch until they've reached their third decade."

"Exactly!" He blew out a frustrated breath. "All that responsibility and then a mate, too? I'd demand things she has no conception of—"

Cian swore, low and pithy. "Isn't that your job as her mate? To demand but to let her demand as much in turn? You're supposed to fucking share the burden, not add to it like you've been doing with your self-pitying bullshit."

"You might be my senior," Nate said, the leopard in his voice, "but you are not my father." His father was long dead, having literally driven himself to an early grave after his wife's death—he'd wrapped his car around a tree. "You want to take me on, go ahead."

"Screw that." Cian shrugged. "If I damaged you, Tammy would have my head."

With that simple comment, the other man defused every bit of Nate's anger. "Tell me where she is. I have to make sure she's safe." The leopard's desperation grew by the minute.

"I don't know." Cian shoved up his sleeves. "To be honest, I don't think you deserve to know, either. And don't bother asking

Nita—she has no idea where Tammy went after getting out of the car."

"What, none of you bothered to ask her?" He couldn't believe that, not with how protective they had become after what had happened to Shayla. As this inquisition clearly proved. "You let her go off on her own without a word of protest?"

Cian's eyes turned opaque. "She's an adult leopard. No one has the right to question her decisions."

And she'd made one to leave him. Nate leaned against a tree and stared up at the dawn sky. It promised to turn a pure, mocking blue. "Where did Nita drop her?" She wouldn't be hard to track—she was carrying his heart with her.

Cian snorted. "Sorry, you're on your own. You made the mess, you can damn well clean it up. But since you look like you've been gut-punched, I will tell you something she said to Lachlan when she made the request to leave and bring Finn in as cover."

Nate straightened. "What?"

"She said you were more important to the pack. Since one of you had to go, she decided it had better be her." The older male shook his head. "My Keelie is the most precious part of my life. How could you let your mate think she was less than you, Nate?"

Nate still hadn't found an answer to that question seven hours later when he finally located the first hint of a trail. He was certain that this was where she'd left Nita's car. He looked up and found himself close to Tahoe. Tamsyn had vanished somewhere in the lake city's streets. Nathan had every intention of hunting her down.

UNFORTUNATELY, WHEN HE RETURNED TO THE DEN TO PICK up his gear, he found another surprise waiting for him, this time in his living room.

"Where's my daughter, Nathan?" was Sadie's first question.

He began to grab what he needed. "I'll find her."

"I don't know if I want you to find her." Tamsyn's mother scowled. "You didn't do a great job of keeping her this time around."

"I'll bring her home."

"Why? So you can make her miserable?" She moved to block the doorway, fierce in her maternal protectiveness. "Let her roam. That's what you've been telling her to do. Well, looks like she listened. Don't you dare go after her."

The blunt words brought him to a halt. "I can't do that."

"Why not? It's *exactly* what you wanted."

"She's mine to protect."

"You gave up that right when you decided you didn't want to be her mate." Sadie shook her head. "You've done enough. Let my baby go."

He stared at her, a sick feeling in his gut. "I never said I didn't want to be her mate. Where the hell did you get that idea?" And did Tammy think the same?

• *Eleven* •

"FROM YOU, NATHAN." SADIE GAVE HIM AN ARCH LOOK AS she shook the foundations of his world. "Tammy was practically screaming for your love and you wouldn't so much as hold her. She got the message—she can't break the bond, but she might be able to mute it with distance."

"What damn message?" Impatience, anger, and a painful hunger for the scent of his mate combined to roughen his tone. "The only thing I wanted to give her was a taste of freedom before—"

"I've heard it all before." She lifted a hand. "If you really mean it, then you'll put down that pack and go sit down. After all, she's free now, isn't she?"

"That's not what I meant," he said between gritted teeth. "I wanted her—"

"You wanted her on your leash—close enough to watch over so you could satisfy your beast." Sadie's eyes went pure leopard. "It didn't matter to you that her need was turning into a kind of slow torture. You are not doing that to my baby again! You let her go. Let her find someone who'll love her for what she is."

Violent rage turned to lethal calm. "What the hell are you talking about? She's my *mate*. That is not negotiable."

"Not if you won't let it be. If you set her free, maybe she'll fall for someone who'll adore her like she's meant to be adored."

"*I* adore her!" he yelled in disbelief. "No one else has that right!"

"Do you?" Sadie's features settled into a resolute expression. "Then show her, for goodness' sake. Otherwise, free her in reality instead of just giving lip service to the idea." She vacated the doorway.

Nate walked out without replying, but her words wouldn't leave his mind, no matter how far he went. Tammy thought he didn't want to be her mate? How could such an idiotic idea have ever entered her head? The second he saw her, he was going to growl the truth to her until she damn well listened.

Well . . . maybe he'd hold her first. He'd made her cry and he hadn't held her. Lucas was right. That was unforgivable. But Tammy was his mate. She had to forgive him. And she had to come home. He couldn't exist without her close to him. Those months she had spent in New York had almost killed him, but at least then he'd been able to tell himself that she was still a girl, not a woman.

But now that he'd felt the lush heat of her, he could no longer kid himself. Tammy had grown up. And she'd left him. "We'll see about that." The leopard snarled, mad as hell.

Not much later, he reached the point where he'd first picked up her trail—close to Tahoe. From there, he could try to track her by scent or . . . or he could do the one thing certain to lead him to her. No choice at all, really.

Taking a deep breath, he released the stranglehold of control he'd held over the mating bond since the day she'd turned fifteen and he'd realized what she was to him. It felt like the whiplash unfurling of a coiled spring—a burst of pure power that actually hurt as it boomeranged off his chest, driving him to his knees.

When his head finally stopped spinning, he felt for the bond and found it stretched out taut and clear, a vibrating cord of need, desire, and belonging. He could feel Tammy deep within his core, as if he had a homing beacon tuned only to her signal. It was perfection. And he wasn't sure he could ever block it again. But he'd think about that later.

Right now, he had to survive the intensity of the emotions shooting down the bond. It felt like he could reach out and touch her. She was sweetness and hope, woman and fire, erotic heat and gentle affection. And she was his. Not fucking negotiable.

IT FELT LIKE GETTING BROADSIDED WITH A BASEBALL BAT.

Tamsyn staggered under the point-blank surge of pure emotion, sliding down the wall to sit with her back braced against it.

Nate had opened the bond.

She rubbed a hand over her chest, then realized the usual persistent ache, the hard knot of dull hurt was simply . . . gone. In its place was the blazing glory of a fully functioning mating bond. She trembled. Why had he taken that step now—after she'd done what he wanted and put distance between them? Surely he wasn't trying to track her?

No, she thought, she wasn't going to believe in fairy tales anymore. Nate had probably done it by accident. Okay, no. That was stupid. No one who'd been as determined as Nate to block their mating would lose that much control by accident. Her eye fell on the small silver phone sitting on the table by the sofa.

Her mother had called soon after Tamsyn arrived at the cabin. Sadie had been distraught to return from her run in the wild and find her daughter gone. Tamsyn had assured her over and over that she was fine, but knowing Sadie, she'd probably ordered Nate to locate her daughter and provide a firsthand report. Tamsyn shuddered, trying to breathe past the impact of the fully flowing bond. She had to think, had to stabilize herself before Nathan arrived, so he'd go back and tell Sadie there was no reason to worry.

That done, he would *think* the bond shut again.

Her blood flushed hot as the vibrant male energy of him raced through her veins. Mates were joined on an incredibly deep level. To other changelings, the scent of one half of a mated pair became difficult to distinguish from the other the longer they were together. Nate's refusal to accept the bond had denied them that closeness, starving her. Now, her senses wanted to gorge.

"No," she said out loud, forcing calm on herself. All healers had to learn such discipline. It allowed them to work in the chaos of a fight or when attempting to heal those they loved—a pack healer didn't have the luxury of passing on the hard cases to another medic. Every one of their cases was hard, because Pack was family.

Finally, after ten long minutes, she could think despite the masculine strength of the emotional connection surging through her. Then, for the first time, she tried to close her end of the exquisite pleasure/pain that was her link to this man she adored beyond life . . . and discovered she couldn't. She fisted her hands. Forget the known wisdom that said the bond couldn't be blocked—if Nate could do it, why couldn't she?

It took her an hour to come up with some sort of answer. She remembered what her mother had said—that Nate had had to learn to suppress his needs in order to allow her the time she needed to come of age. That control seemed to have carried over into everything he did in relation to her. But now he'd thrown off the reins and let the cat out to play.

It might be impossible to put the lid back on that bottle.

Her eyes widened. Nate was not going to be pleased if that proved true. More importantly, she wasn't pleased. She didn't want him to want her because he'd been forced into it by the primal cravings of his beast—cravings her own beast understood far too well. She wanted him to love her.

It was a terribly impractical dream for a practical, sensible healer.

EVEN WITH THE BOND, IT TOOK NATE THREE DAYS TO TRACK Tamsyn to an isolated cottage so far south of the lake, there was nothing else within shouting distance. "What the hell are you doing out in the middle of nowhere?" he said, the second she opened the door.

Her eyes narrowed. "Trying to get away from you." Turning her back, she walked into the house, her hips encased in those damn painted-on jeans.

He was tired, sweaty, and hungry. Not for food. For her. Every soft, curvy, bitable piece of her. His cat wanted to test the resilience of her butt, while his— He slammed the door shut behind himself. "Jesus, Tammy. DarkRiver's operating at red alert while we prepare to take on the ShadowWalkers and you choose this shack to hide in?"

"It's not a shack and I'm not hiding," she said, sitting back down to what appeared to be her breakfast. "It's Cian's place. He likes the water."

Cian had lied to him. Not exactly a surprise. "It's miles from the lake!"

"It's not that far. He likes privacy, too."

Nate dropped his stuff by the door and shoved a hand through his hair. "What, this was some silly little jaunt and no one bothered to tell me?" He saw red.

Then she raised an eyebrow and that red morphed into something darker, more intense, a blatantly sexual surge of dominance. "I'm leaving DarkRiver. Finn's agreed to stay on permanently. His agreement was what I was waiting for."

He didn't believe her. "You're leaving the pack."

"Yes." She put down her uneaten toast and stood. "There, you've seen me. I'm fine." Her smile was sharp enough to cut, her eyes sparking with anger that intrigued the leopard even more than the spicy/wild/hot woman scent of her. "You can leave the same way you came in." She began to clear the table.

"Put those dishes *down*."

She ignored him.

Covering the distance between them, he closed his hand over her wrist. She released the dishes softly to the table but didn't turn to face him. "What do you want, Nate?"

"I want you to talk to me." He found himself pressing against her. It took only a single move to enclose her in the circle of his arms and bury his face against her neck. He was ravenous for the scent of her, the feel of her. "Come on, baby."

Her body trembled so violently he felt her skin move against his caressing lips. "I can't do this anymore." Her voice was a whisper. "Please let me go."

• *Twelve* •

A GROWL ROLLED UP FROM HIS THROAT. "FOR HOW LONG?"

"Why are you asking me that?"

He didn't like the tremor in her voice. "Don't you dare cry, Tammy. That's not fair."

"I won't." But there was a wet kind of pain her words. "I know you don't really want me. I know it's the cat pushing for mating. That's okay. If I go far enough away, maybe you—"

"*What?*" He couldn't believe his ears. "You really believe that load of shit?"

"You made it very clear."

Everything went quiet inside him. Lifting his head, he turned her in his arms. Her head stayed down—she wouldn't look at him. Keeping one arm around her, not sure she wasn't getting ready to bolt, he used the fingers of his other hand to tip up her chin. Her eyes were shiny-wet, but she met his gaze without flinching.

God, she was so proud. Proud and strong and stubborn. And

she'd decided he didn't want her. He intended to teach her the error of her ways once and for all. Holding her gaze, he slid his hand down her neck, over her shoulder, and along her arm until he cupped the back of her hand with his. Then he lifted that feminine hand and placed it on his erection. She jerked in shock. The reflexive tightening of her fingers almost made him cry out.

"Does this feel like I don't want you?" he grit out.

"It's—" She paused, her breath hitching. "It's a result of the mating dance. You don't want me, not really." She pulled away her hand, curling it up to her chest as if it hurt.

Oh Jesus. She was not doing this to him. "Or is it that you don't want *me*?" he asked softly. "Is that it, Tamsyn? Am I too old for you?"

Her head snapped up. "Don't you put this on me!" The first hint of fire entered her tone. "I begged you, *begged* you, to make the bond real, to be my mate in truth. But you said no. You always say no! Well, you know what, I'm through with begging. I'm through with not being good enough for you!"

It felt like she'd stabbed him. "You are the best thing that's ever happened to me," he said, the leopard alive in his voice. "I've spent every day of the past four years thinking of myself as the luckiest man on the Earth—frustrated as hell, but damn lucky."

She shook her head. "Don't. Don't lie."

It was all he could do not to crush his lips to hers and kiss her into accepting his words. "I watch you work and feel such pride, sometimes I think my heart will explode. I look at your body and have to fight the urge to bare my teeth and warn off anyone else from doing the same. You want to know why I lost it when you wore those tight, sexy clothes?

"It was because others could see what was *mine*." It was a possessive, animal reaction, one he usually tempered with human civility. But Tamsyn needed to see the real man, claws and all. "I don't like to share."

Finally a reaction. "You didn't think I looked stupid?"

"I wanted to peel you out of those damn come-to-bed jeans"—something he was definitely going to do today—"and mount you right there in the Pack Circle."

"Nate!"

"I wanted to show everyone that you were mine. I wanted to put my hands on your breasts and my lips on yours and my co—"

She squeaked, slapping a hand over his mouth. "Nate!" The scandalized expression on her face was very Tamsyn. His mate had come back to him.

He pulled away the restraint, using his other hand to manacle her free hand, too. "Where was I? I have wanted you so damn long, my balls are permanently blue. As—"

"I believe you!" A hint of desperation.

"I don't want any mistakes about this." And her time was up. The things he wanted to do to her were probably illegal in some countries. Too bad.

He backed her into a wall with slow deliberation, not stopping until her breasts were crushed warm and tempting against him, her stomach muscles clenching at the granite-hard thrust of his erection. "The sex—hell, yes, I want the sex. I want it so much I could devour you right this second, take little bites out of all those soft, delicate places."

Her breasts rose and fell in a jagged rhythm as she watched him through her lashes.

"But baby, I fell in love with you long before the mating heat kicked in this bad. Do you know why I came to wish you happy birthday when you were fifteen?"

She shook her head, mute.

"Because I adored everything about you as much then as I do now," he whispered, giving her words because she needed them, and because he'd made her cry. There was no excuse for that. "It wasn't sexual—you were too young. It was just this tightness inside my chest. Every time you smiled, my world lit up. All I wanted to do was keep giving you reasons to smile. The day I realized you were my mate, the happiness almost killed me. So don't you *ever* say I don't love or want you. I chose you, Tamsyn Mahaire. I chose you."

Tamsyn wanted to burst out crying. "Oh, Nate." She buried her face against his chest and, when he let go of her hands, wrapped her arms around him as he wrapped his around hers. She had never heard him speak in that impassioned, romantic way, never imagined he would. And to her? To his practical, sensible mate?

"You are not leaving me," he ordered, his voice predator deep. "If you want to go roaming, I'll take you. But you are not leaving me."

She wondered if he expected them to go back to the way things were. If so, he was about to get a surprise. Half of the mess that was their relationship had been her fault. She'd let him think he was the boss. Well, he wasn't. They were a partnership. Breaking the embrace, she pushed off his jacket. He was so surprised, he let her. Then she began undoing his rough wool-blend shirt.

"Tammy." He grabbed at her wrist.

"Forget it, Nathan," she snapped, tearing the shirt down the middle. Buttons went flying every which way. "I'm ready to lose my virginity and you're going to help me do it. I don't care if I have to kidnap you and tie you to the bed."

He opened his mouth as if to speak, but then she flattened her palms on his wonderful, hard chest and he shuddered instead. The same head-spinning rush hit her, powered by the skin to skin contact. *Skin privileges*. She had the most intimate kind.

"What about your freedom?" he whispered in her ear over a minute later, bracing his hands palms down on the wall beside her head. He made no move to stop her as she stroked and petted every inch of that sinfully gorgeous chest, all hard muscle and gleaming skin overlaid with silky-rough strands of dark hair.

"Idiot." She nipped at his jaw with her teeth. "The only freedom I ever wanted was the right to love you."

One of his hands stroked down to slip under her sweater. It was her turn to tremble.

"You're a stubborn woman."

"Yes." The roughness of his skin felt delicious on her.

"You're set on making this real."

"Try and stop me."

He smiled and it was beautiful and strong and quintessentially male. "What, and give up the chance to finally see your pretty breasts? Not a chance."

"Nathan!" And then his hand was squeezing her sensitive flesh and she was drowning in the rush of sensation.

"Why aren't you wearing a bra?" he asked before kissing the wits half out of her.

By the time she could gasp in enough air to breathe, her sweater was in shreds on the floor. Nate had used his claws to slice it to bits. His hand returned to massage and mold flesh that had never known a man's touch. She pushed into the caress. "Um . . . I forgot," she whispered. "I was nervous about you—Oh!"

He'd lifted her up so her legs wrapped around his waist. "You were right to be nervous." He kissed her again, then ran his lips down her neck to nibble on the tender upper slopes of her breasts.

She held on to his shoulders, trying hard to find a sensible thought. "Nervous?"

"I hope you've been exercising." His mouth closed over her nipple.

It might've been hours before she spoke again. "Exercising?" Single words seemed to be all her brain could manage.

He released her sensitive flesh . . . after gripping it lightly between his teeth for a heart-pounding instant. "Because you're going to be indulging in a lot of creative physical activity over the next few days."

Had he said *days*?

Then she lost even that thought and simply felt. Nate didn't ravage her as she'd half expected, given their combined hunger. He was excruciatingly tender and she knew how much that control had to be costing him.

"It's okay," she said several times.

"It's your first time. I'll say when it's okay."

She might have taken that order badly if he hadn't already brought her to orgasm twice by then. His tone may have been rough, but his hands were gentle and his mouth was pure magic. When he did finally decide she'd been pleasured enough, he took her with care that brought tears to her eyes.

The second time, she took him.

• Thirteen •

Solias King did not like to lose. "How much damage?" he asked.

Kinshasa repeated the number. "The missing parts will take weeks to reacquire."

"I thought you said they were a minor pack?" He pinned his aide to the spot with his eyes. "Your risk analysis was faulty."

"My variables were based on the known parameters of changeling intellect."

Solias couldn't fault Kinshasa. The general consensus among the Psy was that the animals weren't that smart. "Find me another site."

As Kinshasa left the suite, Solias wondered which one of his enemies had orchestrated the attack—covert Psy involvement had to be how the changelings had pulled this off. It was preposterous to think he'd been beaten by a pack of animals.

Arrogant in his belief of the Psy race's genetic and intellectual superiority, he never once considered that he might be blind to the truth. The truth that things were changing . . . that the Psy no longer ruled every corner of the planet. And that this minor pack had shown the first signs of the lethal danger it would one day become.

• *Fourteen* •

A WEEK LATER, NATE WATCHED TAMSYN BANDAGE UP A JUVENILE's arm and give the kid a stern warning about rock climbing without gear. She was firm and practical, her hands strong, her body tall. And she had breasts to make a man's mouth water, sweet feminine curves his palms itched to shape.

Then she looked up and smiled and he felt it deep, deep in his core. He wanted to pick her up and kiss her silly, but since the juvenile's eyes were already going wide, he decided to make himself scarce. "I'll see you tonight. I have to make that run into San Francisco."

Another smile. "Don't forget to pick up the things I asked for."

He nodded and left, recalling the list he'd shoved into his pocket. Tammy wanted a few healing supplies, a number of grocery items, and some paint to complete the Christmas decorations. He had the list in hand when he reached the city. It was easy to fill, as she'd included instructions about where to go and had called her suppliers ahead of time to let them know he was coming by.

"For Tammy?" a wizened old man asked as soon as Nate stepped into his tiny store in one of the older parts of Chinatown.

"Yes." His beast picked up a thousand intermingled traces—herbs and spices, medicines and incense, but the mix was strangely soothing. "I'm her mate, Nathan."

The man's smile was fond as he bent under the counter and lifted up a box. "She's a good soul, Tammy. You will protect her, love her. That is your destiny."

Nate looked at the shopkeeper, startled. "Do you see the future?"

"No." The man laughed. "I'm not Psy. Only human."

Only human, and yet there was such ageless wisdom in those dark button eyes. Nate wondered if the Psy, for all their gifts, would ever be able to achieve that look of utter peace. "You're right. About the loving and the protecting."

Wrinkled hands picked up a leather-bound book and consulted something written in a strange, unknown language. "The stars say you'll have a long and happy life."

"I'll take that." Nate grinned.

A hint of mischief entered the old man's eyes. "The women, they don't know what they do to us. It is our secret."

Laughing, Nate exited the shop with Tammy's things and began to walk back to the vehicle. He was putting the box into the trunk when he realized he'd parked in front of a florist's, though he didn't recall seeing it the first time around. Shrugging, he closed the trunk and wandered over to the shop, Tammy on his mind.

There was no stock displayed outside, probably because of the cold, so he pushed open the door. Hothouse air greeted him. The interior was a jungle of flowers, the air thick with their competing perfumes. "Some shop," he muttered, trying to separate out the mingled scents.

"I do try," said a gentle voice.

He turned to find a tiny Chinese woman beside him, her

smile beatific. There was a twinkle in her eye that reminded him of someone. "I don't suppose you know the healer down the road."

"My husband."

Somehow, that seemed right. "Oh." He shifted his feet, slightly uncomfortable in a place that was so intrinsically female. "I want to buy flowers for my mate."

The woman slid her small hands into the front pockets of her apron. "Does she like roses? I just received a new batch."

"She's a healer, too," he found himself saying, never having thought to ask Tammy if she liked roses.

"Ah, a sensible woman." The florist waved him to follow as she weaved through the wild tangle of her shop. "Here." She pointed to a sturdy green potted plant with a few white flowers. "This will last for years with a little water. Doesn't need much care or attention. Practical. It will suit your healer."

Nathan scowled. "No."

She shrugged and moved to another area of the shop, to point at a bunch of daisies. "Sunny, easy to enjoy, but there will be no sadness when they fade."

"No." All of him—man and leopard—was getting angry and he couldn't understand why. "That's not what I want."

Unperturbed, the florist took him around another corner in this shop that was far larger than it appeared from the outside. "Ah, I think this must be what you are searching for." She touched the edges of a rough bouquet. "These flowers will survive no matter what. Very cheap," she said with a shopkeeper's smile. "Common, you know."

"*No.*" The leopard's claws pricked the insides of his skin, a growl building in his throat. "Show me something beautiful, something extraordinary."

"Well . . ." The woman seemed to think for a while before nodding. She took him to the back of the shop, to a small glass case tucked away under special lights. "I have these. They aren't very strong and, as you can see, require much care. But if you love them right, they will reward you with great beauty. They're precious and rare, not easy to find or replace."

"Yes," man and beast said together, fascinated by the delicacy of the blooms he could see beyond the glass. "Give them to me."

"For a healer?" The florist raised a skeptical eyebrow.

"She's not a healer to me. She's my lover, my mate." Unlike these hothouse flowers, she was strong. But just like these rare blooms, she was both irreplaceable and beautiful enough to break his heart. "She's mine to cherish."

This time, the florist's smile was pure brightness. "It is as it should be."

TAMSYN HAD COOKED THE MEAL, SET THE TABLE, AND shimmied into a pretty knee-length dress. She bit her lip and looked in the mirror. The dress was an autumn red-orange that brought out the copper strands in her unbound hair. Shaping her body to the waist, it then flared out in a playful swirl. She'd paired it with heels and a fine gold bracelet.

"I look okay," she told herself, knowing Nate probably wouldn't even notice. It wasn't as if the dress changed who she was. But it made her feel good.

Taking a deep breath, she went into the front room, ready to fluff the cushions for the tenth time. She delighted in living with Nate and wanted to make a good home for him, but had to admit she might be going a bit overboard. The man loved her. He couldn't care less if the pillows were skewed or dinner was late.

She smelled Nathan's wild masculine scent before he knocked. Her heart tripped a beat. Thinking he must have his hands full, she pulled the door open. "Nathan, what—" Her eyes dropped to the flowers in his arms. They were a sumptuous cream color, with gold streaks that shimmered with an almost otherworldly iridescence.

"I thought you'd like these," he said, the cat in his voice.

She touched a hesitant finger to one perfect petal. "For me?"

"Of course they're for you." It was more growl than anything close to human. "Do you think I go around giving other women flowers?"

Shaking her head, she looked up into the velvet blue of his eyes. "You think I'm an orchid kind of girl?"

"Hell yes." He put them into her arms and wiped away the tear she hadn't been aware of shedding. "Stop that."

She sniffed, staring at those precious flowers. *Orchids*. Nathan had given her orchids. Rare and precious and beautiful . . . the kind of flowers a man gave to a girl who was all those things. "Thank you."

"You can thank me later," he murmured against her ear. "When I peel this sexy dress off you." He was behind her now, his hands caressing her hips as he pulled her back against his body. "Or maybe I'll leave the dress on and only take off the underwear."

"You're making me blush." It was a playful rejoinder—she loved his earthy sensuality.

"A dress gives a man ideas." He nibbled at her earlobe.

Her smile turned into a full-fledged grin as her heart filled with so much love she thought it would burst. "What if I took off everything but the heels?"

He groaned. "Put the damn orchids in water."

"They need tender care," she murmured, touching another petal.

"Yes." He kissed the curve of her neck. "But I want to take care of you. Let me."

She blinked. No one had ever offered to take care of her. She was the pack healer—she took care of everyone else. But Nate thought she was an orchid kind of girl. She had the wondrous realization that, to him, that was what she'd always been. He saw the woman behind the healer. Another tear streaked down her cheek. "Always."

His arms came around her tight.

* * *

By the time Christmas rolled around, Solias King was a dim memory. The Psy had removed all his equipment from their land, leaving behind only the ornament and Christmas lights. Tamsyn had been more than happy to use them on her tree, though the chosen fir had no lack of decorations—every one of her packmates had added a piece or ten, so that by Christmas Day, that tree was truly the pack's Christmas tree.

Tamsyn thought Shayla would have been pleased. So many in DarkRiver remained damaged by what had happened, but at least this silly extravagant tree had brought some joy back into their lives. They held the Christmas party under its snow-dusted branches and it was there that Lachlan formally acknowledged her and Nate's mating.

"For me, our anniversary will always be the day you gave me orchids," she said to Nathan as they danced under sparkling tinsel.

He slid his hands down to her lower back. "I vote for the cabin in Tahoe."

She laughed. "What are we going to tell our children when they ask about our mating if we pick Tahoe? Hmm?"

"That DarkRiver looks after its own." Sadie's, Cian's, and even Nita's interference had been born of the ties of Pack, and Nate accepted it. "And that their daddy was a stupid idiot, but one who came to his senses in time." Nate wondered what their cubs would look like. Not that he was going to ask Tammy to have children anytime soon. She was only nineteen . . . and part of him still wasn't sure she wouldn't regret having mated so young. But on this magical Christmas night, he decided to believe in happy endings. "Want a replay?"

"Of the orchids?"

It was such an innocent question he almost missed the mischief in her eyes. "I'll make you pay for that." He stroked his hand over her bottom.

"Behave," she whispered with a blush. "The others will see."

"So?" He turned her until her back was to the tree. "I'm just playing with my mate."

This time, she cuddled into him, her hands sliding up under his sweater. "I want the replay with cream on top."

He grinned. "Why do you think I bought those cans of whipped cream?"

Eyes wide, she licked her lips. "Me first."

• *Epilogue* •

Eighteen Years Later: Year 2079

"Where's the whipped cream?" Nate kissed his way down the naked line of his mate's back.

She glanced over her shoulder, beautiful enough to steal his breath. "Have you forgotten we have guests?"

"They can entertain themselves," he said, referring to the houseful of packmates who'd dropped by for a family dinner.

"They've already been doing that for an hour." She moaned. "Oooh, again."

He complied, kissing the dip at the base of her spine. "I suppose I have to go play host."

"Poor baby," she teased.

He bit the curve of her buttock. "Don't get smart with me, Tamsyn Ryder. I know all your secrets." And after eighteen years together, he knew she was his, body and soul. It had taken him almost two years to really believe that truth—but when she'd only gotten happier and happier as time passed, it had become impossible not to.

She nuzzled at his neck. "Stop seducing me. I need to go finish making dinner."

Rising halfway, he found his gaze caught by a golden envelope on the bureau. "What's that?"

"Card from Nita," she said, referring to the former packmate who'd mated with an outside-Pack male not long after his and Tamsyn's mating. "Her cubs are growing up so fast."

"So are ours." He stroked his hand over the curve where her waist flared into her hip. "God, I'll have to teach them about women soon."

She laughed. "And what do you know about women?"

His reply was a kiss that stole her breath.

THE HOUSE WAS STRANGELY QUIET WHEN THEY WENT DOWN. Tamsyn soon found out why. Lucas and Vaughn were outside playing ball. They'd roped in their own mates and a couple of other sentinels, as well as the kids and several older juveniles.

"See, I told you they'd take care of themselves." Nate kissed the pulse in her neck as they stood on the back doorstep.

She smiled. "More like the women decided we needed privacy." They had been in the kitchen with her when Nate had walked in with the orchids. He did that every year, and every year, she turned to putty in his arms. It was hard not to melt for a man who still saw her as an orchid kind of girl after all these years together.

Her mate's teasing reply was lost in the gleeful cries of their cubs as they spotted their parents. Nate walked out and intercepted the pair, scooping them up and hanging them over his shoulders. In spite of Nate's worries, Roman and Julian were still babies, not even three years old. "Mommy! Help!" they cried now, between giggles.

Nate threw her a grin and something went hot and tight in her stomach. God, she loved him. Walking over, she tilted her head to peer at her babies. That knot in her stomach grew tighter. "I think you look good in that position."

"Mommy!"

Laughing, she freed a wriggling Roman. He peppered her face with kisses before asking to be put down so he could rejoin the game. Julian was playing with his daddy, but waited to give his mom a kiss before chasing off after his twin. "They're so tiny," she whispered, standing in the curve of Nate's arm. "I can't believe they're ours."

"My little pistons," Nate said proudly, watching as Vaughn threw Roman a soft pass. Instead of running, Roman threw a sneaky pass to his twin, who shot off down the field. "See that—a few more years and they'll be pummeling everyone else on the field. So, what about the Christmas tree?"

"I drove out there yesterday." A living Christmas tree had become a tradition, a happy memory that had survived the turmoil of the bleak years after the ShadowWalkers' attack. "Our tree is still going strong."

"Just like the pack," Nate said, echoing her thoughts.

She wrapped her arm around his waist. "Just like us."

He glanced down, a tenderness in his gaze that would have surprised those who saw him only as the most experienced of DarkRiver's dangerous sentinels. "As if I'd ever let you go."

"Sweet talker." She leaned up and kissed him, thinking that her mate was simply getting sexier with age. He now had the darkly sensual beauty of a leopard in the prime of his life, pure hard muscle and a finely honed sexuality that demanded everything she had. She found him irresistible. "I love you."

He nibbled at her lower lip and there was smug male pride in his eyes as he said, "I know."

She laughed. It had taken her years to get him to that point, where he believed she truly was happy with their life. Never once had she regretted mating at nineteen. She'd been one of the lucky ones—she'd found her mate early.

And then he whispered, "Always," and she fell in love with him all over again.

Gifts of the Magi

Jean Johnson

Acknowledgments

I'd like to thank Lady Fi for teaching me how to drive. I didn't learn until I was twenty-nine, and she was an excellent instructor. In fact, I passed with room to spare . . . even though it snowed the day I took the test. It is because of her that I chose Iowa for the setting of this tale; she moved to Rolfe this last winter, and I miss her dearly. So here's hoping that *your* hearthfire never goes out, milady!

—Jean

Prologue

THE CAR JOLTED ONTO THE ROAD IN A SOFT GLOW OF LIGHT, sliding a little over the ice-packed snow. Mike gave Bella a dirty look from his position in the front passenger seat. One of his hands curled around the shoulder strap of his seat belt, dark brown on black, dimly lit by the dashboard lights. "Do you always have to drive like that?"

"Better a few minor bumps than a speeding ticket, O Lead-Footed One," Cassie reminded him from the back seat of the old VW Beetle. "As I recall, you cost us an hour's delay and just under a hundred dollars, the last time you drove."

"Whereas *you* refuse to learn how to drive," Bella quipped, glancing at her companion through the rearview mirror. Cassie's fingers were busy with a wad of saffron-orange yarn and a golden crochet hook, her attention on her task and not on the road ahead. She looked over at Mike and smiled. "Don't worry, Mike. We only have another two miles to go. Besides, cars are much more comfortable than camels. Be grateful we're living in the modern era."

A light in the distance made Mike crane his head that way. "Look, a small town. Probably with a *motel.* Why can't we ever stay at a motel? It's not as if I'm asking for a five-star hotel, you know."

Cassie answered him. "We go where we are needed, we stay where we are welcome, and we do what we must. When you follow the Way, you must follow the path that it dictates."

"Thank you, Ms. Buddhist," he quipped. "You just love to go all Zen on me, don't you?"

The blonde in the backseat merely smiled and flipped her crocheting over, starting on the next row. The three rode in silence for a little while more. Around them, the landscape was lit with an eerie orange-gray glow. It was faint, but the refracted light from that town in the distance was mingling oddly with what little sunlight made it through the thick cloud cover.

Small flakes had already been swirling down out of the sky like granules of sugar on steroids. They now grew to the size of bleached cornflakes, obscuring the vision of the three travelers with disturbing quickness, until it was hard to see more than a hundred feet ahead. The tires slipped on the powder that was accumulating on the packed snow, sending the car skidding sideways.

Mike yelped and clutched at the handle fastened over the upper edge of his door. "Prophet, save us! Can't you drive any more carefully than that?"

"Oh, you fuss over nothing," Cassie soothed him as Bella corrected the vehicle's skid, her attention firmly on her driving. "She has it well in hand!"

Mike shook his head, still clutching the panic-grip over the door with one dark-skinned hand. "To quote Ebenezer Scrooge: 'I am mortal, and liable to fall!' "

"Hah hah, very funny. We're not exactly on a mountainside, Michael, nor staring out a Victorian window," Bella reminded him, her mouth twisted wryly. Since they were out of danger, she was free to speak again. "We're in the middle of Iowa. Flat Iowa, no less."

"Nowhere, Iowa," he muttered. "And those ditches are six feet deep, if you haven't noticed."

"If we were nowhere, then we wouldn't be here, because there wouldn't be a *here* to be," Bella stated.

In the backseat, Cassie pouted and muttered, "Rats. You beat me to it."

"And yes, I noticed the depth of the ditches." Downshifting, Bella carefully turned into a driveway marked by a snow-powdered, ornately carved sign reading "Bethel's Inn—Welcome!" She smiled as she guided the car up the drive. The snow wasn't packed down on the driveway as it had been on the road; the bumper of the rounded car pushed it up in chunks, broke it to either side, and plowed them a path up to the gingerbread-trimmed farmhouse. "Well. Here we are. Time to get going."

"More than get going," Cassie said, freeing a hand from her project to point past Mike's shoulder. "Look."

Two pickup trucks sat at what looked like hastily parked angles mere feet from the covered front porch. Others had arrived ahead of them. From the way the truck lights were still shining on the front windows of the house, it didn't look like their owners were the polite type. Indeed, despite the swirling snowstorm hissing its flakes around them, they could hear shouting from somewhere within the farmhouse.

• One •

"No. No, no, no . . . not this!" Rachel stared in dismay at the small television set perched under the cupboard containing her willowware plates. "Not this, on top of everything else . . ."

The weather report shifted from the weekend to the ten-day forecast, ignoring her pleas. They had eight guests planned to arrive for the Christmas holidays, but with the sudden shift in the jet stream overnight, a huge blizzard was now headed directly their way, rather than bathing the states to the north. Without those eight guests, she and her fiancé wouldn't be able to pay the mortgage at the end of the month, and the country inn that had been in Steven's family for four generations would fail. She stared at the longer forecast, noting with dismay that snow was predicted all the way up through Christmas Night.

The weatherman was cheerfully relating to his viewers that they were definitely going to have a "white Christmas." Rachel didn't find his prognostication the least bit cheering. She flinched when the phone rang, and shifted to pick up the receiver. Sure enough, it was Mrs. Terwilliger, calling to cancel her and her husband's arrival. Opening the day planner, Rachel scratched out the couple's names, feeling depression closing in around her.

Within five minutes, the phone rang again. Billy Platz was calling to let her know that he and his two brothers weren't going to make it; they were stuck at an airport farther north, snowed in and unlikely to go anywhere for a long while. Her hands shook a little as she marked out those names. Three names were left. Mary, Joseph, and Maggie Stoutson; Mary was old Bill Pargeter's granddaughter. Rachel didn't think Joseph would want to travel quite this far in the coming weather with a three-year-old. She flinched when the phone rang again, but it wasn't the Stoutsons, thankfully. Just her future mother- and father-in-law, calling to wish her and their son a quick Merry Christmas before boarding their ship for a holiday cruise in the Caribbean.

Rachel managed to get through the phone call without betraying her inner fears. As soon as she gave an upbeat farewell and hung up the phone, however, she shuddered with the weight of responsibility. It wasn't her fault that the old farmhouse had been partially damaged by a passing tornado. Nor that the insurance company had tried to declare bankruptcy, leaving not only the Bethel Inn but many other homes and businesses in the lurch in the legal tangle that had caused. Nor was it their fault that the estimated costs had grown when the contractors discovered dry rot in some of the main support beams last autumn, requiring extensive repairs.

It was her and Steve's fault for deciding to take out a mortgage on the house, in order to finance those repairs, yes . . . but it wasn't her fault that Mr. Thomas Harrod was such a tight-fisted Scrooge when it came to making payments on time, to the last penny. The Inn *was* profitable; the old house had just run into a bad patch of luck. That was all. It was also more than enough to put the two of them teetering on the brink of ruin. Stress and worry had become a daily part of their lives, and Rachel just wished it would all go away.

The door to the mudroom opened. Her fiancé stepped inside, balancing two pails of milk in his hands. Snow still dusted his light brown hair, though he had removed his boots and overcoat in the mudroom. Setting the covered pails on the counter, he started to grin at her. His smile faltered, seeing her expression. "What's wrong?"

Rachel gestured at the day planner. "Five guests canceled."

Running his hand through his short, crisp locks, Steve winced at the chilly damp his fingers encountered. It was a reminder of the blizzard under way. "Which ones?"

"The Terwilligers and the Platz brothers. I haven't heard from the Stoutsons yet, but it's probably only a matter of time." She sighed and ran her hands over her own hair, dark brown and pulled into a single, sleek braid. "This isn't good, Steve. This isn't good. We're not going to make the mortgage payment, are we?"

"I don't want to ask Mom and Dad for help, but if we can't—" he started to say. Rachel shook her head, cutting him off.

"They just called a few minutes ago. They've probably boarded their ship already. I'm sorry," she added softly. "We won't be able to reach them until they get back."

He spun away from her, hands fisting on the edge of the counter. Frustration alternately boiled and froze in his veins. Steve hated this situation, but he didn't want to loose that anger in front of Rachel. It wasn't her fault. It wasn't his fault . . . well, maybe the mortgage they had cosigned, but considering how many years the Bethel family had partnered with the Harrod Bank, he heartily wished its current owner wasn't such a tightwad.

Rachel crossed to him, lifting her hands to his shoulders. They were knotted with tension. She did her best to massage them, but he was almost a foot taller than her. "Come on; let's get the rest of the milk in the house. And the eggs."

"Oh, that's what I meant to tell you," Steve said, turning around and slipping his arms under hers. He cradled her against him, taking comfort in the feel of her soft curves against his harder muscles, in the trust of her cheek resting on his chest. The hug wasn't as satisfying as it could have been, given how both of them were still stiff with tension. "I had to hang a rope from here to the barn, the snow's threatening to fall that thickly, but I've already got all the eggs gathered. The chickens were cooperating today, not being nearly as nasty as usual. But the really *good* news is that I managed to draw off some colostrum from Ellen. If her first-milk is finally showing up, that means she's getting ready to drop!"

Rachel winced at that, pulling back. "That's *not* good news. We're going to be snowed in, Steve, straight through Christmas! What if she has another breech birth, like the last time?"

"We'll handle it, somehow," Steve reassured her, cupping her shoulders in his palms. He looked down into her brown eyes and managed a smile. "One task at a time. No courting trouble, when we're supposed to be courting each other, got it?"

She managed a smile of her own. Neither of them had been in the mood for "courting" since that tornado had struck last summer. Not for more than halfhearted attempts. "Alright, no courting trouble." She found enough energy to smile and attempt to flirt with her love. "You're certainly cuter."

"Than what, a breech-birthed calf?" he joked.

She chuckled and mock-swiped at him. "Go on, get out there and get the rest of the milk. I'll follow as soon as I can pull on my boots. And don't break any of those eggs. If we don't have any guests, we can at least have a nice quiche for supper."

THE SLEIGH BELLS ON THE FRONT DOOR, HUNG IN HONOR OF the impending holidays, jangled loudly. Rachel, joyful that the Stoutsons had made it safely through the storm, quickly wiped off her hands on her apron, hurrying out of the kitchen and around the bulk of the front stairs. She drifted to a stop, her smile faltering and fading in dismay. The three snow-dusted figures who had walked into her fiancé's home in a swirl of cold air weren't Mr., Mrs., and little Miss Stoutson.

They were Pete, Dave, and Joey. College-aged boys, but none of them college-educated. Their families were close friends of the Harrods, the family that owned the town bank, and with it, the mortgage on the Bethel Inn. Heart pounding in her chest, she dredged something resembling a smile back onto her lips. "Hello, boys. What brings you all the way out here, with a storm on the way?"

Pete—never Petey, that was his dad—closed half the distance between them with an ambling walk that spoke of time spent in a saddle. His father raised pigs, of course, but she had heard he'd spent his summers between school years on his uncle's cattle ranch, farther south. He flashed her a grin. "Now, Miz Rutherford, you ain't that much older'n us. You ain't, what, twenty-five?"

"Twenty-six." Asserting her age allowed her to assert her authority. She spoke the words crisply, too, without any of the local drawl. "And I do not recall inviting you over for a visit."

"Ooh, college-educated," Dave teased; his hair was dark brown, his face less lean and saturnine. He made a pretense of rubbing his jaw, using fingers perpetually stained with the grease from the engines he liked working on in his cousin's garage in town. "Seems a shame ol' Steve had to go all the way to Des Moines to find himself a pretty thing for a future wife. You know what they say: Big city *wimmin* get ideas that are too big for their little-bitty brains."

"At least I *have* a brain that I can use," Rachel retorted. She did her best to keep her smile as Dave stiffened. "But in the spirit of Christmas, I'll be generous, and believe that you have one, too. Now, what are you boys doing in my house? Somehow, I don't think it's to rent any of our rooms."

Joey, the redhead of the trio, finished unbuttoning the puffy front of his blue, down-stuffed parka and hooked his thumbs into his work belt. Of the three of them, he was the most polite and reasonably respectable; he was a journeyman plumber, having apprenticed with his aunt's husband for the last two years. "Now, Miz Rutherford, you know why we're here. You got until the twenty-fourth of each month to come up with the mortgage money. Mr. Thomas wanted us to remind you that, come snow or sleet, hail or dark of night, that money's gotta be delivered this next Monday, or he'll foreclose on this place. You don't wanna be tossed out into the snow on Christmas Day, now do you?"

"We are *not* going to be tossed out," Steve asserted from the top of the stairs. He thumped his way down the stairs, glowering at the trio. "And I thought I told the three of you to stay off my property!"

"Ain't gonna be your property much longer, *Stevie*," Dave drawled, hooking his thumbs into the pockets of his jeans. He rocked on his heels, coolly ignoring the glare the older man aimed at him. "Pretty soon, you won't have a place to lay your head at night . . . and that pretty girl there is gonna come lookin' for a real bed to lay in—something *satisfying*."

He leered at Rachel as he said it. She gasped and stepped back, disgusted by the implication, while her fiancé jumped down the last two steps, anger furrowing his brow.

"Get the hell outta this house!"

"Why doncha try *throwing* me out?" Dave shot back. "There's three of us, an' only one of *you*!"

The door banged open with a vigorous clashing of the sleigh bells, startling everyone. They turned to look at the figure in the opening. The pink, fur-clad figure. At least, the coat was pink, and it had a thick span of high-quality, white faux-fur trim all around the hems, cuffs, and neckline. A fluffy faux-fur hat was perched on the woman's head, and a matching, fuzzy muff dangled from a white cord around her neck. She flung up one hand as they gaped at her, beaming an angelic smile from her pink-painted lips. "We have arrived! Oh, goodness, you wouldn't *believe* how thick the snow is falling out there!"

Her hand slashed down again in a limp-wristed dismissal, showing off her sparkly pink fingernails. Narrow pink heels clicked on the hardwood floor as she crossed from the entry rug to the hallway, brushing between Joey and Pete. Both young men stared at her with wide eyes. She held out her hand to Steve, forcing him to uncurl the fists he had formed in order to shake it. Blue eyes pinned him in place as she did so, and an exotic scent filled his lungs. The combination was too friendly for the anger in his mind to be sustained. He found himself tentatively smiling as she introduced herself.

"You must be Mr. Bethel, owner of this fine establishment. Call me Cassie! We were looking at stopping in the town, but the snow was falling so heavily, it seemed we wouldn't make it—and then we saw your sign, like a miracle from the Buddha himself!" Releasing his fingers, she reached out and clasped Rachel's palm as well, beaming warmly at the two of them.

" 'We'?" Dave managed to ask, not quite as stunned by her appearance as the other two. Until she turned around and smiled at him. He froze in place under the impact of that warm, cheery grin.

"Oh, yes, my traveling companions. Bella," Cassie introduced, gesturing past the three youths, "and Mike."

They turned and saw a dark-eyed, dark-haired woman clad in a black wool coat with flared sleeves and an equally flared hemline that fell almost to her boots. A black fur hat was perched on her head and a muff strung from her neck as well, faux-mink to the faux-fox her companion was wearing. Beside her, closing the front door, stood a dark-skinned gentleman in a marten-fur hat, matching faux-fur muff, and a brown leather trench coat, which he was unbuttoning now that the door was closed, preventing more of the heat in the house from escaping. Doing so revealed the fake sheepskin lining the calf-length jacket.

"Hello," Mike stated, reaching between Pete and Joey to shake Steve's hand. "As she said, my name is Mike, and I'm just as grateful as she is that we have arrived in time. I do hope you have room for us. I would hate to toss anyone out into the blizzard that has formed outside."

"Speaking of which," the woman in black stated, her words accented with a hint of something exotic, maybe Eastern European, "shouldn't you gentlemen go turn off your headlights? Since no one is going to be going anywhere in this weather, there's no point in you killing your batteries."

Joey twisted to peer out the window next to the door and groaned. "Aw, man! We haven't even been here five minutes, and it's already dumped two inches!"

"What?" Dave hurried to the window set to the left of the door. He squinted through the rectangular panes. The only reason why their trucks were still visible was thanks to the headlights shining through the driving mass of snowflakes outside. "Goddammit!"

"*Language*, young man," the woman named Bella snapped, her dark eyes gleaming with outrage. "This is the holy season, and you *will not* take the Lord's name in vain!"

"I'd follow along with what she says," Cassie interjected helpfully, touching Dave's shoulder. "She has quite a temper when it comes to blasphemy."

Dave whirled to tell her something, but her pink-nailed fingers bumped into his cheek, knuckles gently caressing his skin.

"Just mind your manners, be on your best behavior, and enjoy the *peace* that can be found at this time of year," the blond woman suggested, still smiling kindly.

The fight that had been forming drained out of him. There was no point in arguing; the snow was driving too hard and piling too deep to go anywhere safely. "Fine. Then I guess we'll just have to stay here until it stops."

Steve started to open his mouth and argue the point, but Rachel stepped forward, cutting him off. "That'll be a hundred dollars a night, gentlemen. A hundred a night, apiece. Plus the cost of dinner and supper; breakfast does come with the cost of the bed, naturally."

All three youths gaped at her. Pete was the first to regain his voice. "A hundred—*a night?* You can't be serious!"

"Oh, she's quite serious," Mike interjected. "This is a business, and the business is selling rooms and meals. If you wish to stay and eat, you must pay."

"You think I'm gonna pay to help support this place, when my cousin Richie is gonna be running it as soon as they can't pay the mortgage?" Joey demanded.

"Of course; your only other option is to risk driving in this weather, and freezing to death."

"When we want your opinion, we'll beat it out of you!" Pete snapped.

Cassie slipped between the two once again and cupped their jaws gently in her fingers. "Now, boys, this is the season for *peace*. For brotherhood, compassion, and caring. But electricity doesn't come cheaply, and neither do clean linens, or a hot meal. You *will* be gentlemen, and pay for your stay." Releasing their cheeks, she turned and smiled at Rachel and Steve. "Just as we will pay for our own stay. Mike?"

"Why am I the one who always pays for these things?" the dark-skinned man muttered. He touched his chest, then gestured at the dark-haired woman. "Do I *look* like I'm made out of gold?"

"Of course." Bella smirked. She passed between the three boys, bringing with her a sharper, spicier tang to her perfume than the sweeter one her pink-clad companion wore. Glancing over her shoulder, her heart-shaped face thrown into elegant profile, she murmured, "Your headlights? Or do you want to still be stuck here, forced to pay a hundred dollars a night when the roads are cleared in a few more days?"

"To he . . . heck with this," Dave muttered, heading out the door. "I'm not stayin' here!"

Pete, glancing between him and Joey, joined him in slogging through the rapidly forming drifts. Joey exited the house as well, but not to climb into his truck, slam the doors shut, and start up the engine. As the five in the house watched from the front window, he sat there for a moment, the door still opened, barely more than a silhouette glimpsed through the falling flakes. Then the headlights cut off. The other set of headlights swiveled, then vanished into a reflected, swirling glow of lit flakes. The glow dimmed quickly, fading from view.

A figure swirled out of the white, climbing the deep-set porch. Joey opened the door, looking sheepish as he entered far less vigorously than he had originally arrived, keeping one hand on the doorknob so it wouldn't hit the wall. He rubbed at the back of his neck with his free hand, opened his mouth . . . and a crash in the distance, faint but unmistakable, cut him off. Jerking around, he stared out the window next to the doorway. "They must've slid into the ditch! We gotta get to 'em!"

"Joey, stop!" Steve ordered. As the redhead glanced back at him, he explained, "The snow's driving too hard; you get more than twenty yards from this house, you'll never find it again. You *know* what an Iowan blizzard can do."

"We can't leave them out there!" Joey protested. "Look, I know we came out here to give you trouble, but freezin' ain't the way to go."

"I've got some bundles of rope in the mudroom. I brought them in from the barn when I brought in the last of the milk this morning. If we tie them to one of the posts on the porch and keep a hold of the other end, we won't get lost," Steve said.

"They probably misjudged the turn out of the driveway, and hit one of the ditches."

"I *told* you they were six feet deep," Mike whispered to Bella.

She rolled her eyes and waited for their host to come back. He had three bundles of ropes in his hands. Grabbing one of them, she met his startled gaze. "What? It snows like this all the time where I come from. I'm used to maneuvering in the snow."

"I couldn't ask a lady to go out in weather like this," Steve protested, glancing at his fiancée.

"Who said I was a lady? Look, we may need a crowbar as well, depending on how banged up they are. I have one in my car, which is on our way. If that is the case, you'll need someone to hold the rope to make sure it doesn't get blown away while the two of you gentlemen pry open the doors," she instructed Steve and Joey, giving them equal time under the weight of her dark brown gaze. "And if both boys are injured, each of you can carry a man, and I can reel in the rope and keep track of the four of you, to make sure no one gets lost."

"You'd better give in, Mr. Bethel," Mike advised wryly. "There was never a more stubborn or opinionated being in all of creation, once Bella makes up her mind to help someone." He flashed the dark-clad woman a white-toothed grin. "At least she uses her powers for good."

Cassie laughed at his quip, and Bella smirked. No one else chuckled. Considering her offer carefully, Steve finally handed the second bundle of rope to Joey. "Fine. You reasoning is sound. But you follow orders. I don't know where you're from, but I doubt you've seen a snowstorm like the ones we get around here. There's a porch on the second floor, at the back of the house. There have been times when my family has had to clear *that* of two feet of snow."

"Mr. Bethel, it can drop an average of half a meter overnight where I come from. And the landscape is a lot more mountainous than this."

"Where's that?" Joey muttered, eyeing her all-black outfit warily. "Transylvania?"

"Yes, actually." She parted her lips, licking her teeth, as if her canines were about to grow a lot longer and pointier than their normal appearance would seem.

"Oh, be nice!" Cassie chided, flipping her hand at her companion. As the three rescuers headed out the front door, the pink-clad woman turned to Rachel, patting her hand. "Don't you worry, Mrs. Bethel. Bella will make sure they all get back here nice and safely."

"I'm not Mrs. Bethel yet," Rachel found herself compelled to admit. "I'm going to be, soon."

"A nice, big wedding?" Mike asked her, distracting their hostess from the danger of the storm. "With a huge feast and lots of relatives?"

"Actually . . . a small, quiet civil ceremony, New Year's Day," Rachel found herself confessing as Cassie drew her into the sitting room next to the front hall. "Just his parents and mine as witnesses. We originally thought of having a big wedding, but had to scale back when the Inn was damaged last summer. Repairs are more important than parties, after all."

"Well, that's a shame," Cassie commiserated. "Mind you, the Buddhist way is about as simple as a civil ceremony can get, but most cultures like to indulge in lavish displays of hospitality and festivity. And as prominent business owners, it would also be a good way to spread awareness of just how fine your inn is, if you were to host a reception here."

She gestured at the warm oak wainscoting and pale, calico-sprigged walls lining the front parlor, with darker versions of calico-covered furniture amply cushioned for comfort. Efforts had been made to festoon the room with red and gold ribbons, artificial greenery, and a Christmas tree in the bay window off to one side. Even the Franklin stove boasted a set of sleigh bells, wrapped around the stovepipe on a metal chain that would tolerate the heat of a fire better than the velvet ribbon supporting the ones hung from the front door.

"Yes, it's very warm and inviting," Mike agreed, taking one of the stuffed armchairs while Cassie sank onto the sofa with their hostess. "Are all of the furnishings new?"

"This side of the house was badly hit in a tornado last summer," Rachel found herself explaining. "We took out a mortgage on the Inn to make the necessary repairs, since the insurance company tried to go bankrupt, and all the funds are still tied up in litigation. The house is on the Historic Registry waiting list, so we did our best to have the structure repaired very close to what it originally was, in case it does make it onto the list of important buildings for this region. But our guests prefer more comfortably padded furniture."

"Fascinating. Has it always been an inn?" the dark-skinned gentleman inquired.

"From within the first eight years of its construction," Rachel agreed, glad she had asked Steve about the Inn's history. "It was a part of the railroad expansion. There used to be a set of tracks that ran near the property line, and the owners realized that if they invested in lumber and some bed frames, they could house first the workers, then the people who traveled through here. They made sure to bill it as a family establishment, a place for the husbands to bring their wives and children, as opposed to the bachelor quarters offered in town—no single men allowed. When the railroad was built, and the main depot installed at the edge of town, they had a buggy specifically built to escort the women travelers out to the Bethel Inn so that they could sleep in chaperoned safety."

A beeping noise cut off any further explanation. Mike gave her a sheepish look as he extracted an electronic day planner from his pocket. "Please forgive me. It is time for my devotions."

"Oh. Are you a minister, then?" Rachel asked him, curious.

"No, just a faithful Muslim—you aren't going to be serving a lot of pork, are you?" he asked with a wry smile. "I realize that Iowa is pork central, of course, but while I'm not absolutely strict in my diet when I'm traveling, I do try to avoid alcohol and pork."

"Ah. Well, if you're snowed in with the rest of us through Christmas, I had planned to carry on the tradition of the famous Bethel Inn ham . . . but I suppose I could roast a chicken as well."

"That would be very kind of you," Cassie replied, smiling. "I know Bella would be grateful, too."

"Is she also a Muslim?" Rachel inquired politely.

"No, she's a Reform Jew," Mike corrected.

Blinking, Rachel looked between him and Cassie, who was finally unbuttoning her fluffy-edged pink coat. "A Buddhist, a Muslim, and a Reform Jew, traveling together? . . . Listen to me," she scoffed in the next moment, smiling ruefully. "I made that sound like the opening to a bad joke, or something. Next thing you know, you'll be walking into a bar!"

Cassie and Mike both laughed at that. Ruefully, Mike shook his head in the next moment. "As much as I'd like to continue to chat, I really do need to attend to my midmorning devotions. If I give you my debit card, could you show me to a room, and perhaps process it while I pray?"

Having been raised a Christian herself, Rachel had heard only bits and pieces about how the faith of Islam worked, but she did know those who were devout to it prayed five times a day. Though it wasn't her own system of beliefs, she would be an innkeeper's wife, and that meant welcoming not only a diverse number of travelers, but a diverse number of faiths. Rising, she nodded cordially to him, adding a smile. "I think that can be arranged. I can scrounge up another rope to go out to your car to safely fetch your bags, if you like."

"Oh, there'll be no need," Cassie reassured her, rising from the sofa as well. "They're out in the hall."

Rachel headed through the greenery-framed door, frowning softly. Sure enough, three sets of bags rested around the foot of the coat rack, like presents around a Christmas tree. One set was vinyl pink, one set was cloth black, and one set was leather brown. She was *sure* they hadn't brought their luggage in with them, and *reasonably* sure she hadn't heard the front door open and close . . . somewhat sure? Maybe Bella had directed the other two to bring in their bags while Rachel was distracted with the tale of the Inn . . .

Shaking it off, she picked up the brown cloth bags and mounted the stairs. "This way, please; I presume you'll each want separate bedrooms?"

"Of course," Mike agreed. "When you've traveled together for as long as we have, you tend to want some privacy now and then."

"Have you been together long, then?" Rachel asked next, leading him toward the bedroom overlooking the front of the house. "Oh, the bathroom is that door there, conveniently labeled as such. There are two more further down the hall, each with its own sign, in case this one is busy at some point."

"Yes, I see," Mike confirmed, nodding his head at the carved and painted sign. "We've gone on holiday voyages like this one for many years now. Sort of a *hajj* of friendship, as it were—I've already been to Mecca, so that journey is complete. We travel for other reasons these days."

"I hope you don't mind our Christmas celebrations," Rachel offered politely, entering the bedroom and crossing to the four-poster bed, setting his two suitcases on the padded bench at its foot.

"Why should I? Christ was one of the most important Prophets to appear before Mohammed's time. The traditions of

Christmas celebrate the exact same spirit of unity and brotherhood that the followers of Islam embrace at this time of year—in fact, today is the last day of hajj on our holy calendar," Mike added, smiling at her. "Not to mention the Winter Solstice, an important holy-day for those who revere nature. Though the coldest days of winter still lie ahead of us, today is the darkest, longest night, the shortest, dimmest day of the whole year . . . and it is a time when all of us in the Northern Hemisphere are reminded that, no matter how bleak things look today, tomorrow *will* be a little brighter than today, and the day after will be even brighter than before.

"And so here we are," he stated, spreading his arms with a smile. "Bringing you customers for your business, when it seems likely that the storm has chased everyone else away."

Her cell phone rang, startling Rachel. She hadn't realized what a mesmerizing speaker her guest was until then. Pulling it out of her pocket, she flipped it open. "Bethel Inn, how may I help you?"

"*Rachel? This is Bill Pargeter. I just wanted you to know that my granddaughter and her family have arrived safely at my house. It's going to be a tight squeeze, what with my two daughters and their own broods, plus my grandson . . . but I wouldn't put a rabid dog out in weather like this, let alone make 'em drive all the way out to your place. I'd shoot the rabid dog to put it out of its misery, but I wouldn't put it out in this weather.*"

Rachel made a face at the wall. *So much for tomorrow being a little brighter than today* . . . "I'm glad to hear that Joseph, Mary, and the baby are safe and sound at your place, Bill. Thanks for letting me know."

"*Wait, there's more!*" Bill's voice interrupted her before she could tell him good-bye. "*I know Mr. Harrod's being, well, the backside of a front-ugly cow right now about that mortgage of yours. Joseph and I talked it over, and we're both in agreement. We're gonna pay you the full price for their ten-day stay, half from him, an' half from me. That's on the hope that this storm will be less severe than the weather guys keep claiming it'll be. By paying you a retaining fee, they can at least guarantee a room to escape to, once it's safe to drive again—and* no *arguing, young lady. Consider it a Christmas gift from the Pargeters and the Stoutsons, a thank-you for hosting little packets of our family whenever we have 'em over for a holiday.*

"Now, if you'll excuse me, I gotta get off-line so my own daughter can teach me how to use that newfangled computer-thing she got me for my birthday last month. Beth says there's a way we can transfer the money to you online, so you'll get it into your account right away. Richie's a good enough boy, but that father of his would have him cuttin' corners an' driving the Inn into bankruptcy."

"Th-thank you!" Rachel stammered, too shocked by the generosity to protest. Not that she had much of a chance for it, since the old farmer hung up before she could even try. Returning the phone to her pocket, she blinked a few times, then drew a deep breath and let it out. With the income from six guests, plus the income from the Stoutsons . . . they would have enough to pay the mortgage for this month, and their other bills as well. Their savings had been whittled down during the months Steve and she had spent doing all those repairs, unable to operate the Inn. With the boys replacing the Platz brothers, they'd not only have the mortgage and the electricity paid, but enough set aside to start feeding those depleted accounts.

Maybe today was one of the darkest days of the year; it had certainly been darkening metaphorically around her and her fiancé up until this point, as well as physically. But with one phone call and six unexpected visitors, Rachel felt like the sun was finally returning to her and Steve's life. Remembering her guest, who was rolling out a small prayer rug taken from one of his suitcases, she quickly murmured her excuses and left the room, giving him privacy for his faith.

Six guests . . . God bless them all, Rachel thought, amazed that she would find herself thinking such a thing after the way the boys had arrived. *It's going to be interesting, entertaining that many when they can't go off and visit other people. Maybe some party games in between meals?* She could still do a quiche for supper, if she stretched it with cheese and vegetables and added a few more dishes, but Rachel also had a much bigger lunch to plan. Head full of ideas, she returned to the kitchen.

• *Two* •

Steve wasn't sure what to make of the woman, Bella. Ignoring the biting, breath-stealing cold, she used her muff to dust the snow off the front of the rounded lump that was her car, extracted the crowbar with black-gloved hands, and trudged alongside him and Joey through the increasingly deep drifts without any problems, despite the slenderness of her frame. Joey, bundled up once again, kept slipping her glances, too. Of the three of them, she seemed almost happy to be out in the deepening drifts. Sandwiched between the two men, she forged onward, somehow guiding them in what had to be the straightest line Steve had ever seen anyone take in a blizzard, as if drawn by some sort of beacon.

Not that there was much to see beyond the swirling, falling snow and misty white puffs of their own breath, of course, but when something reddish-gray loomed up out of the grayish-white surrounding them, it took Steve a moment to realize the reddish thing was the plastic of his newspaper box, advertising the name of the local tribune, and the gray bits belonged to the metal mailbox and the weathered-wood post supporting both. The object looked oddly short, until he realized how deep the drifts had packed up under their feet.

The snow was coming down even harder now, blowing sideways in disorienting swirls before angling the other way. Without the rope playing into the distance behind them, Steve doubted they would be able to make it back at all, straight-line march or otherwise; he couldn't even see the far side of the road from here. From the way the cold seeped into his boots and gloves, how the wind stole into every gap and sucked heat from every thin spot in his clothes, if they didn't make it back to the house, they would freeze to death. No, Joey was right; this wasn't the way anyone should die.

"My guess," Bella enunciated over the hissing of the wind and its swirling burden of flakes, "is that they pulled out of the driveway, then slid into the far side of the ditch. Which way would they have turned, do you know?"

"The nearer of the two is Pete's place," Joey offered, speaking over the scarf wrapping the lower half of his face. "Off to the left."

Bella and Steve looked at each other. He looked down at the rope in his hands. Having already tied two lengths together, he took the third coil, knotted them stoutly, then handed her the rope and put her on the end. "Let's check that way first. I'll take point. Joey, you take the middle and make sure you hold my hand, and Miss Bella, don't you let go of either him or that rope!"

"Don't worry; you can trust me," she returned stoutly.

Hoping that everyone, sensible or otherwise, had found shelter and gotten themselves off the road, Steve inched out across the highway, trying to spot signs of the ditch on the far side before he found it the hard way. If it weren't for the mittened hand gripping his, he wouldn't have known he wasn't alone. The world had turned white and violently empty with the onset of this blizzard. Cold seeped through his clothes in little patches of discomfort. All he wanted to do was go back and warm up by the woodstove, cuddling on the couch with his soon-to-be wife and a hot cup of cider, rich with spices.

It was her cider that had first made him realize he was in love with her. They had met in college in business class. He had offered to buy her a cup of coffee and chat in his dorm room, and she had countered with an offer of home-brewed cider in her apartment. An offer that he had ended up accepting several times. The spices she used reminded him of her eyes, cinnamon-warm and nutmeg-bright. Their courtship had progressed slowly, since she had accepted an internship for two years at a hotel down in California after getting her MBA, with a minor in the hospitality industry. But Steve had been willing to be patient.

Stress over their finances had dampened some of their prewedding enthusiasm, and certainly curbed their original, pre-tornado plans for a better wedding. Inching his way across a snow-obscured road, Steve just wanted to get back to her. But there were two young fools somewhere out here. He couldn't leave them to freeze to death.

His feet found the edge of the ditch, blanketed into a mere dimple by the drifting snow. The moment he felt the curve, he shifted to the left, crowbar in one hand, the other tugging Joey behind him. It didn't take more than another two minutes to find the truck, though at first he couldn't make out what he was seeing; tilted firmly on its side, Dave's black pickup sat under an obscuring blanket of white at least three inches deep. Part of it was due to the way the wind swirled snow up off the road, driving it until it hit the vehicle and formed the start of a snowdrift, but part of it was just the heavy, icy downpour of flakes all around.

"Here it is!" Steve told the others, restraining the impulse to hurry to the front of the truck. With the road slick from compressed snow underneath the freshly deposited stuff, he didn't want to risk stepping wrong and twisting an ankle, or worse. As soon as he was even with the back of the pickup bed, he whacked the truck with the crowbar, clanging metal against metal. "Hopefully, that'll wake 'em up!"

"I'll stay at the bumper with the rope," Bella told him, releasing Joey's hand. "Don't go further away than you can touch this thing, or you'll be lost!"

Nodding, the two men moved up along the length of the truck. They reached the door, designated by a peak in the blanketing white that was the side mirror, and heard a thumping and yelling noise from within. Scraping the snow from the window, Steve saw Dave and Pete inside. With Joey's help, he cleared off the rest of the snow, finding the door handle. It seemed to be stuck. Joey took the crowbar from him and, with Steve gripping the latch to release its lever, helped to pry the thing open. Dave helped by shoving from the inside.

Holding the door open against the wind, Steve watched as Joey assisted his two friends in scrambling out. It was awkward, since the moment Dave released his seat belt, he slid right into Pete, who yelped at being squished. But the boys sorted themselves out. Gesturing at the back of the truck, Steve shouted over the wind.

"Bella's at the back of the truck. She's got a rope that'll lead us right back to the Inn. Everybody, grab hands and work your way back there together. Don't let go!"

Joey took point, pulling Pete along behind him. Dave hesitated a moment, then gripped Steve's hand. "Thanks."

Steve almost didn't hear the words, but knew it must have cost the younger man a bit to say them. He held his tongue, saving his breath and his energy for the trek back to the Inn. He let Bella take the lead, reeling in the rope as she walked steadily through the thickly falling flakes, retracing their path through the snow. Joey had one hand tucked into the belt wrapped around the waist of her overcoat, the other forming the rest of the chain of men. All Steve had to do was follow in the wake of the others, holding

Dave's gloved hand as he trudged through the gap in the drifts that had been churned and trampled into their path home.

Inside the front room, Cassie peered through the glazed front of the woodstove. The flames were burning merrily enough, but eventually the fire would die down. Peering at the logs stacked in the nearby basket, she smiled and selected a rounded one, then used a nearby pot holder to open the metal door.

Long ago, the people of the Scandinavian lands had ceremonially lit a log like this one—only much, much bigger, the entire trunk of a tree—to celebrate Thor, god of lightning, at this time of the year. The object was to burn a single tree for the entire length of the old celebrations. The Celts had also lit a log much like this one as well, to entice the sun to grow strong once again, shedding more and more light. But the tradition involving flames she thought most fondly of, as she tenderly placed the rounded bit of trunk into the heart of the fire, was the one Bella would think of, too: that of the miracle of the temple lamps, in the ancient land of the Hebrews. At the darkest time of the year, it was important to remember that light *would* come back into their lives, no matter how gloomy things might seem.

"Shalom," she breathed into the metal box, before closing the door. Inside the stove, the log slowly caught fire, burning with a steady golden light. The Franklin stove was as far as one could get from a menorah, but in a storm like this, it was just as important to warm the body as to warm the spirit.

This had to be the snowstorm to end all snowstorms; by the time they reached the front porch of the converted farmhouse, it was nearly three steps shorter than it should have been, and all of them were chilled to the bone, shivering inside their clothes. A pink-clad figure met them on the porch, dusting each of them off in a fluttering bustle of pink-gloved hands before allowing them into the house, so that the caked snow on their clothes wouldn't melt and soak them into a worse chill, or so Cassie chattered. The boys accepted her fussing with wide eyes, and Steve with an impatient sigh, wanting only to rejoin his fiancée. Bella accepted it with a roll of her eyes as she finished coiling the last bit of rope.

As soon as they were inside, Rachel met them with a tray loaded with steaming mugs. The spicy scent warmed Steve's heart just as much as his lungs. As soon as he had shed his outer coat and his gloves, he wrapped his hands around the almost-too-hot mug, letting the heat sink into his chilled fingers. For a moment, he wanted to tell her how much he loved her. It felt too awkward, though. Professing his love in front of strangers was bad enough, but in front of three unwelcome guests, boys who would snicker and make fun of his feelings . . . he couldn't do it.

Mike came down the stairs, dressed in a deep brown sweater-vest, tan shirt, and chocolate trousers. "I'm glad to see all of you made it back safely. Allah's blessings upon you, and those of the Prophet Emmanuel."

Pete blinked and frowned at him. "You ain't a Christian?"

Bella smacked him on the back of the head with her muff. "No, he isn't! And neither am I, though I'm willing to admit your Christ was probably a True Prophet of God, if not the Messiah."

"God is God," Cassie interjected smoothly, favoring Pete with a smile. "Whether you dress Him up in an aba, a sari, or a three-piece suit, God is God."

"And this time of the year has been set aside for the celebration of kindness, tolerance, unity, and brotherhood," Mike agreed as he finished descending the last few steps. Reaching for one of the mugs, he lifted it from the tray in Rachel's hands. "A toast: to the enlightenment that comes from opening our minds to *knowledge*. May we all know the Creator a little better, through getting to know each other."

Bella plucked a mug from the tray, holding it high. "May we

all enjoy the *comfort* of a solid roof over our head, good food in our bellies, and friendships—both new and old—warming our hearts."

"To *peace*, in this holiest of seasons," Cassie agreed, taking the second-to-last mug. She looked expectantly at Steve, who realized she wanted him to add a toast.

"Uh . . . to finding these two young gentlemen alive."

"And to making it back alive," Joey added, clinking his mug against his friends'.

David blinked, then nodded. "To being rescued, even when I made an a—" He caught Bella's pointed glare and changed his wording. "A donkey of myself."

"To, um . . . tolerance, and the holiday spirit," Pete agreed.

"To a Merry Christmas, a happy hajj, and a joyous Hanukkah," Rachel offered. Then blinked and looked at Cassie. "Um . . . what celebrations do Buddhists hold at this time of the year?"

"The day the Buddha began his search for Enlightenment, but that was earlier in the month," she dismissed with a smile. "I'm perfectly fine with the idea of toasting happiness, merriment, and joy, since you're all safe and sound."

"Then to happiness, merriment, and joy," Rachel allowed, clinking her mug with the others.

"Good! Now it should be cool enough to drink," Mike told the others, smiling. They lifted their mugs to their lips, finding the cinnamon-laced apple juice just on the tolerable side of hot.

Rachel lowered her mug and gestured everyone into the front parlor. "Come, sit! Shed a few more layers as soon as you've warmed up enough. If anyone needs a hot shower, we have three of them available, but the water tanks can only reheat so much at one time."

"That's assuming the power doesn't go out," Pete muttered, taking a seat on a padded calico footstool. "Storm this bad'll probably knock out a substation somewhere, plus all them power lines coming down."

"Naw, the county got smart along this stretch of road, an' buried all the lines," Joey reminded his friend, stretching out his legs. He'd claimed the rocking chair in the corner by the stove. "Power'll only go out if the substation goes. Of course, that makes it a pain in the b—uh, backside when it comes to findin' the road if the drifts get deeper than the ditches, since there's no poles to watch for."

"Well, if the power goes out, we've got a portable generator in the lean-to, just off the mudroom out back," Steve told the others from his seat on the sofa, freeing one hand from the mug of cider so that he could tuck his wife-to-be closer against him. Having cheated a frozen, swirling death, he appreciated Rachel a whole lot more today.

"Speaking of which . . . shouldn't at least one of you gentlemen cough up a credit or debit card, so that our hostess can register you for your stay?" Mike inquired gently, giving the three boys a pointed look.

"You can't be serious about that," Dave scoffed.

"Quite serious," Bella stated before Rachel or Steve could speak. "Two of you owe your very lives to Mr. Bethel and that rope of his that guided us safely back to this shelter."

They looked at each other, then Joey grumbled under his breath, pulling his wallet out of his back pocket. "You can put it on mine, Miz Rutherford. I'll beat it outta the other two later."

Pete snorted. "As if you could!"

"Let us not test that theory in person," Mike chided them. He turned to their hostess, who had leaned fully into her fiancé's side, her slippered feet curled up next to Bella's hip. "So, what shall we be having for our lunch?"

"Tomato soup, grilled cheese sandwiches, and steamed vegetables," Rachel replied promptly. "With more cheese smothered over the top."

Dave scratched his chin. "Well, if it's the Bethel Inn cheese, I suppose I could stomach 'em . . ."

"It is," Rachel promised, reluctantly uncurling from Steve's side to take the credit card Joey extended her way. There was a credit reader in the kitchen she could use to bill him with. Credit wasn't quite as good as debit, since it wasn't an instant transfer of funds, but it would have to do.

"Well, in the meantime, why don't we play a game?" Cassie offered. "Something to warm us up in both body and mind, like charades!"

The others groaned, but conceded the idea. With the snow swirling outside the house, the front room was cozily warm in contrast, thanks to the cheerfully burning woodstove. Bella volunteered to go first, rising to her feet and holding up three fingers.

"Okay, three words," Mike agreed.

She held up two fingers, and Joey said, "Second word."

Two more fingers, and Pete offered, "Two syllables?" Bella shook her head, so he changed it to, "Two letters?"

A nod and a tug of her ear, then a fluttering of her fingers, her thumbs intertwined, forming the shape of a bird. Steve narrowed his eyes. "Sounds like . . . dove—*of*!"

The black-clad woman nodded, unbuttoning her overcoat. Naturally, she was wearing an all-black ensemble of wool slacks and an angora sweater underneath. She held up her first finger after passing her coat to Dave, who draped it over the arm of his chair, and then she held up four fingers.

"First word, four letters," the dark-haired youth offered, and received a nod.

A tug of her ear, and she stretched her hands out, as if expanding something. Steve tried to guess it. "Sounds like . . . stretch. Expand?"

Bella shook her head twice. Mike tried a guess next. "Lengthen?"

She swirled her fingers, encouraging that line of thought. Pete blurted out, "Long?"

Grinning, Bella tugged on her ear and pointed to him.

"Wrong, bong, thong," Dave muttered.

"Song?" Steve asked, and received a sharp nod, three fingers, and then seven more in reply. It popped into his head. "'Song of Solomon'?"

"You got it!" Applauding him, Bella reseated herself on the other end of the couch. "Your turn, Mr. Bethel!"

"Steve, please," he urged. Thinking for a moment, he rose and began his own charade attempt with a smile and six fingers.

By the time Rachel returned, the others were laughing at her betrothed, who was flapping his elbows and making faces.

"Six words, Miz Rutherford!" Joey gasped, wiping at the tears in his eyes. "We can't figure it out!"

"One Flew Over the Cuckoo's Nest," she stated, and grinned as the others gaped. "He did the exact same one when we first played charades together at a party back in college."

"Cuckoo?" Mike snorted. "He looked more like a drunken chicken! No offense meant."

"None taken," Steve agreed, straightening with a grin. He took his fiancée's hand and kissed it impulsively, remembering that party and how she had found his silliness endearing rather than off-putting. "Your turn, love."

"HEY."

The soft-spoken word turned Steve's head. Pete stood in the doorway to the mudroom, watching him tug on his boots. "What do you want?"

"That gal, Bella, is right. I owe you my life. Me an' Dave both do." He scratched at the back of his head for a moment, then asked, "You gotta go milk your cows, right?"

"That's right," Steve agreed. "It's almost time for their afternoon milking."

"Well, I can help you. I've done it before, at my uncle's place,"

Pete offered with a diffident shrug. "If nothin' else, you'll need help clearin' a path to th' barn."

Steve hesitated only a moment before nodding his head. "There's only the four of them that need full milking; one of them's at the first-milk stage, so that'll need to be set aside; there's a bottle of colostrum started in the dairy's fridge. But the offer is appreciated. Get your things, and put them on in here. I've already strung a rope from the house to the barn, so we'll be following that from here."

Nodding, looking relieved at having his offer accepted, Pete vanished from the doorway. Steve finished settling his snow boots on his feet, and hoped that this peaceful coexistence would continue. The two boys did owe him their lives, true, but he didn't do things like that to hold any favors over the heads of others. He had done it because it was the right thing to do.

STEVE GROANED AS HE SETTLED BETWEEN THE FLANNEL sheets next to Rachel. It had been a long day, and he was tired from slogging through the snow. The radio on the far side of the bed from him played softly, letting them know there was still electricity to the house. Rachel had picked a classical music station, something soothing, relaxing.

"How are the cows doing?" she asked him. "Do you need to watch Ellen yet?"

"If this one's anything like the last five calvings, she'll have two more days to go before she's ready to drop. Butt first," he added, gesturing with his hand. "But she'll drop. Probably the night before Christmas Eve."

"And unless a miracle happens, this storm will keep the vet away for longer than those three days," Rachel sighed, twisting onto her side so she could snuggle close. "You'll have to start sleeping out in the barn tomorrow night, just in case . . . and I'll miss you."

A smile quirked the corner of his mouth. He twisted his head, kissing her dark hair. "Actually, Pete is going to be sleeping out there. We'll trade off during the day, but he's volunteered to watch during the night. He's had to turn breech-birth calves half a dozen times before, with his uncle's guidance. And he says the cot we have out there is nicer than having to doss down in the hay like at his uncle's place. I made sure he had extra blankets. He'll be fine."

"It's a nice turnaround from him and his friends coming here to bully us earlier," Rachel sighed. "And it takes one of our worries off the mind. Depending on whether or not the credit companies can give us a fast turnaround on processing Joey's card before noon, we should have enough in the bank for the automatic withdrawal of the mortgage. If not . . ."

"If not, then there's nothing we can do about it. Except pray for a miracle that Mr. Harrod gets that stick unwedged from his butt," Steve muttered.

Rachel shoved at him lightly for the vulgarity, and he kissed her on the lips to soothe her protest. It had been a while since they had last kissed in bed. Stress had taken its toll on their urge for intimacy, submerging their desires under the weight of their worries. With some of that weight lifted, and with memories stirred of how they had first gotten together, Steve felt his body quickening with a half-forgotten thrill of desire. So what started out as a simple, loving kiss grew a bit warmer.

His hand slid from her shoulder to her breast. Rachel sucked in a startled breath, pulling her head back. He hadn't touched her like that in a few weeks, and truth be told, she hadn't been in the mood for it herself. Until now, that was. Brown eyes stared at hazel for a long heartbeat, then they both squirmed under the covering quilts, Steve removing his pajamas, Rachel her long-sleeved nightgown.

Shoving the garments under their pillows so they could be found again, Rachel squeaked when Steve pounced on her, his hands just a little too chilly for comfort. He tickled her ribs, making her giggle, then muffled the noise with his lips, recapturing their kiss. She returned the favor, brushing her fingertips over the hairs dusting his chest. He retaliated by cupping her breast.

The soft, moaning sigh that escaped Rachel's lungs made Steve remember that sound, back when they had first been intimate. It reminded him how much she had enjoyed the way he had stroked and savored her curves. The last time they had made love, he had only played with them a little, wanting to move on to the rest of her body. Only he hadn't really moved on to the rest of it. Not her legs, not her arms . . .

I've been neglecting her, he thought, pulling back from their kiss. She gave him a puzzled look, so he gave her a reassuring smile in return. *I should not neglect the woman I love.*

Catching her hand, he brought it to his mouth, nipping gently at her skin. From the flush of her cheeks, she still enjoyed having her fingers nibbled and licked. That made him dredge through the rest of his memory, recalling every little caress she had ever enjoyed at his hand. The suckling of his lips at the soft inner bend of her elbow. The lapping of his tongue over the tender flesh of her wrist. The worshipful caress that palmed the outer curve of her breast.

Rachel moaned again, enjoying his touch. She couldn't remember the last time he had pampered her like this. As he worked his way down her torso, teasing around her nipples rather than going straight to their crinkled tips, she knew she would reward him once he was done with her. It would be rude to interrupt him before he was done, after all.

When he kissed her belly, she giggled. It was too ticklish a sensation not to react—mainly because he lapped like a kitten around the rim of her navel. But rather than continuing on to her core, he squirmed into a lump under the covers that had enough room to nibble on the soft skin of her thighs. Aroused more than she could remember, Rachel moaned softly with each breath. With their room on the ground floor, she didn't fear the softer sounds of lovemaking. Only if he provoked her into a loud cry would she worry, though they had invested some of their renovations in filling the spaces between the walls with plenty of insulation.

Oh! Oh . . . there . . . Her breath groaned out of her when she felt his tongue tickling the edges of her folds. Hands curling into the feather-stuffed pillows, Rachel twisted, arching her hips up and splaying her knees out. *There, there, there . . . ohhh, yes, this man deserves a big reward for thi—wait, he's stopping.*

Disoriented by the sudden cessation of pleasure, she lifted her head, feeling him squirming an arm up the length of her body—and not to grope her breasts. He batted instead at the edge of the covers, lifting them up. A moment later, Rachel heard a deep inhalation. She giggled, divining his problem.

"Can't breathe down there, my love?" she asked her lover, amused.

"No, I can't," came his half-muffled reply. "A little help with the air, please?"

"And let myself freeze from the cold draft?" she joked, shifting the bedding so that it formed what she hoped was an adequate tunnel.

"I'll make sure you're kept nice and warm," Steve murmured, returning to his task. A moment later, he paused in his savoring to add, "Mm, tasty."

That made her laugh. It was what he'd first said about her recipe for cider, and for the first meal she had made for him . . . and the first time they had made love. No, she didn't mind the cold, after all; not when he resumed flicking his tongue between her nether lips, sending a flush of pleasure out across her body.

He knew her very well. In fact, Steve could usually make her climax within minutes once he began tasting her down there. This time, he took his time, using his knowledge to tease, not just to please. A flick here, a suckle there, a bit of lapping, a swirling lick. Gentle stroking from his fingers, counterpoint to the nibbling of his lips. One of those fingers slipped inside, carefully twisted around, and pressed upward in a fluttering movement. Stars exploded silently behind her eyes, making her cry out.

When he added an equally rapid flicking of his tongue to the peak of flesh overlooking his finger, Rachel shattered deliciously, arching her neck and twisting her body, before relaxing gradually under the easing of his touch.

Steve couldn't breathe; her brief writhe had been just enough to collapse the tunnel of the bedcovers that had been providing him with fresh, cool air. Squirming carefully up the length of her body, he poked his head out with a gasp of relief, flushed from the heat the two of them had generated under the thickly layered quilts. He grinned as he gulped in the crisp, cool air. In fact, he was surprised he still fit in the bed, given the dreamy, dazed look on his fiancée's face.

What a way to make a man feel ten feet tall! Damn, I've missed totally scattering her wits like that. What a fool I was, letting the grind of daily life drive our love down into something ordinary . . .

Rachel came back to herself with a double blink, finally realizing her fiancé was beaming at her like a lit-up Christmas tree. She thought briefly about twitting him for being so smug, but conceded that it was well-deserved smugness. That, and it was much easier to whisper a simple "Wow."

"Mm-hmm," Steve agreed smugly, cupping her damp mound under the layers of bedding. His groin twitched with desire, feeling how slick he had made her, but he told that part of himself to hush. Tonight was for his future wife to enjoy. If she wanted more, she'd let him know. If not, it was enough to have pleased her so thoroughly. She deserved being pleased.

Thankfully, his loins agreed with that decision; Rachel was worth far more to him than the proverbial quick roll in the hay.

His quietude puzzled Rachel. Arching a brow, she asked, "Is that it? No pouncing on me?"

The curve of his mouth deepened from a smirk to a leer. "If you want more of the same, I'd love to do it all over again."

Oh. She blinked at him, thought about him suckling her again, and of him not being that eager to release himself. Since she could feel his erection prodding her hip, she knew he was eager physically, but he hadn't even hinted at his own need. "Why? I mean, why pamper me, and not take any pleasure for yourself?"

"Who said I don't enjoy that?" Steve countered, propping his head up on his hand. The air was cold against his arm, but he was still a bit heated from being buried under the covers. "It pleases me a lot to pleasure you. Tonight is *your* night. Anything you want," he promised impulsively, almost rashly, "and if it's within my power, I'll give it to you."

And I thought he'd melted my body into warm goo with that mouth of his, she thought distractedly. *Who knew he could melt my heart, too, after all these years together?* Thoughts whirling, she settled on what she really wanted, and slid a hand onto his shoulder, pushing him over. "What I *want*, right now . . . is to please you as thoroughly as you have just pleased me. So kindly make an air tunnel for me."

Grinning at the ceiling, Steve complied, first making sure the quilts and sheet stayed high on his chest while she squirmed underneath, then rumpling them just so to ensure that she could breathe as she kissed her way down his chest. He didn't want his fiancée to suffocate, after all. Especially with her mouth full.

• *Three* •

The alarm clock rang all too early, as it usually did, but both Rachel and Steve woke with that wonderful, must-stretch-under-the-covers sensation of having had a truly good and relaxing night's sleep. Rachel winced as Steve turned on the lamp by the bed, smirked as he slapped off the alarm, and kissed him with closed lips when he leaned over her. Morning breath was always a worry, but a peck on the lips was a very nice way to start the morning in a good frame of mind.

Good enough that the chill in the air only made both of them gasp and hurry to dress for the morning's chores. Even with Pete out in the barn, ready to help shift the cows from their stalls to the attached dairy annex and give them their morning feed, it would still be a chore. Since he could still hear the wind whisking the snow around the house, Steve crossed to one of the heavily draped windows and peeked between the velveteen curtains. He frowned, trying to make sense of what he saw.

With his and Rachel's bedroom being on the ground floor,

with the understanding that the "ground floor" technically started two feet above the actual level of the ground, it took him a few moments to process what he was looking at in the sliver of light that shone through the windowpanes: snow that had piled up to the bottom edge of the window.

Six feet of snow.

There had been about eight to ten inches of snow left over from previous storms, compacted by time, wind, and almost-thawing before freezing again. It usually didn't snow more than a few inches, half a foot at most per snowstorm, but it rarely thawed in Iowa long enough for all of the snow to melt away, just compact down. By the time spring rolled around, it would be a couple feet thick, but that was at the end of winter. This much snow in a single fall was almost surreal.

"Six feet . . ."

Rachel, tugging her head through the sweater she was pulling on over a long-sleeved knit shirt, padded over to join him. "What did you say?"

"Six feet!" He held the curtain back so that she could see for herself. It was somewhat dark outside, though still lit by a faint, almost sourceless, orange-peach glow that undoubtedly came from the lights over by the barn, and the streetlamp glow from the nearby town. "Assuming it hasn't drifted up on this side of things, that's six feet of snow out there! This is one of those storms that only comes along once every half-century!"

"Wow," she breathed, staring at the still-falling flakes, which didn't have quite so far to fall anymore.

"You're only allowed to say that after I give you mindless pleasure," Steve teased her, drawing her into his arms as he let the curtain fall back into place. They shared a loving but brief kiss before he set her free with a sigh. "I'm going to have to crawl through the snow to get to the barn, then shovel my way back again. I told Pete the milking starts at five o'clock sharp; I hope he has the sense to start without me, or the girls will get off their schedule and stop producing as much milk."

"You'll need a hearty meal when you're done. I'll start making sausage . . . um . . . chicken gravy and buttermilk biscuits for breakfast," Rachel amended, thinking of the two guests who wouldn't be able to eat pork.

"I'll need a hearty meal *before* I'm done," Steve quipped, shifting to pull on a second layer of wool socks. The rest of him might get warm from the exertion of all that shoveling, but his toes would freeze if he didn't take care of his feet.

Rachel jerked to a stop by the partially open study door. Frowning, she poked her head inside, searching the brightly lit room for its occupant, which shouldn't have been brightly lit at all. The nubbly black curls and chocolate-colored nape of their tan-clad guest met her gaze. He was doing something on their computer, checking something online. Stepping inside, Rachel caught his attention. "Excuse me, but this room is off-limits to guests."

He turned to face her with an apologetic smile. "I'm terribly sorry; I didn't realize. I just saw the computer and the router, and thought I could check my e-mail. Um . . . while I was online, your instant messaging thingy popped up a little window. You've received an e-mail from someone about a Mr. Swanson. The subject line looked rather urgent—I'm done here, so you can check it out yourself," he added, closing out the last window and rising from her office chair. "Forgive me my meddling, but I wanted to make sure my business was running smoothly."

"What sort of business?" Rachel found herself asking in curiosity as he moved out of her way.

Mike smiled warmly. "*Knowledge*. It is important to learn, and it is vital to understand. I am something of a teacher, and something of an information broker, a researcher. But then, you already know an education is important; after all, you wouldn't be so successful as a bed-and-breakfast owner if you and your impending husband hadn't gone to college . . . and met there, and fallen in love. I'll leave you to your work, and go sit in the front parlor."

Rachel blushed as she smiled. Settling into the chair, she started to face the monitor, then turned back. "Oh—I need to stoke and build up the fire in that room first."

"No need," Mike reassured her. "I checked on it when I got up, and saw that someone had done it earlier."

Puzzled, Rachel frowned at him. "Earlier? It's nine minutes to five a.m.—who would be up this early?"

"Oh, we're all early risers. Especially when motivated. Don't forget your e-mail," he instructed her, nodding at the computer screen. "It looked urgent, and we don't know how long the power from the county can be maintained, what with this storm and all."

Bemused, Rachel turned back to the screen, clicked on the appropriate icon, and started sorting through the list of e-mails received. The latest one puzzled her even more than her early-rising guests. It was from "Lappschaum & Assoc." and the subject line read "Pursuant to the Request of Mr. Theodore Swanson." Teddy Swanson was one of their longest-standing guests, according to Steve. He came every single summer, stayed for four weeks, visited all his friends and relatives in the area, then went back to Minneapolis–St. Paul. He was something of a local legend, too, for he had been doing so for most of his eighty-four years, ever since graduating from the local high school and going off to college three hours to the north, where he had found a wife and started a family.

Opening the e-mail, Rachel read the contents. Her hand crept up over her mouth, tears prickling in her eyes. Someone had written to inform them that Mr. Swanson had died in his sleep. Steve would be devastated, as would his parents, who had hosted Teddy for decades. As had the previous generation of Bethels.

She forced herself to read on . . . and the hand covering her mouth to hold back her grief now covered up its urge to gape. It seemed that Mr. Lappschaum was Teddy Swanson's executor for his will . . . and that Teddy had left a trust fund for Steve's future children, to ensure they would have a college education, whenever Steve and she got around to having them. It wasn't a huge amount of money, but with compound interest, it would be enough to ensure at least two offspring had the chance to attend some college or university somewhere across the States.

It was an incredibly generous gift from a man who had been a delight for the Bethels to host. Even though she personally had known him only a few summers, she had enjoyed taking care of the elderly gentleman's needs. He would be missed, but remembered for a long time, especially with this unexpected piece of philanthropy. Closing the browser window, Rachel made her way to the kitchen in a daze. The sad and the happy news could wait until Steve returned from the barn; she had breakfast to make.

Adjusting his knit cap on his head one last time, Steve opened the door of the lean-to, ready to grab his snow shovel and start forging a path to the barn. The shovel wasn't there, however. Neither snow shovel hung on their assigned pegs hammered into the board running along the outer wall, nor was the regular shovel, which should have been hanging in the toolshed-style room. Confused, he closed the lean-to door, then opened the back door to the mudroom, expecting to have to climb up over the couple of feet of snow that had piled up over the back porch.

A snow-dusted trench greeted his eyes, wide enough for two people to pass, and the faint sound of voices in the distance met his ears. Bitter cold seeped into his lungs, and swirling white still fell from the dark sky. Treading over the crunchy, squeaky snow that had begun to reaccumulate at the bottom of the artificial, somewhat broad, curving canyon, he found the source of the cleft in the drifts when he was within viewing distance of the bright glow from the large fluorescent light hung at the peak of the barn roof. Three bodies worked in rotating tandem as he stopped and watched, goaded by the accented voice of the slender woman in black. They had followed the path of the rope he had strung, straight to the barn entrance.

"That's it! Put your back into it! Four more shovels to go! Keep it up, David; you're doing well! Three more shovelfuls! Watch that clump, Joey, it's about to fall! Two more shovels . . . and it's my turn again!"

Joey stepped to the right as Dave stepped back, and Bella stepped up into Joey's place on the left. She hacked at the snow with her spade-tipped shovel while Joey scooped up the broken chunks of snowbank and tossed them up over the head-high snowbank enfolding them. Breathing hard, David leaned on his shovel and watched them for a moment, then idly glanced behind him. He blinked at the sight of Steve standing there, watching them, then straightened and held out the shovel.

"Here. Your turn. I'm bushed."

"Nonsense!" Bella asserted as she lunged the implement in her hands at the wall of snow between them and the small side door set in the end of the barn wall, next to the larger, sliding doors. "Exercise is good for you! All those endorphins, pumping through your blood! Plus it will make us appreciate our breakfast all the more. Five more shovelfuls, Joey, then it'll be our host's turn!"

Guessing what was expected of him, Steve stepped up behind them, waited for his turn, and slotted himself on the left as Joey stumbled back, breathing just as hard as his friend had. "Man!" He gulped, his breath steaming in the snow-swirled air. "Where does she get all that energy?"

Steve found himself hard-pressed to keep up with her, even though he was fresh and she must have been working the two boys for at least half an hour. She continued to chop into the snow with the spade in her hands, switching sides with him so that he could scoop away the loosened snow. Joey stepped back in after a few more minutes, having regained some energy. Within a minute after that, they reached the door and had to take more care so as not to damage the wooden planks of the siding, scraping more than shoveling.

Grinning, Bella twisted open the door as soon as the way was mostly clear, and gestured Steve into the warmth of the building. "There you go! Mind you, I want to enjoy fresh milk and eggs for my breakfast when you are through. Come along, boys. Unless you want to muck stalls and pitch hay while you're at it?"

Muttering their refusals as politely and quickly as they could pant, the two youths followed her, taking the shovels back with them. Amazed at how the odd, black-clad woman could get such honest work out of the local pack of troublemakers, Steve shook his head and stepped inside. It was only a couple minutes after five, and he could hear the lowing of the ladies in their byres. Or rather, not in their byres, he noted with satisfaction. Pete was already leading what looked like the second cow out of her stall, taking her to the dairy room for food and milking, just like he had the previous afternoon. It was a relief for Steve to see that their girls would've been fine without him.

Shedding a layer as the heat of the barn seeped into him, Steve headed for Ellen's stall; she needed to be hand-milked for the colostrum, rather than put on the machine that would send her first-milk into the same pails as the rest. But when he got to her, he found she'd already been milked. When Pete came back, he grinned shyly at Steve, who was straightening from checking the now slack udder.

"Already done it, Mr. Bethel; she gave it up easy, too. Of course, I was smart enough to wash my hands in hot water so they'd still be warm when they touched her. It's in the fridge with the rest, in the processing room. I wasn't sure you'd make it out here in less than three hours, given how deep th' snow got overnight; then I heard Miz Bella yelling at Dave an' Joey, making 'em clear a path to the barn. Made me right glad, too," he added, taking Eliza's halter and backing the lowing cow out of her stall. "I mean, you showed me the microwave and the frozen stuff in the deep-freeze, but I ain't so good at cookin', even with prepackaged stuff. Miz Rutherford's cookin' beats my own hands-down, any day."

"It also beats my own," Steve agreed, entering the last stall and taking the halter of the remaining cow. "And she loves doing it, too, which is the important part. We're having chicken gravy on homemade buttermilk biscuits once we're done cleaning, milking, and cleaning again in here."

"Well, I'm glad you're here; that machine ain't too familiar," Pete admitted. "You did show me, and I could figure out whatever I couldn't remember, but I'd rather trade you; I'll muck out the stalls as clean an' fresh as can be, while you take care of these ladies in the dairy. Deal?"

"Deal," Steve agreed. Nearly ten minutes of shoveling had been more than enough for him; not having to change out the bedding in the stalls was a very welcome offer. "Don't forget, we'll need to gather the eggs in the henhouse, which is through that door over there . . ."

"AND THE YEAR AFTER THAT, WE WERE TRAVELING IN THE Bahamas," Bella related as the others finished laughing, "so those lavi-lavi turned out quite useful as makeshift sarongs, but I'll never stop teasing Mike about having to wear what we think of as a skirt over his trousers!"

"It's a good thing I can enjoy a laugh at my own expense," Mike warned her, passing along the bowl of fried potatoes they were sharing at the dinner table, "or I'd have to retaliate with the tale of you and the fresh coconut halves you wore for a hula dancer's top at that costume party that one Christmas Eve two years ago. It turns out she's allergic to fresh coconut milk," he confided to the others. "But only when it's allowed to dry on her skin."

"That was me," Cassie interjected, lifting her finger while Joey and Pete eyed her speculatively. "Not Bella. And that is too painful a subject to discuss at the dinner ta—"

The lights went out, stopping the chatter around the long oak table. With the cessation of speech came an awareness of the cessation of the furnace that had been blowing its heat in a subtle background whoosh, easily missed until it went missing. They could hear the wind still blowing outside, and the hiss of snow on the upper half of the windows, since it had drifted and covered the lower half already. It was a poignant moment, dark and quiet. Then Steve scraped back his chair, clearing his throat.

"If everyone will stay here, I'll go get a flashlight and some candles, then start up the generator once we can see."

Bella's voice broke the quiet following the footsteps of his cautious exit. "Well. At least we finished our supper first. And with the snow halfway up the house, it should help to insulate us against some of the cold outside."

"Coconut halves, huh?" Dave's voice asked archly. Something *whapped* a moment later, making him yelp. "You tossed a bun at me!"

"You're still in your seat, and I have a very long memory," Cassie quipped back. She giggled after a moment. "This is turning out to be a very special holiday, that's for sure!"

Steve came back with the glowing beam of a flashlight in one hand, a pair of candelabras in the other, and a plastic sack swinging from his arm. "Well, I suppose candlelit meals could be considered 'ambience.' We'll have you lit in a jiffy so you don't bump around; then I'll get the generator going. Rachel, if you can get the votive holders off the sideboard there, in case they need to get to the bathroom before the lights are back on; I've got the candles for 'em here."

It didn't take long to set up the candles in their holders, nor to light them. Steve waited long enough for Rachel to get started on illuminating the room, then took himself and a jacket upstairs. The exhaust chimney for the generator was hooked up to a long, tall stovepipe with a sharp, conical peak for a roof. It was designed to take several feet of snow on the lean-to roof and still be able to vent, but with the snow still coming down, Steve didn't quite trust it to remain clear.

Grabbing a broom from the upstairs closet, he made his way to the covered balcony, which overlooked the mudroom and lean-to below. Snow had stacked up at a fairly steep angle to the balcony railing. More snow fell, glittering as it swirled into the glow of the flashlight he set on the wrought-iron chair in the corner, pointing it out into the snow. As beautiful as the flakes were to watch, they were interfering with his employment; he had guests to keep warm.

Balancing carefully, he climbed high enough to check the snow on the lower roof. It was within a foot or two of the top of the pipe. Poking at the snow with his broom, Steve tried to dislodge it. For a moment, nothing moved, then a good chunk of it broke off and slithered down the sloped surface, taking more and more snow with it. It splattered somewhere below, falling from most of the roof in a rough wedge shape, warning him that he would probably have to shovel the chunks out of the trench to the barn, but it did clear the lean-to roof nicely around the exhaust pipe.

The last thing they needed was to asphyxiate on diesel fumes, after all. Sweeping the snow from his feet, he picked up the flashlight again, returned inside, hung the broom in the closet again, and headed back downstairs, dusting the snow from his short locks. Inside the dining room, he could hear the others playing some sort of game, and paused to check on them. Mike was explaining that the book-sized box in his hands, wrapped in something white printed with golden bells and ribbons on its paper, was a Guessing Box game; they could shake the box, tilt it, turn it, even weigh it, and each person would write down on a piece of paper what they thought was inside the box. Whoever guessed right would win a bar of Swiss chocolate.

It was the perfect dinner game to play in the dim glow of candlelight. Wishing he could join them, since he knew Rachel loved Swiss chocolate, Steve continued on to the mudroom. It was chilly enough, so he kept on the jacket . . . because if the mudroom was chilly, the lean-to was positively freezing. Crossing to the generator, he played the flashlight over it, checked the gas gauge, and followed the instructions to start it.

Nothing happened.

Frowning, Steve tried again. Nothing happened. He unscrewed the tank cover, checked to make sure it had diesel inside, closed the cap tightly, pressed all the right buttons, pulled on the lever, and . . . Nothing happened.

Frustrated, he turned away before he could smack the machine. A house full of *paying* guests, and he couldn't get the generator to work. This was not good. *One problem at a time, one solution at a time*, he reminded himself. *Of course, the problem is I don't know much about fixing engines. Milking machines, yes. Generator machines—wait . . .*

Walking back into the house, he poked his head into the dining room. Everyone was still eating and playing the game; the box was now in Joey's hands, and he was making a show of carefully tipping it just so, to see at what angle the object inside would either roll or slide.

"Dave? You work on engines, right?"

"Yeah," Dave admitted, lowering his cup of cider. "What's up?"

"I, ah, can't get the generator to start," Steve forced himself to admit. "Maybe, if you took a look at it . . ."

Shrugging, the youth abandoned the dining table. Borrowing a jacket in the mudroom, he followed Steve into the lean-to. He, too, tried the buttons and the lever, checked the tank, tapped the gauge, then checked over the cables. Digging around on the tool bench in one corner, he came back with a screwdriver and removed the engine cover, checking it over. It didn't take long for him to figure out the problem.

"Here it is. It's the spark plugs. They're all corroded," the dark-haired youth stated, removing each one for a closer inspection.

"Ah. Well, can they be cleaned up?" Steve asked him. "With some soda pop or something?"

Dave examined each plug, then shook his head. "I doubt it. When was the last time you had this thing serviced?"

"Um . . ." Steve hated to say, "Never," but the younger man got the message.

"We're screwed," he stated bluntly, handing Steve the ruined plug.

"Now, wait a minute," a familiar, accented voice stated from the doorway. They both turned and blinked at Bella, who was holding a lit votive candle in a blue glass holder. "Do you mean to tell me, young man, that you work on car engines all the time, as you told us earlier this afternoon, and you *don't* have any spare parts in your truck?"

"If I *did* have any, and *if* they were the right type, you forget my truck is all th' way out there, on the far side of the road, lyin' in a ditch, lady," Dave reminded her pointedly.

"Well, then, what is the problem? We know it takes two and a half lengths of rope to get from the porch to the bed of your truck, and we have a flashlight to see our way there. Put on your snow boots, gentlemen!" Bella ordered them. "If there is a packet of spark plugs that will work in that truck, now is the time to go find them. Not five hours from now, when we are freezing in our beds. If you want the *comfort* of a warm home, you must exert yourselves to attain it—he who cuts his own wood is twice warmed, and all of that. Come along!"

Dave shot Steve a sardonic look. "Ever get the feeling she was a drill instructor in a former life?"

"I heard that!"

At least the snow hadn't piled any deeper than the bottoms of the ground-floor windows, though the wind still swirled it around like it was a full-blown blizzard. No one could tell if it actually was snowing from the clouds somewhere overhead, or if it was all ground drift. It also took a lot longer to get from the front porch to the truck and back, but at least breaking a trail through such deep drifts meant they had an easier time finding their way back. The sight of the mound that was Joey's truck greeted them first, lit by the plying of two flashlights through the night. Once past the view-blocking mound, they could see the glow of candlelight in the front window, and the figures of Rachel and the others waiting to open the door for them.

Dave was still muttering to himself as he started stripping off his down jacket inside the foyer, letting Steve hang it on the coat rack by the front door. "I don't believe it . . . I just don't believe it . . ."

"Don't believe what?" Joey asked his friend, watching the other two removing their gear as well.

"We got there, I climbed down inside, and I immediately found a pack of four spark plugs that can fit the generator, a ten-dollar bill, a rolled-up pair of sweat socks, that old road map I've been looking for, and a *weenie whistle*," he told his redheaded friend, wrinkling his nose. "A *weenie* whistle? You know, one of them hotdog-shaped plastic things?" From the blank look on Joey and Pete's faces, reflected in the light of the votives they were holding, they didn't know what he was talking about. "Ah . . . never mind. The point is, we got what we need."

"What's wrong with finding a weenie whistle?" Bella asked him, her accent muffled by the way she had bent over to tug off her snow boots.

"I have never in my life owned a weenie whistle, that's what!" Dave retorted. "I tell you, there's somethin' weird goin' on."

"What's weird about finding what you need when you need it?" Mike asked, his dark skin blending him into the doorway of the front parlor.

"Yeah," Cassie agreed, her blond curls very visible next to his shoulder as she leaned past her friend. " 'Tis the season for miracles, and all that!"

"Well, maybe it dropped outta someone's pocket when they were ridin' with you," Pete offered. "Dad found a one-dollar coin from Canada in his car about three years after he bought it from his cousin, who had gone up North a couple years before that."

Grunting, unable to deny the logic of that possibility, Dave followed Steve back to the lean-to and the waiting generator. Both men groaned, then grumbled, realizing they had to shrug back into their jackets, given the breath-frosting chill in the mudroom; the lean-to was achingly cold in comparison, making their coats a necessity even for such a short task. Once the plugs were installed and the cover resecured, it was simply a matter of pushing a few buttons, pulling on the lever, and starting up the generator. Pleased with their efforts, the two males slapped hands in a high five, shed their things in the mudroom, and returned to the front room, where the others had gathered.

"Just to let you know," Rachel was cautioning the others, "we cannot run a lot of electricity off that generator, and it only has so much fuel, anyway. It's only good for a few lights at a time, for the heater out in the barn, and for the furnace and hot water tanks. And when it's milking time, the dairy gets priority on the electricity, so there'll be a ban on using it from five to six in the morning, and from three to four in the afternoon. So if you leave a room, turn off the lights behind you if you're the last one out of there . . . and enjoy a nice long snuggle under the covers in the mornings."

"Reading by candlelight can be cozy," Cassie offered, cheerful as ever. She had brought out her tangle of bright orange yarn again, and was busy crocheting away on something smallish. "And Mike's little box game is fun, and doesn't require a lot of bright light. We can keep doing some of that to conserve power in the afternoons."

"Is she always this cheerful?" Pete asked Bella.

"Yes. You get used to it after a while."

"A long while," Mike added dryly. Cassie only laughed and continued playing with her yarn.

"Well," Rachel stated. "Now that everyone is back, and we have a bit of power for lights, I'm going to bring out the apple crumble I baked earlier. And some of our famous Bethel Inn cheese from the curing cupboards down in the basement. We can heat the crumble on the woodstove here and serve it piping hot, if you're willing to wait a few minutes. Does that sound good?"

"That, and some of that magnificent spiced cider of yours sounds delicious," Mike praised, voicing the enthusiasm of the others, who were all nodding.

"Then I'll be right back."

It didn't take long for Rachel to bring out the casserole pan with the apple crumble, nor to set it on the woodstove to heat. Heading down into the basement, she entered the room where the cheese was made and turned to the curing cupboards. The sweetness of the apple crumble would be best offset with a sharp flavor, so she turned toward the cupboards holding the rounds that had aged the longest.

It was very chilly down there, colder than expected. So cold that her breath frosted almost as badly as if she had stepped outside. That meant when Rachel heard a *ting-ting* followed by a *crack* and a *pshhhhhhh* off in the distance, she guessed instantly what had happened. Dismayed, she abandoned the cheese room, hurrying through the other rooms comprising the basement.

The busted pipe was in the laundry room, of course. It sprayed water down from one of the pipes crossing the ceiling. There was a drain pipe in the tiled floor, but with the ground ice-cold under all that snow, it would soon freeze and clog up. Biting back a curse, Rachel hurried for the stairs.

She couldn't shut off the water, since if it stopped flowing, it would freeze that much faster elsewhere in the house. Once Joey was ready to work, then it could be shut off. She couldn't even put a space heater into the room to keep the other pipes in there from freezing until the water was cleared up, and not just because of the electricity hazard. Space heaters drained a sizable chunk of the generator's power; it would be better to just let the furnace do its work.

"Joey? Joey!" She found him headed her way in the front hall, trailed by the others. "You brought your work truck, right?"

"Yeah, I did," he agreed, jerking his thumb at the front door behind him. "It's not ten feet from th' porch, buried under all that snow."

"Well, unbury it as fast as you can and get your toolbox," Rachel ordered him tightly. "The blizzard just busted a pipe in the laundry room, and since you're here, I need you to fix it."

"You know, who's gonna pay for all these things we're supplyin'?" Dave asked her and Steve as Joey stood up. "Help in the barn, shovelin' all that snow, those spark plugs, and now a busted pipe?"

"We haven't charged you for your extra meals yet," Steve pointed out. "Why don't we call it services in trade?"

"You gotta admit, the food is worth it, Dave," Joey allowed, hurrying to get into his winter clothes. Bella, ever willing to go out into the snow, was already pulling on hers.

"I'll get the snow shovels," Steve sighed.

Rachel caught his hands as he started for the mudroom. Tugging him close, she kissed him on the lips, then leaned back with a smile. "One problem at a time."

"Yeah, but it's one problem after another," Steve muttered back, feeling the tension from earlier in the week returning to his shoulders. He hadn't realized just how much he had relaxed in the last twenty-four hours, thanks to a nearly full inn. Having all these new troubles piling on top of him threatened to grind him right back down again.

"So think of our blessings. The power would have gone out, regardless . . . and we'd be without a functional generator, and the pipe would have frozen and busted anyway. But we've got a full enough house to pay the mortgage, a mechanic who had the spark plugs necessary, a plumber who can fix our pipes . . . and plenty of heating oil in the furnace, so long as we have the power to run it," she reminded him. "And plenty of wood for the woodstoves here and in the kitchen, just in case."

Bella poked her head into the front room. "Are you getting the snow shovels or not?"

Sighing, Steve nodded. He did spare a moment for another quick kiss with his fiancée, then followed their dark-haired guest back to the mudroom. Rachel watched him go, thinking of all the exercise he'd been doing. Deciding he needed rewarding, she started planning what could be done, once the latest problem was fixed.

• *Four* •

Joey not only had the tools and the piping to make the necessary repairs, he also had a roll of insulation, white on one side, shiny on the other, and fibrous in the middle. Steve and Rachel had pooled their resources for the renovations, even to the point of draining the money originally set aside for a wedding, but they hadn't been able to insulate all the pipes in the basement. With the power lines buried underground, the electricity rarely went out in the winter; in fact, it was far more common for the Inn and its neighbors in that corner of the county to lose power in the summer from various repairs and construction projects.

The chance of a storm knocking out the electricity had been weighted against the presence of the generator and the fact that the basement rarely got cold enough to freeze. It was a gamble they had lost this time around. But with the pipe repaired and the now-functional generator helping the furnace to blow heat into the rooms once more, it was thankfully not as bad as it could have been. The furnace burned oil, yes, but it operated electronically, an irony not lost on anyone thanks to the storm.

Aware of how much these sort of repairs would cost normally in labor as well as materials, Rachel and Steve conferred quietly, then asked the young man what he would want in additional trade for the work and materials. He thought for a moment, then shrugged and said, "A wheel of your cheese. Mom and Gran are always going on about it, and I think it'd make a nice Christmas present for 'em."

Considering the youth had managed to make his insulation roll stretch to cover three rooms of piping so far, Steve didn't think that was adequate. "*Two* wheels of cheese."

Joey grinned at the offer, pulling more binding tape from the roll in his hands while Dave held the insulation in place. "Well, now . . . if *that's* the price you're offerin', I should have a look at all th' washers and drainpipes in this place, make sure the seals are good and the U-bends are unclogged."

"I won't object to that," Steve laughed, reaching out to shake the younger man's hand as soon as he was done taping the latest section of insulation.

"I wouldn't object to some of that hot apple crumble we were promised, neither," Dave stated, climbing down the other half of the two-sided ladder.

"As soon as we've run out of insulation," Joey promised his friend. "I'll make a plumber's apprentice out of you in the meantime, if you don't watch out!"

"And I'll make a grease monkey outta *you*," Dave quipped back, helping him shift the ladder. He waited for Joey to measure off a manageable length of the insulation, cutting it into strips that would just fit around the pipes with a little bit of overlap. "Aren't you done with that thing yet?"

"I'm still cuttin' it out," Joey retorted, working the shears through the material.

"No, I mean, haven't you run *out* of it?"

Steve frowned in thought. Dave was right; the roll shouldn't have been that bountiful, even with the journeyman plumber cutting it as economically as possible. It looked almost as thick as it had when he first started. Then again, the stuff was thin, especially when compressed into a tightly rolled cylinder like that. Shaking his head, he left the two to their work in the basement. *Maybe it is the season for miracles . . .*

He met a puzzled-looking Rachel in the hallway. She saw him closing the door to the basement and smiled, then frowned softly again, beckoning him into the kitchen. It was dark, with only the light from the hall to illuminate them; with the generator rumbling out in the lean-to, they had a measure of privacy. The dinner dishes had been washed by hand while he, Dave, and Bella had gone out to the truck. Rachel moved automatically to the drying rack to check if they were ready to be put back, and Steve followed her.

Sliding his hands up her arms, he kneaded the muscles to either side of her nape. "Is something bothering you?"

"Yeah . . . It's the stove in the parlor. Every time I've gone in there to check on it since last night, it's been burning merrily away, not needing any tending whatsoever. The one in here does, which I started when the three of you went back out to Dave's car," Rachel admitted, turning her head to look at the old-fashioned, cast-iron cookstove Steve's great-grandmother had cooked upon when the Inn had first opened. She had started it to keep the house warm while they looked for spark plugs outside, and had put a quartet of water-filled milk pails on the stovetop to slowly heat. "Every time I ask the others, either they don't know when it was last stoked, or they say they saw one of the others feeding it earlier. It's nice to know they're keeping it going for me, but . . ."

"But what?" Steve asked his love. "There's something nagging at you about it. What is it?"

"There's always this one log in there, whenever I go to check.

It could be a series of them, since we did cut up the limbs of that old alder that came down in the tornado and put them in the woodpile, but . . . there's always this one round log just burning away every time I go to look. Sometimes it's to the front, sometimes it's to the back, or sometimes it's crosswise. But it's always in there among the others."

He laughed softly, half in amusement and half in wonder. "And here I was, just thinking as I came up the stairs that it's a miracle Joey has so much of that insulation stuff he's been putting on the pipes downstairs. By rights, he should be almost done with the roll, except it looks like he's only used a quarter of it. Which makes me want to believe in miracles again. And . . ."

"And?" Rachel prompted him, turning around in her beloved's arms.

"And it makes me remember how much I still love you, now that the burdens are being lifted from our shoulders," Steve whispered, looking down into Rachel's brown eyes. His smile faded, replaced by a sober look. "I forgot that, because of all our troubles. I didn't *stop* loving you, but I did forget to *tell* you how much I still love you. And how much I appreciate you being here, working so hard right beside me. If there's any miracles happening in this house, *you* are one of them. I don't know how else to tell it to you, to make you believe . . . except . . ."

Backing up from her, he lowered one knee to the linoleum-covered floor, holding her hands in his. His legs ached from all the work he'd done, climbing through all that snow and back, but that didn't matter. It was the look on her face, surprised yet tender, that provided all the cushion he needed.

"Rachel Rutherford, love of my life . . . will you still marry me?" Steve asked her. "For richer or poorer, for better or worse, in sickness and health . . . and in spite of tornado and blizzard?"

His wry question chased away her tears, though her smile was still tremulous. "Of course I will. God couldn't keep me from marrying you . . . and He wouldn't stop it, either." Freeing one hand, she ran her fingers through his crisp curls, loving their springy texture. "You're a *good* man, Steven Bethel. The only man for me. I'm sorry I forgot to show my own deep love and appreciation of you, too."

Kissing her other hand, Steve pushed back onto his feet. He groaned as he did so, his muscles sore, then smiled at her, pulling her into a hug that was a lot less tense than the one they had shared the previous day. "It's been a rough five months, hasn't it? But if we think about it, if we can survive all of *this*, then we can survive marriage together."

"Yes, we can," Rachel sighed, snuggling her cheek into his shoulder.

A voice cleared itself back at the doorway. Steve twisted the two of them a little, so they could both see who it was. Mike stood in the doorway, looking apologetic for interrupting their privacy, yet somehow pleased by the sight of them embracing tenderly. "Pardon the intrusion, but the apple crumble is bubbling, the cheese is melting, and I have only twenty minutes before giving my last devotions for the evening. My stomach politely reminds me that it is not necessary for me to fast before doing so at this time of the year."

His grin made the other two smile ruefully. Squeezing his fiancée, Steve let go with a sigh. "I'll call the boys up from the basement."

"I'll bring the plates," Rachel agreed, and smiled as Mike offered his assistance.

WITH THE LAST OF THE DESSERT DISHES HAND-SCRUBBED—the dishwasher took up too much energy to run—and all of the dishes dried and stacked in the cupboards, with their guests retired for the night and nothing more needing to be done until morning, Rachel nudged her fiancé toward the kitchen woodstove and the four milk pails set on its surface. "Grab a pot holder and help me carry these pails, will you?"

Quirking a brow, Steve did as she bid. "What are they for?"

"Well, I didn't want to run too much water from the tanks, what with the power coming from the generator for both the heating units, and the well pump. And I wasn't sure how many of our guests would want a hot shower before going to bed," Rachel explained, taking a couple of pads to lift the handles on two of the pails herself. "I turned the sink on a trickle while you were out, to try to keep the pipes from freezing—yes, I know that didn't quite work—but it had to be done, and since I lit a fire in the stove to heat the back end of the house, I thought, why put both of them to waste?

"I was going to just draw a regular bath, but it all came together nicely enough," she added, voice tight as she hauled the heavy pails across the hall, into their own ground-floor bedroom.

With the door shut and the heat out for a while, the room was chilly. She manipulated the lever-style handles for both bedroom and private bath, stopping only when she reached the old-fashioned, big, deep claw-footed tub, with its sloped back and refinished porcelain surface. It had been restored as an engagement gift from Steve's parents, since it was just big enough for the two of them to nestle in like spoons.

Rachel had blushed when that had been explained to her, but it had told her just how much his parents supported the thought of her as their daughter-in-law. Setting down her pails, she made sure the tub was stoppered, shook some sandalwood-scented bath salts into the tub, then lifted the first pail over the rim, pouring its steaming contents into the basin. If she hadn't grown used to hauling the heavy pails around in the last several months, helping Steve occasionally in the dairy, her task would have been that much harder.

"What, no bubble bath?" Steve quipped, copying her by pouring one of his own pails into the tub. The water was quite hot, though not scalding; it quickly perfumed the air with scented steam.

"Oh, it's not for me," Rachel demurred, smiling to herself. "It's for you."

"Me?" He stared at her as the last of the water dripped into the tub, hazel eyes wide and brows quirked, bemused.

"Yes, you," she confirmed with a feminine smile. "You've worked very hard today, and I'm very proud of you. So I'm going to bathe you. Pamper you, like you did me last night."

He smirked at that. "If I'm in the tub when you're trying that, you might drown."

She gave him a mock dirty look and took the pail from his hands, setting it back by the other empty canisters, out of her way. The fourth pail, she left full for rinse water later. "Strip, mister!"

"Your command is my wish," he said, still smirking. Pulling his sweater over his head, he sat on the edge of the tub to unlace his boots. Rachel dropped to her knees in front of him, batting his fingers away so that she could perform the task herself. It felt nice, being pampered. Even when she peeled down his socks and briefly massaged his feet, it felt good. She was even careful to lower his soles to the fuzzy green bath mat, rather than letting his feet touch the cold vinyl of the floor.

Smiling, he let her unbutton his shirt cuffs, then work her way down his chest. Shifting back, she silently urged him to stand, then unfastened his jeans. He had to help her push down the denim, since they clung to his long johns underneath. While he pulled off the undershirt, she started to lower the silk-knit leggings.

That brought a certain part of his anatomy into view, reminding her of what she had done with him last night. Grinning, Rachel lifted his shaft, pressing a kiss to its tip. Steve groaned softly, stroking her dark brown hair with one hand. He stopped her after a few more moments, if reluctantly. "It may have warmed up in here, with all that water heating the place, but I'm going to freeze if I don't get into the bath. And if I freeze," he stated wryly, "I'll shrivel up and won't be of any use to you tonight."

"Well, we can't have that," Rachel agreed, amusement coloring her reply. "Into the bath with you. I need to shed a layer or two so I can bathe you without overheating or getting too wet."

"So long as you get nicely wet . . ."

She smiled as she pulled off her own sweater, watching him climb into the tub once her face was free. The water was hot enough to make him hiss through his teeth, but not so hot that he couldn't sink down into it with a groaning sigh. The bliss smoothing the furrows in his brow made her glad she had thought of doing this for him. Stripping to her undershirt and long johns, Rachel tossed their clothes in the hamper, took their boots back into the bedroom, rearranged the milk pails a little more out of the way, then found the sea sponge he had given her for her birthday two years ago. She hadn't used it in about seven months, which meant it was long overdue. That it was for him instead of her didn't matter; it was the ritual of the thing that made it special.

Steve knew she liked using it for special occasions, for when she wanted to feel extra-feminine and pampered. When he spotted it in her hands, he blushed a little. Not that he thought she was going to make him more feminine by using it, but because she was going to spoil him by association with her favorite bathing ritual. He watched her dip the sponge into the bathwater, then anoint it with some of her body wash, working the sponge into a lather.

When she picked up his near arm and began gently scrubbing his muscles, Steve let her manipulate him as she willed. The combination of slick suds and scratchy sponge relaxed and invigorated him. Coupled with the attention she was giving him, he felt a renewal of the love he knew she held for him. He had given her care and attention last night, reasserting what had been suppressed by the troubles in their lives. Now she was giving it back to him.

"I don't know . . ." He trailed off, unsure if he should say it.

Rachel looked up from his shoulder and upper chest, working her way across to his other arm. "You don't know . . . what?"

"I don't know if you're just reviving my deep love for you, or making me fall in love with you all over again," he murmured diffidently, and watched her blush with pleasure. He smiled. "I think a little of both."

"Good. We've forgotten to do things like this," Rachel said, reaching across him to scrub at his other arm. Soap smeared across one breast from his closer arm, dampening and turning her undershirt translucent. "We were on a pattern spiraling down into dullness, weren't we? I mean . . . not that you're *dull*, but that we'd gone and forgotten how special we are together."

"I was thinking the exact same thing," Steve agreed, admiring the way the dampened silk permitted the darkness of her nipple to show. Tracing the little peak made her glance at him. "You'd better take that off before it gets too wet and soapy to wear, in case we can't do laundry for a few more days."

"But then I'll freeze," she pointed out. "You're the one in the water, not me."

"Then come in here, and straddle me," her fiancé coaxed. "I'll keep most of you warm."

Stripping off her remaining clothes, Rachel found herself asking skeptically, "*Most* of me warm?"

He grinned, looking at her breasts. "I like certain parts of you best when they're cold. It's so much more fun that way."

Considering how her areolas had puckered, she couldn't blame him. Chuckling, she finished removing her undergarments and stepped carefully into the tub with him. The heat from the water was heavenly. Kneeling carefully, she scrubbed his abdomen with the sponge, then sat back and worked on his legs, taking her time to refamiliarize herself with every inch of his skin she could reach.

Her fiancé had a decent body; working in the dairy had kept him reasonably fit, and there was just enough hair on his chest and legs to say he was a man, but not enough to suggest he was a beast. Some women liked their men to be downright furry; Rachel just wanted a little bit of curl on her man's chest, and not much elsewhere. The texture of Steve's sparsely dusted skin was just the way she liked a man to feel: warm and silky in some spots, warm and crinkly coarse in others. Perfect.

Leaning forward, she made him sit up, then wrapped her arms around him, kissing him somewhat awkwardly while she scrubbed at his back. Getting him to stand, she scrubbed the parts the water had covered, then urged him back down again, rinsing and using the sponge to trickle water over his body. Midway through her task, he stole the brown sponge from her.

Against her protests, he lathered it up again and scrubbed her in turn from neck to toes, shushing her mouth with kisses. Catching on to his silencing scheme, Rachel mumbled a few more protests, making him kiss her again. The water had turned too murky to rinse with, but she had anticipated that. Standing, Rachel urged Steve to his feet, and with his help, lifted the final milk bucket over both their heads. It was still full of hot, clean water. Steve helped her pour it over both of them for a rinse while the tub drained at their feet.

Steve laughed when the last of the water was done dripping out of the can. "We still have soap on our bodies. I think we'll need to risk a brief shower."

Rachel nodded. It was now late; if any of the other guests had taken a shower, there might not be much hot water left, but it also shouldn't be a strain on the generator to siphon some from the tanks. Letting him pull the curtain into place, she turned and worked with the faucet, waiting until warm water spilled forth. The position left her bent over at the waist. She didn't know why she was surprised when he grasped her hips, but she was. Pleasantly, at least.

The sight of her stooped over like that excited him. Being bathed had been more sensuous, like a backrub, but this was just too sexy to resist. Swaying closer, Steve teased her flesh with his own. He didn't have a condom handy, so he wasn't going to penetrate her . . . mostly wasn't going to penetrate her . . . she pushed back, slotting him into position, then into place with a soft, feminine groan. A spasm of lust twitched through his entire body. Gritting his teeth, he held back, held himself still within her.

"Rachel . . . I'm not wearing a condom," Steve managed to warn her.

"We're getting married in less than ten days," she reminded him, grinning over her shoulder. "I won't tell if you won't!"

"Well, since not even the worst blizzard in the history of the whole Midwest would stop me from marrying you," he conceded, pulling out almost all the way before pushing back in again, nice and slowly, "I think we can keep our mouths shut."

She turned off the tub faucet again to conserve the hot water; they could always rinse off *after* making love, but not if they ran out first. From the slow pace he was setting, she figured they'd definitely run out of hot water if she left the taps open. Not that slow was a bad thing . . . but it was getting cold in the bathroom without the shower running. Changing her mind, Rachel stood up, letting him slip free. Turning, she silenced his wordless protest with a kiss, looping her arms around his shoulders. "Let's finish rinsing off, then get dirty in bed, under the nice, warm covers."

As much as he wanted to just take her, Steve conceded not only the increasing chill in the air, but also the slipperiness of their location. Kinky was only okay if it didn't lead to a broken neck, in his book. "Alright. Rachel . . . I've been thinking," Steve added as she turned on the taps and lifted the lever for the shower head. "I kind of miss the way we used to, you know, court each other. Not that I'm aiming to be spoiled or anything, but I liked you pampering me just now, and I liked doing it to you last night."

Turning to face him, Rachel let the hot water rinse any lingering soap from her back. "I liked it, too. I missed doing things like that."

He nodded. "That's what made me think. What if we set aside one weekend each month, or a weeknight, whatever works with the rest of our schedule . . . and just make sure to pamper each other on that day?"

Considering the idea, Rachel finished washing off the soap, then shifted out of his way so he could rinse himself, too. "It's not a bad idea at all. But I'd rather spend one day on one of us, and the other day on the other person—the one being lavished with love can reciprocate if they want on their day, but it's their day."

" 'Lavished with love,' " Steve repeated over his shoulder, twisting under the spray. "I like the sound of that. And a day apiece, that's good. Nothing too extravagant—we live in Iowa, so no buying either of us a yacht," he teased, making her laugh. "But little things, we can do that. Things we can do around the needs of the Inn. And we could even space it out every few weeks between the two of us. Say, you get the first and I get the sixteenth of each month?"

Rachel thought about it as she twisted off the taps again. "No, that runs up against New Year's Day. That conflicts with our wedding, which is supposed to be about both of us. How about the fifteenth and the thirtieth? That way, it's separate from any possible holidays or anniversaries, and makes the days in question ours alone for a celebration."

Stepping out of the tub, Steve fetched a large towel from the stack on the shelves in the corner and enfolded her in it with a hug, before fetching one for himself. "I like it. The fifteenth and thirtieth it is. And you get the thirtieth, so I can spoil you before our wedding day." He paused, then added quietly, looking off to one side, "I wish we could still afford a big wedding, then I could've spoiled you on that day, too."

Tucking her finger under his chin, Rachel turned his gaze to her. "I'm marrying you. That's the important thing. If we can survive tornadoes and mortgages and once-a-century blizzards—and we have—then the rest of our lives will be good, and that's all I could ask for. So long as I get to spend the rest of my life with you."

Steve ducked his head, kissing the tip of her finger. "I don't deserve you, woman."

"Every fifteenth of the month, you will," she returned, grinning. "Now, dry off so the important bits don't freeze before we can get into bed. I'm still in the mood to start a family with you, mister!"

"Yes, ma'am!" Grinning back, he complied.

CROCHETING IN THE LIGHT OF THE FOUR VOTIVE CANDLES she had brought upstairs with her, Cassie blinked sleepily. The infant-sized jumper suit was almost done. Just a few more rows to finish the collar, and she'd be finished. Which was just as well, since she was almost out of pink yarn in the skein she had brought.

Pink.

Blinking again, this time to clear the sleep from her eyes, she grinned and crawled out of the quilt-covered bed. Padding out of her room, jumper and skein wadded in one hand, a candle in its glass holder carried in the other for illumination, she tapped lightly on the door across the hall from hers with a knuckle. Bella opened it after a moment, one of her dark brown eyebrows arched in silent inquiry. Still grinning, Cassie lifted the jumper into view, displaying it to her longtime friend.

For a moment, Bella squinted in confusion. Then her brow cleared, her eyes widened, and she smiled as well. Tipping her head to the left, she indicated Mike's door, there at the end of the hall. A nod and Cassie moved over to that panel, rapping quietly on the painted wood. It opened after a moment. Lifting the votive holder and the nearly finished jumper, Cassie displayed it to him as well.

He grinned and nodded, speaking softly. "Everything will be taken care of on my end. Don't worry. Just keep up your own work. I trust the snow will end in time for us to get going."

Cassie nodded, clutching the pink jumper to her chest with that same pleased smile. "Everything will work out, I'm sure of it."

"When does it not?" Bella murmured from the doorway of her room. "Good night, you two."

SOME OF THE SNOW HAD SWIRLED INTO THE TRENCH BETWEEN the farmhouse and the barn, and some of the snow had swirled away from the house, reducing the six feet of snow in the drifts around them to about five and a half. But it was still passable when Steve slogged through the knee-high powder and wind-blown flakes on his way to help Pete with the morning's milking. The air was still bitingly cold, too, threatening to freeze him from nostrils to lungs with each cautious breath.

He wanted to be back in bed with his wife-to-be, but tending animals was a responsibility, with cattle to milk and chickens to feed. He did allow thoughts of last night's unfettered coupling to keep him warm, since the wind was blowing hard. Of how deliciously naughty it had felt to enter her without any protection . . . of how she had laughed at one point during a position shift when he complained about the cold drafts down his back, since the covers had also shifted.

Opening the barn door, he stepped inside, and heard an unexpected sound. The lowing of the girls in their stalls was joined by the bleating, higher bawl of a calf. Blinking, Steve closed the door behind him. There, in Ellen's stall on the other side of the barn, was a newborn calf! And a very tired but pleased-looking Pete, seated on a stool as he fed the hungry thing from the oversized baby bottle of colostrum they had collected.

The slats of the stall were angled wrong for Steve to tell if it was a future bull or heifer. Joining the younger man, he saw the gender. "A boy. Ah, well."

"Something you don't need in a dairy herd. Not when it's the offspring of one of these ladies," Pete agreed. "It's hard not to get attached to 'em when they're newborns. A girl, you could've kept. What'll you do with him?"

Steve always hated this part, but he knew he had to be practical. They had room for six cows, in the count of the stalls and the milking machine stations in the dairy; if the calf had been a heifer, they could've kept her. "Same as the last one, I guess. Raise to the point of weaning, then sell for veal, and keep the stomach for the rennet."

"Rennet?" Pete asked, curious.

"The stomach lining of a milk-fed calf has enzymes that help turn milk into cheese," Steve informed him. "A lot of the enzymes are vegetable-based these days, and we mix it in, but there's no sense in wasting the calf rennet, either. Didn't you ever read the Laura Ingalls Wilder books when you were going up?"

"Nope; I was more into books with talkin' animals. I figured you'd raise him for veal," Pete replied, getting back to the subject. He scratched the top of the calf's head. "That's why I resisted naming him. This is the part about dairy farming I don't like. The rest of it, I do. Much more than pig farming.

"I've been thinking, out here at night," he added, adjusting his grip on the bottle, tilting it higher so the calf could suckle the remaining milk. "I think I should go back to my uncle's place and hire on as a hand. He's always been grateful for the help in the summers. Joey's turning into a real good plumber, an' Dave's got an offer in the works for the garage of the dealership in the next town. It's time I did something with my own life, rather than just drift an' make trouble. An' I'm sorry I came here to make trouble for you an' Miz Rutherford. I shouldn't have done it."

"I think you just finished growing up, Pete," Steve observed softly. "And your apology is accepted. It takes a man to admit when he's been wrong. Anyone who can't do it is still just a boy, no matter how many years under his belt." From the shy smile Pete gave him, Steve knew his compliment had driven home. "But I'm not too sorry you three came out here. Dave helped with the generator, Joey with the plumbing, and now you with the calf. Was it a hard birth?"

"Breech, like you thought; her lowing woke me up," Pete admitted. "But it was easy enough to scrub up, reach in, and turn 'im around." He paused and laughed. "I almost went up to th' house to wake you up, make a city-educated boy like yourself learn how do it . . . but I thought of all that sloggin' through the snow you did yesterday, gettin' the spark plugs an' such, an' I didn't have the heart to wake you so early. Besides, it was an easy turnin' to do."

A yawn followed his words. Steve took pity on him. "Why don't you finish up with the calf, then go on back to bed for a nap? I'll do the milking and the mucking, then wake you up when it's breakfast time."

Pete smiled at him. "I'll take that offer. This little boy's almost done, anyway. Darn near drained Mama dry when he first latched on, too, so I thought I'd offer him what was in the bottle."

Nodding, Steve went to work.

The winds continued to scour down the drifts of snow, but at least more didn't seem to be coming down from the thinning clouds in the sky. At the rate it was vanishing, somewhat slower than it had arrived, Rachel figured the roads should be reasonably drivable by Christmas morning. They couldn't get out to church for Sunday services, but that was alright, in a way; Cassie found a book of hymns in the small, family-style library the Inn boasted, and coaxed the others into singing carols with her. It filled the old farmhouse with joy and tranquility, that eight people, three with diverse faiths, could enjoy such a simple yet uplifting task together while they waited for the last of the storm to abate. And with the drifts gradually blowing away, they'd be able to go into town for Christmas services.

Mike suggested it to the others, in fact, the afternoon of Christmas Eve. After peering out at the rumpled, shrinking mound that was Joey's half-undug truck, he came back to the others. "I think," the dark-skinned man stated with a smile, "that we will all be able to go to your church tomorrow morning."

" 'We'?" Joey asked, arching a brow his way. "Ain't you a Muslim?"

"Yes, but we do honor Christ in our own way. His birth is worthy of celebrating." Mike looked at Bella, who shrugged.

"I'm willing to admit he was special, even if I don't know personally if he was the Messiah my people prophesied, or merely a prophet of God." She looked at Cassie. They all looked at her. The faiths of Judaism, Christianity, and Islam all shared common beliefs at their foundation, but Buddhism was different.

"What?" the vivacious blonde asked, glancing at the others in the front parlor. "There's nothing in the writings that say I cannot also revere Christ. Buddhism is an *addition* to one's faith. Besides, between Joey and Steve's trucks, and our Bug, we can make it just fine, I'm sure of it. And it'll be nice to interact with other people," Cassie added. "As nice as we've all been to each other, it'll make an equally pleasant change."

A beeping sound in the distance jerked Steve onto his feet. Dave looked up at him, curious. "What is it?"

"That's the generator's alarm." He grinned at the others. "Ladies and gentlemen, we have power! I'll just go shut off the generator, to conserve what's left of the fuel in the tank."

"If it wouldn't be too much of an imposition," Mike offered politely, looking Rachel's way, "could I possibly check my e-mail? I have some very important messages I've been waiting for."

"I suppose it wouldn't hurt," Rachel allowed. "I'm glad you

asked me this time around." She gave him a wry smile. "Steve and I were going to put WiFi into the house for our guests, but that got derailed by more important things last summer. Don't take too long; I still need to check and make sure we've enough in our bank balance to cover the mortgage withdrawal."

"I'm sure it will be fine," Bella offered, smiling. " 'Tis the season for brotherhood, kindness, and miracles, after all."

THE CHURCH WAS CROWDED WHEN THEY ARRIVED THE NEXT morning. The sky was still overcast and the wind was still blowing, but the weather wasn't hampering travel anymore. In fact, it looked like the only people missing were Steve's parents, but they would've been gone through the whole of the holiday season anyway, including missing out on their son's quiet wedding. Steve and Rachel had urged them to go, however; a Caribbean cruise was an opportunity not to be missed. So, though both of them missed the elder Bethels, they had a good time greeting everyone in the community with hugs and introducing their three out-of-town guests, before settling into the padded pews for the service.

Steve knew the big miracles of his faith were worthy of honoring, but as Rachel snuggled into his side during the reading of the nativity scene, he thought that the woman at his side was his own personal miracle. She wasn't a large miracle, but she was his fiancée, his soon-to-be wife, a woman willing to stand beside him through thick and thin, and that was miraculous enough. From the way her hand crept up to cover her stomach, he could guess she was thinking about a different sort of miracle, the possible creation of life between the two of them. Happier than he had been in a long time, he returned his attention to the service.

At the end of the closing prayer, rather than giving the final parting words of peace and fellowship he usually did, Pastor Jonathan lifted one of his hands and said something unexpected.

"And now, for the other thing that drew so many of you out here, despite the lingering snow and the icy roads. Not quite so important as the birth of Our Lord, but important enough to this community to make the effort to stay just a little longer. Will Steven Bethel and Rachel Rutherford please stand?"

Startled, Rachel and Steve exchanged looks before complying; they felt the eyes of the rest of the congregation upon them as they did so, as well as the warmth of everyone's smiles.

"As we all know, the Bethel Inn has hit some hard times in recent months. Including to the point that this loving couple gave up their dreams of holding a big wedding, because they couldn't afford it anymore. Well, it being the season for miracles . . . and aided by the modern miracle of e-mail"—Pastor Jonathan chuckled—"we have managed to pull off a small miracle of our own. Steve, Rachel . . . if you will permit your friends here in the community to do so, we'd like to *give* you a big wedding day, right here, right now!

"We already have the civil paperwork from the county, since you picked it up last week . . . and our three newest guests managed to smuggle in your best outfits," he added, smiling and nodding at Bella, Cassie, and Mike, who gave unrepentant little smiles and waves to the startled couple. "And since everyone is already here, we all thought, why not celebrate not only a birth, but a wedding as well today? What do you say?" the pastor asked them.

Encouraging words were called out from the sea of faces lining the church. "Go on!" "Do it!" "Don't let 'er get away!" "Don't let *him* get away!"

Laughter greeted that last outburst; then the congregation quieted, waiting for their reply. Rachel glanced at their three conspirator guests, then looked up at Steve. "Well, you want to get hitched a few days early?"

"More than anything in the world," Steve agreed, before pulling her close enough to kiss. The sound of the pastor clearing his throat broke them apart. Keeping one arm around his fiancée's shoulder, Steve looked at the community members gathered in the church around them, warmed beyond words. "Thank you all for this incredible surprise. I—"

Several arriving figures at the entry doors caught his attention. And Rachel's. She squinted, then widened her eyes. "Mom? Dad?"

"We weren't sure we'd make it, the roads are that messy!" Rachel's mother called out from the back of the sanctuary, unwrapping the scarf covering her face. The others resolved themselves into Rachel's siblings. "Sorry we couldn't make it for the service."

"God forgives when it's with good intentions. You're just in time to get ready for the wedding. Everyone else, there will be a half-hour break while beautiful things are done to the bride, and the groom is wrestled into his suit," Pastor Jonathan joked. "Tea and coffee are waiting in the fellowship room. God bless you and hold you in His heart!"

A hand on his elbow distracted Steve from following Rachel as she made her way toward her family, somehow brought all the way out from Des Moines for the occasion. Turning, he saw it was Mr. Thomas Harrod, the mustached, stiffly postured bank owner. Fear raced through him. *Didn't we have enough to pay the mortgage?*

The older, graying gentleman cleared his throat with a touch of awkwardness. "My, ah, wife pointed out to me that our son, Richard, cannot make cheese. If he cannot make cheese, she cannot *eat* cheese. Not the Bethel Inn Blue Ribbon Cheese, at any rate. And then she gave me a half-hour lecture on how long the Bethel Inn has been operating, how prosperous it normally is, and . . . well, she made a lot of sense, once my ears stopped ringing.

"So I'm letting you know that I am going to give the Bethel Inn special dispensation, a full month's leeway in its mortgage payments. Of course, you didn't need it for this month," Mr. Harrod added under his breath. "But the offer stands. My wife said, you don't make a business prosperous by trying to pretend your best clients aren't all that good . . . and your family has been very good to mine for a very long time. She said I owe *you* . . . and I find I'm inclined to agree."

"She did?" Steve asked, too startled to say anything else, though he did manage to shake the hand the bank owner offered to him.

"She did. That, and she called me nothing but Ebenezer this, and Mr. Scrooge that, for the whole length of the storm," he muttered, smiling slightly, wryly. "May your own wife not have quite so sharp a tongue, whenever she's upset with you. Or at least, may you give her no reason to use it on you."

"Thank you—and a Merry Christmas to you, Mr. *Harrod*," Steve enunciated carefully, making the man laugh. As the bank owner left him, a touch on his other elbow turned him back around. It was Mike; his two traveling companions had vanished, no doubt to bring Rachel her clothes.

Mike clasped his hands firmly, then nodded politely. "I just wanted you to know that Cassie, Bella, and I will not be returning to the Inn after the wedding. It's time for us to be on our way. But we enjoyed our stay very much, and we're very happy for the two of you. May the blessings of God—by whichever name you call Him—shine upon you and your new family like the Star of Bethlehem. Love is a miracle we must not forget to honor. It has been a pleasure seeing you honor that love with your wife-to-be."

"Thank you. Are you sure you cannot stay?" Steve found himself asking. "We've enjoyed hosting you very much."

"Alas, no. We have a long way to go, to get to our next destination," Mike demurred. "But it was good to see you and your impending bride getting a little good fortune back into your lives."

"Will you at least come back?" he asked next. He wanted to ask, *Did you cause all of these miracles that have been happening?* But there were too many people around, and Steve wasn't going to spoil it by looking the proverbial gift horse in the mouth. It was enough to know that subtle miracles had happened . . . like this big Christmas Day wedding everyone else had planned.

Mike merely smiled. "If we can, it would be a delight. Now, if you don't mind, I have your suit waiting in the men's room. I trust I will not have to 'wrestle' you into it?"

Steve laughed at that. "Believe me, I'm more than eager."

Rachel gave her situation a lot of thought, as her two guests, her mother, and her sisters fluttered around her, helping her into her dress, then fixing her hair and face. It wasn't until they were almost ready that she had a moment alone with Cassie and Bella. "How did you do it?"

The two women exchanged looks before Bella asked, "Do what?"

"Steve and I had a talk the other night. About the one log in the front woodstove that just keeps burning. The spark plugs that were an exact match. The insulation that wouldn't run out. Having on hand the three helpers we needed to keep our inn running. And now, getting my family here in time for an unexpected wedding on the tail end of a big blizzard—Mike using my e-mail, and the pastor saying it was all arranged via e-mail!" She looked up into Cassie's blue eyes. "*You* somehow did it all, didn't you? Or at least had a hand in it. It *had* to have been you. How? And why?"

The two women exchanged looks. Cassie sighed and shrugged. "We do this every winter solstice, that's why. Northern or Southern Hemisphere, we seek out miracles that need to happen, and make sure they happen."

"Sometimes they happen on their own, and sometimes we just . . . help them along," Bella admitted with a shrug of her own. "It's been our joy, and our assignment, for as long as we can remember."

"Assignment?" Rachel asked, confused. "From who?"

Both women just looked upward for a moment, then back at Rachel again with identical smiles. Cassie reached over to where she had laid her coat and muff on the counter in the ladies' room, pulling a small, roundish, wrapped present out of one of her coat pockets. "Here. One more gift for the two of you. It's not frankincense, but then that fell out of fashion ages ago. And it's far more practical for you."

Curious, Rachel carefully opened the package. A bundle of pink fabric came out, resolving itself into a finely crocheted baby suit, the kind with little footies on the leggings, and little steel snaps up the torso. For a moment, she was confused at why it was such a practical gift . . . and then blushed bright red. Cassie grinned at her, patting her on the shoulder. Bella smiled and straightened.

"Don't you worry about a thing. When the world has reached its darkest point, just remember that the light *will* come back into your lives once again," the dark-haired woman said. "And now, we must be going."

"Wait—one question. If you're . . . you know, *you*," the bride-to-be asked, "the Three Magi . . . aren't you all supposed to be males? And why are calling yourselves a Buddhist, a Muslim, and a Reform Jew?"

"Because miracles happen all the time, regardless of whatever faith you follow," Bella told her.

"And gender does not matter," Cassie added. "Only love, unity, compassion, and brotherhood. So long as the teachings are good, does it matter who delivers them? Merry Christmas, Rachel."

"Don't ever forget how much you love each other—and have a good life together. That's an order," Bella added. She grinned. "Now, go and marry that wonderful man."

Rachel started to rise from the chair that had been brought in for her to sit in while having her hair and face done, then looked up at Cassie. "How long *will* that log burn?"

"Until the end of tonight. I was going to make it last eight days, but since you figured it out . . ." The blonde shrugged. "Well, some of the magic goes out of it when people do that."

"A little mystery in life is necessary, to slip the miracles through the cracks in people's attention spans," Bella said. "By the way, that idea you have, to pamper each other one day a month, that's a very good idea. I think we'll keep it in mind for our next visit, and suggest it to others in the future. Just make sure *you* don't forget to do so, hmm?"

"Yes, keep the love alive," Cassie agreed. "It'll light up your lives, even on the darkest of nights."

Rachel would have asked more, but her mother poked her head through the door, murmuring that it was time. She looked at Cassie, who lifted a pink-nailed finger to her lips, and understood the two women wanted her to keep quiet about what she had figured out. Deciding she would comply, Rachel nodded her head, acquiescing. One task at a time, as her groom-to-be liked to say . . . and that task was now for her to marry him.

• *Epilogue* •

"A BUDDHIST, A MUSLIM, AND A REFORM JEW," MIKE stated with a laugh as he escorted his friends out to their car. "We sound like the start of a bad joke—hey, maybe I can come up with the rest of it?"

Bella snapped her fingers. A length of pipe materialized midair, just in time for their friend to walk into it with a *bonk*. "There's your 'rest of it.' "

Cassie giggled, watching Mike grimace and dissolve the apparition with a snap of his own fingers.

"*Very* funny, Balthazzar. Watch it, or I'll sic a camel on you!"

"No, thank you." Bella shuddered. "I still remember the trouble we had with them, and the delay we suffered over two thousand years ago."

"Me, too," Cassie agreed. "I much prefer modern conveniences."

Bella nodded. "Well. Next time, I think I'll be a female Baptist. You, Melchior?"

"I was thinking a female Pagan. Caspar?" Mike asked their third member.

"Greek Orthodox. And I want to be a man next time. Where are we going, anyway?" Cassie asked him.

Pulling out his electronic notebook, Mike consulted it with a few taps from the stylus. "Argentina. A city called Rosario, which is located on the western banks of the Rio Paraná, at the edge of the State of Santa Fe. We'll be looking for a dance instructor, and the arrival of his long-lost childhood sweetheart."

"Sounds like fun." Peering all around them, Cassie gestured at their snow-dusted car. The wind was still blowing, but only lightly this time. The blizzard she had arranged was now over. "No one is watching. Shall we just go?"

"I don't feel like driving, so why not?" Bella shrugged.

All three laid their hands on the vehicle. It vanished with a soft white glow. Mike held out his hand to the two ladies. "See you in six months, then?"

"At the next winter solstice," Bella agreed with a smile, reaching to shake his proffered hand. Cassie, never one to stand on formality, pulled both of them into a group hug, making her friends laugh. Like the car, they vanished in a soft glow of light. The wind stirred for a moment, swirling rapidly through the parking lot. It covered their tracks, obscuring the fact that the VW Bug hadn't backed out or driven away, then gentled back down into a winter zephyr, stirring only a few flakes here and there.

From somewhere within the church, the strains of the "Wedding March" could be heard all the way out by the parking lot . . . had anyone been outside to hear them.